PREVIOUS BOOKS
BY NICK BERTOZZI

LEWIS & CLARK

THE MASOCHISTS

PERSIMMON CUP

THE SALON

SHACKLETON: ANTARCTIC ODYSSEY

with Pierce Hargan:
BECOMING ANDY WARHOL

with Kim Chaloner:
DIABETES AND ME

with Jason Lutes:
*HOUDINI:
THE HANDCUFF KING*

with Boaz Yakin:
*JERUSALEM:
A FAMILY PORTRAIT*

with Glenn Eichler:
STUFFED!

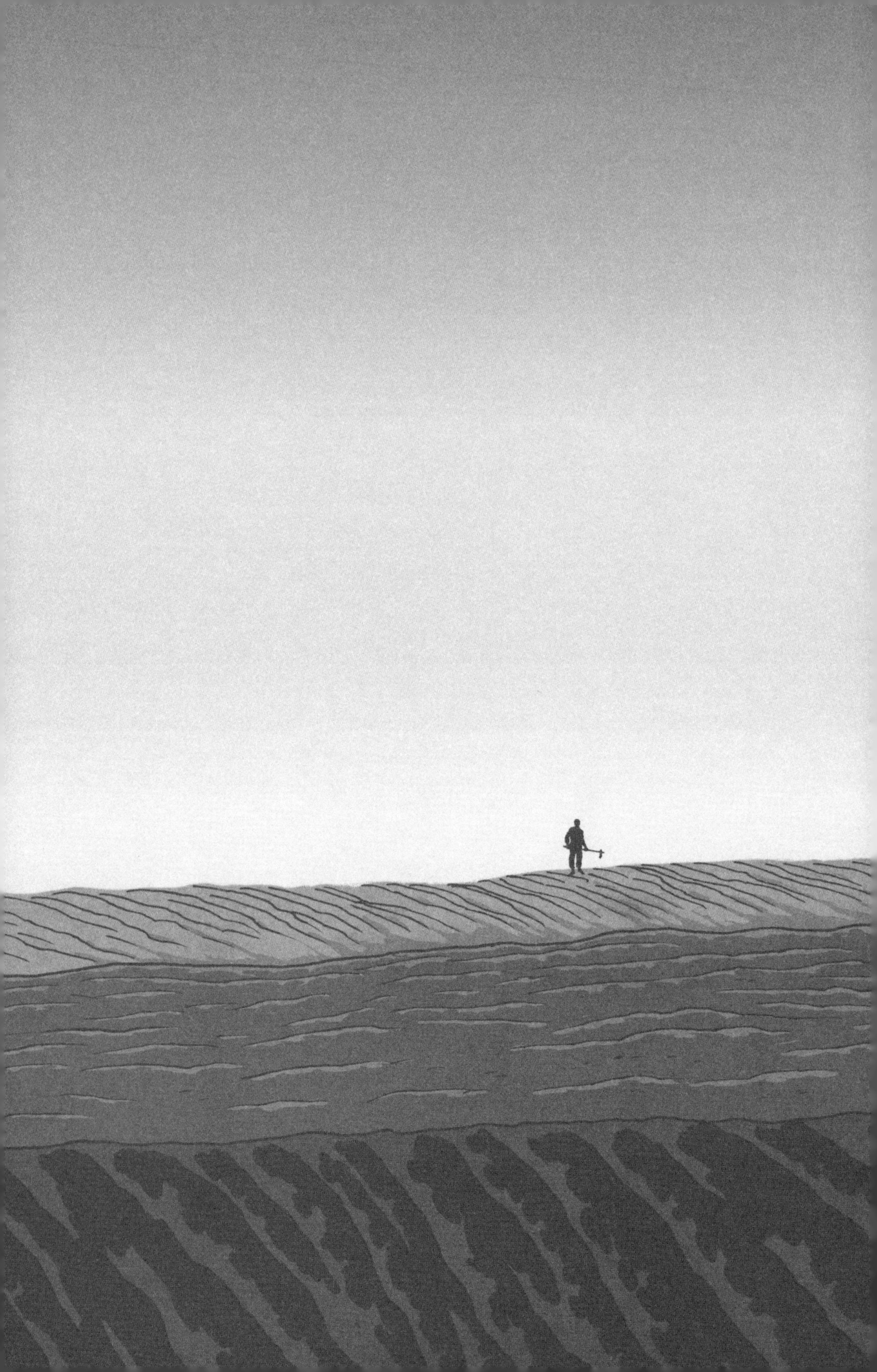

THE GOOD EARTH

by

PEARL S. BUCK

Graphic Adaptation by

NICK BERTOZZI

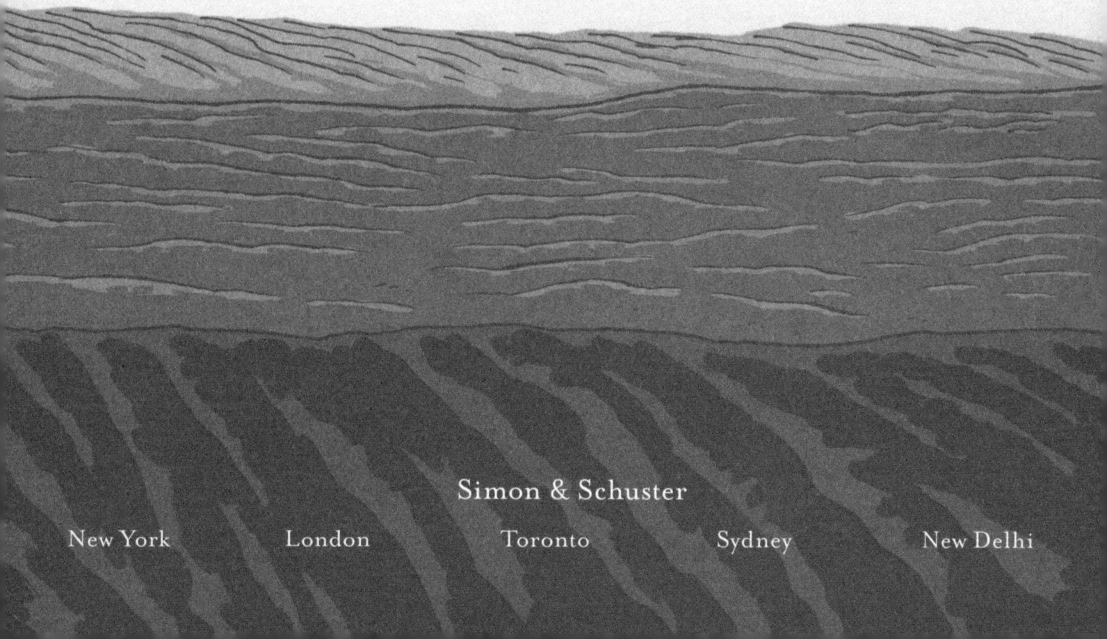

Simon & Schuster

New York London Toronto Sydney New Delhi

Simon & Schuster
1230 Avenue of the Americas
New York, NY 10020

First Simon & Schuster hardcover edition July 2017

SIMON & SCHUSTER and colophon are registered trademarks of Simon & Schuster, Inc.

For information about special discounts for bulk purchases, please contact Simon & Schuster Special Sales at 1-866-506-1949 or business@simonandschuster.com.

The Simon & Schuster Speakers Bureau can bring authors to your live event. For more information or to book an event, contact the Simon & Schuster Speakers Bureau at 1-866-248-3049 or visit our website at www.simonspeakers.com.

Interior design by Pete Friedrich
Jacket design by Pete Friedrich and Nick Bertozzi
Jacket art by Nick Bertozzi

Manufactured in the United States of America

10 9 8 7 6 5 4 3 2 1

Library of Congress Cataloging-in-Publication Data is available.

ISBN 978-1-5011-3276-6
ISBN 978-1-5011-3278-0 (ebook)

ACKNOWLEDGMENTS

Joan Hilty and Pete Friedrich
at PageTurner

Edgar Walsh

Charlie Olsen

Amar Deol

Brit Hvide

Kim Chaloner

and all of my family and friends

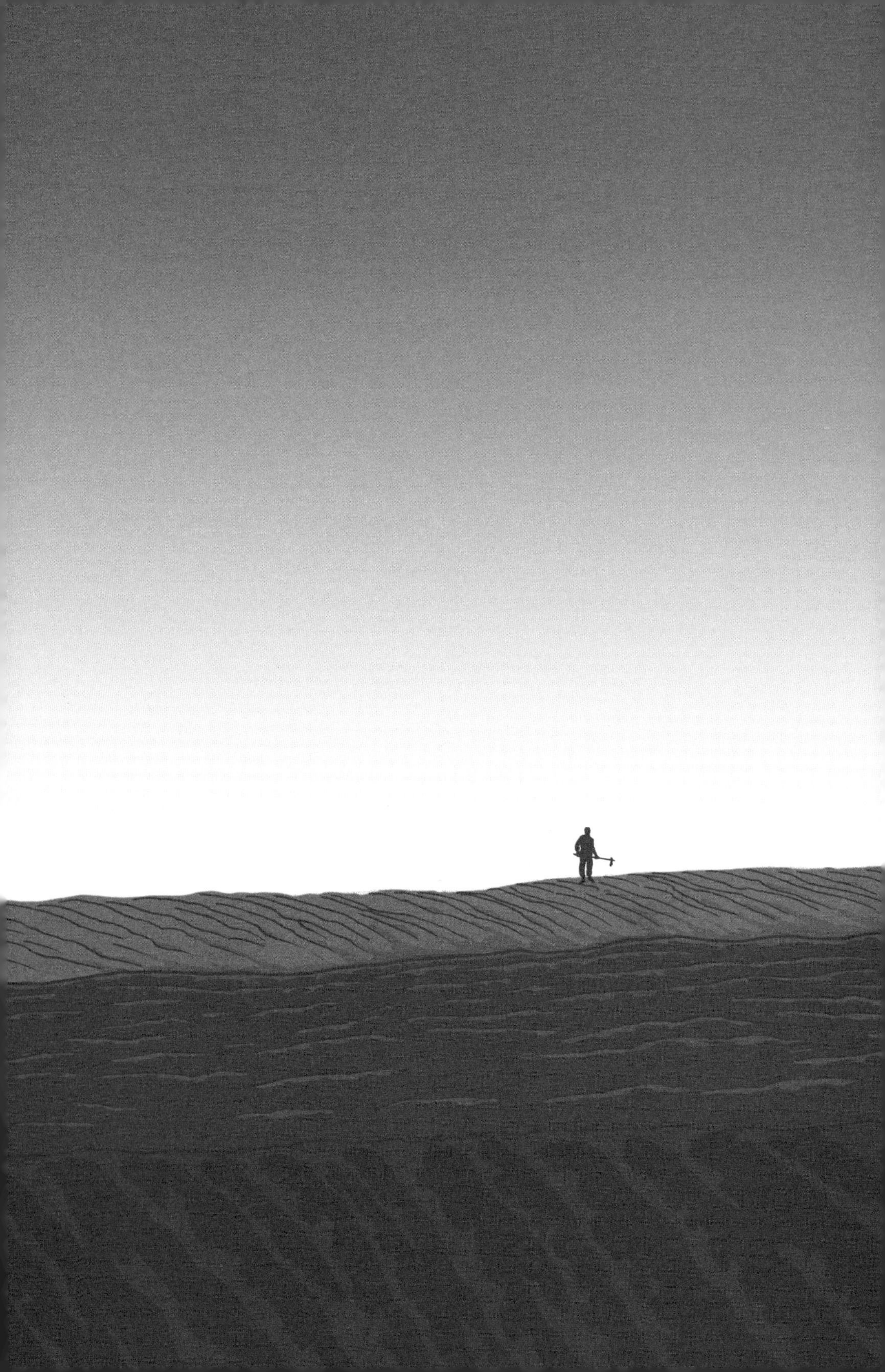

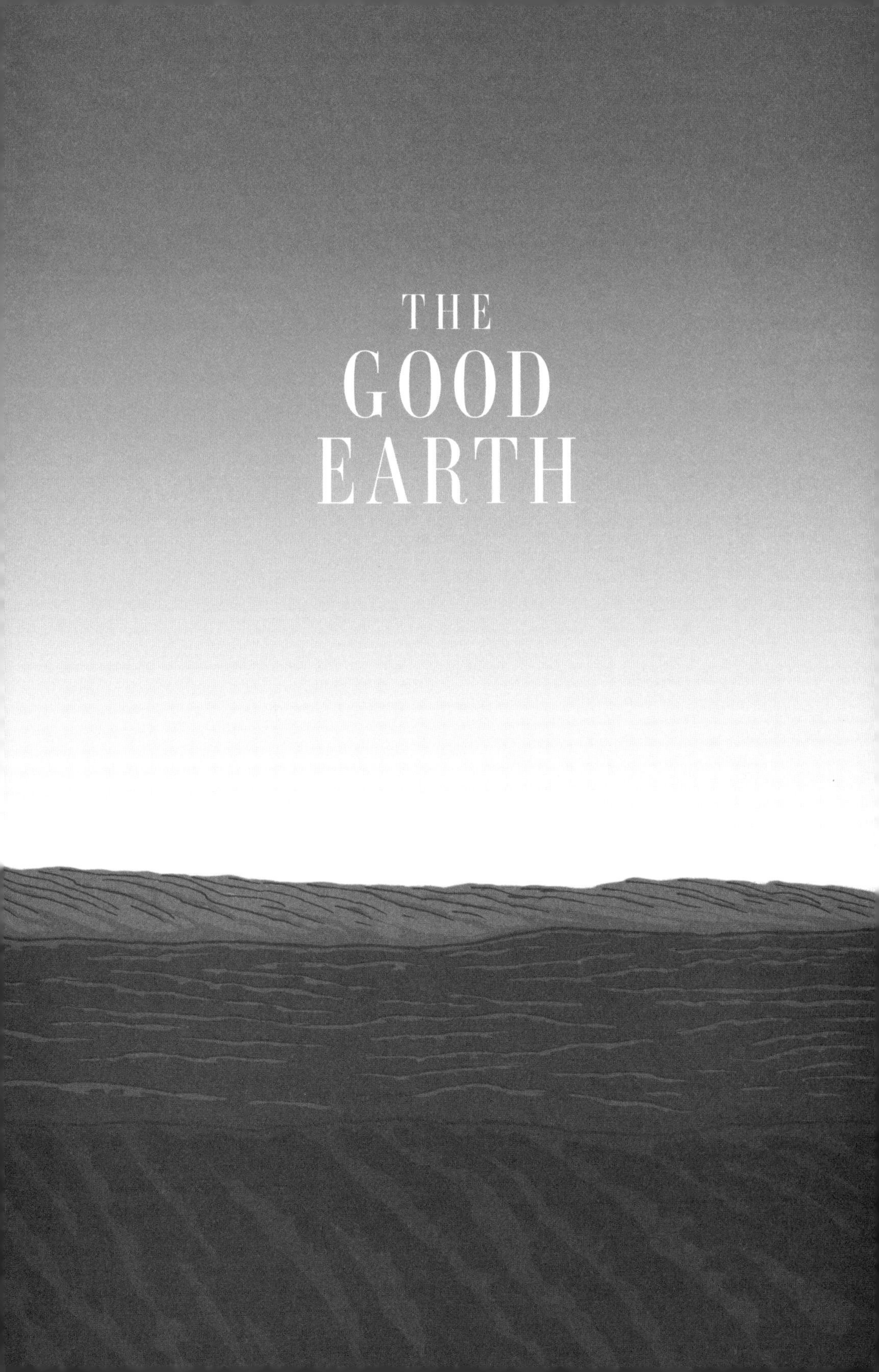
THE
GOOD
EARTH

1

This was the last morning he would have to light the fire. He had lit it every morning since his mother died six years before.

Every morning for these six years the old man had waited for his son to bring in hot water to ease him of his coughing.

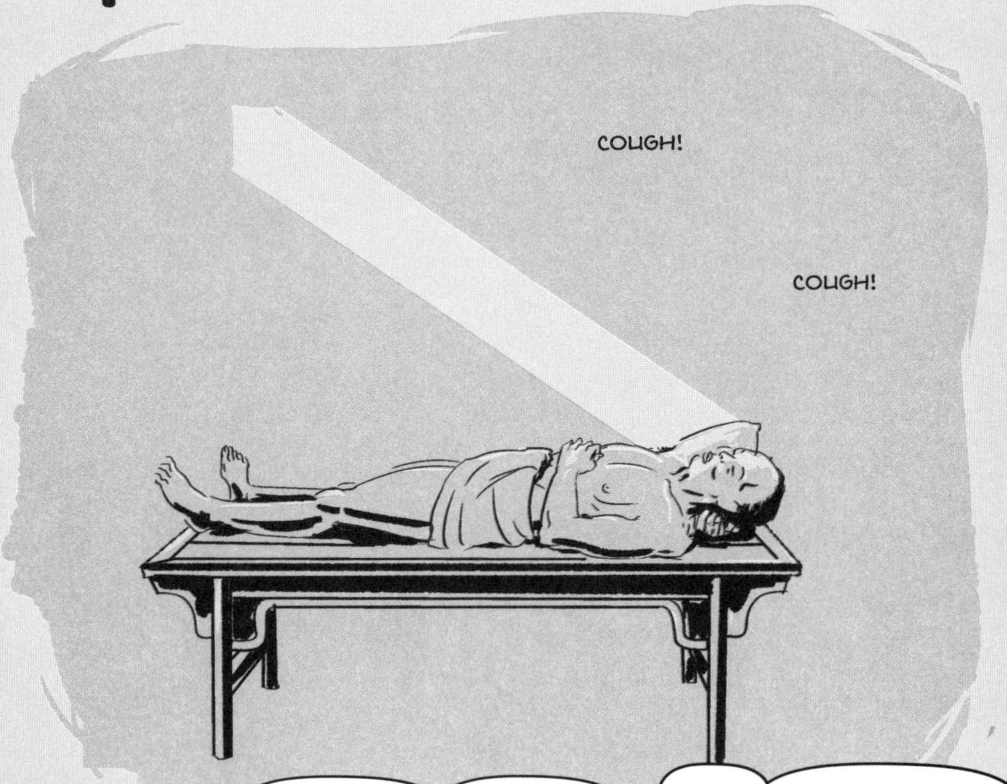
COUGH!
COUGH!

Now father and son could rest.

There was a woman coming to the house.

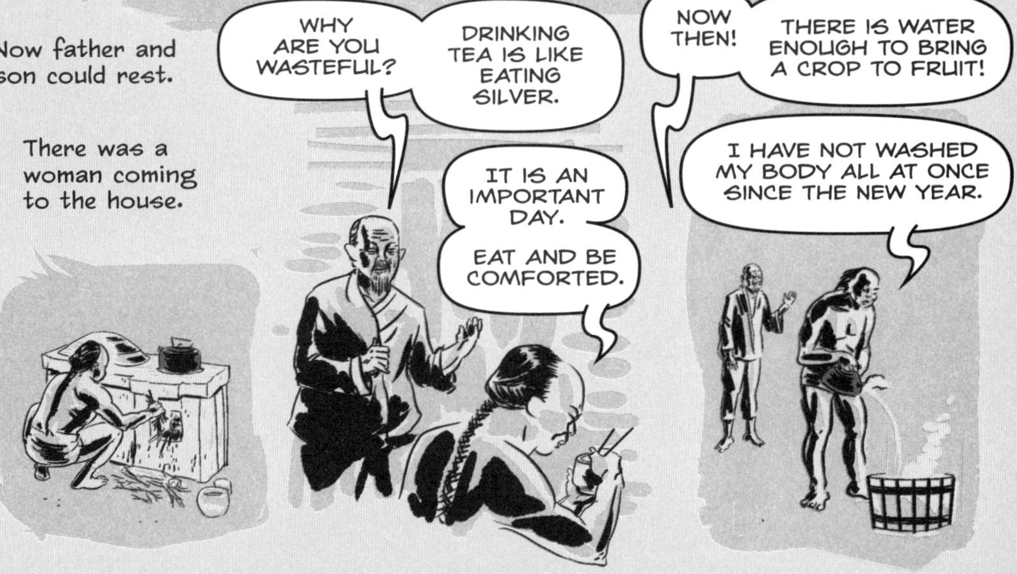
WHY ARE YOU WASTEFUL?
DRINKING TEA IS LIKE EATING SILVER.
IT IS AN IMPORTANT DAY.
EAT AND BE COMFORTED.
NOW THEN!
THERE IS WATER ENOUGH TO BRING A CROP TO FRUIT!
I HAVE NOT WASHED MY BODY ALL AT ONCE SINCE THE NEW YEAR.

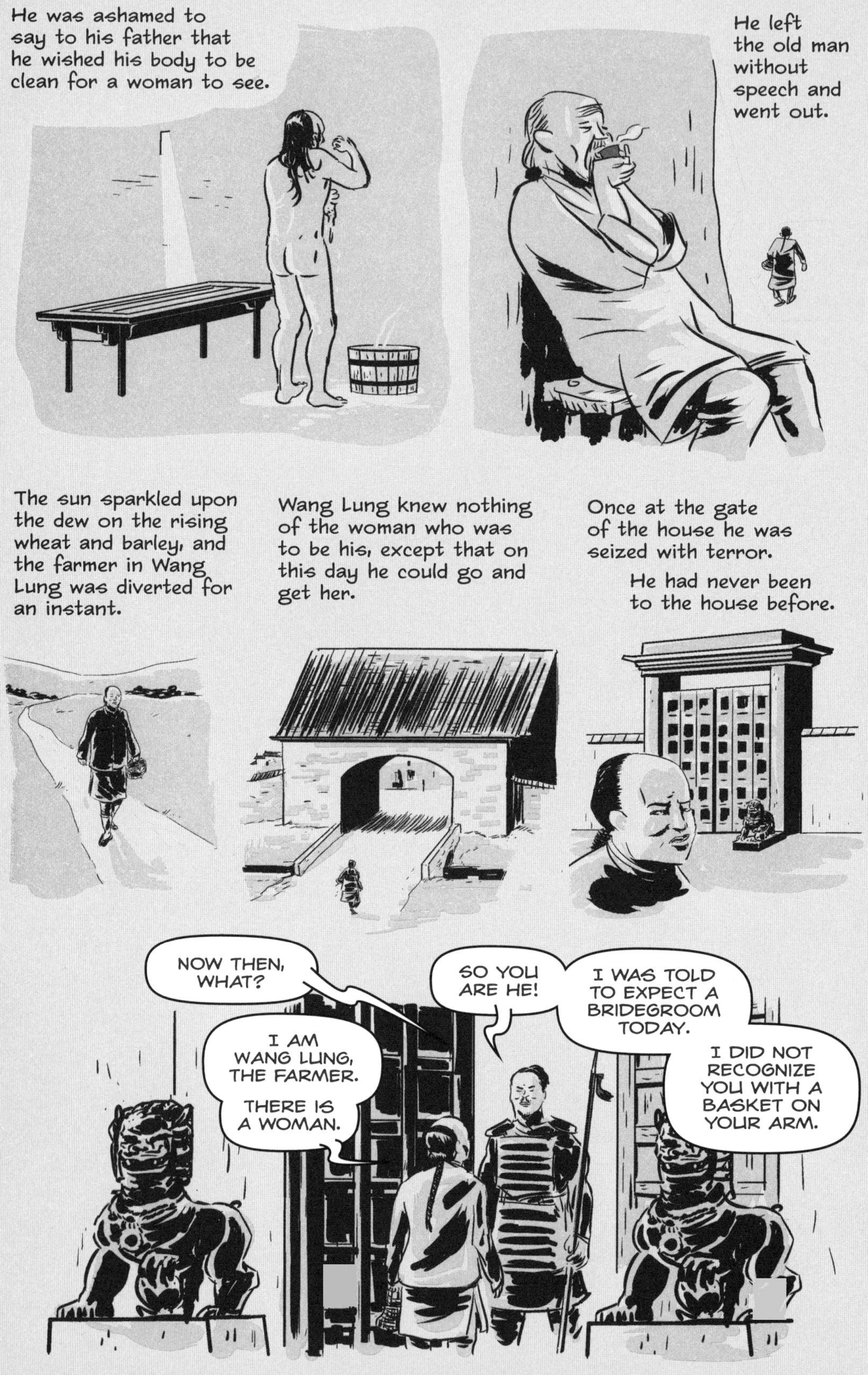
He was ashamed to say to his father that he wished his body to be clean for a woman to see.
He left the old man without speech and went out.
The sun sparkled upon the dew on the rising wheat and barley, and the farmer in Wang Lung was diverted for an instant.
Wang Lung knew nothing of the woman who was to be his, except that on this day he could go and get her.
Once at the gate of the house he was seized with terror.
He had never been to the house before.
NOW THEN, WHAT?
I AM WANG LUNG, THE FARMER.
THERE IS A WOMAN.
SO YOU ARE HE!
I WAS TOLD TO EXPECT A BRIDEGROOM TODAY.
I DID NOT RECOGNIZE YOU WITH A BASKET ON YOUR ARM.

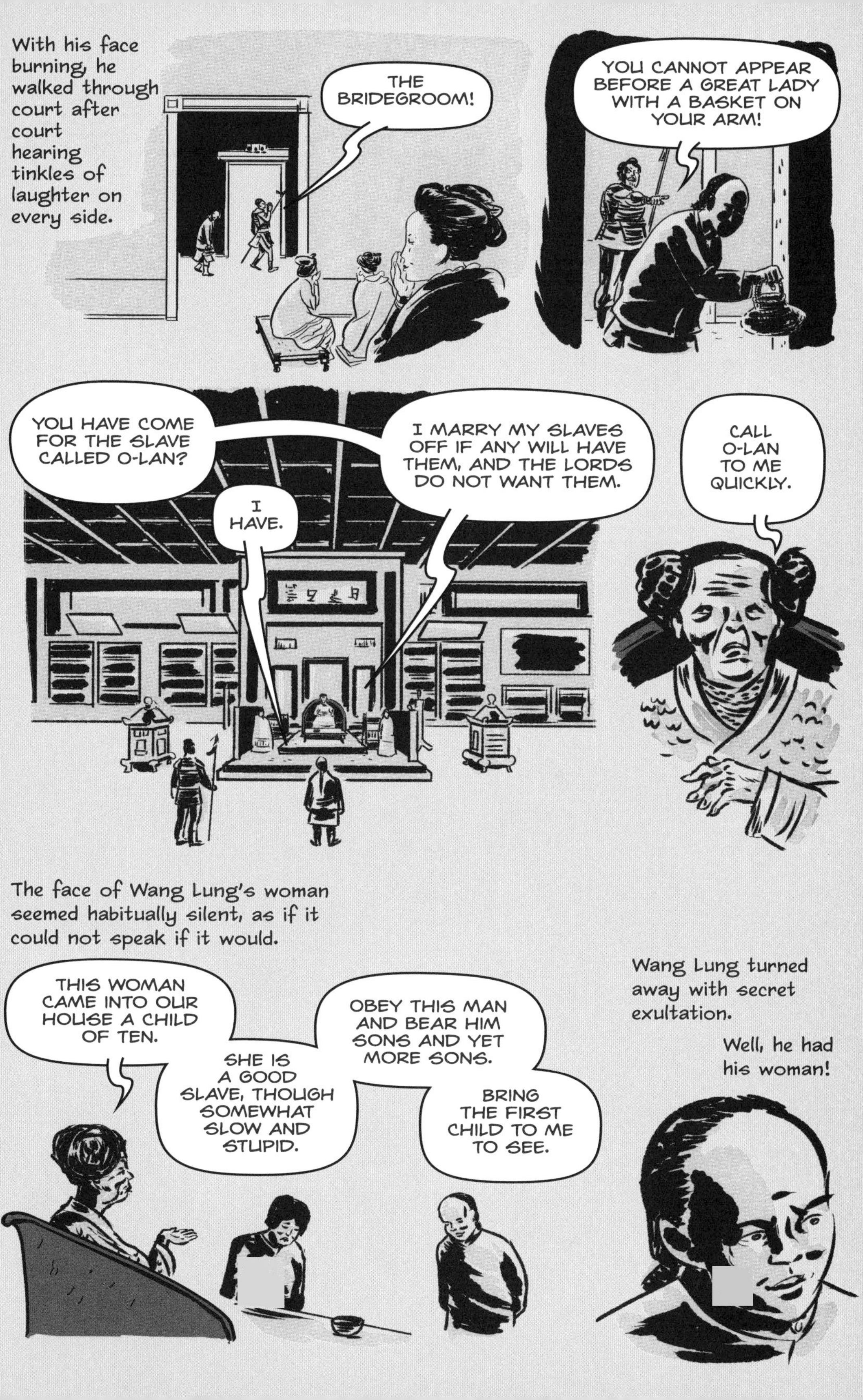

With his face burning, he walked through court after court hearing tinkles of laughter on every side.
THE BRIDEGROOM!
YOU CANNOT APPEAR BEFORE A GREAT LADY WITH A BASKET ON YOUR ARM!
YOU HAVE COME FOR THE SLAVE CALLED O-LAN?
I HAVE.
I MARRY MY SLAVES OFF IF ANY WILL HAVE THEM, AND THE LORDS DO NOT WANT THEM.
CALL O-LAN TO ME QUICKLY.
The face of Wang Lung's woman seemed habitually silent, as if it could not speak if it would.
THIS WOMAN CAME INTO OUR HOUSE A CHILD OF TEN.
SHE IS A GOOD SLAVE, THOUGH SOMEWHAT SLOW AND STUPID.
OBEY THIS MAN AND BEAR HIM SONS AND YET MORE SONS.
BRING THE FIRST CHILD TO ME TO SEE.
Wang Lung turned away with secret exultation.
Well, he had his woman!

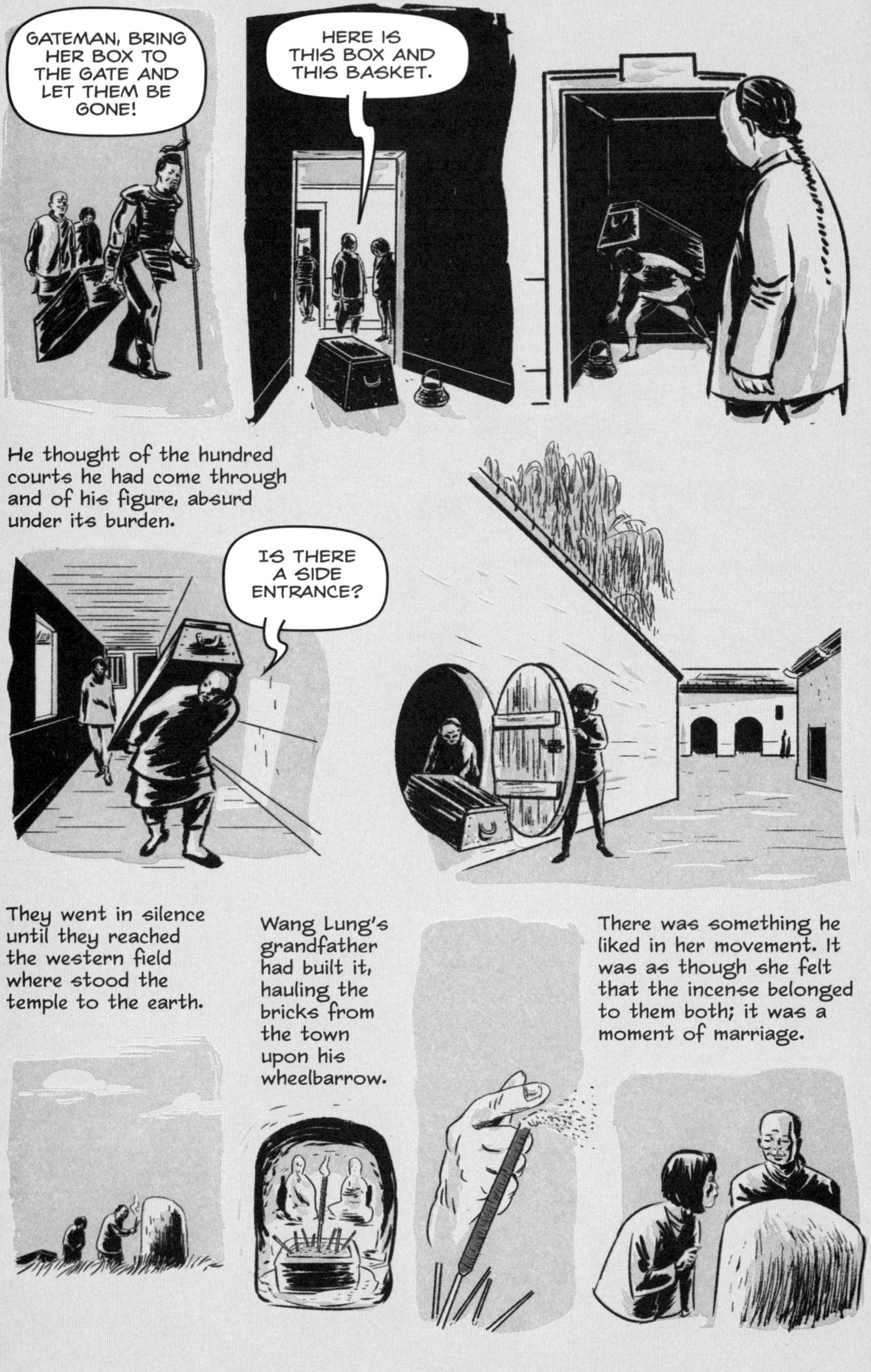
GATEMAN, BRING HER BOX TO THE GATE AND LET THEM BE GONE!
HERE IS THIS BOX AND THIS BASKET.
He thought of the hundred courts he had come through and of his figure, absurd under its burden.
IS THERE A SIDE ENTRANCE?
They went in silence until they reached the western field where stood the temple to the earth.
Wang Lung's grandfather had built it, hauling the bricks from the town upon his wheelbarrow.
There was something he liked in her movement. It was as though she felt that the incense belonged to them both; it was a moment of marriage.

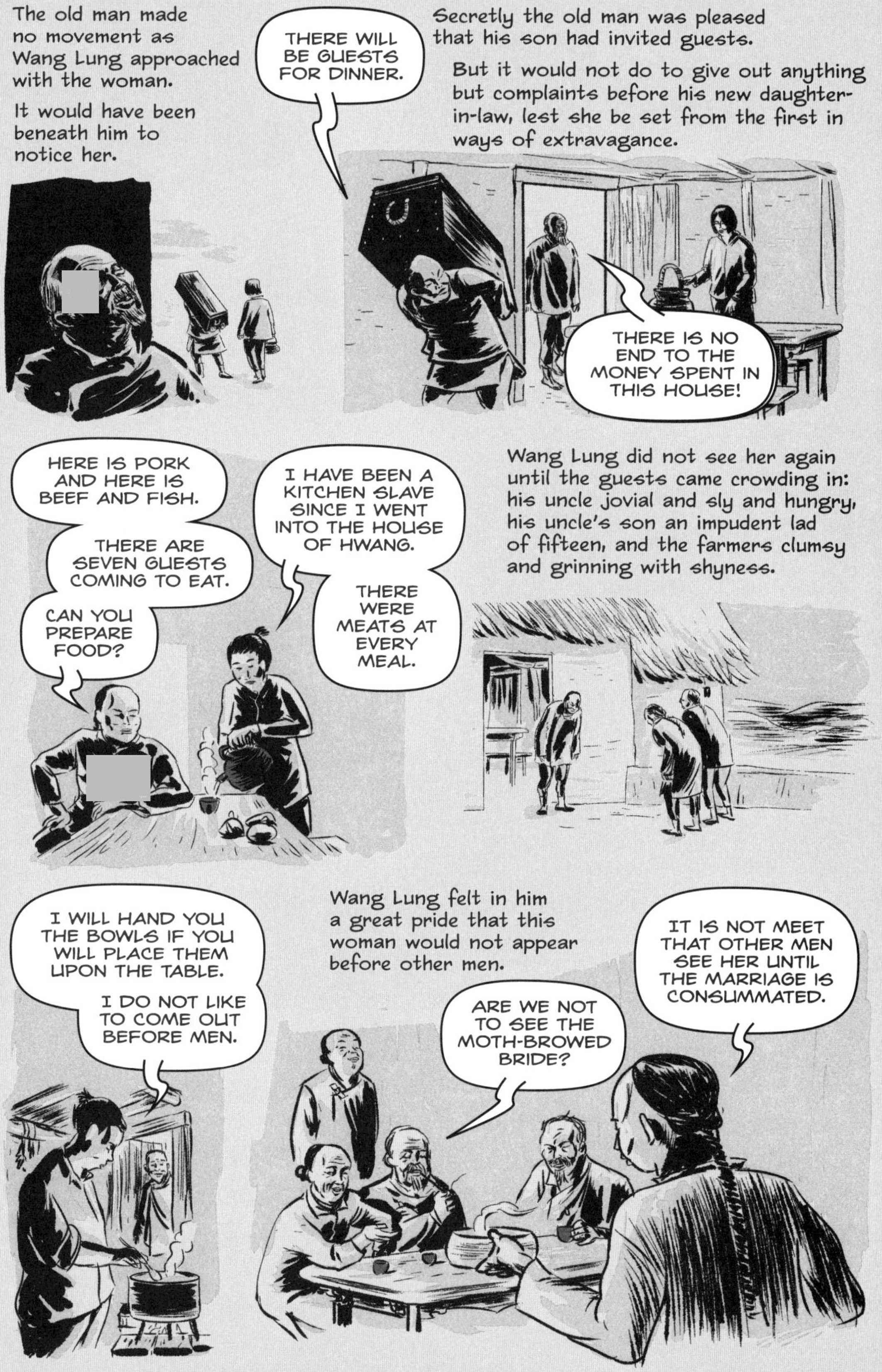
The old man made no movement as Wang Lung approached with the woman.
It would have been beneath him to notice her.
THERE WILL BE GUESTS FOR DINNER.
Secretly the old man was pleased that his son had invited guests.
But it would not do to give out anything but complaints before his new daughter-in-law, lest she be set from the first in ways of extravagance.
THERE IS NO END TO THE MONEY SPENT IN THIS HOUSE!
HERE IS PORK AND HERE IS BEEF AND FISH.
THERE ARE SEVEN GUESTS COMING TO EAT.
CAN YOU PREPARE FOOD?
I HAVE BEEN A KITCHEN SLAVE SINCE I WENT INTO THE HOUSE OF HWANG.
THERE WERE MEATS AT EVERY MEAL.
Wang Lung did not see her again until the guests came crowding in: his uncle jovial and sly and hungry, his uncle's son an impudent lad of fifteen, and the farmers clumsy and grinning with shyness.
I WILL HAND YOU THE BOWLS IF YOU WILL PLACE THEM UPON THE TABLE.
I DO NOT LIKE TO COME OUT BEFORE MEN.
Wang Lung felt in him a great pride that this woman would not appear before other men.
ARE WE NOT TO SEE THE MOTH-BROWED BRIDE?
IT IS NOT MEET THAT OTHER MEN SEE HER UNTIL THE MARRIAGE IS CONSUMMATED.

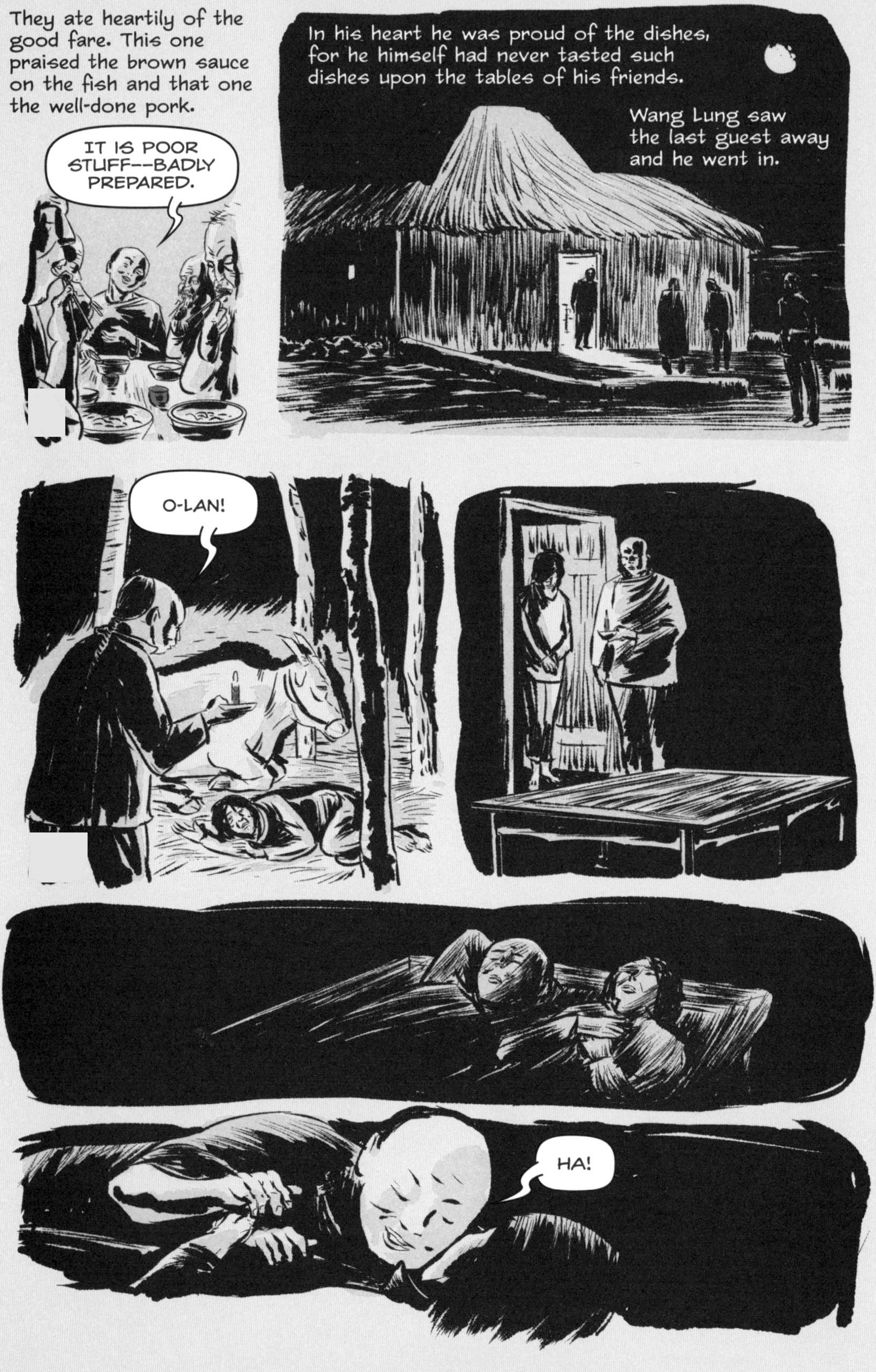
They ate heartily of the good fare. This one praised the brown sauce on the fish and that one the well-done pork.
IT IS POOR STUFF--BADLY PREPARED.
In his heart he was proud of the dishes, for he himself had never tasted such dishes upon the tables of his friends.
Wang Lung saw the last guest away and he went in.
O-LAN!
HA!

2

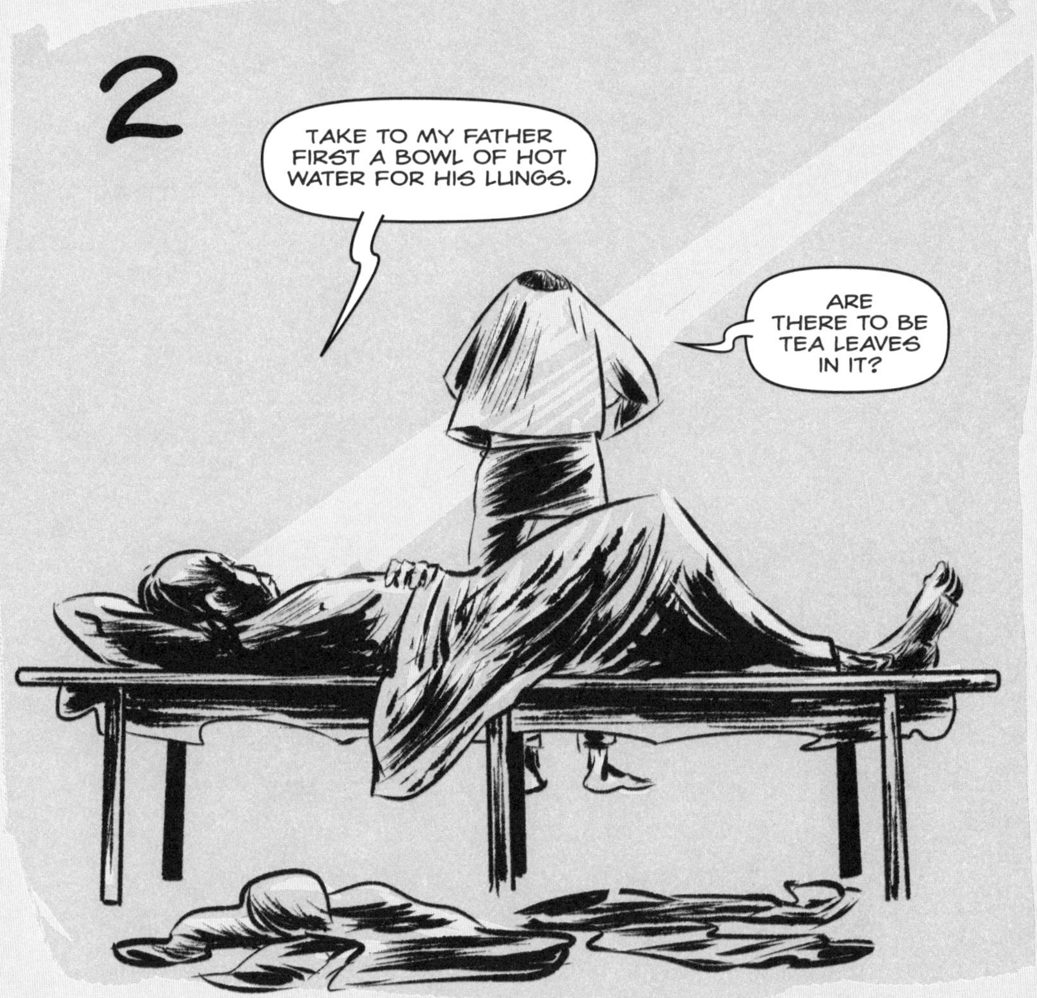
TAKE TO MY FATHER FIRST A BOWL OF HOT WATER FOR HIS LUNGS.
ARE THERE TO BE TEA LEAVES IN IT?

This simple question troubled Wang Lung as they really were not rich.

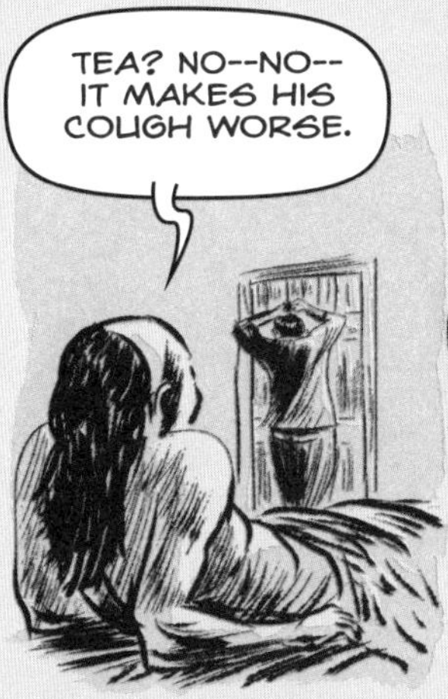
TEA? NO--NO-- IT MAKES HIS COUGH WORSE.

He lay there, tasting and savoring in his mind and in his flesh his luxury of idleness.

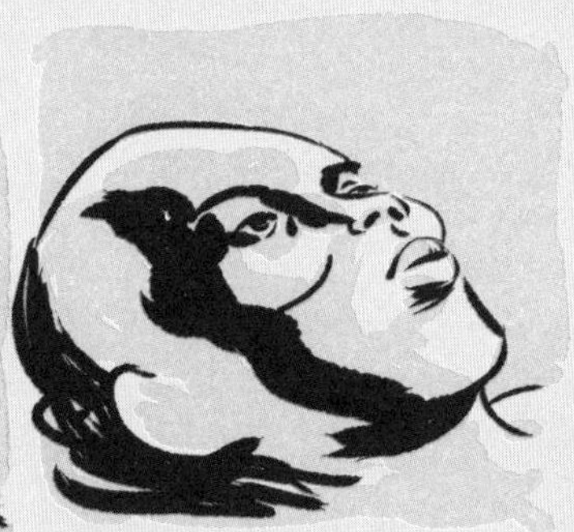

It occurred to him suddenly, thinking of the night, to wonder if she liked him.

And then he was ashamed of his own curiosity, and of his interest in her.

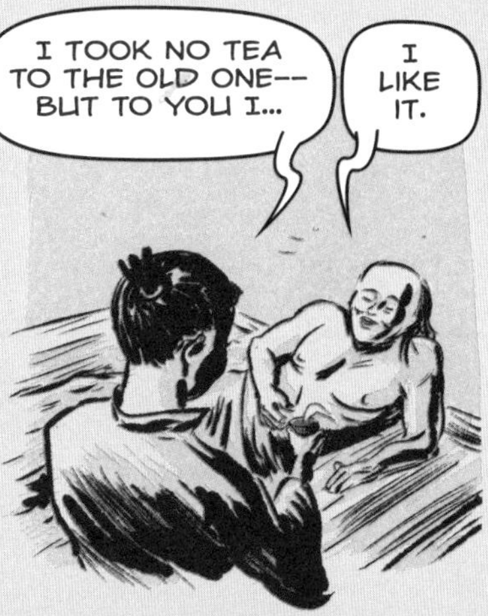
I TOOK NO TEA TO THE OLD ONE-- BUT TO YOU I...
I LIKE IT.

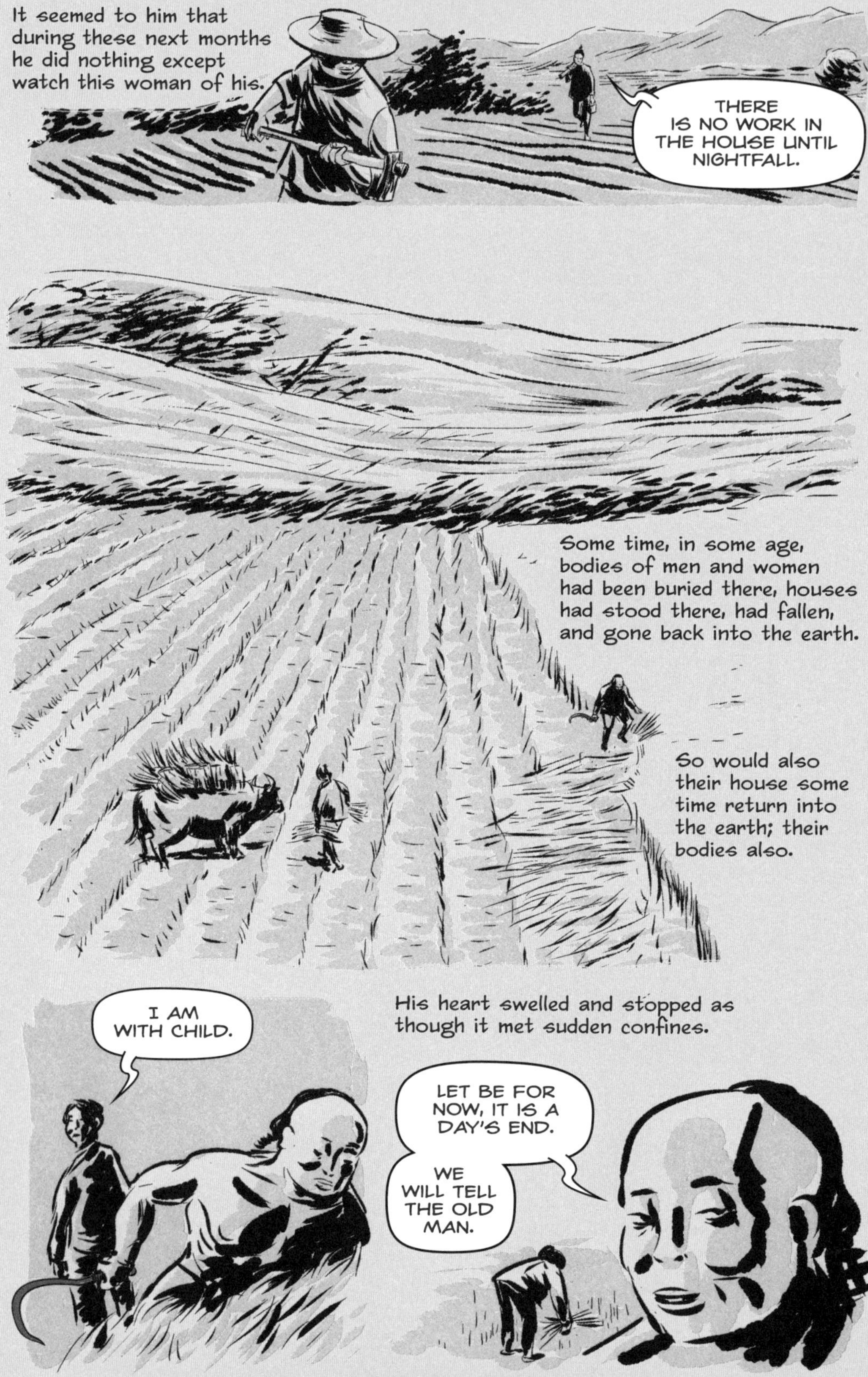
It seemed to him that during these next months he did nothing except watch this woman of his.
THERE IS NO WORK IN THE HOUSE UNTIL NIGHTFALL.
Some time, in some age, bodies of men and women had been buried there, houses had stood there, had fallen, and gone back into the earth.
So would also their house some time return into the earth; their bodies also.
I AM WITH CHILD.
His heart swelled and stopped as though it met sudden confines.
LET BE FOR NOW, IT IS A DAY'S END.
WE WILL TELL THE OLD MAN.

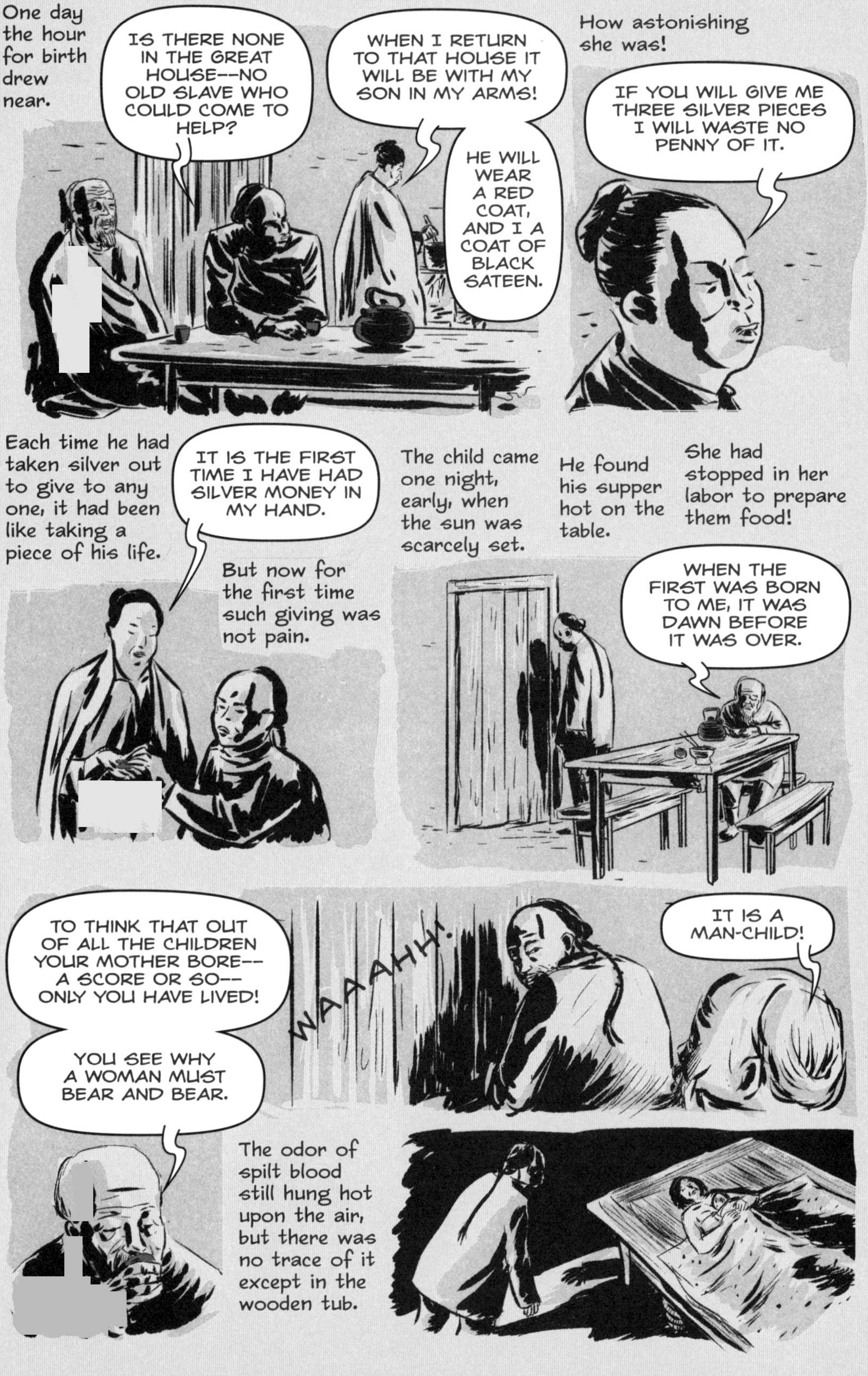
One day the hour for birth drew near.
IS THERE NONE IN THE GREAT HOUSE--NO OLD SLAVE WHO COULD COME TO HELP?
WHEN I RETURN TO THAT HOUSE IT WILL BE WITH MY SON IN MY ARMS!
HE WILL WEAR A RED COAT, AND I A COAT OF BLACK SATEEN.
How astonishing she was!
IF YOU WILL GIVE ME THREE SILVER PIECES I WILL WASTE NO PENNY OF IT.
Each time he had taken silver out to give to any one, it had been like taking a piece of his life.
IT IS THE FIRST TIME I HAVE HAD SILVER MONEY IN MY HAND.
But now for the first time such giving was not pain.
The child came one night, early, when the sun was scarcely set.
He found his supper hot on the table.
She had stopped in her labor to prepare them food!
WHEN THE FIRST WAS BORN TO ME, IT WAS DAWN BEFORE IT WAS OVER.
TO THINK THAT OUT OF ALL THE CHILDREN YOUR MOTHER BORE--A SCORE OR SO--ONLY YOU HAVE LIVED!
YOU SEE WHY A WOMAN MUST BEAR AND BEAR.
WAAAHH!
IT IS A MAN-CHILD!
The odor of spilt blood still hung hot upon the air, but there was no trace of it except in the wooden tub.

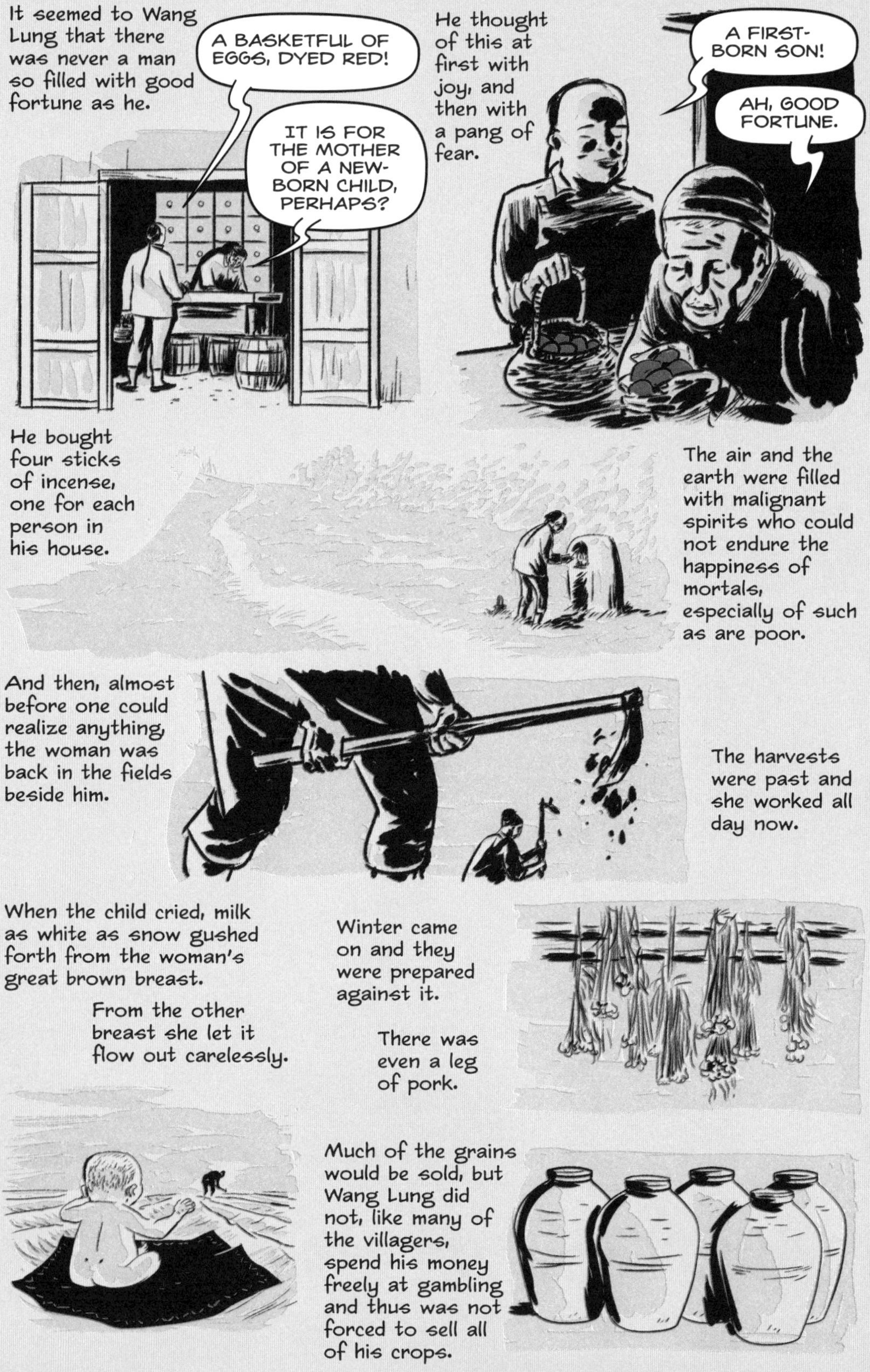
It seemed to Wang Lung that there was never a man so filled with good fortune as he.
A BASKETFUL OF EGGS, DYED RED!
IT IS FOR THE MOTHER OF A NEW-BORN CHILD, PERHAPS?
He thought of this at first with joy, and then with a pang of fear.
A FIRST-BORN SON!
AH, GOOD FORTUNE.
He bought four sticks of incense, one for each person in his house.
The air and the earth were filled with malignant spirits who could not endure the happiness of mortals, especially of such as are poor.
And then, almost before one could realize anything, the woman was back in the fields beside him.
The harvests were past and she worked all day now.
When the child cried, milk as white as snow gushed forth from the woman's great brown breast.
From the other breast she let it flow out carelessly.
Winter came on and they were prepared against it.
There was even a leg of pork.
Much of the grains would be sold, but Wang Lung did not, like many of the villagers, spend his money freely at gambling and thus was not forced to sell all of his crops.

He saved it and sold it when the snow came on the ground or at the New Year when people in the towns will pay well for food at any price.

His uncle was always having to sell his grain before it was even well ripened.

Sometimes, to get a little ready cash, he even sold it standing in the field to save himself the trouble of harvesting and threshing.

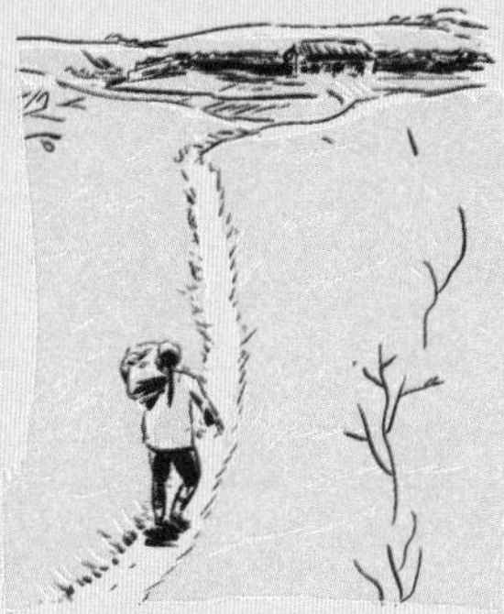

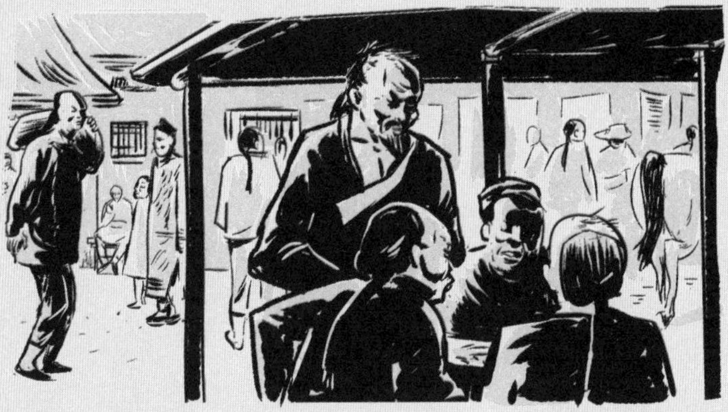

The leaves were soon torn from the date tree on the threshold and from the willow trees and the peach trees near the fields.

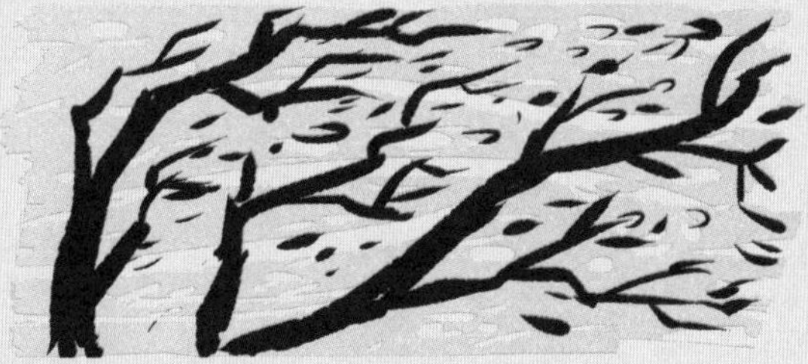

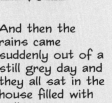

And then the rains came suddenly out of a still grey day and they all sat in the house filled with well-being.

And in the fields the wheat seed sprouted and in the village there was visiting.

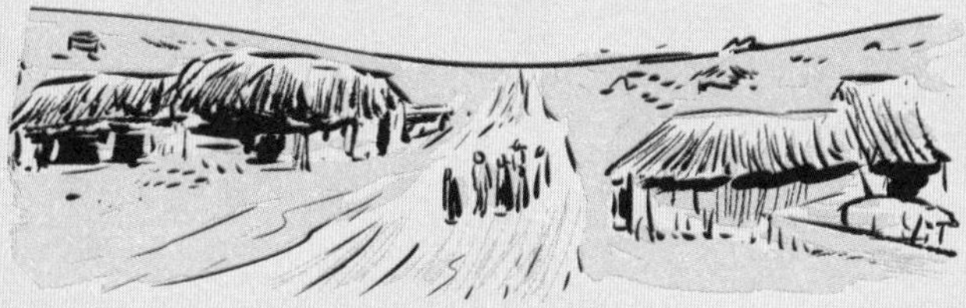

But Wang Lung and his wife were not frequent at visiting. He felt that if he became too intimate with the others there would be borrowing.

From the produce, Wang Lung in this good year had a handful of silver dollars over and above what they needed.

He was fearful of keeping them in his belt or of telling any except the woman what he had.

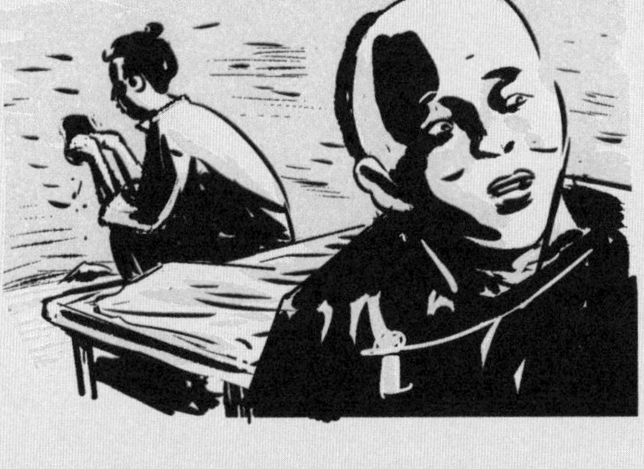

She cleverly dug a small hole in the inner wall of their room behind the bed.

Wang Lung walked among his fellows with a secret sense of richness and reserve.

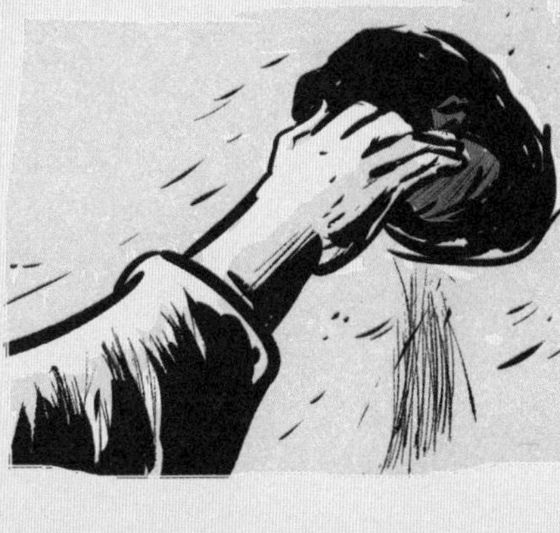

3

The New Year approached and in every house in the village there were preparations.

Wang Lung went into the town and he bought squares of red paper on which were brushed in gilt ink the word for happiness and some with the word for riches.

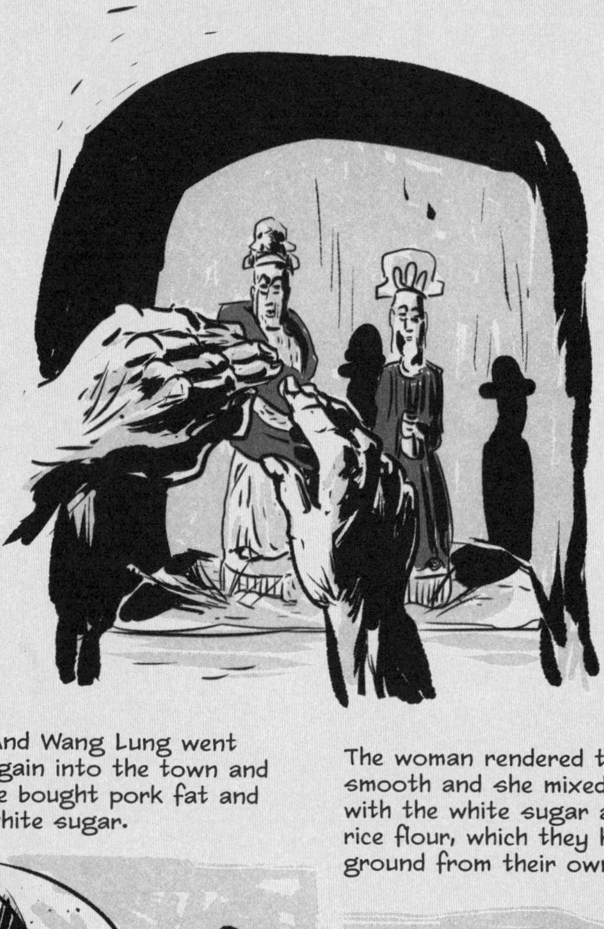

These squares he pasted upon his farm utensils to bring him luck in the New Year.

And he bought red paper for his father to make new dresses for the gods.

And Wang Lung went again into the town and he bought pork fat and white sugar.

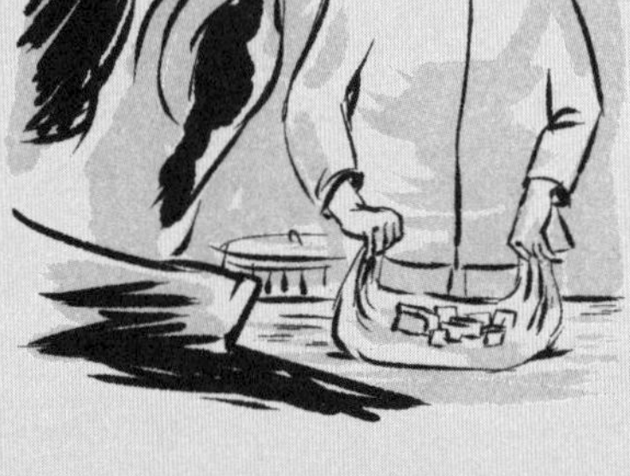

The woman rendered the fat smooth and she mixed it with the white sugar and rice flour, which they had ground from their own rice.

The woman kneaded rich New Year's cakes, called moon cakes, such as were eaten in the House of Hwang.

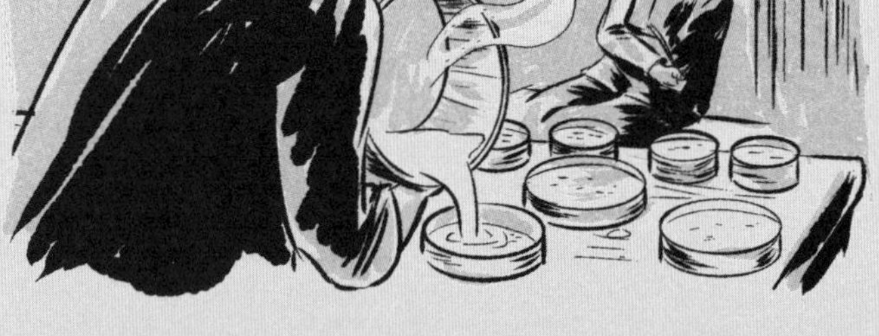

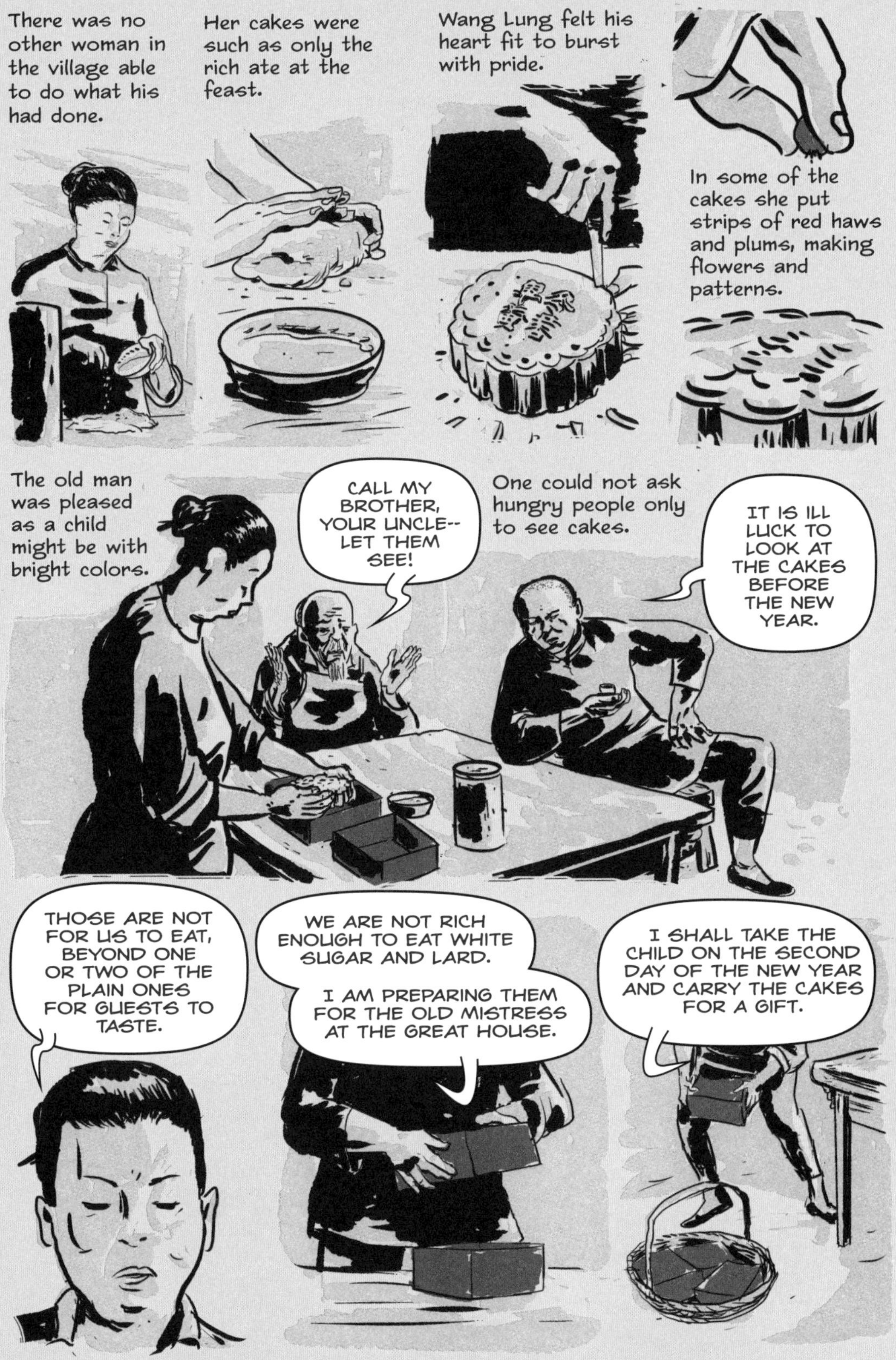
There was no other woman in the village able to do what his had done.
Her cakes were such as only the rich ate at the feast.
Wang Lung felt his heart fit to burst with pride.
In some of the cakes she put strips of red haws and plums, making flowers and patterns.
The old man was pleased as a child might be with bright colors.
CALL MY BROTHER, YOUR UNCLE-- LET THEM SEE!
One could not ask hungry people only to see cakes.
IT IS ILL LUCK TO LOOK AT THE CAKES BEFORE THE NEW YEAR.
THOSE ARE NOT FOR US TO EAT, BEYOND ONE OR TWO OF THE PLAIN ONES FOR GUESTS TO TASTE.
WE ARE NOT RICH ENOUGH TO EAT WHITE SUGAR AND LARD.
I AM PREPARING THEM FOR THE OLD MISTRESS AT THE GREAT HOUSE.
I SHALL TAKE THE CHILD ON THE SECOND DAY OF THE NEW YEAR AND CARRY THE CAKES FOR A GIFT.

Wang Lung was pleased that to the great hall where he had stood with timidity and in such poverty his wife should now go.

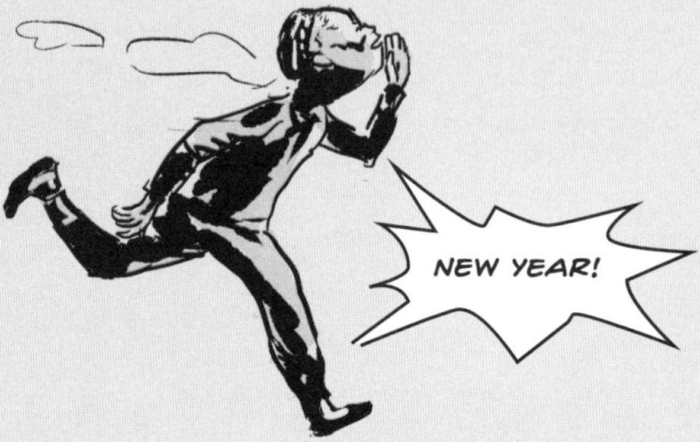
NEW YEAR!

All else at that New Year sank into insignificance beside the visit.

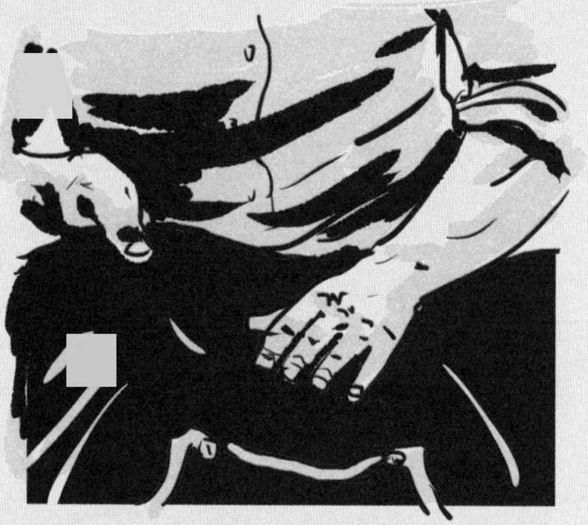

O-lan made him a new coat of black cotton cloth which made him say to himself:

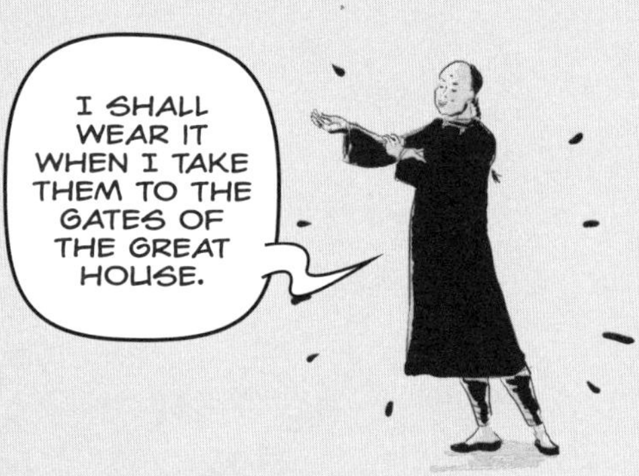
I SHALL WEAR IT WHEN I TAKE THEM TO THE GATES OF THE GREAT HOUSE.

When his uncle and neighbors came to the house, he found it very hard not to cry out:

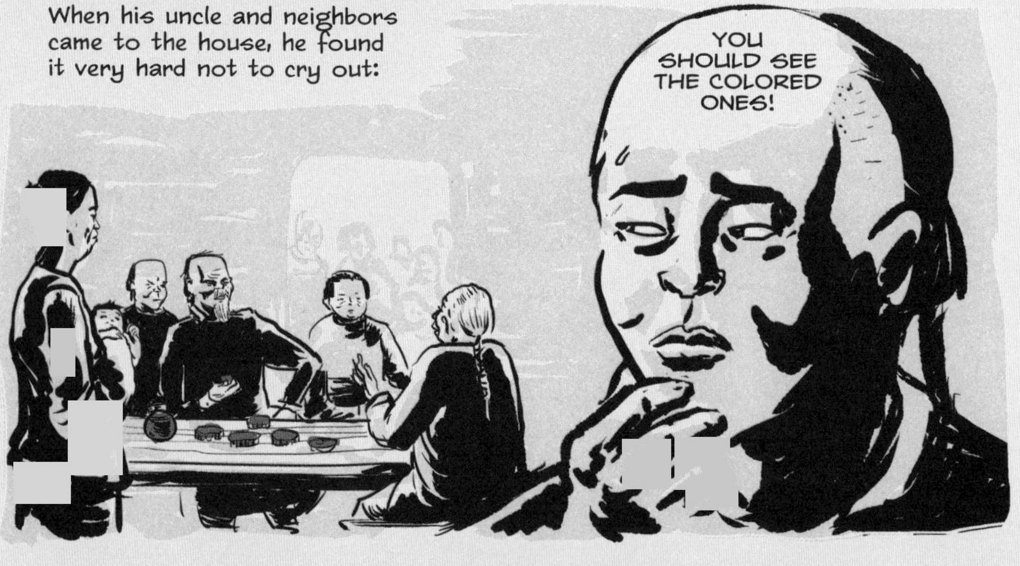
YOU SHOULD SEE THE COLORED ONES!

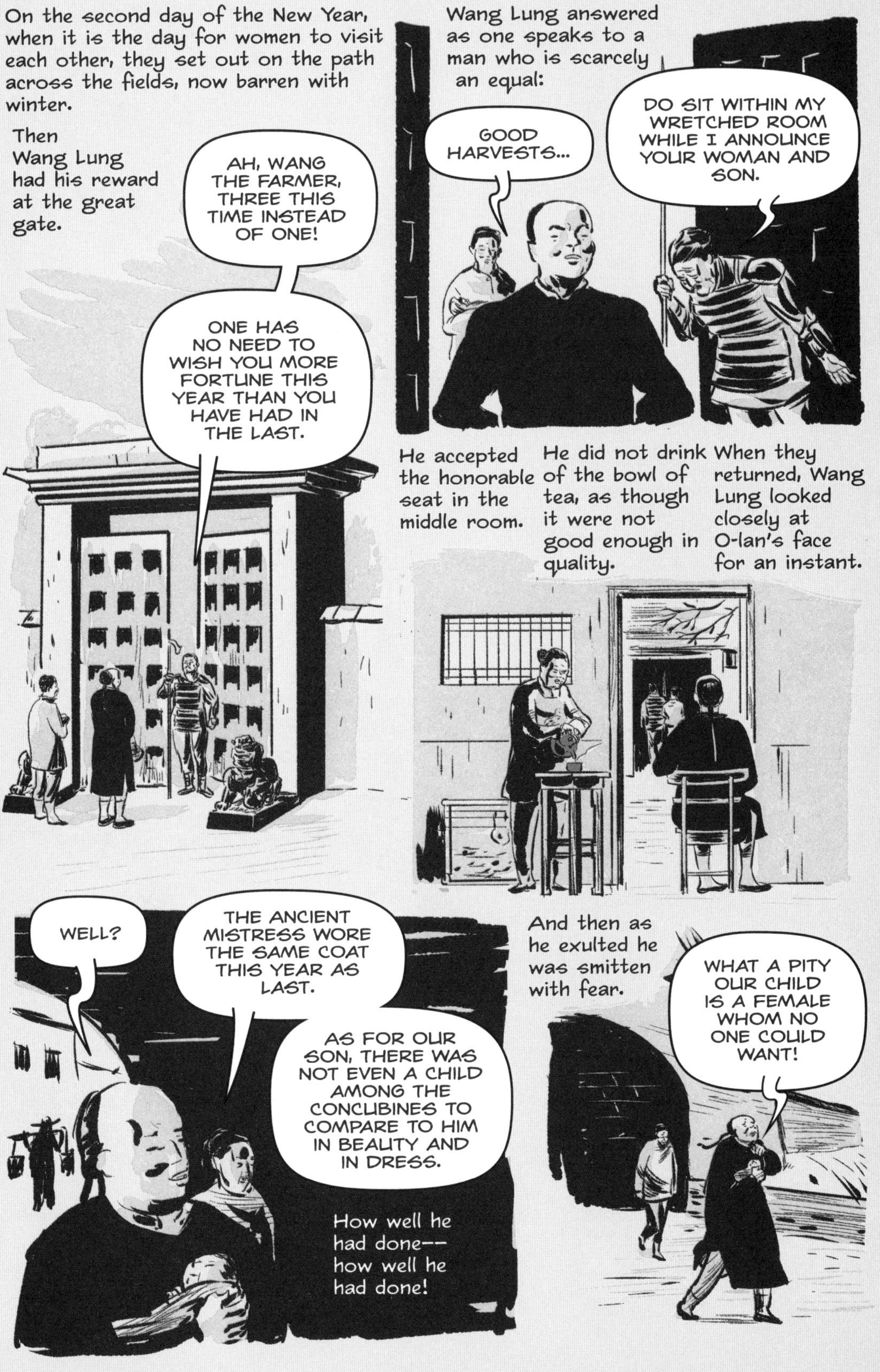
On the second day of the New Year, when it is the day for women to visit each other, they set out on the path across the fields, now barren with winter.
Then Wang Lung had his reward at the great gate.
AH, WANG THE FARMER, THREE THIS TIME INSTEAD OF ONE!
ONE HAS NO NEED TO WISH YOU MORE FORTUNE THIS YEAR THAN YOU HAVE HAD IN THE LAST.
Wang Lung answered as one speaks to a man who is scarcely an equal:
GOOD HARVESTS...
DO SIT WITHIN MY WRETCHED ROOM WHILE I ANNOUNCE YOUR WOMAN AND SON.
He accepted the honorable seat in the middle room.
He did not drink of the bowl of tea, as though it were not good enough in quality.
When they returned, Wang Lung looked closely at O-lan's face for an instant.
WELL?
THE ANCIENT MISTRESS WORE THE SAME COAT THIS YEAR AS LAST.
AS FOR OUR SON, THERE WAS NOT EVEN A CHILD AMONG THE CONCUBINES TO COMPARE TO HIM IN BEAUTY AND IN DRESS.
How well he had done-- how well he had done!
And then as he exulted he was smitten with fear.
WHAT A PITY OUR CHILD IS A FEMALE WHOM NO ONE COULD WANT!

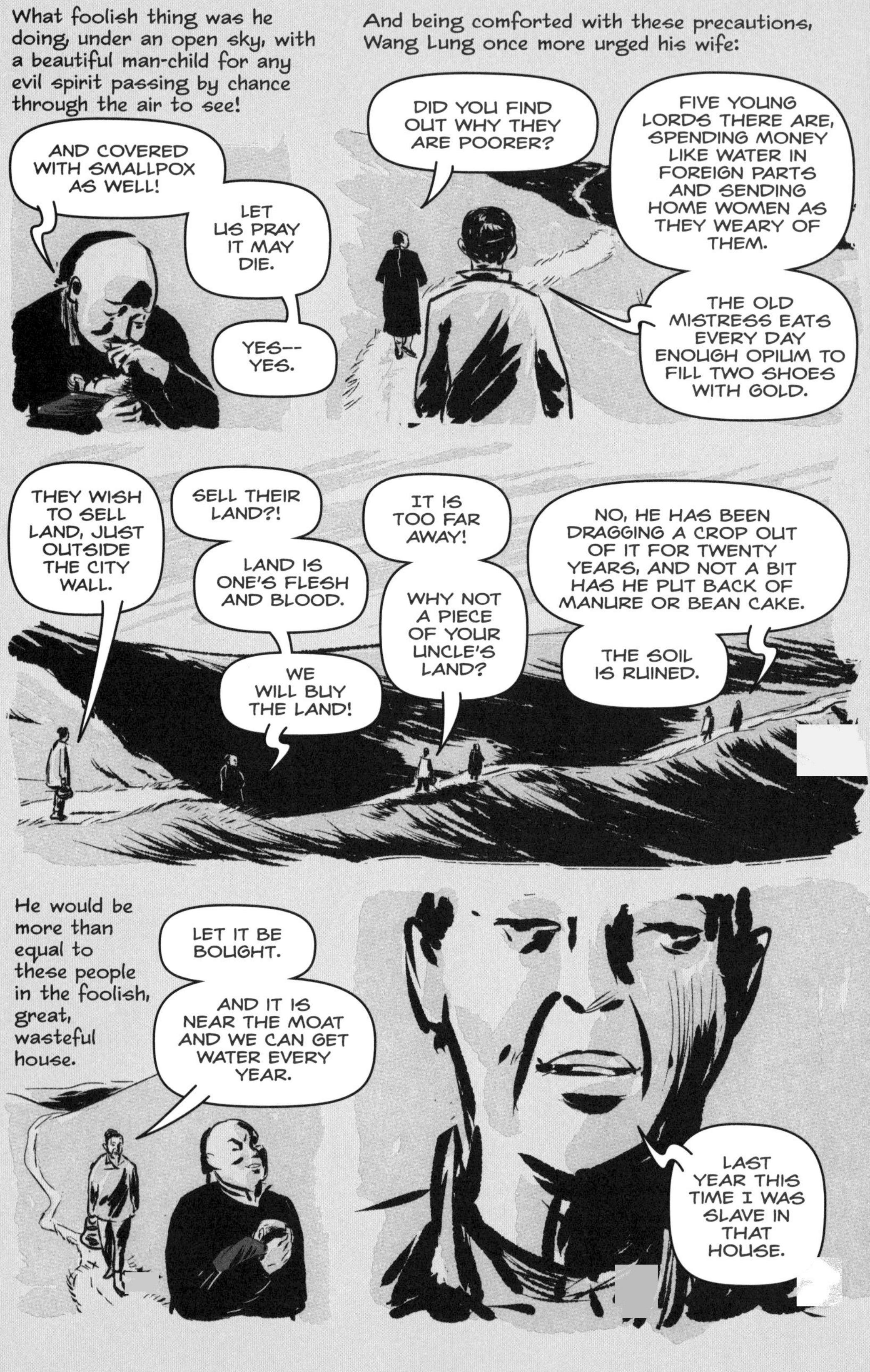
What foolish thing was he doing, under an open sky, with a beautiful man-child for any evil spirit passing by chance through the air to see!
AND COVERED WITH SMALLPOX AS WELL!
LET US PRAY IT MAY DIE.
YES-- YES.
And being comforted with these precautions, Wang Lung once more urged his wife:
DID YOU FIND OUT WHY THEY ARE POORER?
FIVE YOUNG LORDS THERE ARE, SPENDING MONEY LIKE WATER IN FOREIGN PARTS AND SENDING HOME WOMEN AS THEY WEARY OF THEM.
THE OLD MISTRESS EATS EVERY DAY ENOUGH OPIUM TO FILL TWO SHOES WITH GOLD.
THEY WISH TO SELL LAND, JUST OUTSIDE THE CITY WALL.
SELL THEIR LAND?!
LAND IS ONE'S FLESH AND BLOOD.
WE WILL BUY THE LAND!
IT IS TOO FAR AWAY!
WHY NOT A PIECE OF YOUR UNCLE'S LAND?
NO, HE HAS BEEN DRAGGING A CROP OUT OF IT FOR TWENTY YEARS, AND NOT A BIT HAS HE PUT BACK OF MANURE OR BEAN CAKE.
THE SOIL IS RUINED.
He would be more than equal to these people in the foolish, great, wasteful house.
LET IT BE BOUGHT.
AND IT IS NEAR THE MOAT AND WE CAN GET WATER EVERY YEAR.
LAST YEAR THIS TIME I WAS SLAVE IN THAT HOUSE.

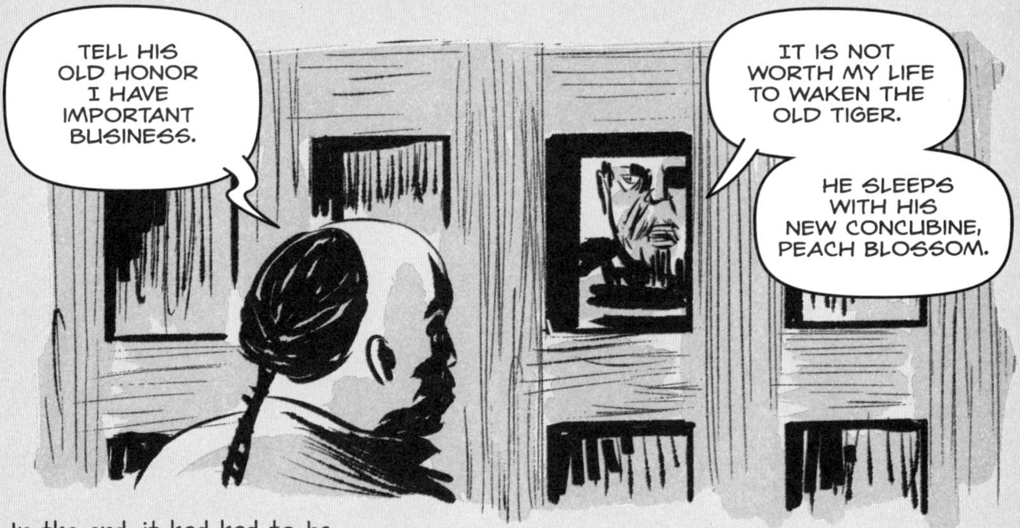
TELL HIS OLD HONOR I HAVE IMPORTANT BUSINESS.
IT IS NOT WORTH MY LIFE TO WAKEN THE OLD TIGER.
HE SLEEPS WITH HIS NEW CONCUBINE, PEACH BLOSSOM.

In the end, it had had to be managed with the Old Lord's agent, an oily scoundrel.

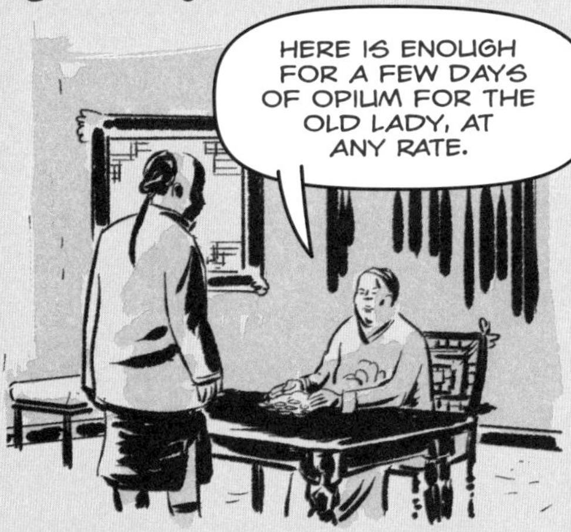
HERE IS ENOUGH FOR A FEW DAYS OF OPIUM FOR THE OLD LADY, AT ANY RATE.

He paced the land off carefully, three hundred paces lengthwise and a hundred and twenty across.

None knew yet that it belonged to him.

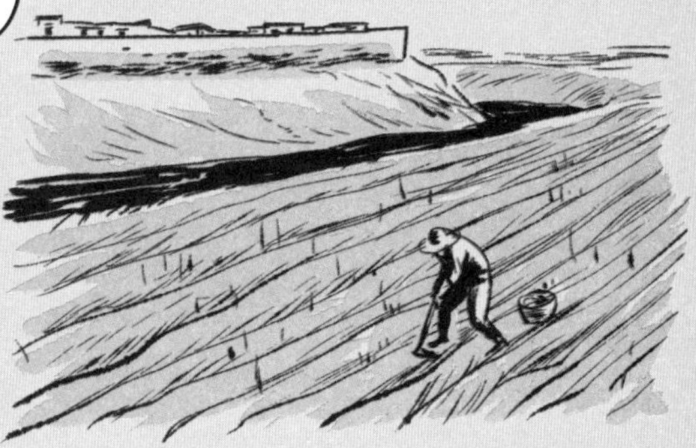

He was filled with an angry determination then, that he would buy from the House of Hwang so much land that his own would be less than an inch in his sight.

And so this parcel of land became to Wang Lung a sign and a symbol.

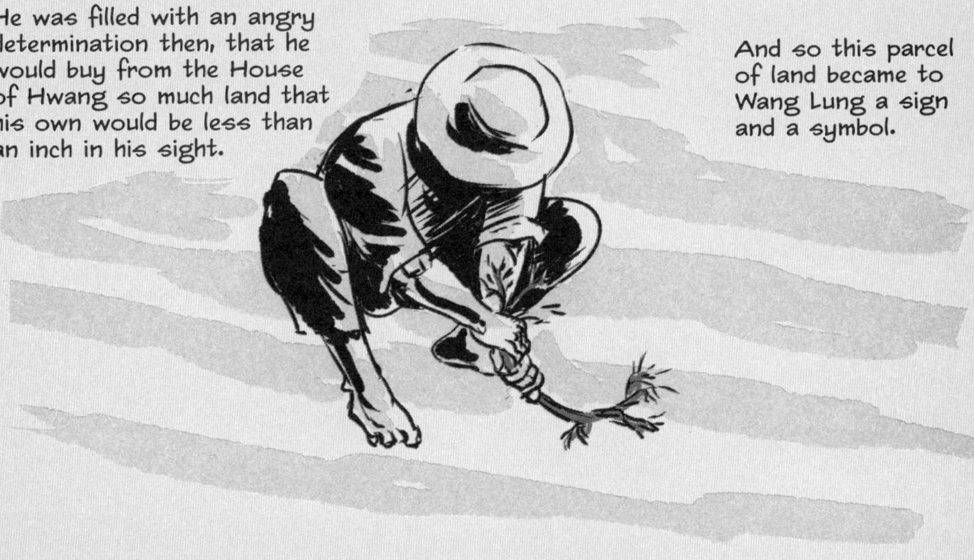

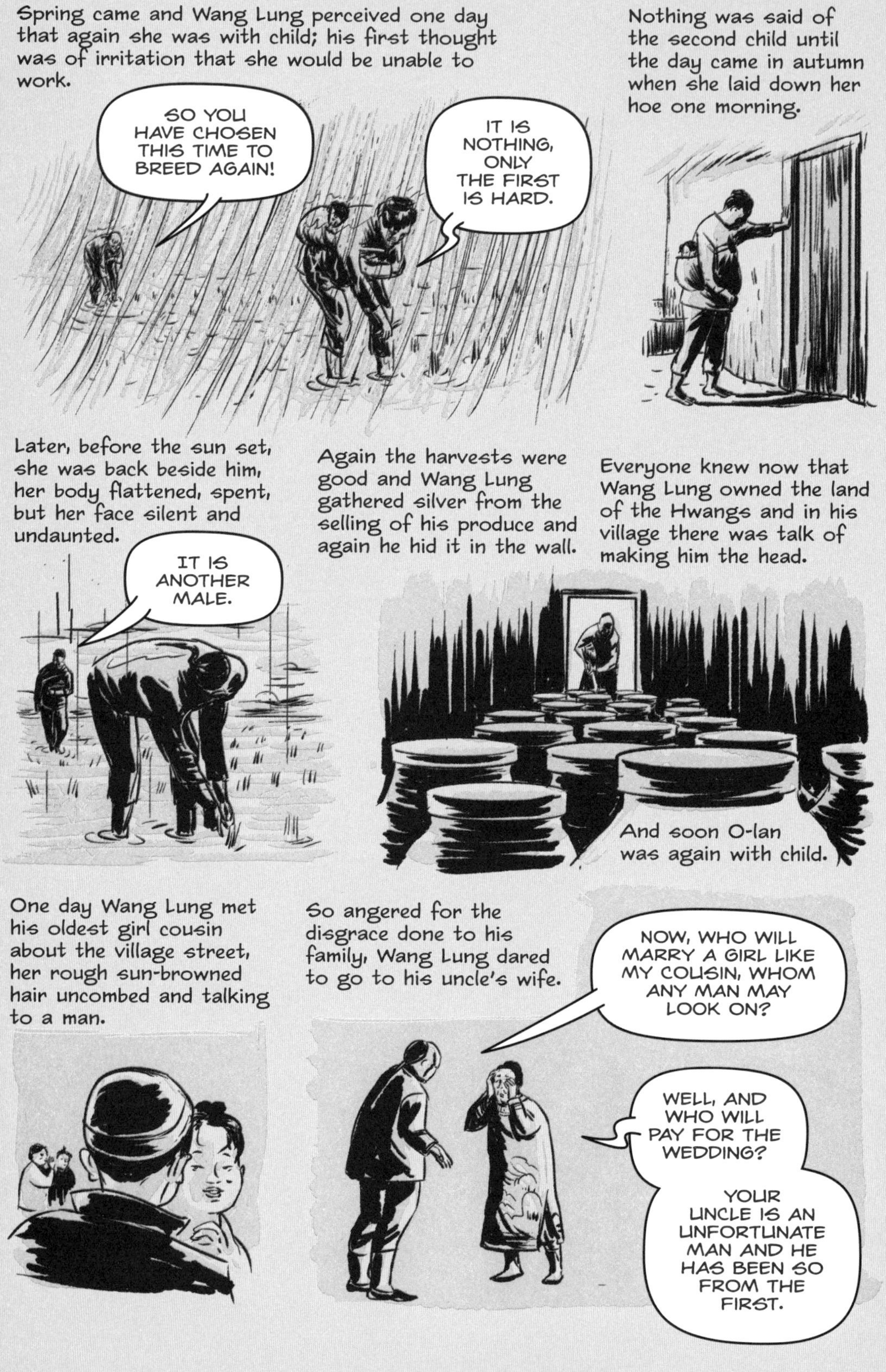
Spring came and Wang Lung perceived one day that again she was with child; his first thought was of irritation that she would be unable to work.
SO YOU HAVE CHOSEN THIS TIME TO BREED AGAIN!
IT IS NOTHING, ONLY THE FIRST IS HARD.
Nothing was said of the second child until the day came in autumn when she laid down her hoe one morning.
Later, before the sun set, she was back beside him, her body flattened, spent, but her face silent and undaunted.
IT IS ANOTHER MALE.
Again the harvests were good and Wang Lung gathered silver from the selling of his produce and again he hid it in the wall.
Everyone knew now that Wang Lung owned the land of the Hwangs and in his village there was talk of making him the head.
And soon O-lan was again with child.
One day Wang Lung met his oldest girl cousin about the village street, her rough sun-browned hair uncombed and talking to a man.
So angered for the disgrace done to his family, Wang Lung dared to go to his uncle's wife.
NOW, WHO WILL MARRY A GIRL LIKE MY COUSIN, WHOM ANY MAN MAY LOOK ON?
WELL, AND WHO WILL PAY FOR THE WEDDING?
YOUR UNCLE IS AN UNFORTUNATE MAN AND HE HAS BEEN SO FROM THE FIRST.

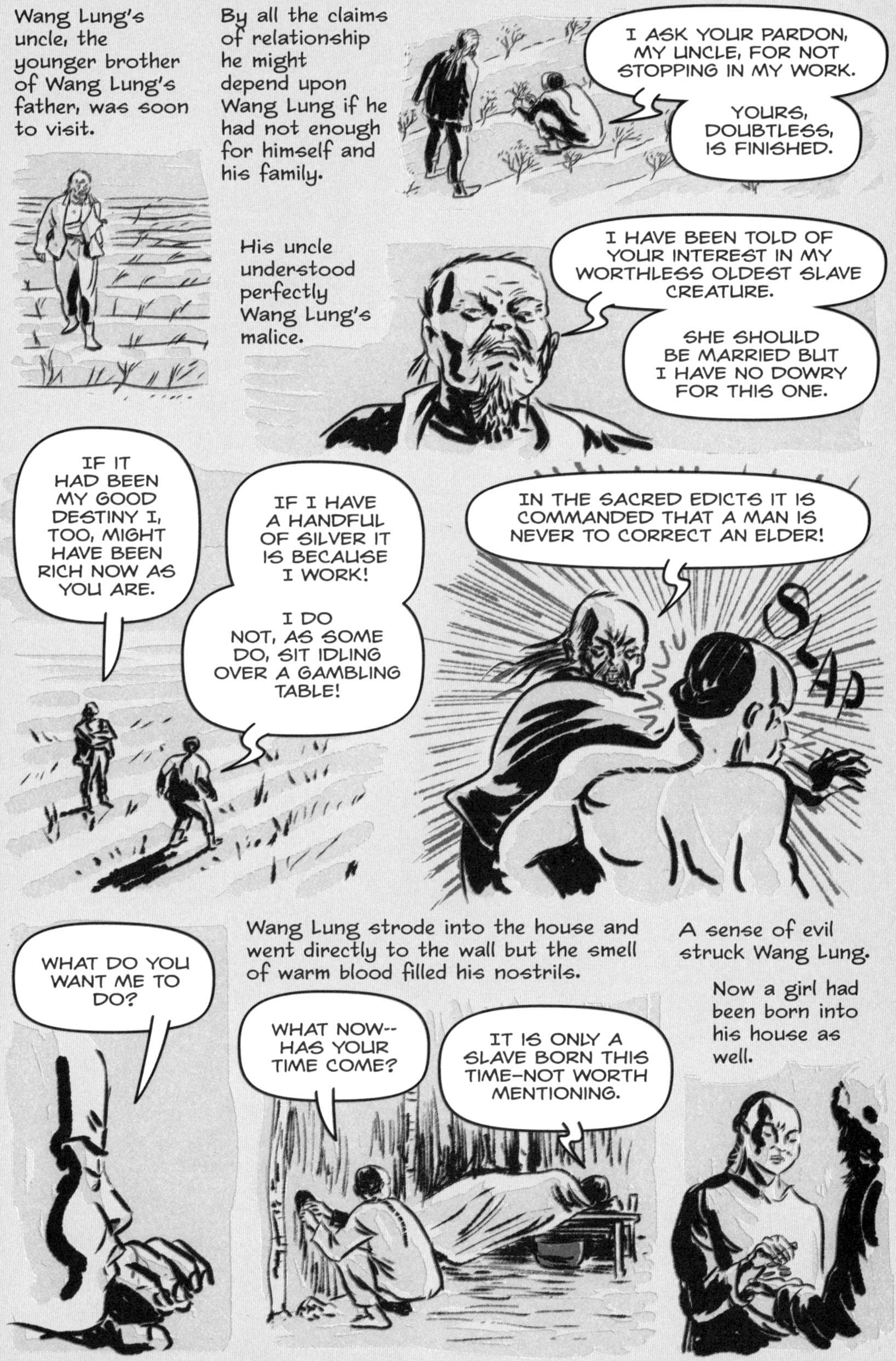
Wang Lung's uncle, the younger brother of Wang Lung's father, was soon to visit.
By all the claims of relationship he might depend upon Wang Lung if he had not enough for himself and his family.
I ASK YOUR PARDON, MY UNCLE, FOR NOT STOPPING IN MY WORK.
YOURS, DOUBTLESS, IS FINISHED.
His uncle understood perfectly Wang Lung's malice.
I HAVE BEEN TOLD OF YOUR INTEREST IN MY WORTHLESS OLDEST SLAVE CREATURE.
SHE SHOULD BE MARRIED BUT I HAVE NO DOWRY FOR THIS ONE.
IF IT HAD BEEN MY GOOD DESTINY I, TOO, MIGHT HAVE BEEN RICH NOW AS YOU ARE.
IF I HAVE A HANDFUL OF SILVER IT IS BECAUSE I WORK!
I DO NOT, AS SOME DO, SIT IDLING OVER A GAMBLING TABLE!
IN THE SACRED EDICTS IT IS COMMANDED THAT A MAN IS NEVER TO CORRECT AN ELDER!
SLAP
WHAT DO YOU WANT ME TO DO?
Wang Lung strode into the house and went directly to the wall but the smell of warm blood filled his nostrils.
WHAT NOW-- HAS YOUR TIME COME?
IT IS ONLY A SLAVE BORN THIS TIME—NOT WORTH MENTIONING.
A sense of evil struck Wang Lung.
Now a girl had been born into his house as well.

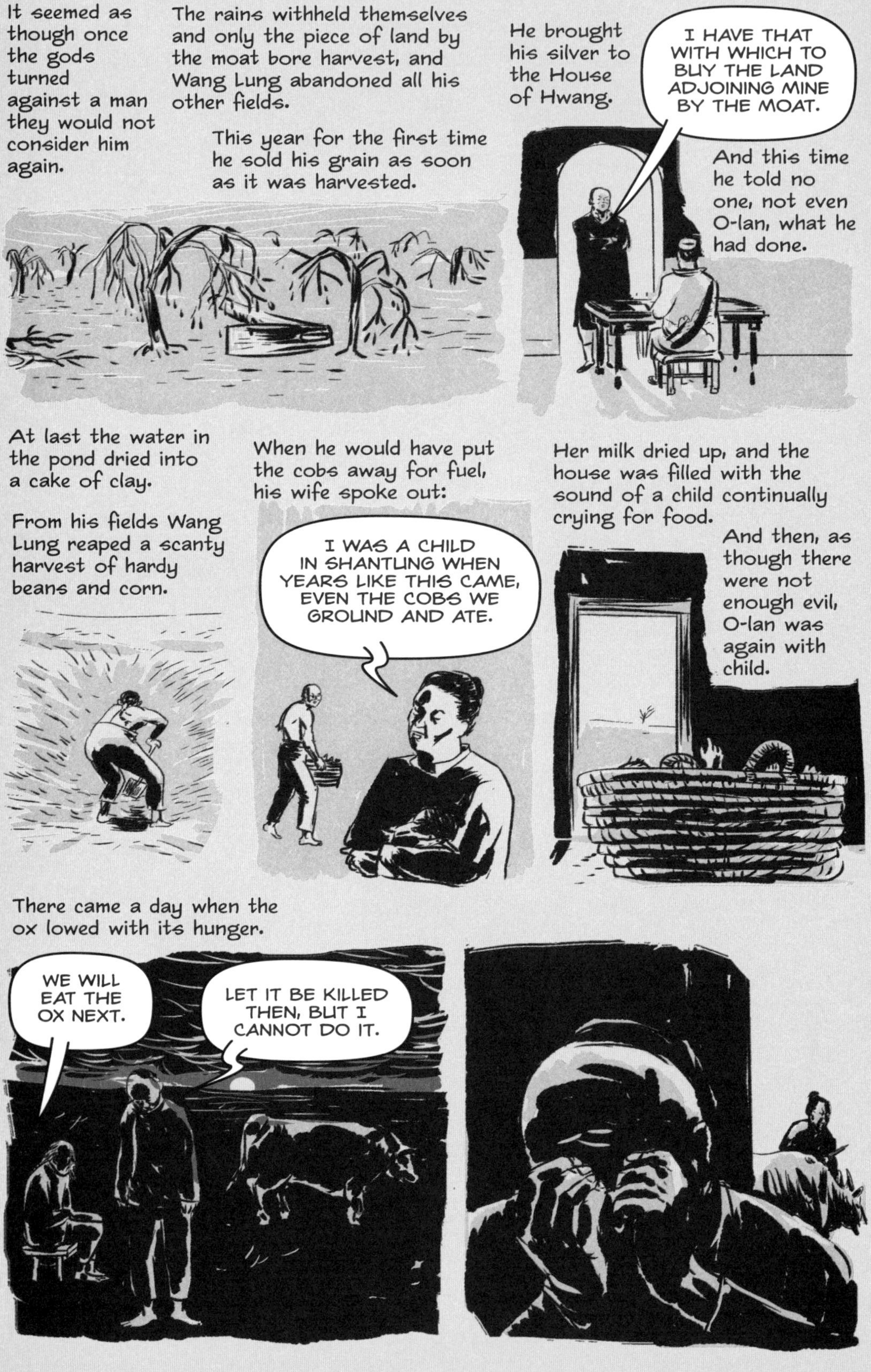
It seemed as though once the gods turned against a man they would not consider him again.
The rains withheld themselves and only the piece of land by the moat bore harvest, and Wang Lung abandoned all his other fields.
This year for the first time he sold his grain as soon as it was harvested.
He brought his silver to the House of Hwang.
I HAVE THAT WITH WHICH TO BUY THE LAND ADJOINING MINE BY THE MOAT.
And this time he told no one, not even O-lan, what he had done.
At last the water in the pond dried into a cake of clay.
From his fields Wang Lung reaped a scanty harvest of hardy beans and corn.
When he would have put the cobs away for fuel, his wife spoke out:
I WAS A CHILD IN SHANTUNG WHEN YEARS LIKE THIS CAME, EVEN THE COBS WE GROUND AND ATE.
Her milk dried up, and the house was filled with the sound of a child continually crying for food.
And then, as though there were not enough evil, O-lan was again with child.
There came a day when the ox lowed with its hunger.
WE WILL EAT THE OX NEXT.
LET IT BE KILLED THEN, BUT I CANNOT DO IT.

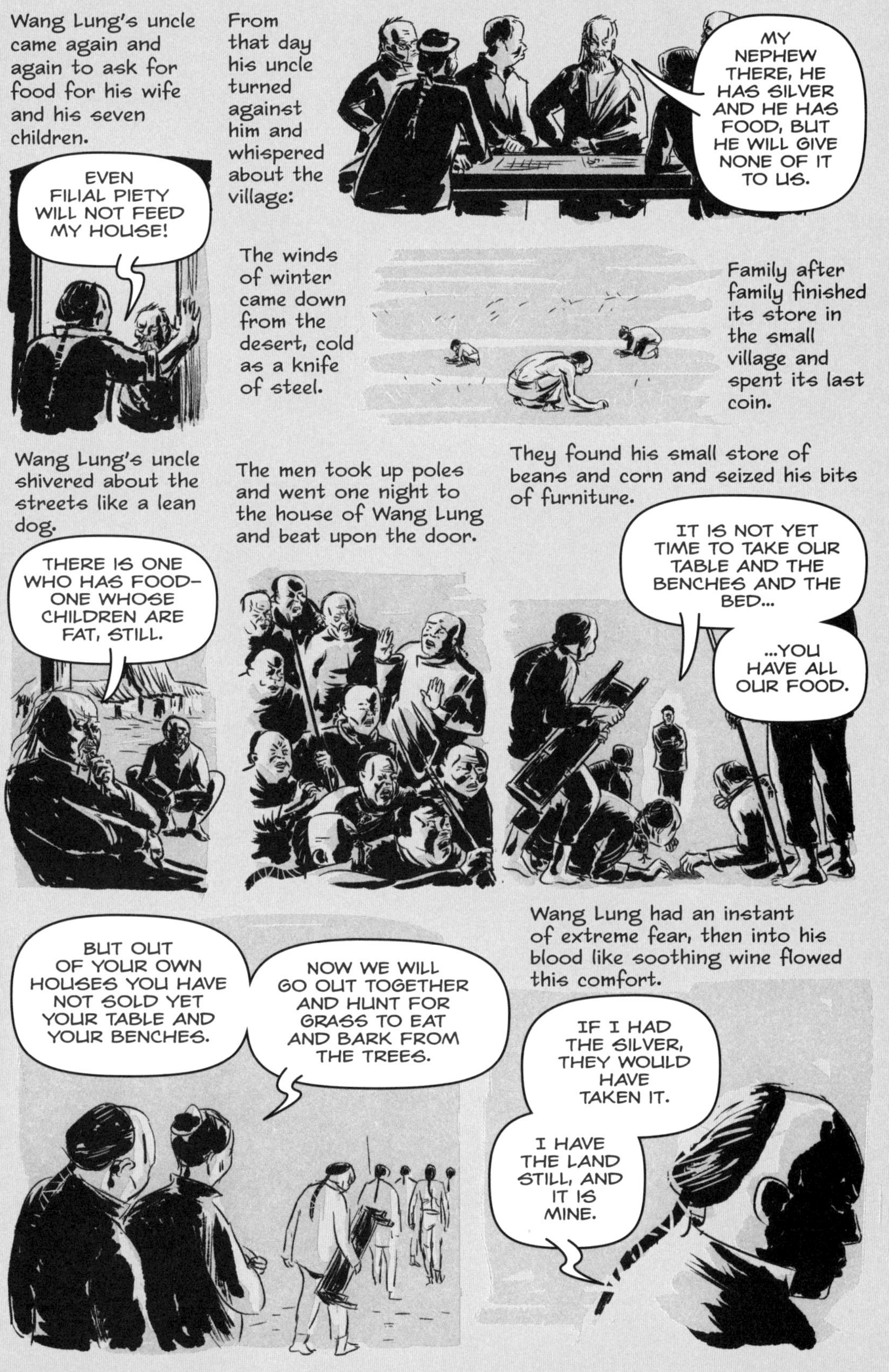
Wang Lung's uncle came again and again to ask for food for his wife and his seven children.
EVEN FILIAL PIETY WILL NOT FEED MY HOUSE!
From that day his uncle turned against him and whispered about the village:
MY NEPHEW THERE, HE HAS SILVER AND HE HAS FOOD, BUT HE WILL GIVE NONE OF IT TO US.
The winds of winter came down from the desert, cold as a knife of steel.
Family after family finished its store in the small village and spent its last coin.
Wang Lung's uncle shivered about the streets like a lean dog.
THERE IS ONE WHO HAS FOOD— ONE WHOSE CHILDREN ARE FAT, STILL.
The men took up poles and went one night to the house of Wang Lung and beat upon the door.
They found his small store of beans and corn and seized his bits of furniture.
IT IS NOT YET TIME TO TAKE OUR TABLE AND THE BENCHES AND THE BED...
...YOU HAVE ALL OUR FOOD.
BUT OUT OF YOUR OWN HOUSES YOU HAVE NOT SOLD YET YOUR TABLE AND YOUR BENCHES.
NOW WE WILL GO OUT TOGETHER AND HUNT FOR GRASS TO EAT AND BARK FROM THE TREES.
Wang Lung had an instant of extreme fear, then into his blood like soothing wine flowed this comfort.
IF I HAD THE SILVER, THEY WOULD HAVE TAKEN IT.
I HAVE THE LAND STILL, AND IT IS MINE.

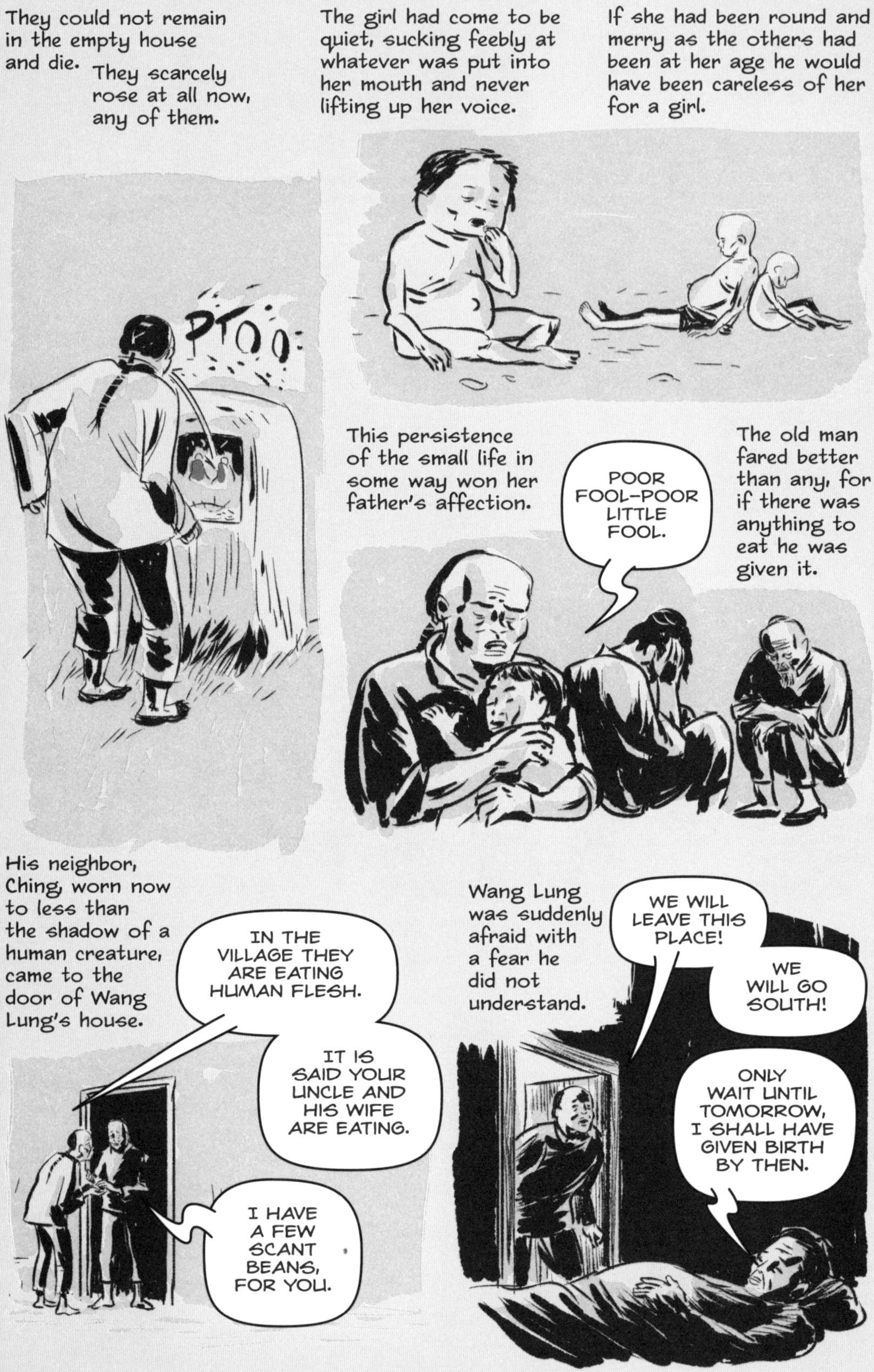
They could not remain in the empty house and die.
They scarcely rose at all now, any of them.
PTOO
The girl had come to be quiet, sucking feebly at whatever was put into her mouth and never lifting up her voice.
If she had been round and merry as the others had been at her age he would have been careless of her for a girl.
This persistence of the small life in some way won her father's affection.
POOR FOOL—POOR LITTLE FOOL.
The old man fared better than any, for if there was anything to eat he was given it.
His neighbor, Ching, worn now to less than the shadow of a human creature, came to the door of Wang Lung's house.
IN THE VILLAGE THEY ARE EATING HUMAN FLESH.
IT IS SAID YOUR UNCLE AND HIS WIFE ARE EATING.
I HAVE A FEW SCANT BEANS, FOR YOU.
Wang Lung was suddenly afraid with a fear he did not understand.
WE WILL LEAVE THIS PLACE!
WE WILL GO SOUTH!
ONLY WAIT UNTIL TOMORROW, I SHALL HAVE GIVEN BIRTH BY THEN.

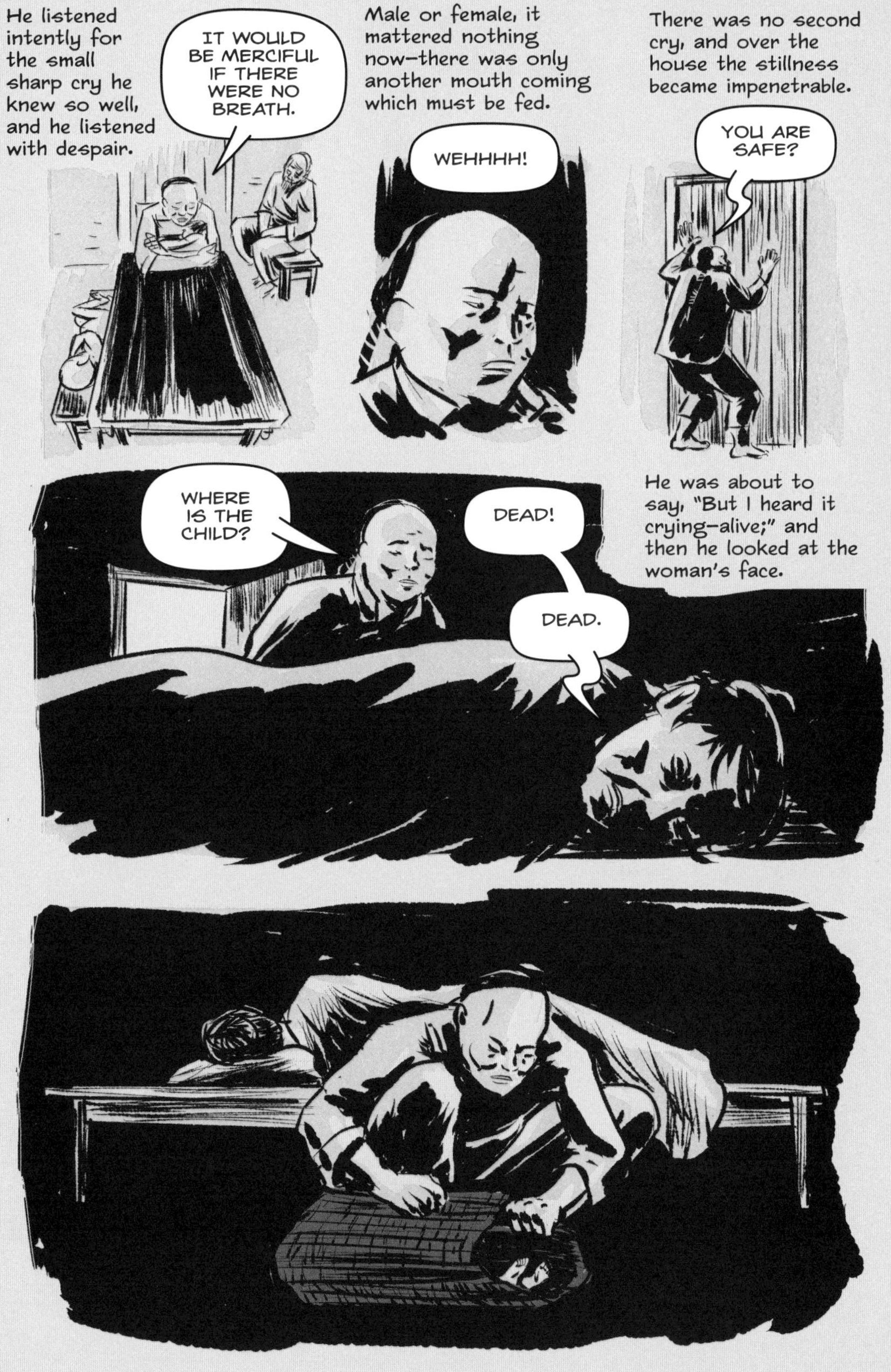
He listened intently for the small sharp cry he knew so well, and he listened with despair.
IT WOULD BE MERCIFUL IF THERE WERE NO BREATH.
Male or female, it mattered nothing now—there was only another mouth coming which must be fed.
WEHHHH!
There was no second cry, and over the house the stillness became impenetrable.
YOU ARE SAFE?
WHERE IS THE CHILD?
DEAD!
DEAD.
He was about to say, "But I heard it crying—alive;" and then he looked at the woman's face.

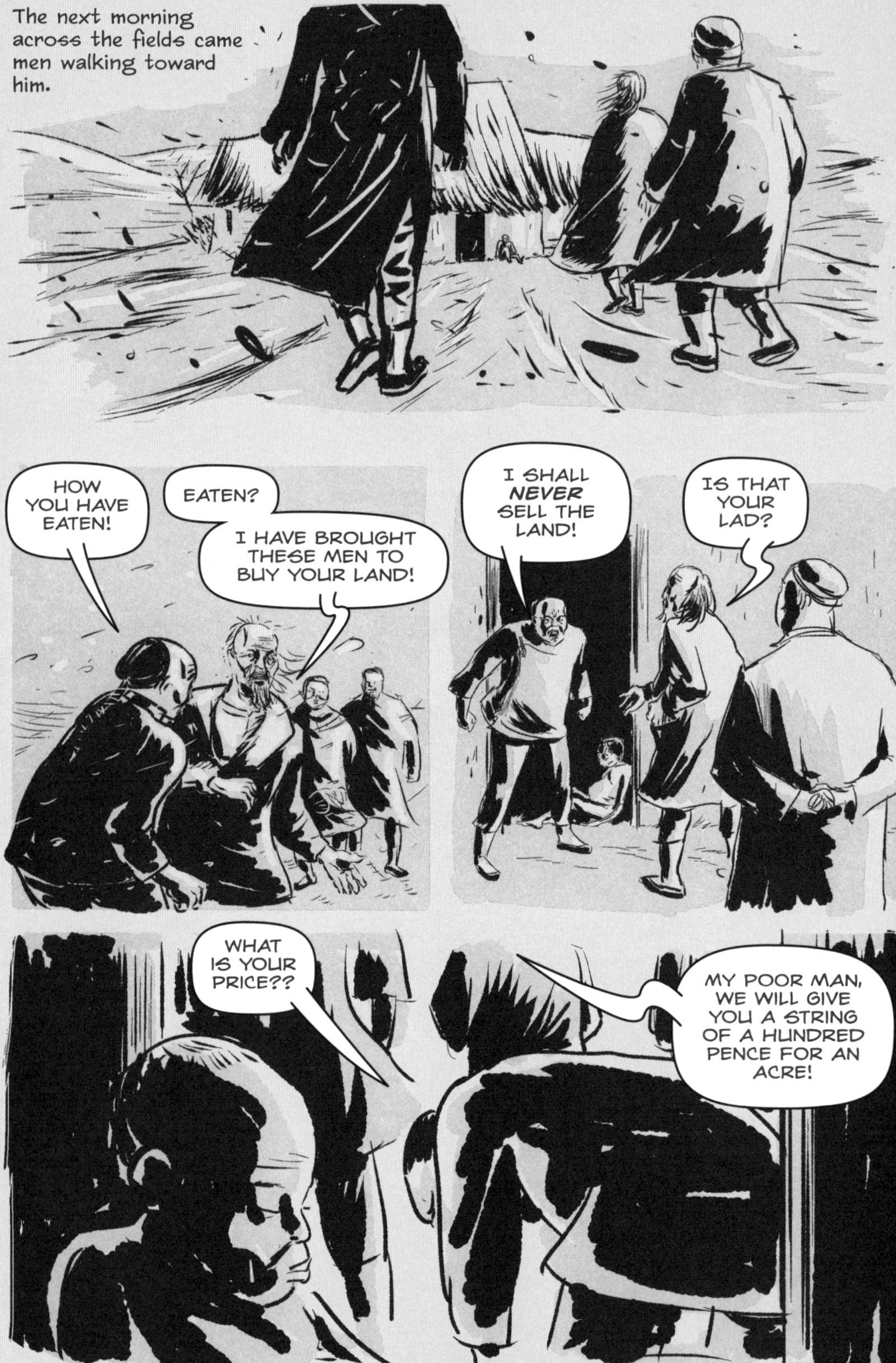
The next morning across the fields came men walking toward him.
HOW YOU HAVE EATEN!
EATEN?
I HAVE BROUGHT THESE MEN TO BUY YOUR LAND!
I SHALL NEVER SELL THE LAND!
IS THAT YOUR LAD?
WHAT IS YOUR PRICE??
MY POOR MAN, WE WILL GIVE YOU A STRING OF A HUNDRED PENCE FOR AN ACRE!

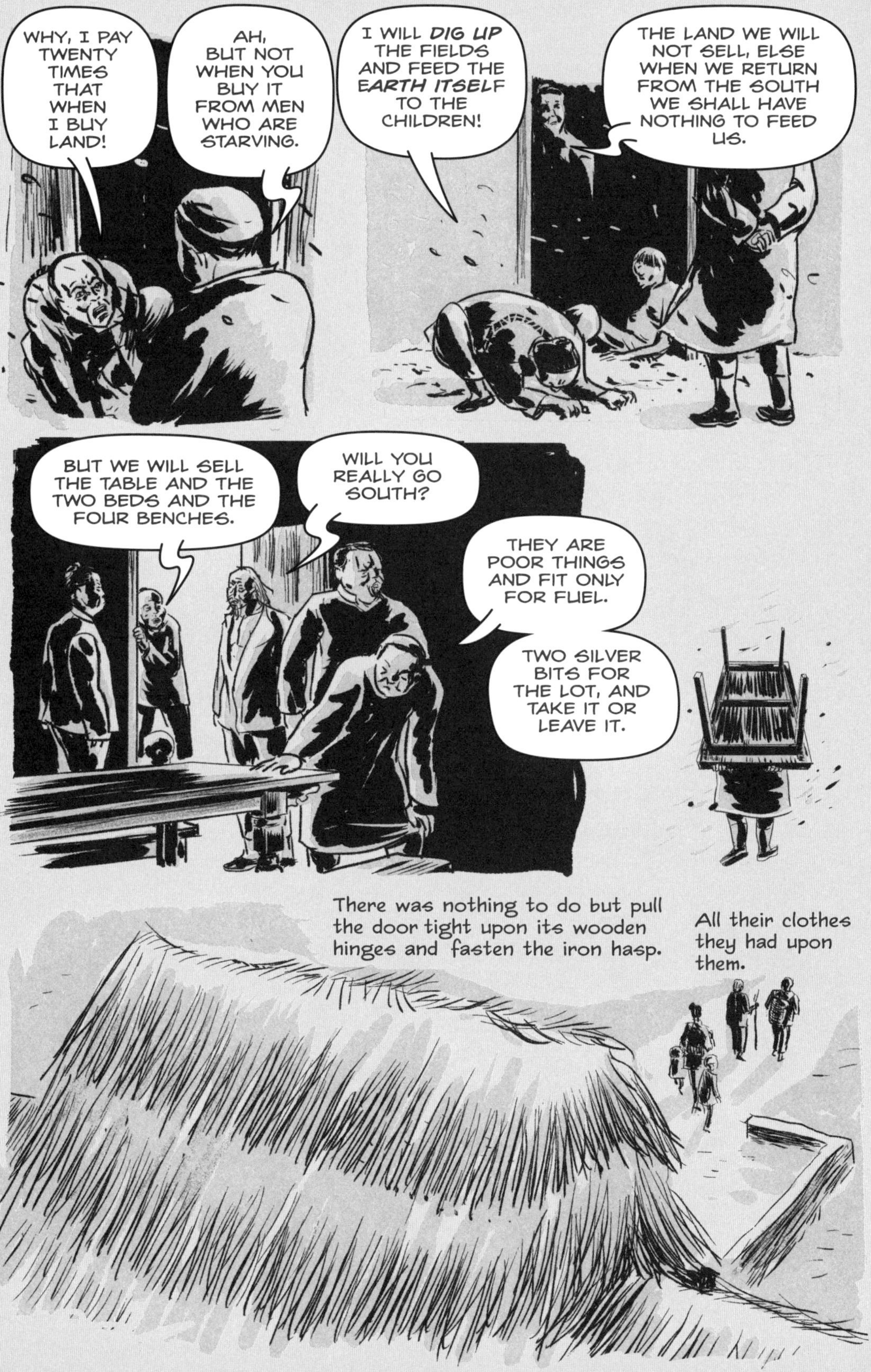
WHY, I PAY TWENTY TIMES THAT WHEN I BUY LAND!
AH, BUT NOT WHEN YOU BUY IT FROM MEN WHO ARE STARVING.
I WILL DIG UP THE FIELDS AND FEED THE EARTH ITSELF TO THE CHILDREN!
THE LAND WE WILL NOT SELL, ELSE WHEN WE RETURN FROM THE SOUTH WE SHALL HAVE NOTHING TO FEED US.
BUT WE WILL SELL THE TABLE AND THE TWO BEDS AND THE FOUR BENCHES.
WILL YOU REALLY GO SOUTH?
THEY ARE POOR THINGS AND FIT ONLY FOR FUEL.
TWO SILVER BITS FOR THE LOT, AND TAKE IT OR LEAVE IT.
There was nothing to do but pull the door tight upon its wooden hinges and fasten the iron hasp.
All their clothes they had upon them.

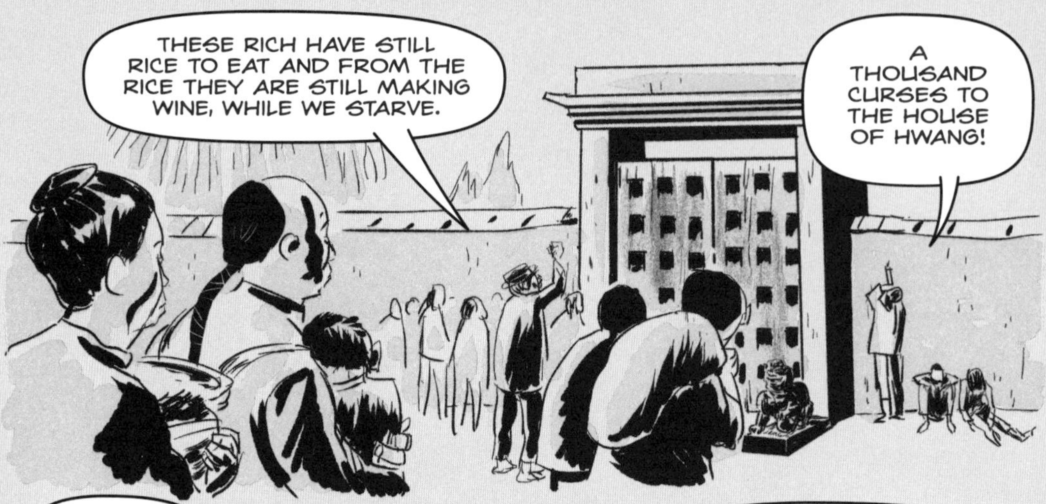
THESE RICH HAVE STILL RICE TO EAT AND FROM THE RICE THEY ARE STILL MAKING WINE, WHILE WE STARVE.
A THOUSAND CURSES TO THE HOUSE OF HWANG!

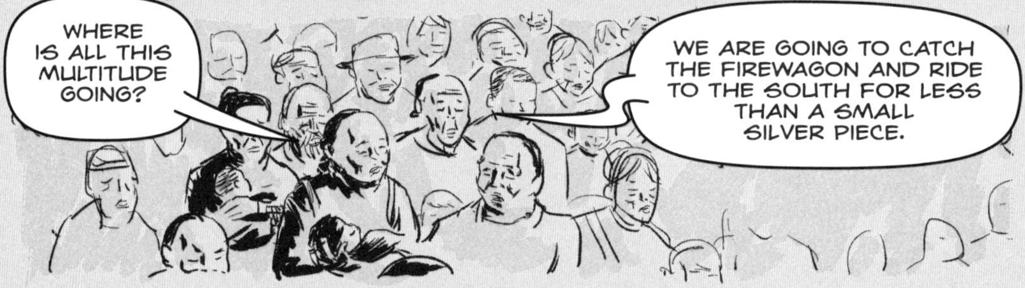
WHERE IS ALL THIS MULTITUDE GOING?
WE ARE GOING TO CATCH THE FIREWAGON AND RIDE TO THE SOUTH FOR LESS THAN A SMALL SILVER PIECE.

And pressing forward in the confusion they were pushed somehow into a small open door and into a box-like room.

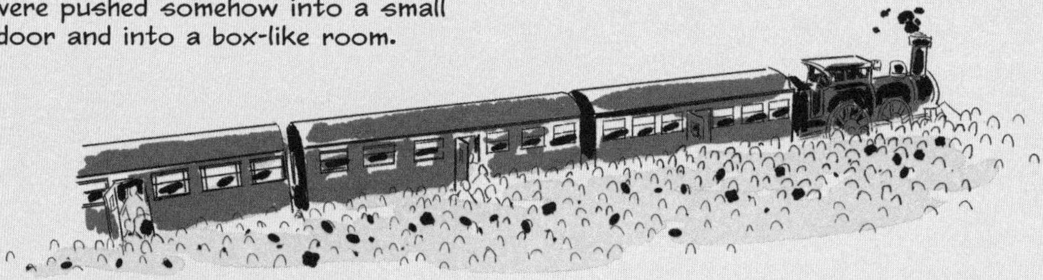

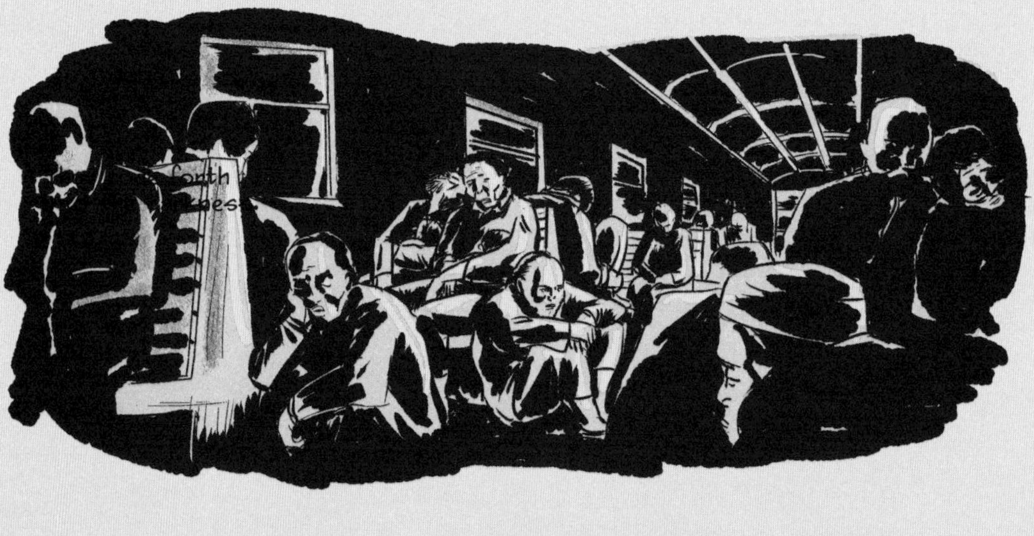

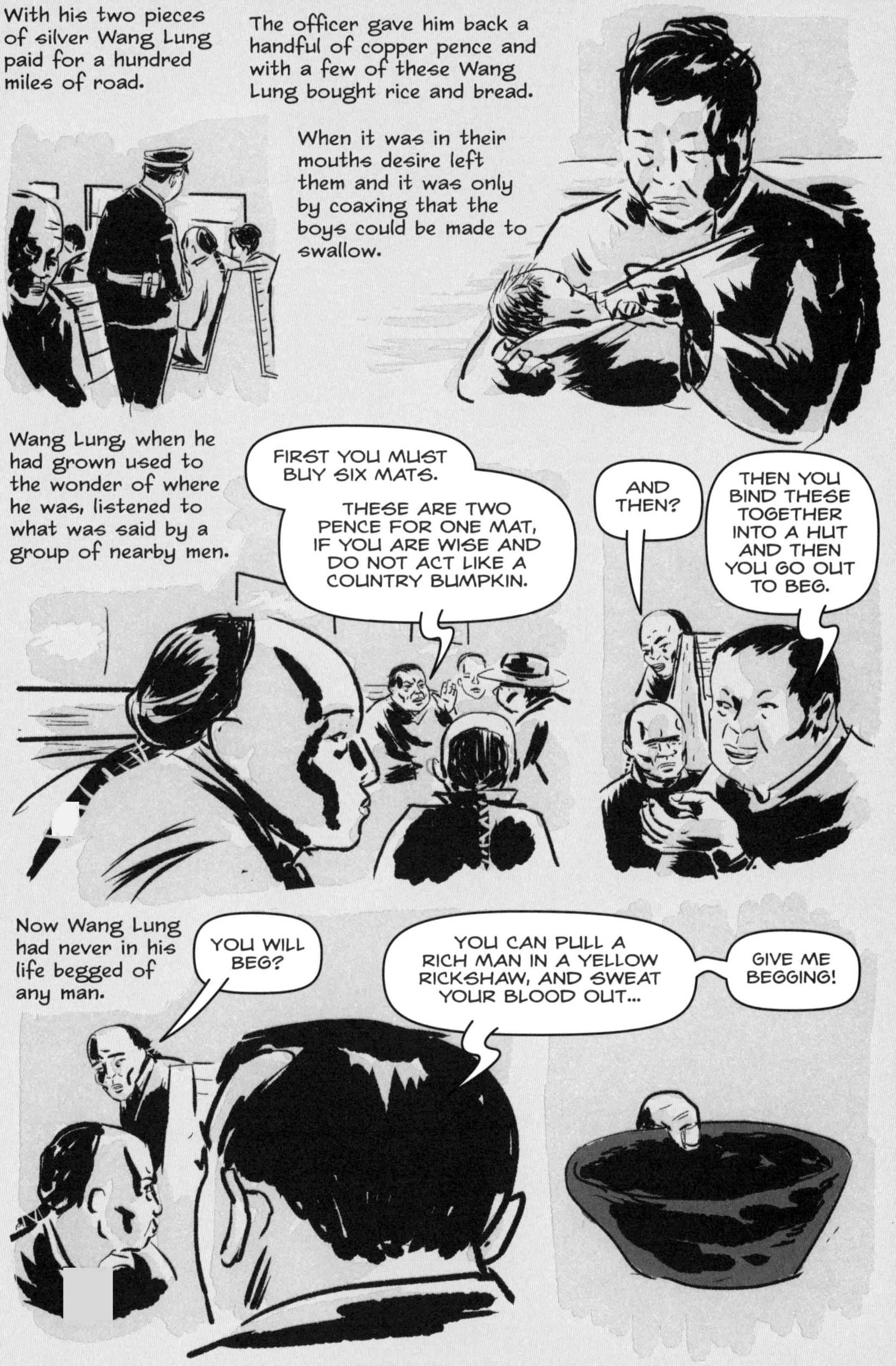
With his two pieces of silver Wang Lung paid for a hundred miles of road.
The officer gave him back a handful of copper pence and with a few of these Wang Lung bought rice and bread.
When it was in their mouths desire left them and it was only by coaxing that the boys could be made to swallow.
Wang Lung, when he had grown used to the wonder of where he was, listened to what was said by a group of nearby men.
FIRST YOU MUST BUY SIX MATS.
THESE ARE TWO PENCE FOR ONE MAT, IF YOU ARE WISE AND DO NOT ACT LIKE A COUNTRY BUMPKIN.
AND THEN?
THEN YOU BIND THESE TOGETHER INTO A HUT AND THEN YOU GO OUT TO BEG.
Now Wang Lung had never in his life begged of any man.
YOU WILL BEG?
YOU CAN PULL A RICH MAN IN A YELLOW RICKSHAW, AND SWEAT YOUR BLOOD OUT...
GIVE ME BEGGING!

4

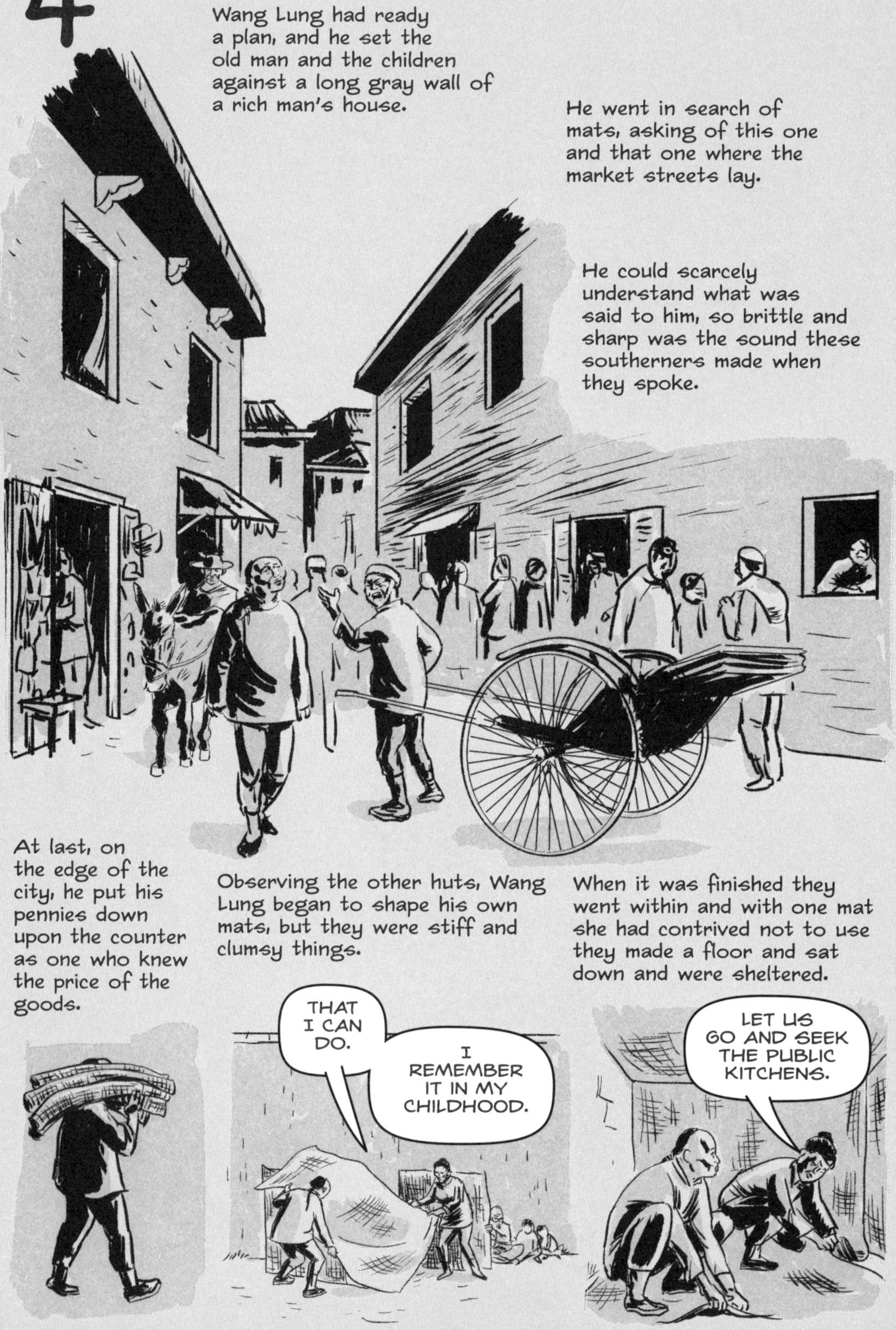
Wang Lung had ready a plan, and he set the old man and the children against a long gray wall of a rich man's house.
He went in search of mats, asking of this one and that one where the market streets lay.
He could scarcely understand what was said to him, so brittle and sharp was the sound these southerners made when they spoke.
At last, on the edge of the city, he put his pennies down upon the counter as one who knew the price of the goods.
Observing the other huts, Wang Lung began to shape his own mats, but they were stiff and clumsy things.
THAT I CAN DO.
I REMEMBER IT IN MY CHILDHOOD.
When it was finished they went within and with one mat she had contrived not to use they made a floor and sat down and were sheltered.
LET US GO AND SEEK THE PUBLIC KITCHENS.

The next day they spent the last copper coin upon the morning's rice.

I AND THE CHILDREN CAN BEG AND THE OLD MAN ALSO.

Wang Lung found a place where rickshaws were for hire.

He waited half the day for a fare, and just as he said to himself in despair that he had better beg:

TAKE ME TO THE CONFUCIAN TEMPLE.

At the temple gates the rider handed Wang Lung a small silver coin.

NOW I NEVER PAY MORE THAN THIS, AND THERE IS NO USE IN COMPLAINT.

Another driver asked Wang Lung how far he had pulled the old head, and Wang Lung told him.

A COUNTRY LOUT YOU ARE, PIGTAIL AND ALL!

HE GAVE YOU ONLY HALF THE PROPER FARE.

At night, when he counted out all his money he had only a penny above the rent of the rickshaw.

Angry as he was he thought suddenly of his land lying back there, far away, and it filled him with peace.

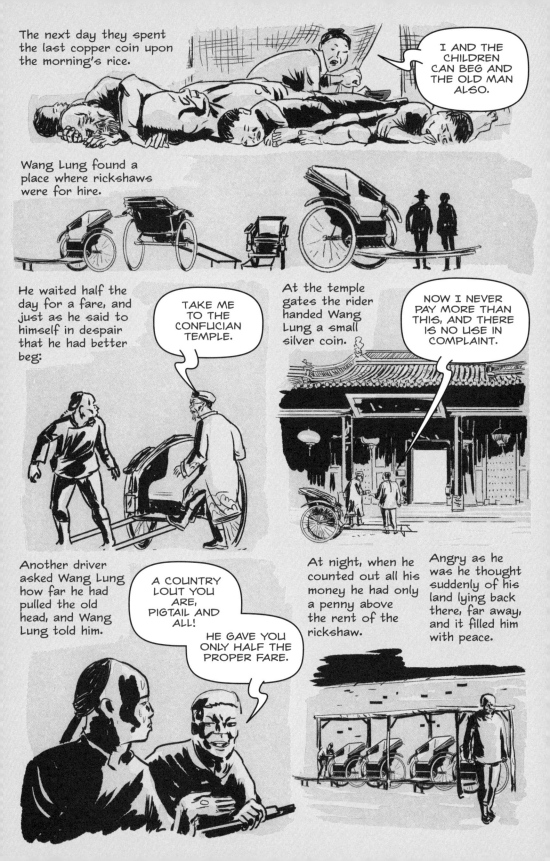

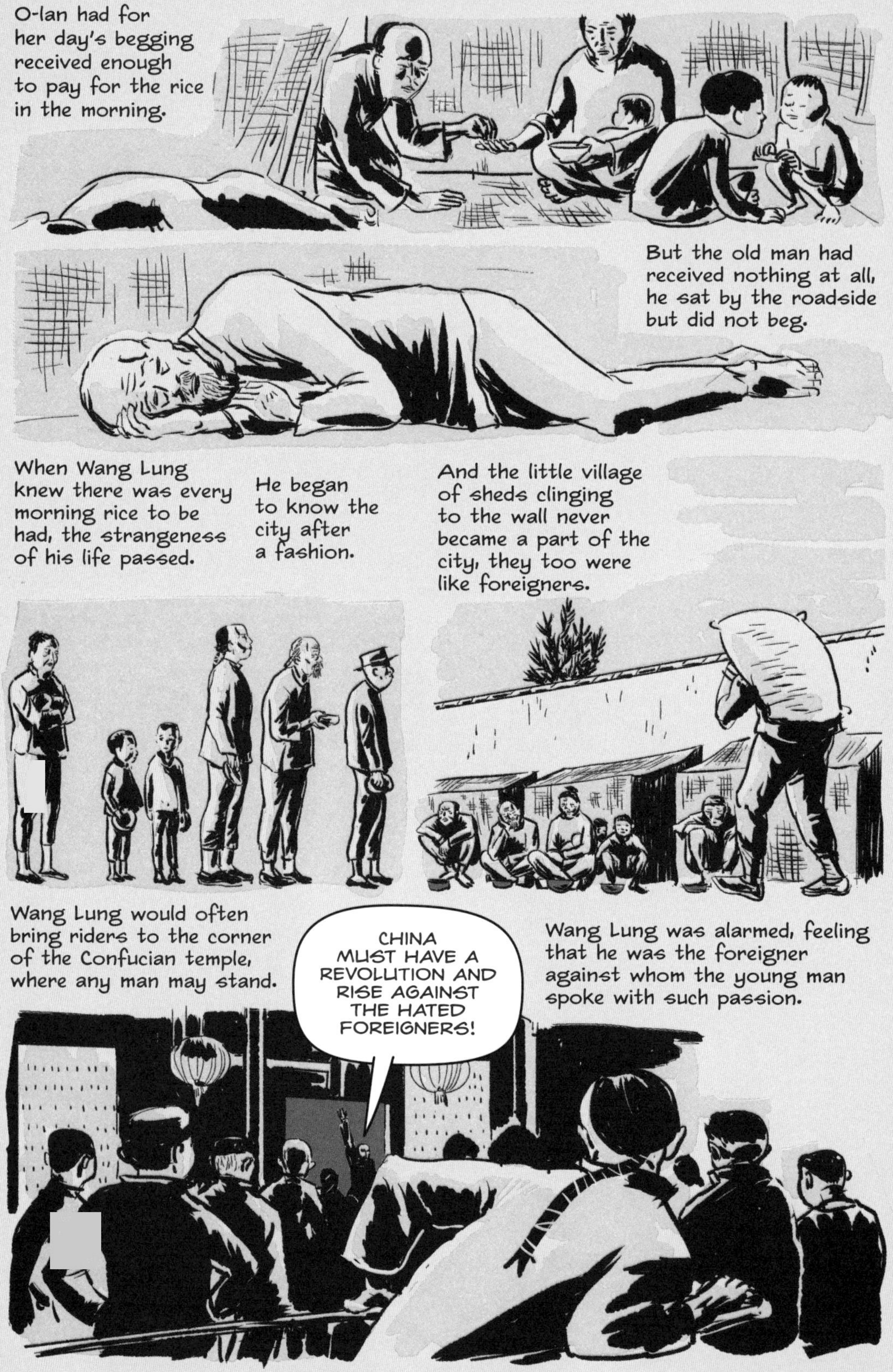
O-lan had for her day's begging received enough to pay for the rice in the morning.
But the old man had received nothing at all, he sat by the roadside but did not beg.
When Wang Lung knew there was every morning rice to be had, the strangeness of his life passed.
He began to know the city after a fashion.
And the little village of sheds clinging to the wall never became a part of the city, they too were like foreigners.
Wang Lung would often bring riders to the corner of the Confucian temple, where any man may stand.
CHINA MUST HAVE A REVOLUTION AND RISE AGAINST THE HATED FOREIGNERS!
Wang Lung was alarmed, feeling that he was the foreigner against whom the young man spoke with such passion.

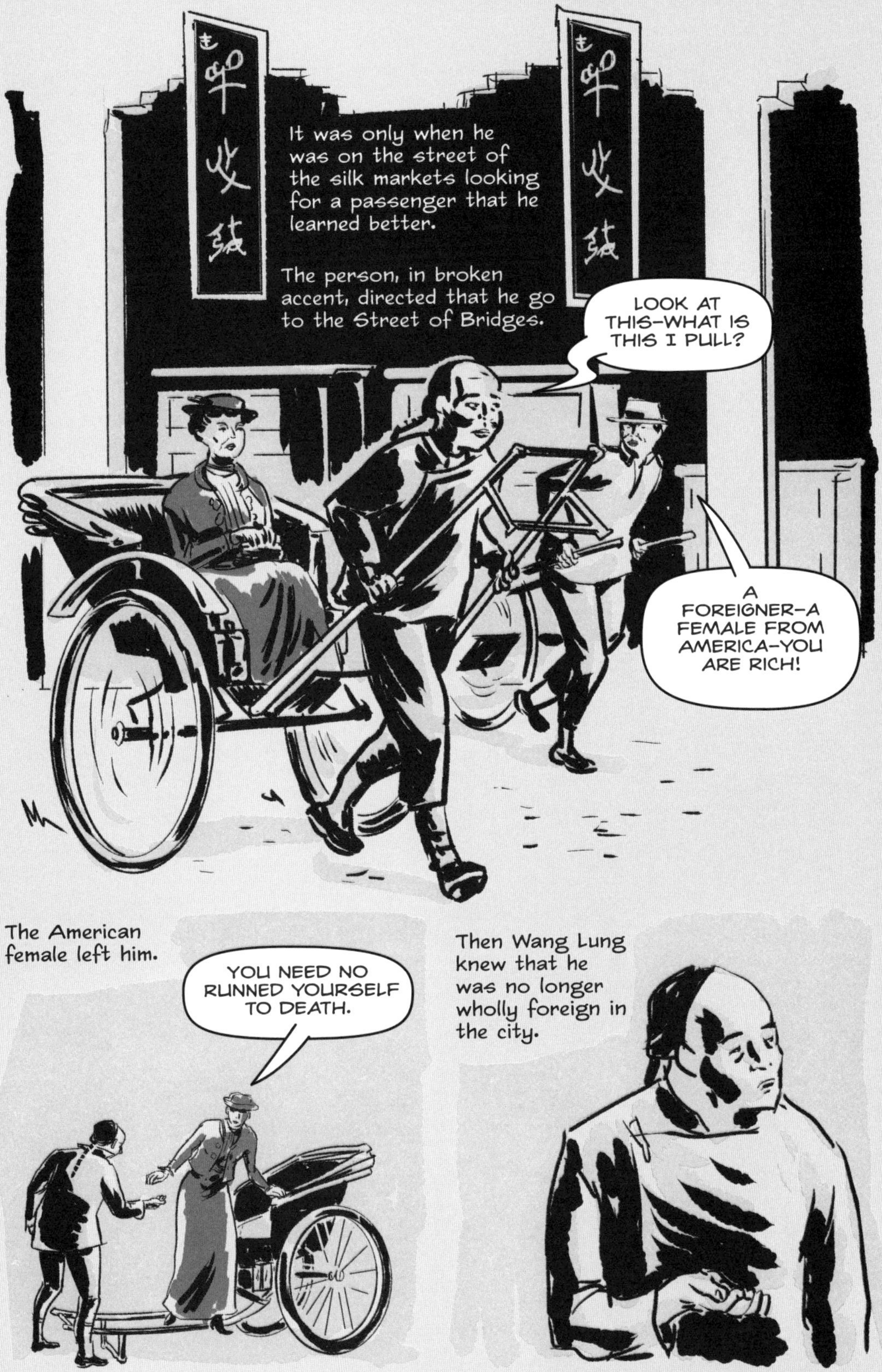
It was only when he was on the street of the silk markets looking for a passenger that he learned better.
The person, in broken accent, directed that he go to the Street of Bridges.
LOOK AT THIS–WHAT IS THIS I PULL?
A FOREIGNER–A FEMALE FROM AMERICA–YOU ARE RICH!
The American female left him.
YOU NEED NO RUNNED YOURSELF TO DEATH.
Then Wang Lung knew that he was no longer wholly foreign in the city.

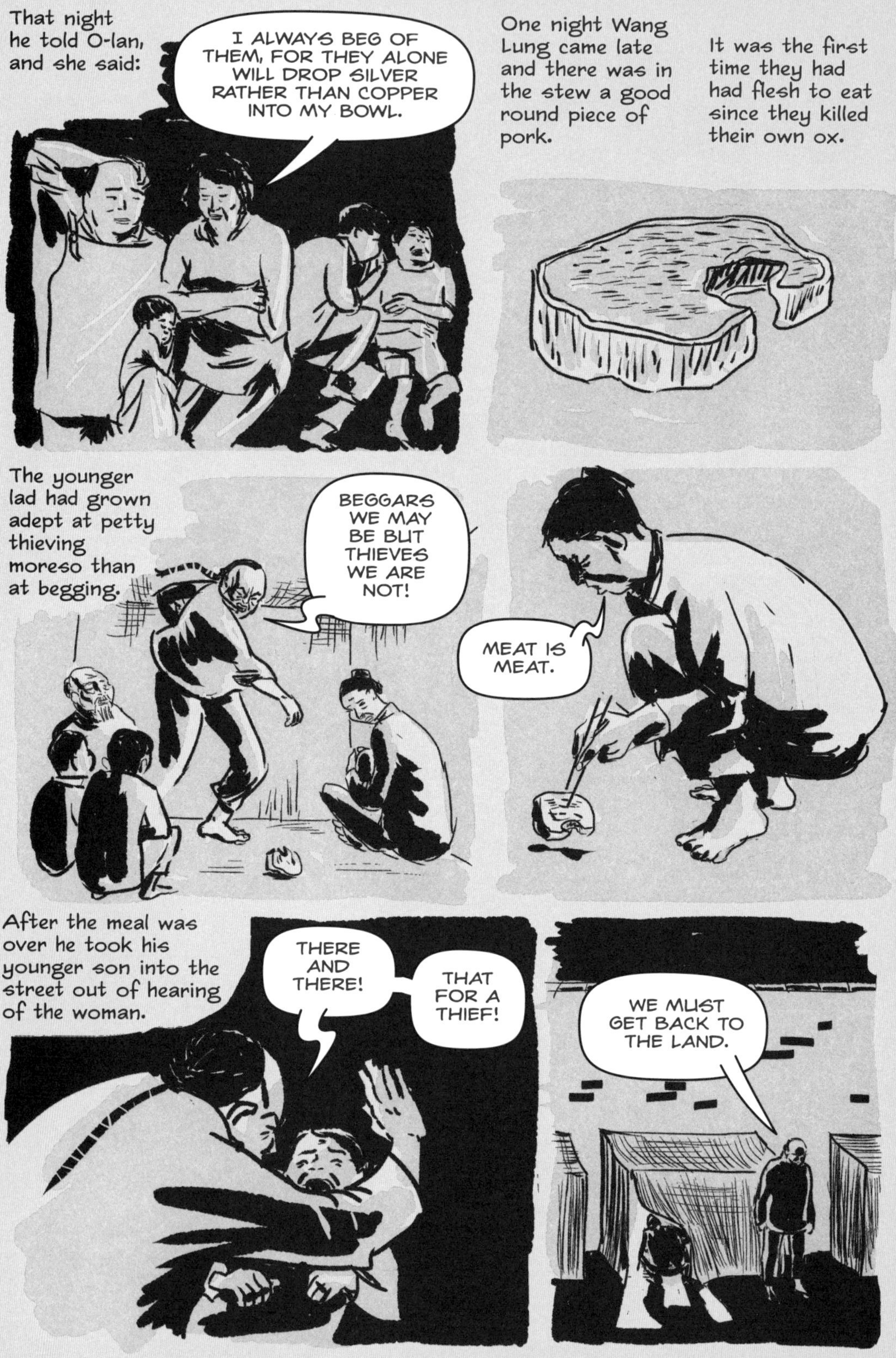
That night he told O-lan, and she said:
I ALWAYS BEG OF THEM, FOR THEY ALONE WILL DROP SILVER RATHER THAN COPPER INTO MY BOWL.
One night Wang Lung came late and there was in the stew a good round piece of pork.
It was the first time they had had flesh to eat since they killed their own ox.
The younger lad had grown adept at petty thieving moreso than at begging.
BEGGARS WE MAY BE BUT THIEVES WE ARE NOT!
MEAT IS MEAT.
After the meal was over he took his younger son into the street out of hearing of the woman.
THERE AND THERE!
THAT FOR A THIEF!
WE MUST GET BACK TO THE LAND.

Day by day, beneath the opulence of this city, Wang Lung lived in the foundations of poverty upon which it was laid.

Men labored all day at the baking of breads and cakes for the feasts for the rich.

Children labored from dawn to midnight, and slept all greasy and grimed as they were upon the floor, and staggered to the ovens the next day.

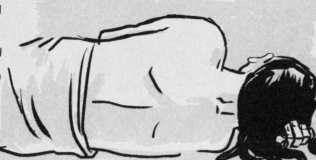

There was not money enough given them to buy a piece of the rich breads they made.

In late winter the ground about the huts was still muddy with the melting snow, and the water ran into the huts.

A soft mildness in the air made Wang Lung exceedingly restless.

ON SUCH A DAY AS THIS THE FIELDS SHOULD BE TURNED, AND THE WHEAT CULTIVATED.

Now that O-lan was again with child the old man looked after the girl.

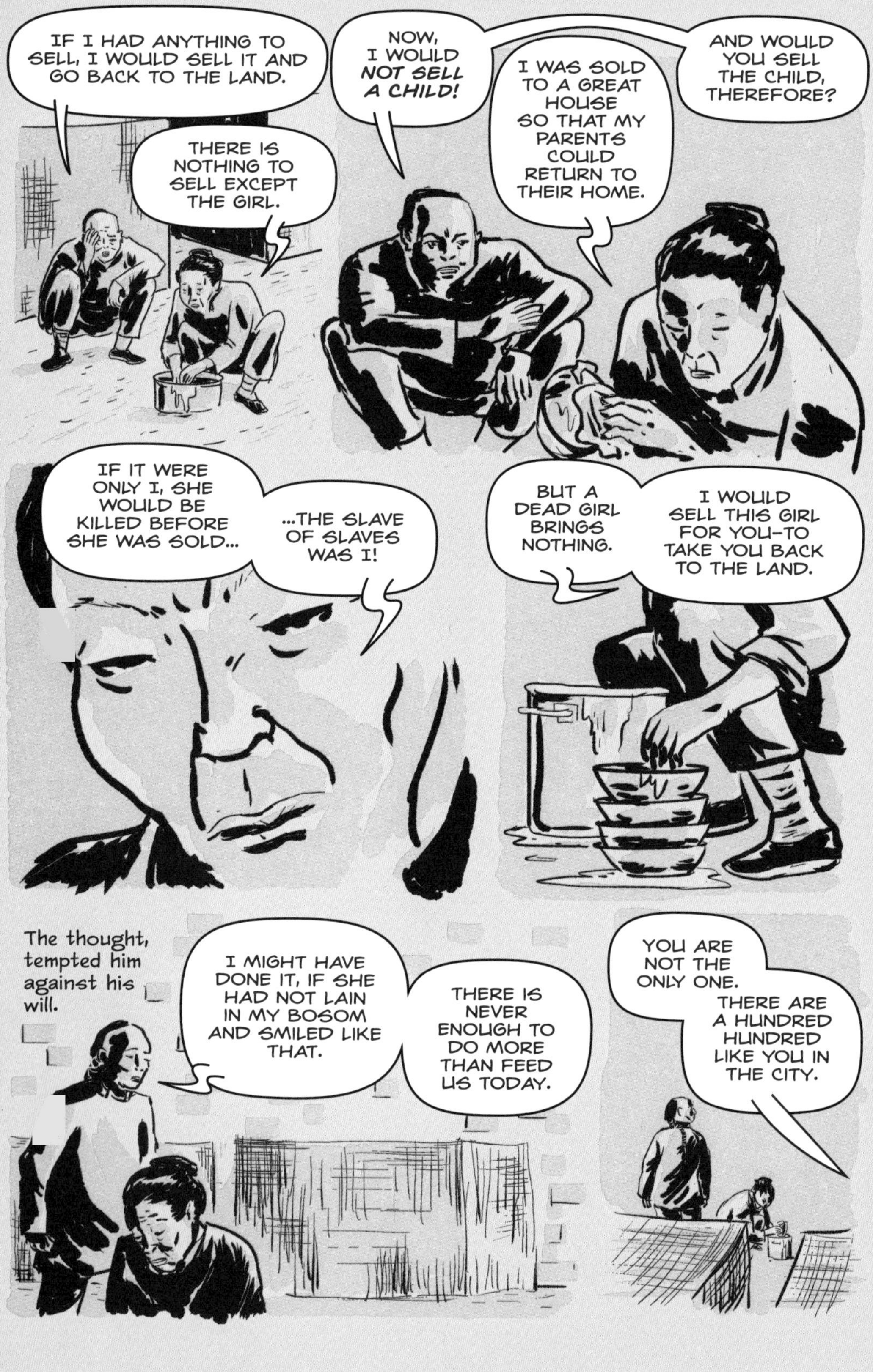
IF I HAD ANYTHING TO SELL, I WOULD SELL IT AND GO BACK TO THE LAND.
THERE IS NOTHING TO SELL EXCEPT THE GIRL.
NOW, I WOULD NOT SELL A CHILD!
AND WOULD YOU SELL THE CHILD, THEREFORE?
I WAS SOLD TO A GREAT HOUSE SO THAT MY PARENTS COULD RETURN TO THEIR HOME.
IF IT WERE ONLY I, SHE WOULD BE KILLED BEFORE SHE WAS SOLD...
...THE SLAVE OF SLAVES WAS I!
BUT A DEAD GIRL BRINGS NOTHING.
I WOULD SELL THIS GIRL FOR YOU—TO TAKE YOU BACK TO THE LAND.
The thought, tempted him against his will.
I MIGHT HAVE DONE IT, IF SHE HAD NOT LAIN IN MY BOSOM AND SMILED LIKE THAT.
THERE IS NEVER ENOUGH TO DO MORE THAN FEED US TODAY.
YOU ARE NOT THE ONLY ONE.
THERE ARE A HUNDRED HUNDRED LIKE YOU IN THE CITY.

It was the father of the family in the hut next but two to Wang Lung's hut.

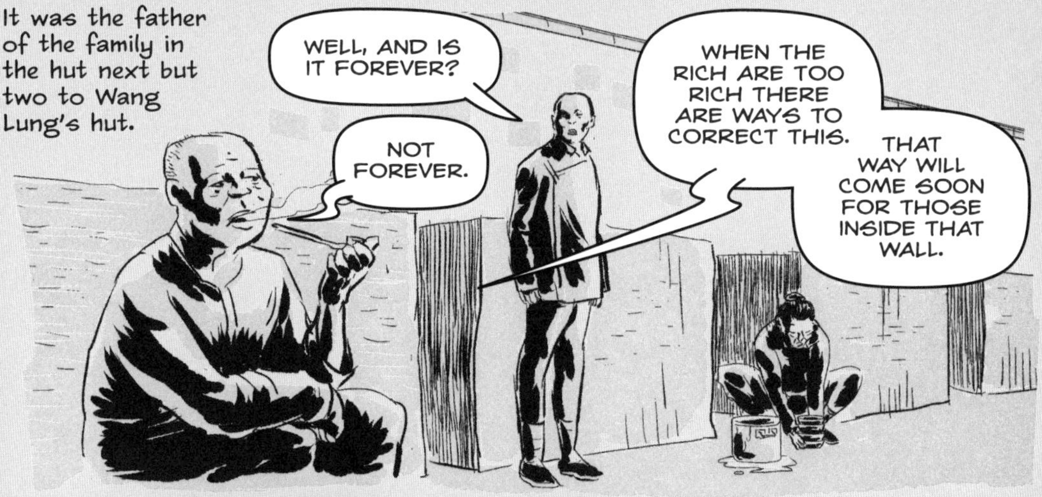
WELL, AND IS IT FOREVER?
NOT FOREVER.
WHEN THE RICH ARE TOO RICH THERE ARE WAYS TO CORRECT THIS.
THAT WAY WILL COME SOON FOR THOSE INSIDE THAT WALL.

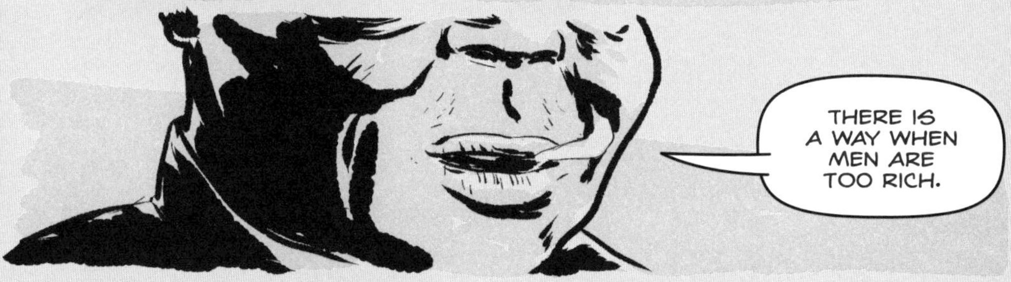
THERE IS A WAY WHEN MEN ARE TOO RICH.

The lengthening warm days and the sunshine and sudden rains filled everyone with longings and discontents.

Alongside the discontent there was a paper that men gave out here and there, and sometimes even to Wang Lung.

Now Wang Lung had never learned the meaning of letters upon paper and he discussed its possible meaning with the old man.

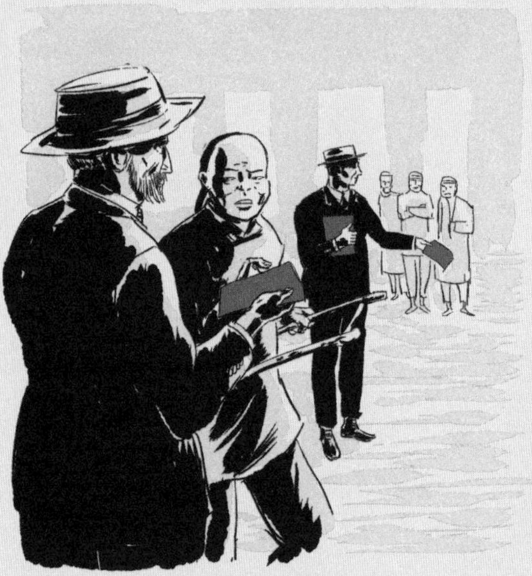

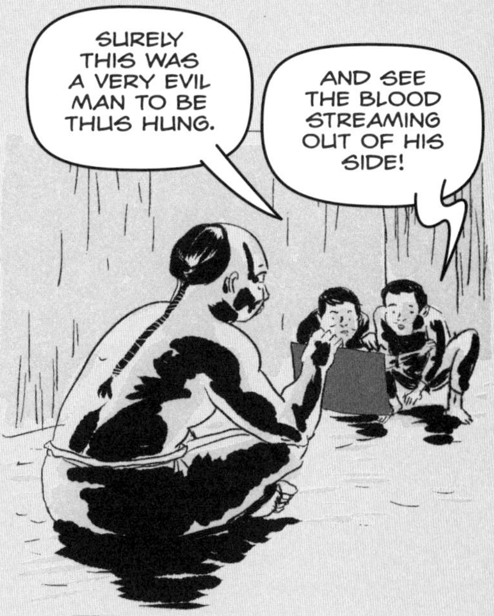
SURELY THIS WAS A VERY EVIL MAN TO BE THUS HUNG.
AND SEE THE BLOOD STREAMING OUT OF HIS SIDE!

Wang Lung was fearful of the picture, but O-lan took it and sewed it into a shoe sole.

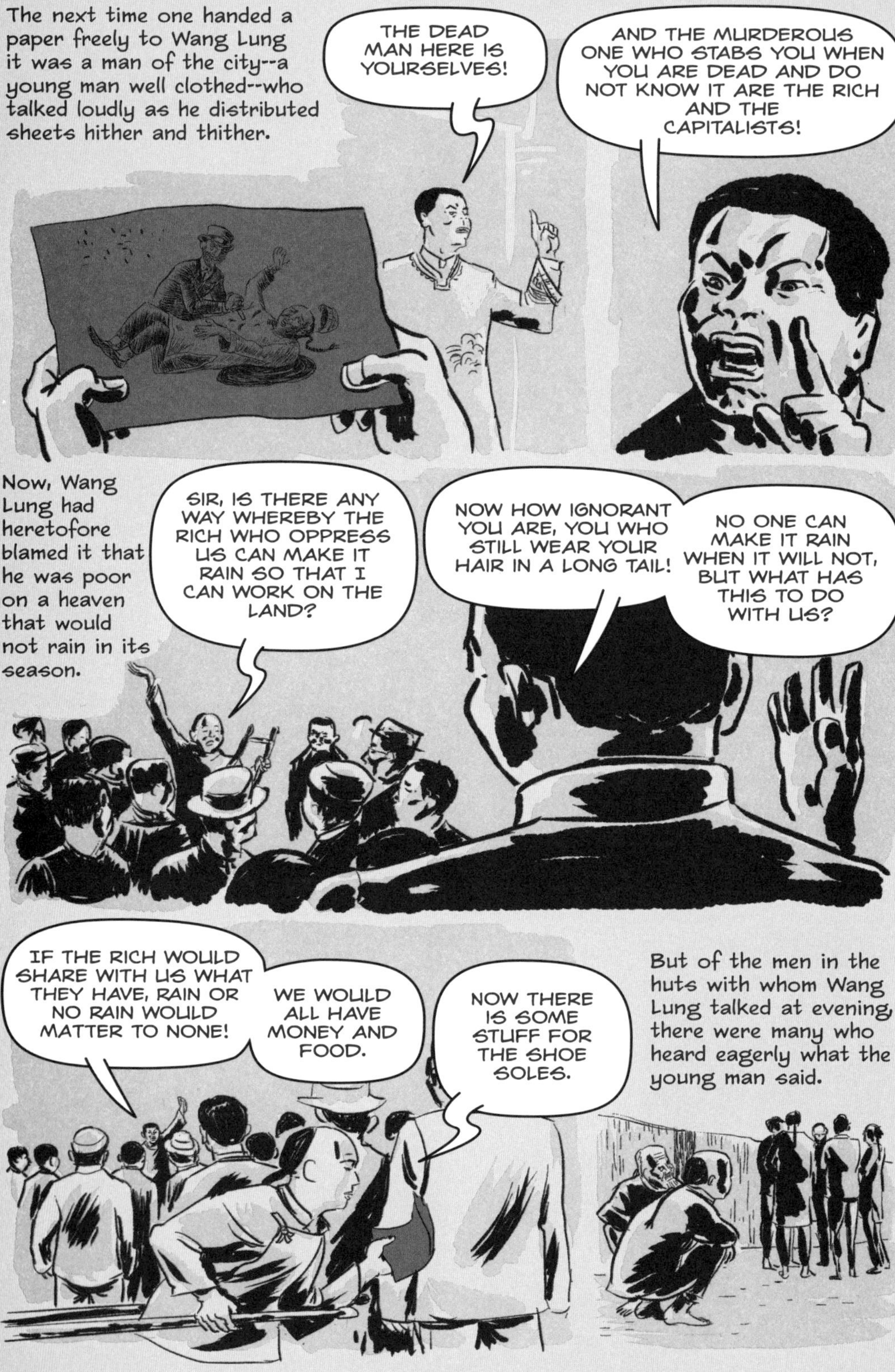
The next time one handed a paper freely to Wang Lung it was a man of the city--a young man well clothed--who talked loudly as he distributed sheets hither and thither.
THE DEAD MAN HERE IS YOURSELVES!
AND THE MURDEROUS ONE WHO STABS YOU WHEN YOU ARE DEAD AND DO NOT KNOW IT ARE THE RICH AND THE CAPITALISTS!
Now, Wang Lung had heretofore blamed it that he was poor on a heaven that would not rain in its season.
SIR, IS THERE ANY WAY WHEREBY THE RICH WHO OPPRESS US CAN MAKE IT RAIN SO THAT I CAN WORK ON THE LAND?
NOW HOW IGNORANT YOU ARE, YOU WHO STILL WEAR YOUR HAIR IN A LONG TAIL!
NO ONE CAN MAKE IT RAIN WHEN IT WILL NOT, BUT WHAT HAS THIS TO DO WITH US?
IF THE RICH WOULD SHARE WITH US WHAT THEY HAVE, RAIN OR NO RAIN WOULD MATTER TO NONE!
WE WOULD ALL HAVE MONEY AND FOOD.
NOW THERE IS SOME STUFF FOR THE SHOE SOLES.
But of the men in the huts with whom Wang Lung talked at evening, there were many who heard eagerly what the young man said.

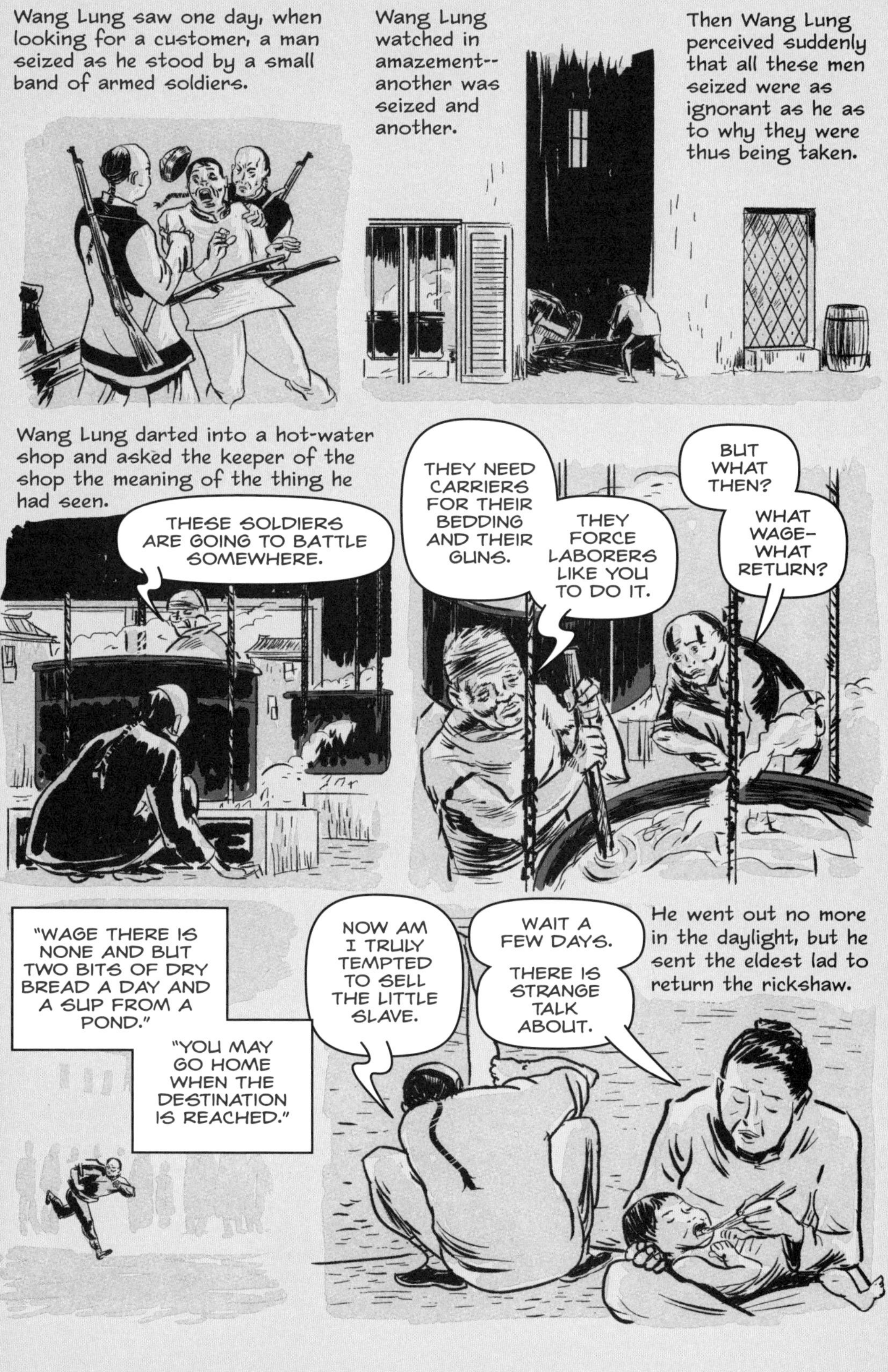

Wang Lung saw one day, when looking for a customer, a man seized as he stood by a small band of armed soldiers.
Wang Lung watched in amazement--another was seized and another.
Then Wang Lung perceived suddenly that all these men seized were as ignorant as he as to why they were thus being taken.
Wang Lung darted into a hot-water shop and asked the keeper of the shop the meaning of the thing he had seen.
THESE SOLDIERS ARE GOING TO BATTLE SOMEWHERE.
THEY NEED CARRIERS FOR THEIR BEDDING AND THEIR GUNS.
THEY FORCE LABORERS LIKE YOU TO DO IT.
BUT WHAT THEN?
WHAT WAGE– WHAT RETURN?
"WAGE THERE IS NONE AND BUT TWO BITS OF DRY BREAD A DAY AND A SUP FROM A POND."
"YOU MAY GO HOME WHEN THE DESTINATION IS REACHED."
NOW AM I TRULY TEMPTED TO SELL THE LITTLE SLAVE.
WAIT A FEW DAYS.
THERE IS STRANGE TALK ABOUT.
He went out no more in the daylight, but he sent the eldest lad to return the rickshaw.

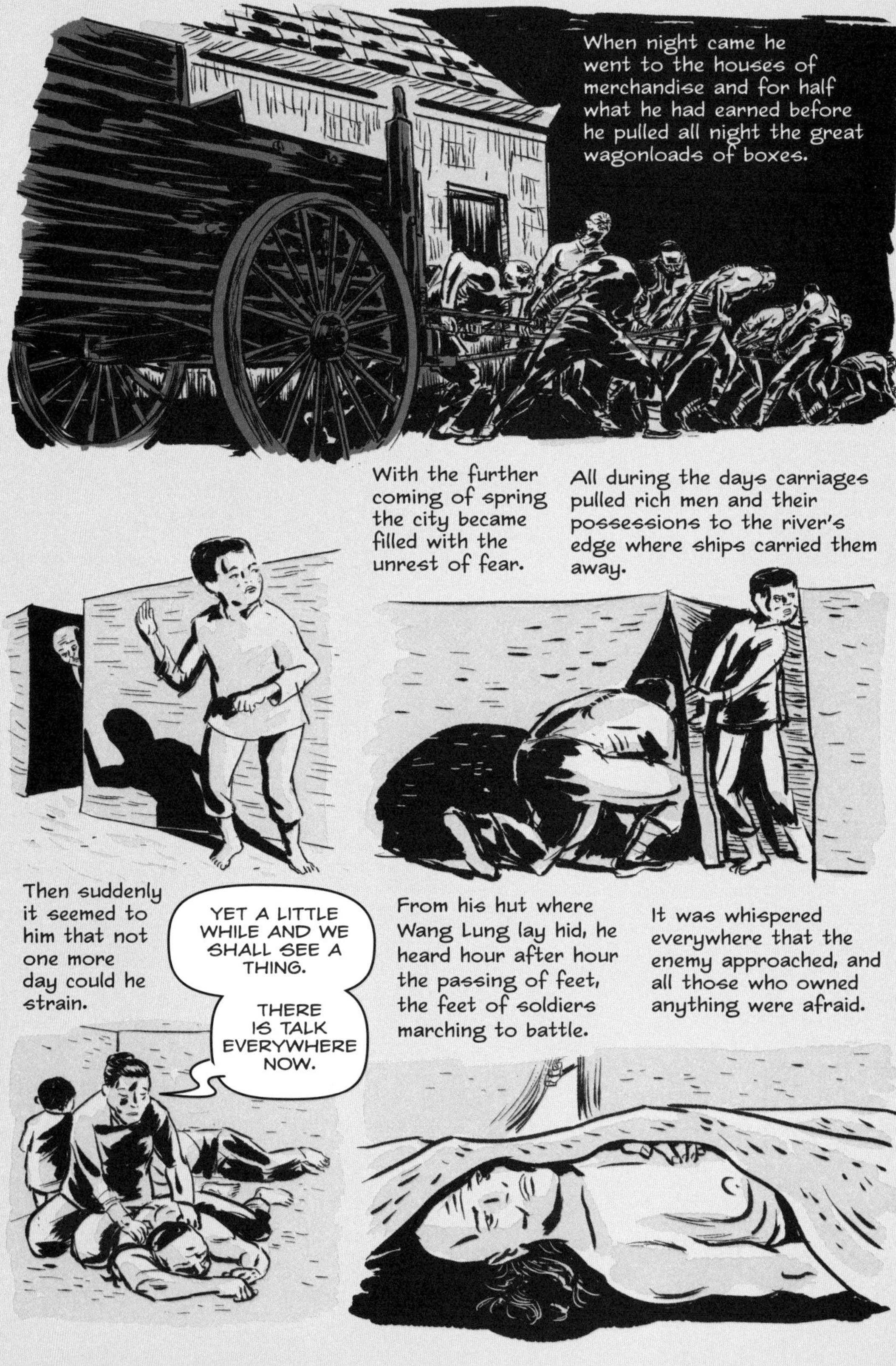
When night came he went to the houses of merchandise and for half what he had earned before he pulled all night the great wagonloads of boxes.
With the further coming of spring the city became filled with the unrest of fear.
All during the days carriages pulled rich men and their possessions to the river's edge where ships carried them away.
Then suddenly it seemed to him that not one more day could he strain.
YET A LITTLE WHILE AND WE SHALL SEE A THING.
THERE IS TALK EVERYWHERE NOW.
From his hut where Wang Lung lay hid, he heard hour after hour the passing of feet, the feet of soldiers marching to battle.
It was whispered everywhere that the enemy approached, and all those who owned anything were afraid.

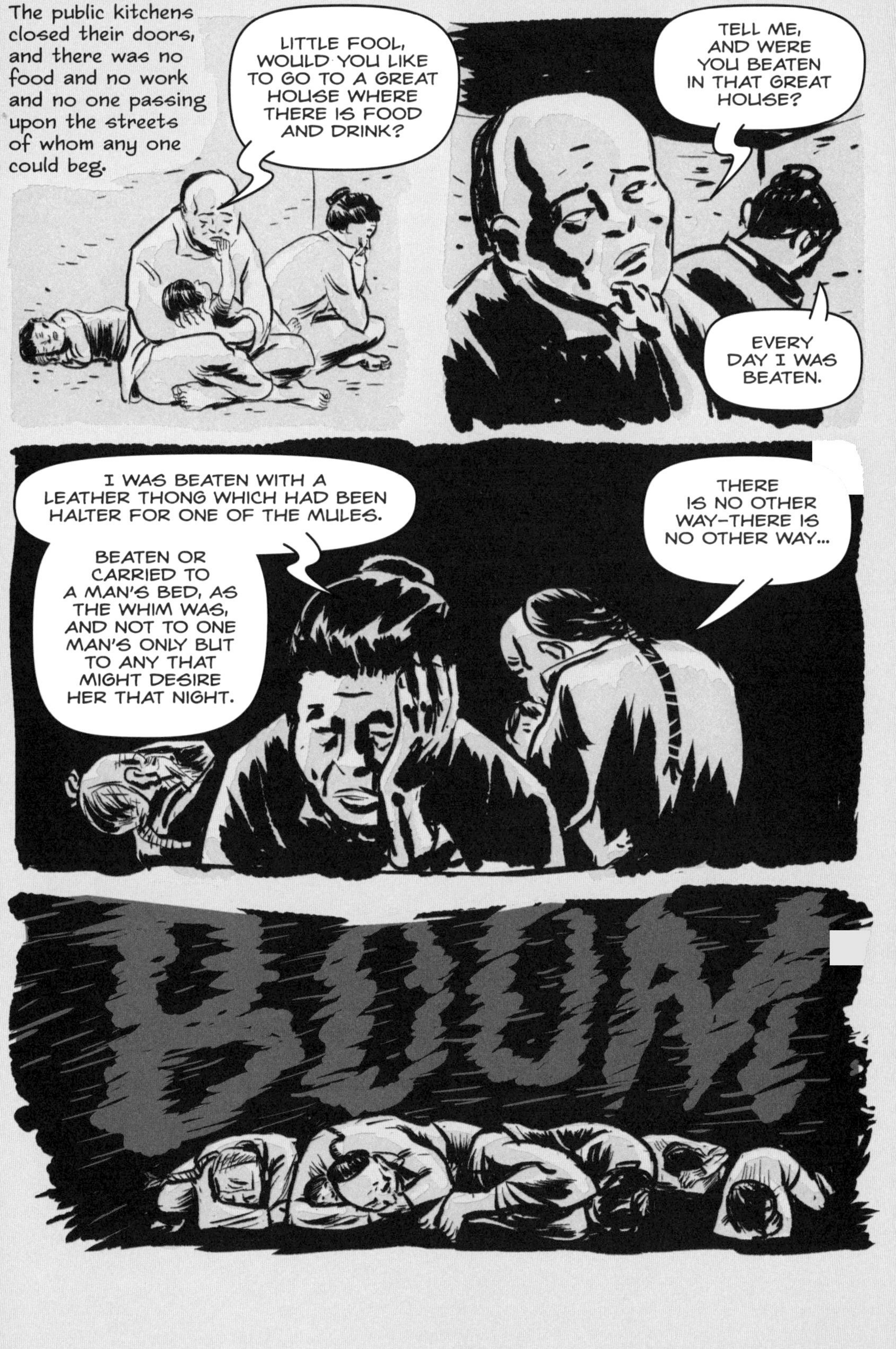
The public kitchens closed their doors, and there was no food and no work and no one passing upon the streets of whom any one could beg.
LITTLE FOOL, WOULD YOU LIKE TO GO TO A GREAT HOUSE WHERE THERE IS FOOD AND DRINK?
TELL ME, AND WERE YOU BEATEN IN THAT GREAT HOUSE?
EVERY DAY I WAS BEATEN.
I WAS BEATEN WITH A LEATHER THONG WHICH HAD BEEN HALTER FOR ONE OF THE MULES.
BEATEN OR CARRIED TO A MAN'S BED, AS THE WHIM WAS, AND NOT TO ONE MAN'S ONLY BUT TO ANY THAT MIGHT DESIRE HER THAT NIGHT.
THERE IS NO OTHER WAY—THERE IS NO OTHER WAY...

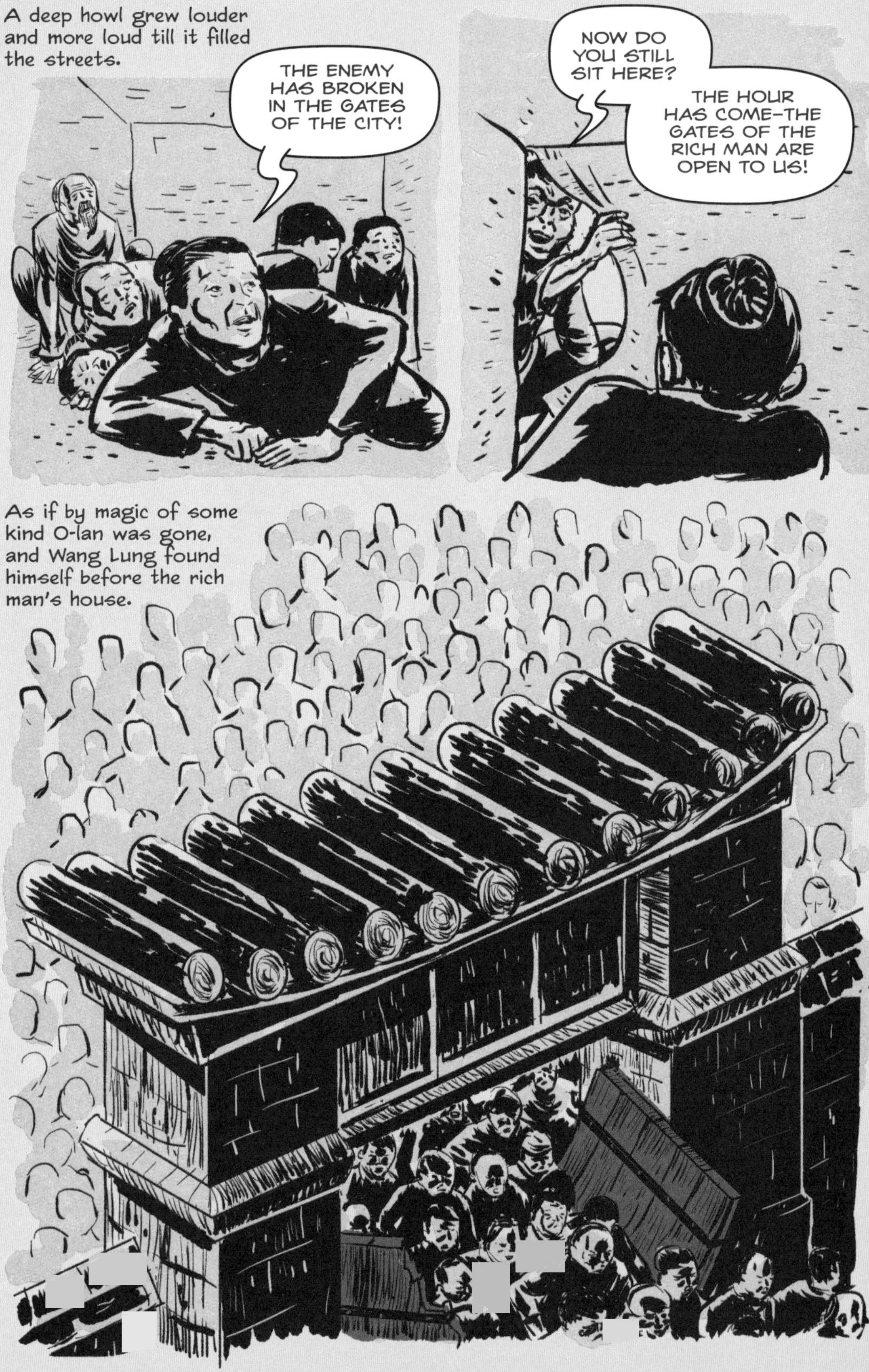

A deep howl grew louder and more loud till it filled the streets.
THE ENEMY HAS BROKEN IN THE GATES OF THE CITY!
NOW DO YOU STILL SIT HERE?
THE HOUR HAS COME—THE GATES OF THE RICH MAN ARE OPEN TO US!
As if by magic of some kind O-lan was gone, and Wang Lung found himself before the rich man's house.

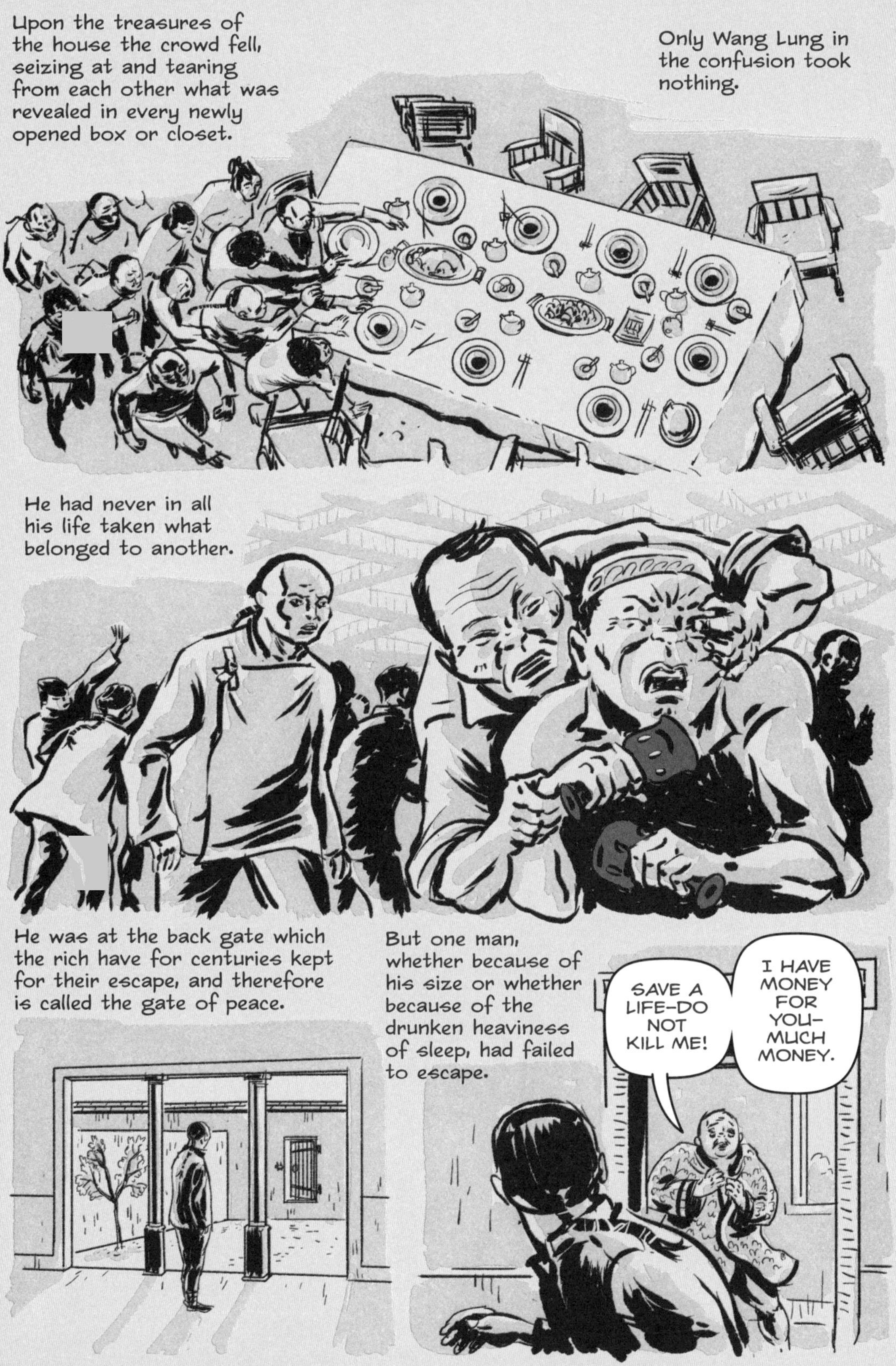
Upon the treasures of the house the crowd fell, seizing at and tearing from each other what was revealed in every newly opened box or closet.
Only Wang Lung in the confusion took nothing.
He had never in all his life taken what belonged to another.
He was at the back gate which the rich have for centuries kept for their escape, and therefore is called the gate of peace.
But one man, whether because of his size or whether because of the drunken heaviness of sleep, had failed to escape.
SAVE A LIFE–DO NOT KILL ME!
I HAVE MONEY FOR YOU– MUCH MONEY.

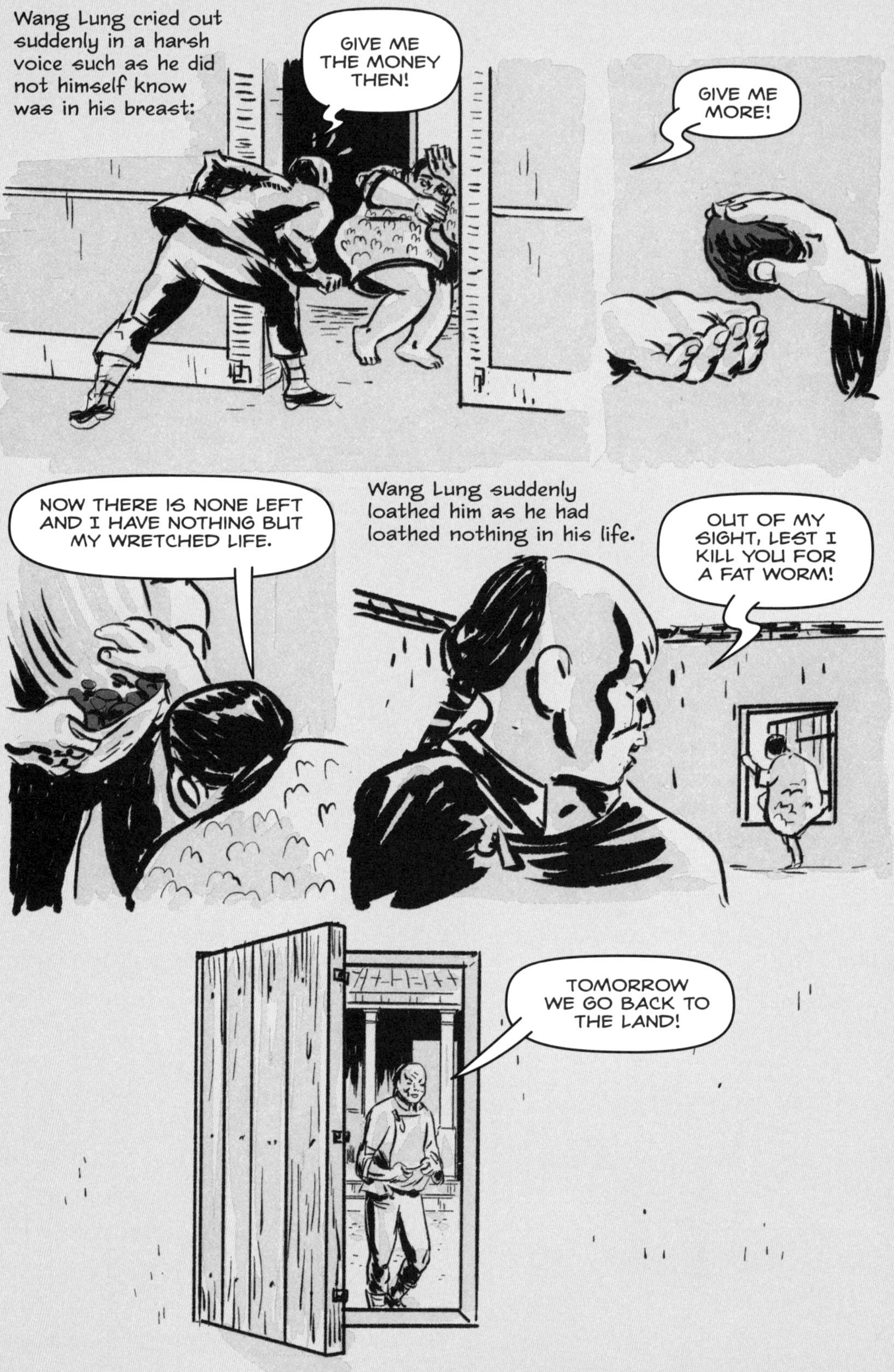

Wang Lung cried out suddenly in a harsh voice such as he did not himself know was in his breast:
GIVE ME THE MONEY THEN!
GIVE ME MORE!
NOW THERE IS NONE LEFT AND I HAVE NOTHING BUT MY WRETCHED LIFE.
Wang Lung suddenly loathed him as he had loathed nothing in his life.
OUT OF MY SIGHT, LEST I KILL YOU FOR A FAT WORM!
TOMORROW WE GO BACK TO THE LAND!

Before a handful of days had passed, it seemed to Wang Lung that he had never been away from his land.

5

With three pieces of the gold he bought good seed from the south.

For very recklessness of riches he bought seeds the like of which he had never planted before, celery and lotus for his pond and great red radishes.

Before ever he reached his own land he stopped.

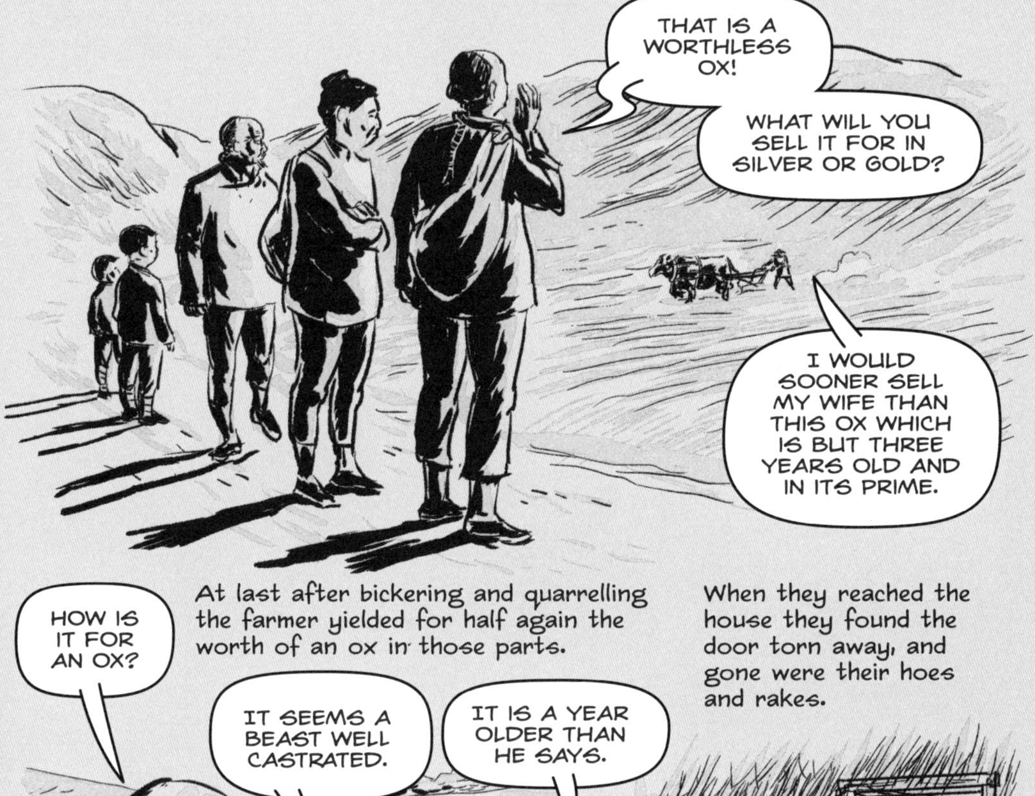

THAT IS A WORTHLESS OX!
WHAT WILL YOU SELL IT FOR IN SILVER OR GOLD?
I WOULD SOONER SELL MY WIFE THAN THIS OX WHICH IS BUT THREE YEARS OLD AND IN ITS PRIME.

At last after bickering and quarrelling the farmer yielded for half again the worth of an ox in those parts.

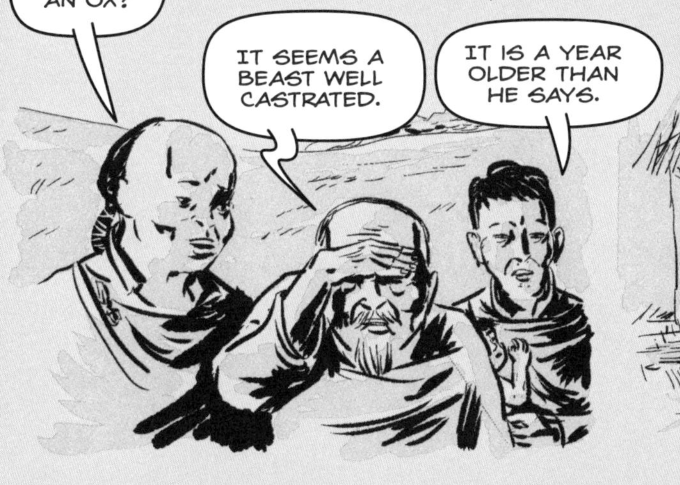

HOW IS IT FOR AN OX?
IT SEEMS A BEAST WELL CASTRATED.
IT IS A YEAR OLDER THAN HE SAYS.

When they reached the house they found the door torn away, and gone were their hoes and rakes.

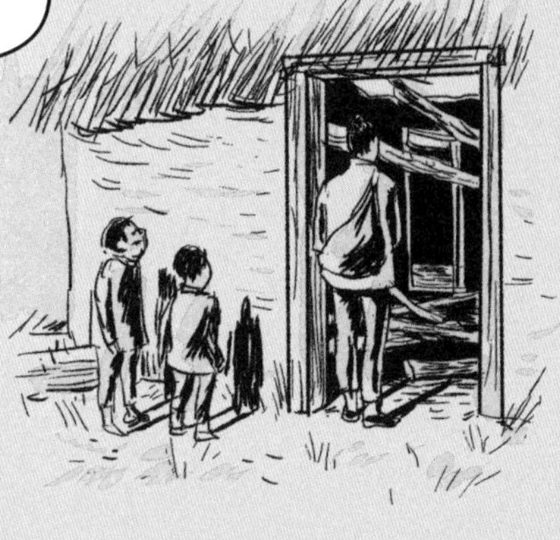

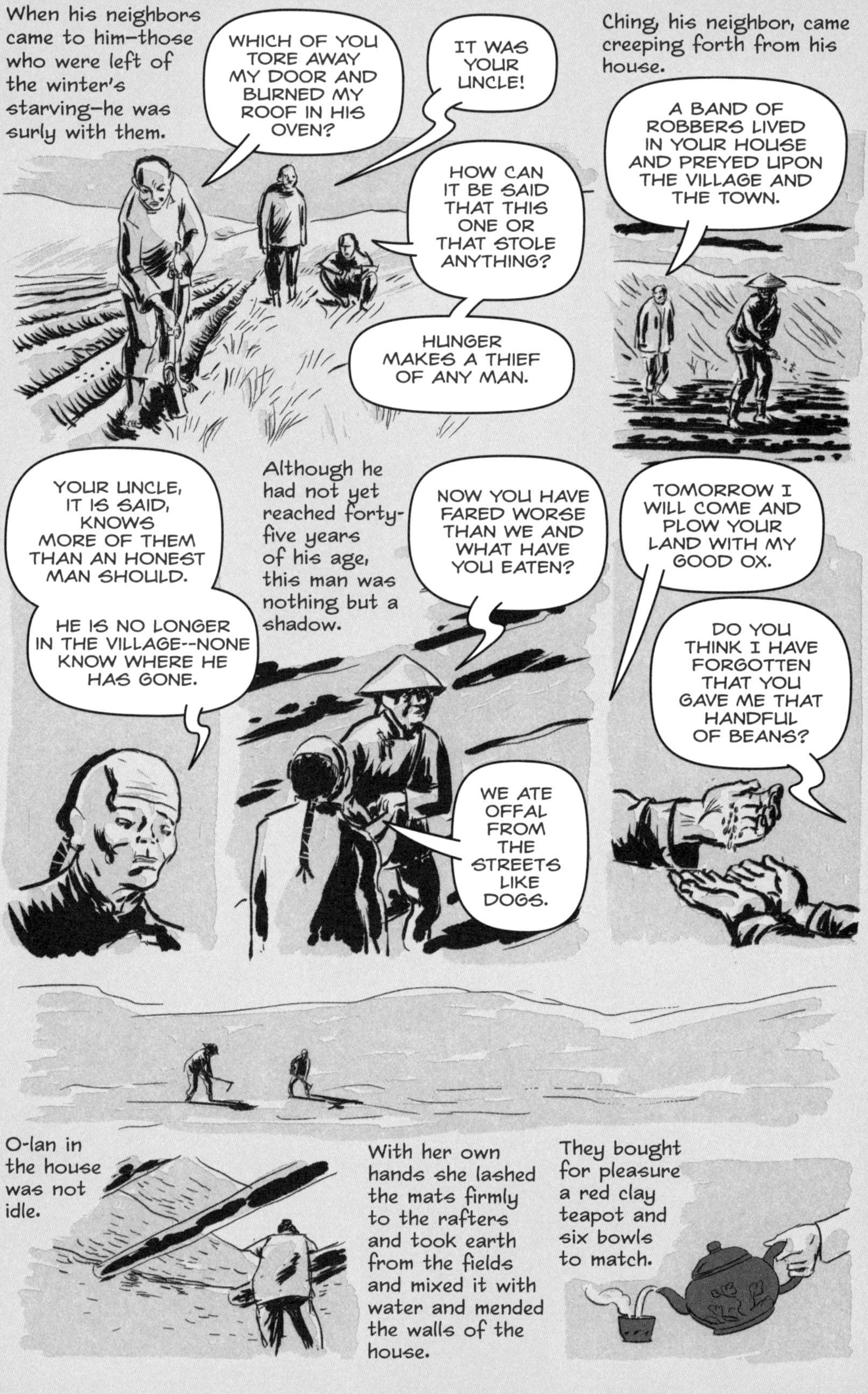

When his neighbors came to him—those who were left of the winter's starving—he was surly with them.
WHICH OF YOU TORE AWAY MY DOOR AND BURNED MY ROOF IN HIS OVEN?
IT WAS YOUR UNCLE!
HOW CAN IT BE SAID THAT THIS ONE OR THAT STOLE ANYTHING?
HUNGER MAKES A THIEF OF ANY MAN.
Ching, his neighbor, came creeping forth from his house.
A BAND OF ROBBERS LIVED IN YOUR HOUSE AND PREYED UPON THE VILLAGE AND THE TOWN.
YOUR UNCLE, IT IS SAID, KNOWS MORE OF THEM THAN AN HONEST MAN SHOULD.
HE IS NO LONGER IN THE VILLAGE--NONE KNOW WHERE HE HAS GONE.
Although he had not yet reached forty-five years of his age, this man was nothing but a shadow.
NOW YOU HAVE FARED WORSE THAN WE AND WHAT HAVE YOU EATEN?
WE ATE OFFAL FROM THE STREETS LIKE DOGS.
TOMORROW I WILL COME AND PLOW YOUR LAND WITH MY GOOD OX.
DO YOU THINK I HAVE FORGOTTEN THAT YOU GAVE ME THAT HANDFUL OF BEANS?
O-lan in the house was not idle.
With her own hands she lashed the mats firmly to the rafters and took earth from the fields and mixed it with water and mended the walls of the house.
They bought for pleasure a red clay teapot and six bowls to match.

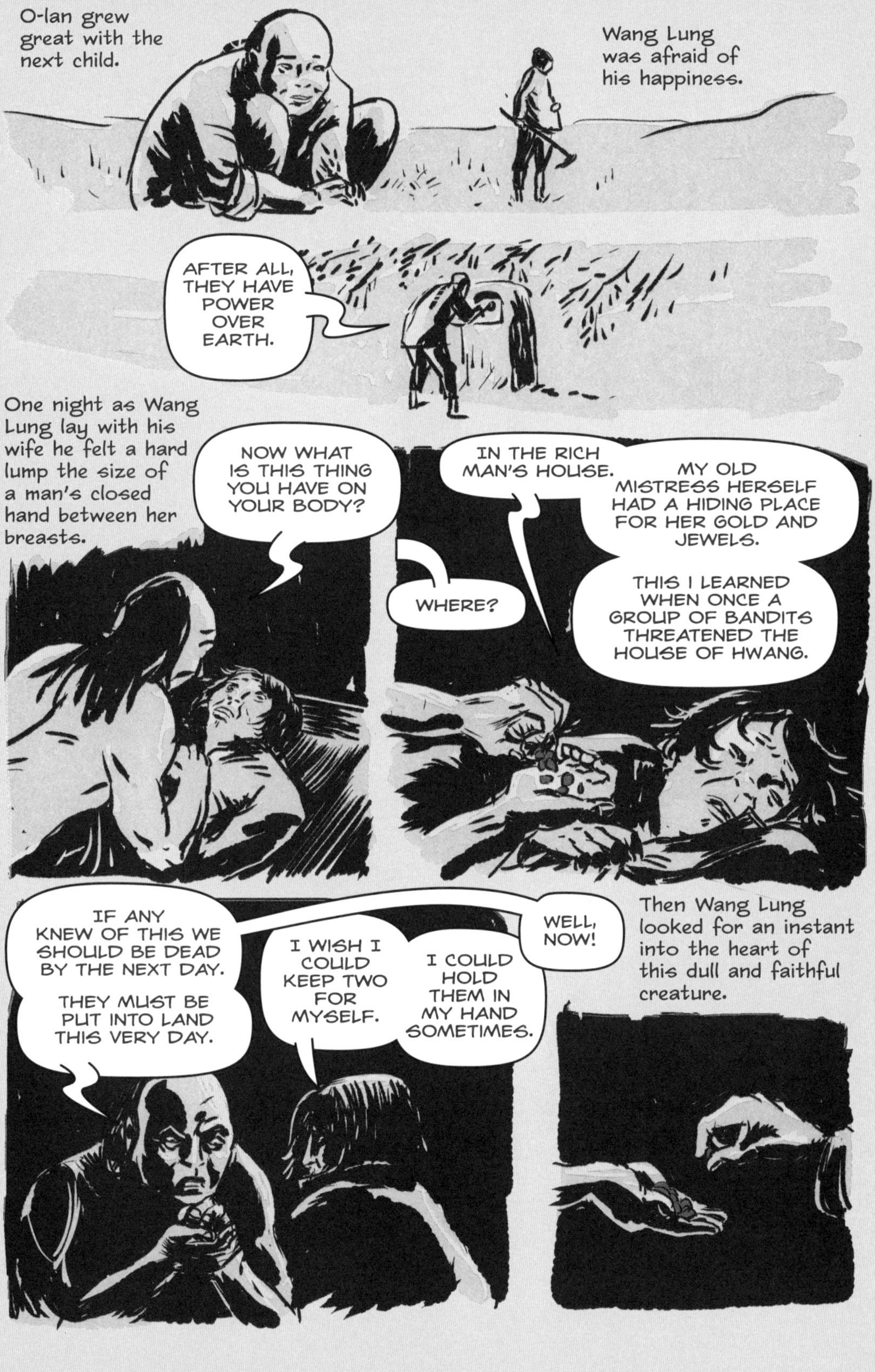
O-lan grew great with the next child.
Wang Lung was afraid of his happiness.
AFTER ALL, THEY HAVE POWER OVER EARTH.
One night as Wang Lung lay with his wife he felt a hard lump the size of a man's closed hand between her breasts.
NOW WHAT IS THIS THING YOU HAVE ON YOUR BODY?
WHERE?
IN THE RICH MAN'S HOUSE.
MY OLD MISTRESS HERSELF HAD A HIDING PLACE FOR HER GOLD AND JEWELS.
THIS I LEARNED WHEN ONCE A GROUP OF BANDITS THREATENED THE HOUSE OF HWANG.
IF ANY KNEW OF THIS WE SHOULD BE DEAD BY THE NEXT DAY.
THEY MUST BE PUT INTO LAND THIS VERY DAY.
WELL, NOW!
I WISH I COULD KEEP TWO FOR MYSELF.
I COULD HOLD THEM IN MY HAND SOMETIMES.
Then Wang Lung looked for an instant into the heart of this dull and faithful creature.

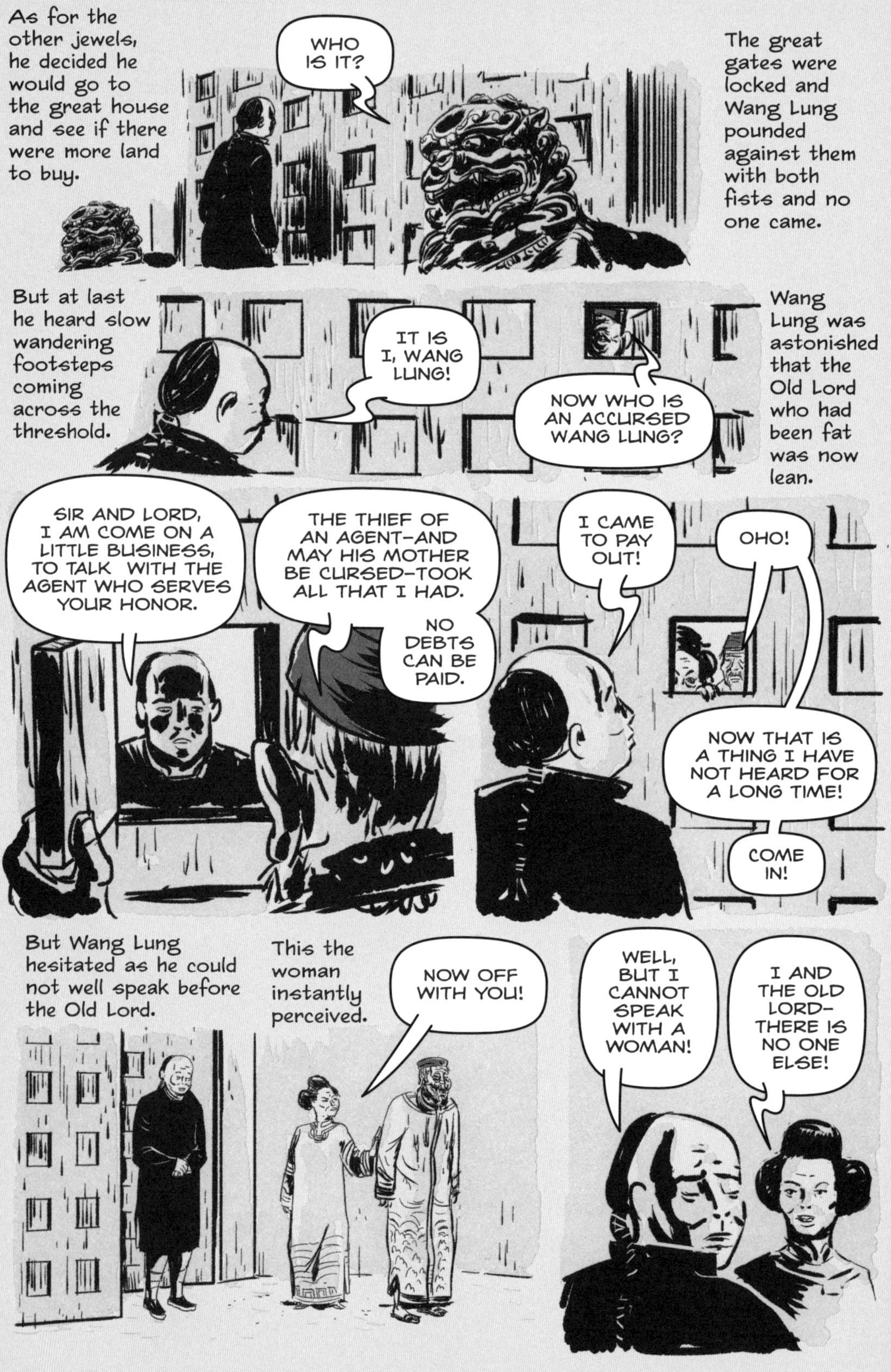
As for the other jewels, he decided he would go to the great house and see if there were more land to buy.
WHO IS IT?
The great gates were locked and Wang Lung pounded against them with both fists and no one came.
But at last he heard slow wandering footsteps coming across the threshold.
IT IS I, WANG LUNG!
NOW WHO IS AN ACCURSED WANG LUNG?
Wang Lung was astonished that the Old Lord who had been fat was now lean.
SIR AND LORD, I AM COME ON A LITTLE BUSINESS, TO TALK WITH THE AGENT WHO SERVES YOUR HONOR.
THE THIEF OF AN AGENT—AND MAY HIS MOTHER BE CURSED—TOOK ALL THAT I HAD.
NO DEBTS CAN BE PAID.
I CAME TO PAY OUT!
OHO!
NOW THAT IS A THING I HAVE NOT HEARD FOR A LONG TIME!
COME IN!
But Wang Lung hesitated as he could not well speak before the Old Lord.
This the woman instantly perceived.
NOW OFF WITH YOU!
WELL, BUT I CANNOT SPEAK WITH A WOMAN!
I AND THE OLD LORD—THERE IS NO ONE ELSE!

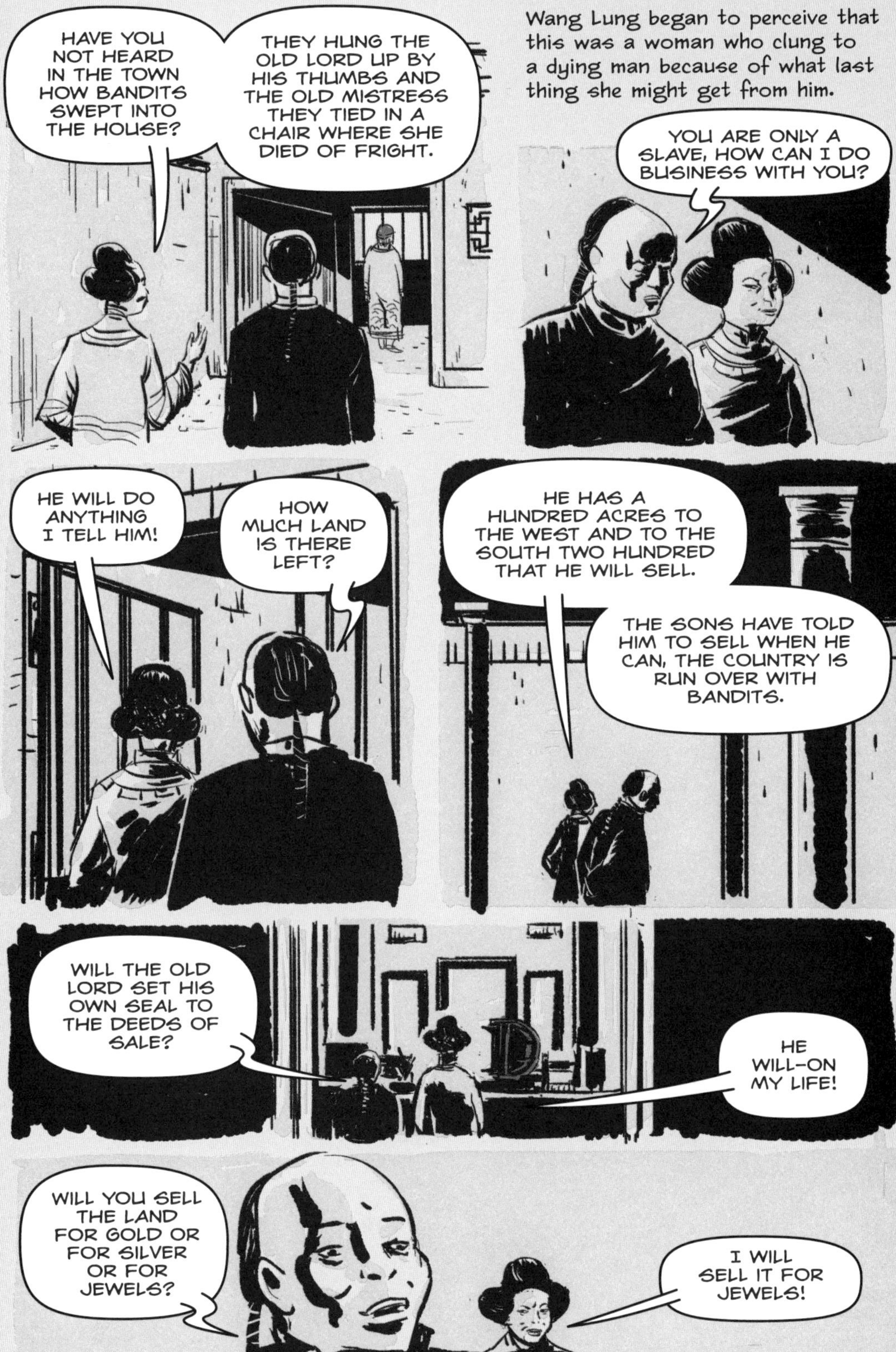
HAVE YOU NOT HEARD IN THE TOWN HOW BANDITS SWEPT INTO THE HOUSE?
THEY HUNG THE OLD LORD UP BY HIS THUMBS AND THE OLD MISTRESS THEY TIED IN A CHAIR WHERE SHE DIED OF FRIGHT.
Wang Lung began to perceive that this was a woman who clung to a dying man because of what last thing she might get from him.
YOU ARE ONLY A SLAVE, HOW CAN I DO BUSINESS WITH YOU?
HE WILL DO ANYTHING I TELL HIM!
HOW MUCH LAND IS THERE LEFT?
HE HAS A HUNDRED ACRES TO THE WEST AND TO THE SOUTH TWO HUNDRED THAT HE WILL SELL.
THE SONS HAVE TOLD HIM TO SELL WHEN HE CAN, THE COUNTRY IS RUN OVER WITH BANDITS.
WILL THE OLD LORD SET HIS OWN SEAL TO THE DEEDS OF SALE?
HE WILL—ON MY LIFE!
WILL YOU SELL THE LAND FOR GOLD OR FOR SILVER OR FOR JEWELS?
I WILL SELL IT FOR JEWELS!

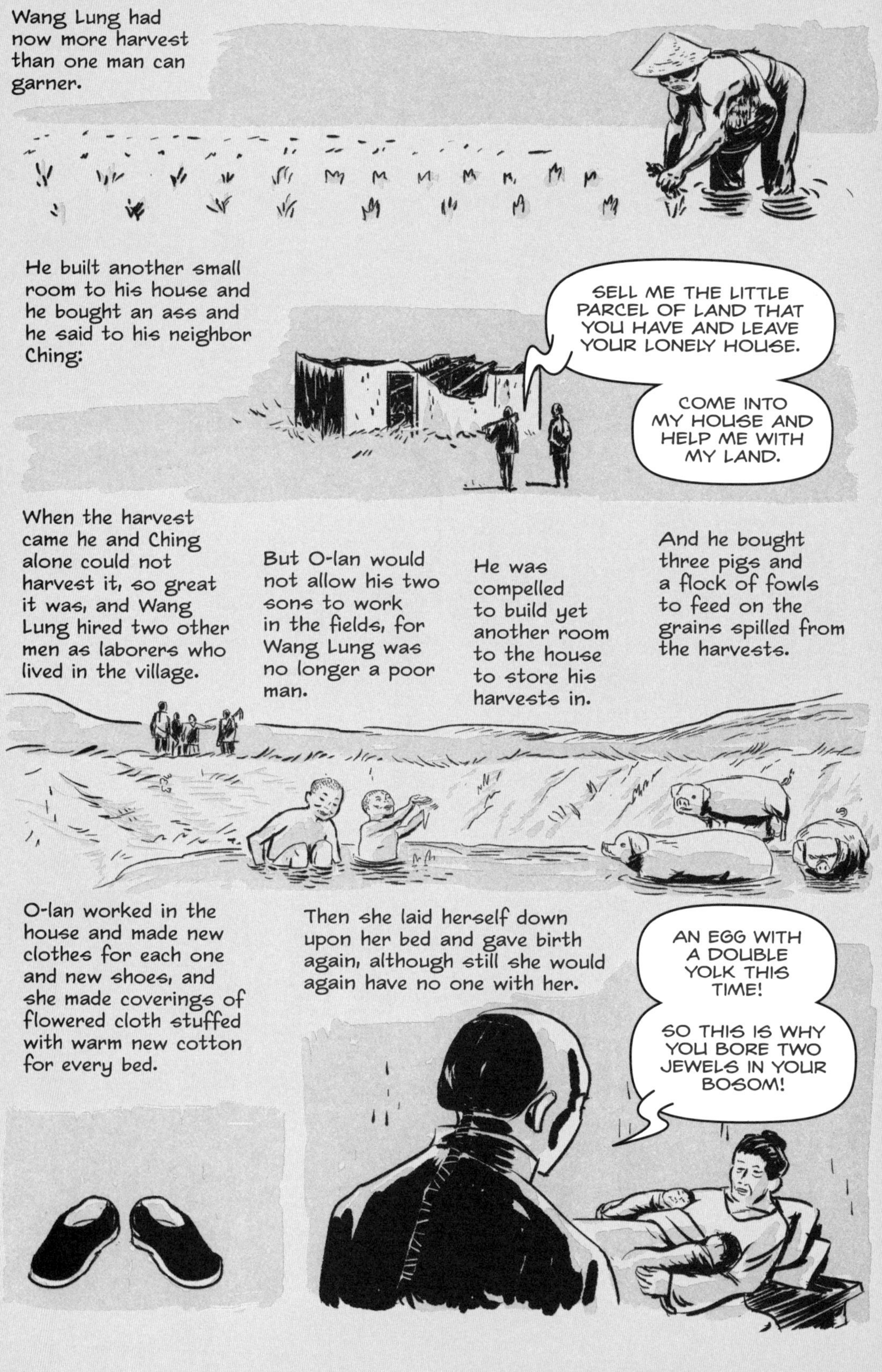
Wang Lung had now more harvest than one man can garner.
He built another small room to his house and he bought an ass and he said to his neighbor Ching:
SELL ME THE LITTLE PARCEL OF LAND THAT YOU HAVE AND LEAVE YOUR LONELY HOUSE.
COME INTO MY HOUSE AND HELP ME WITH MY LAND.
When the harvest came he and Ching alone could not harvest it, so great it was, and Wang Lung hired two other men as laborers who lived in the village.
But O-lan would not allow his two sons to work in the fields, for Wang Lung was no longer a poor man.
He was compelled to build yet another room to the house to store his harvests in.
And he bought three pigs and a flock of fowls to feed on the grains spilled from the harvests.
O-lan worked in the house and made new clothes for each one and new shoes, and she made coverings of flowered cloth stuffed with warm new cotton for every bed.
Then she laid herself down upon her bed and gave birth again, although still she would again have no one with her.
AN EGG WITH A DOUBLE YOLK THIS TIME!
SO THIS IS WHY YOU BORE TWO JEWELS IN YOUR BOSOM!

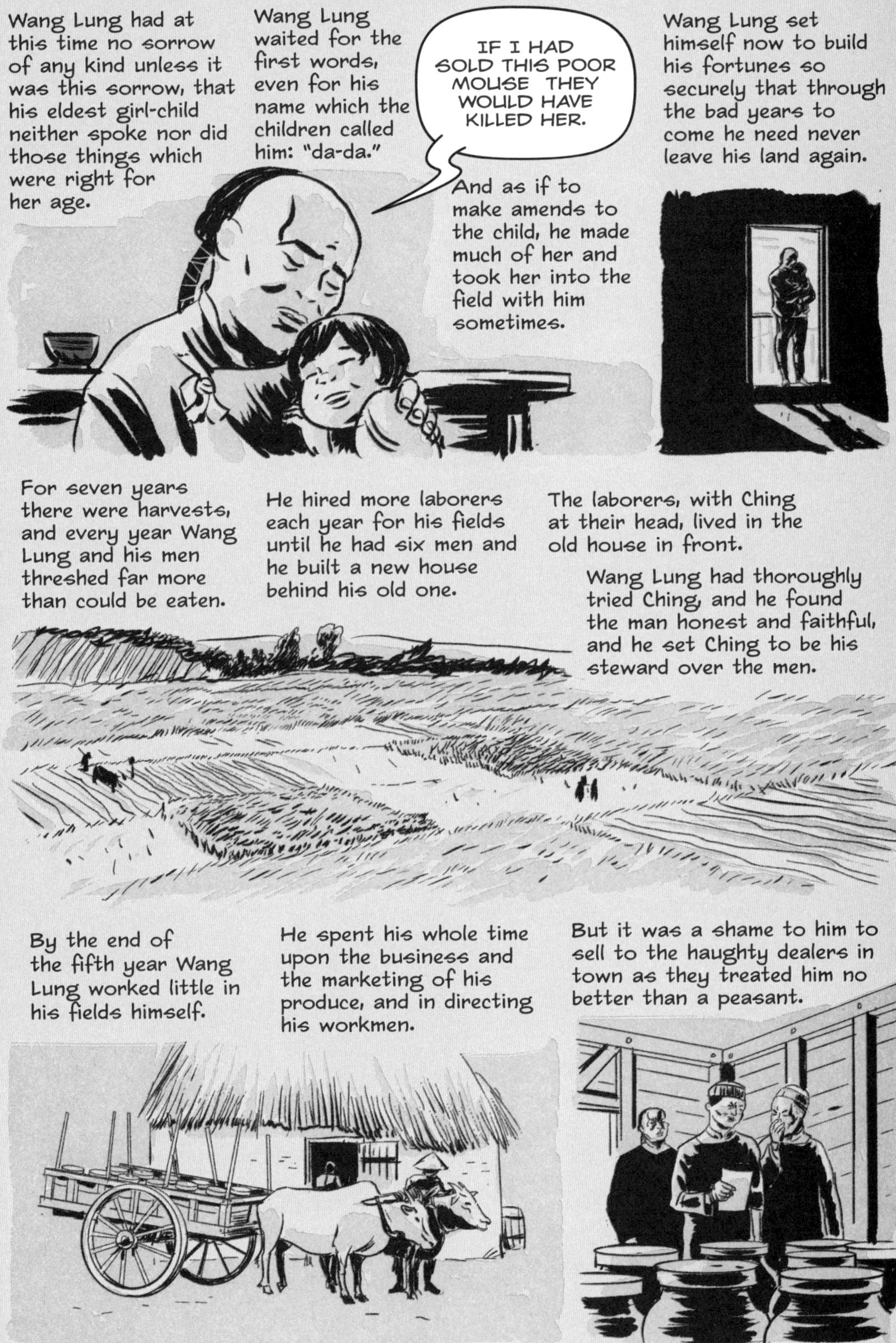
Wang Lung had at this time no sorrow of any kind unless it was this sorrow, that his eldest girl-child neither spoke nor did those things which were right for her age.
Wang Lung waited for the first words, even for his name which the children called him: "da-da."
IF I HAD SOLD THIS POOR MOUSE THEY WOULD HAVE KILLED HER.
And as if to make amends to the child, he made much of her and took her into the field with him sometimes.
Wang Lung set himself now to build his fortunes so securely that through the bad years to come he need never leave his land again.
For seven years there were harvests, and every year Wang Lung and his men threshed far more than could be eaten.
He hired more laborers each year for his fields until he had six men and he built a new house behind his old one.
The laborers, with Ching at their head, lived in the old house in front.
Wang Lung had thoroughly tried Ching, and he found the man honest and faithful, and he set Ching to be his steward over the men.
By the end of the fifth year Wang Lung worked little in his fields himself.
He spent his whole time upon the business and the marketing of his produce, and in directing his workmen.
But it was a shame to him to sell to the haughty dealers in town as they treated him no better than a peasant.

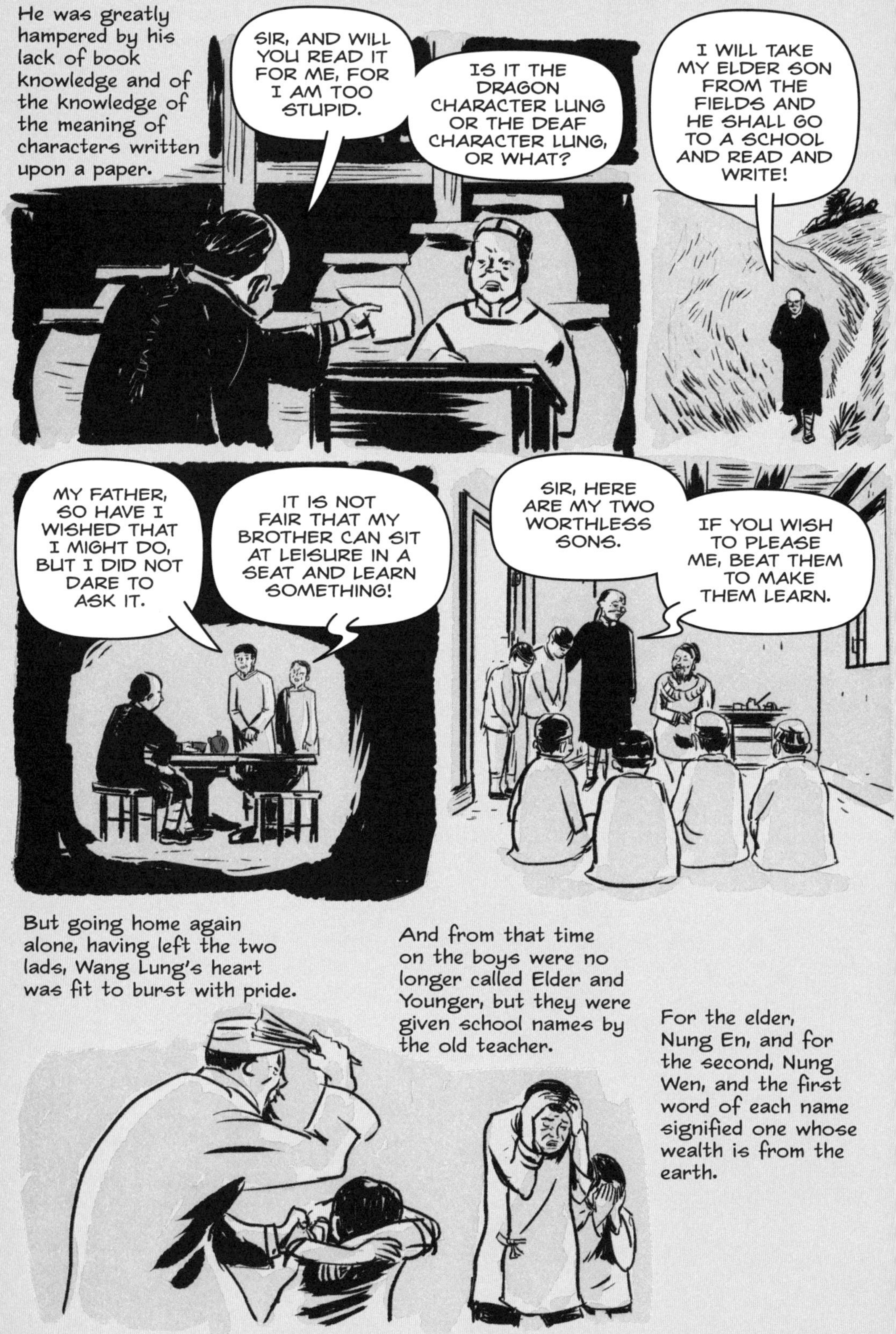
He was greatly hampered by his lack of book knowledge and of the knowledge of the meaning of characters written upon a paper.
SIR, AND WILL YOU READ IT FOR ME, FOR I AM TOO STUPID.
IS IT THE DRAGON CHARACTER LUNG OR THE DEAF CHARACTER LUNG, OR WHAT?
I WILL TAKE MY ELDER SON FROM THE FIELDS AND HE SHALL GO TO A SCHOOL AND READ AND WRITE!
MY FATHER, SO HAVE I WISHED THAT I MIGHT DO, BUT I DID NOT DARE TO ASK IT.
IT IS NOT FAIR THAT MY BROTHER CAN SIT AT LEISURE IN A SEAT AND LEARN SOMETHING!
SIR, HERE ARE MY TWO WORTHLESS SONS.
IF YOU WISH TO PLEASE ME, BEAT THEM TO MAKE THEM LEARN.
But going home again alone, having left the two lads, Wang Lung's heart was fit to burst with pride.
And from that time on the boys were no longer called Elder and Younger, but they were given school names by the old teacher.
For the elder, Nung En, and for the second, Nung Wen, and the first word of each name signified one whose wealth is from the earth.

When the seventh year came, the great river to the north burst its bounds and came sweeping and flooding all over the lands of that region.

All through the late spring and early summer the water rose and there were those who starved as they ever had.

But Wang Lung was not afraid, although two-fifths of his land was a lake as deep as a man's shoulders and more.

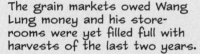

The grain markets owed Wang Lung money and his store-rooms were yet filled full with harvests of the last two years.

But since much of the land could not be planted he was more idle than he had ever been in his life.

The old man grew very feeble now, half-blind and almost wholly deaf.

It made Wang Lung impatient that the old man could not see how rich his son was.

The elder girl, never spoke at all but sat beside her grandfather hour after hour, twisting a bit of cloth, and smiling at it.

These two had nothing to say to a man prosperous and vigorous.

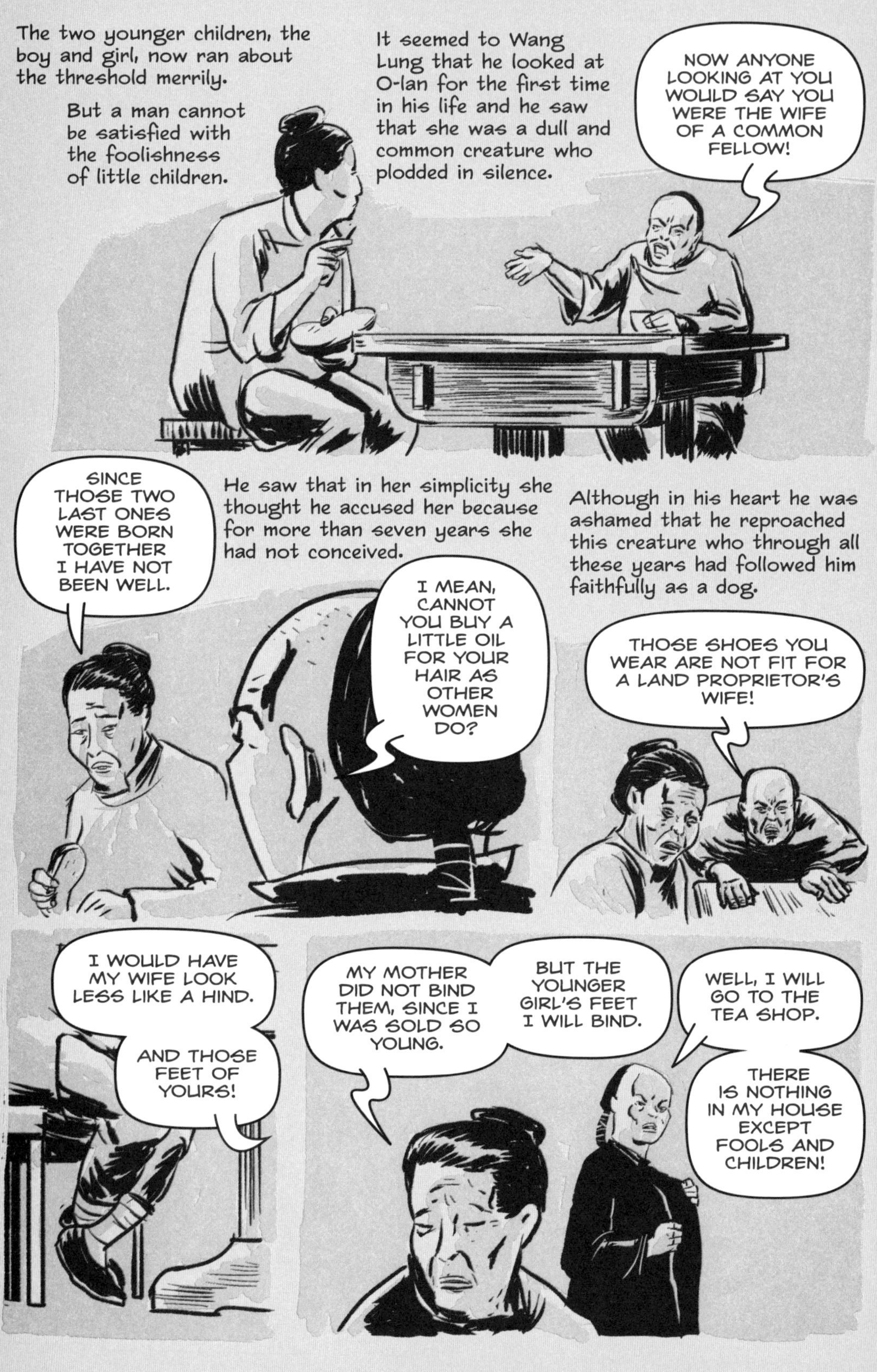
The two younger children, the boy and girl, now ran about the threshold merrily.
But a man cannot be satisfied with the foolishness of little children.
It seemed to Wang Lung that he looked at O-lan for the first time in his life and he saw that she was a dull and common creature who plodded in silence.
NOW ANYONE LOOKING AT YOU WOULD SAY YOU WERE THE WIFE OF A COMMON FELLOW!
SINCE THOSE TWO LAST ONES WERE BORN TOGETHER I HAVE NOT BEEN WELL.
He saw that in her simplicity she thought he accused her because for more than seven years she had not conceived.
I MEAN, CANNOT YOU BUY A LITTLE OIL FOR YOUR HAIR AS OTHER WOMEN DO?
Although in his heart he was ashamed that he reproached this creature who through all these years had followed him faithfully as a dog.
THOSE SHOES YOU WEAR ARE NOT FIT FOR A LAND PROPRIETOR'S WIFE!
I WOULD HAVE MY WIFE LOOK LESS LIKE A HIND.
AND THOSE FEET OF YOURS!
MY MOTHER DID NOT BIND THEM, SINCE I WAS SOLD SO YOUNG.
BUT THE YOUNGER GIRL'S FEET I WILL BIND.
WELL, I WILL GO TO THE TEA SHOP.
THERE IS NOTHING IN MY HOUSE EXCEPT FOOLS AND CHILDREN!

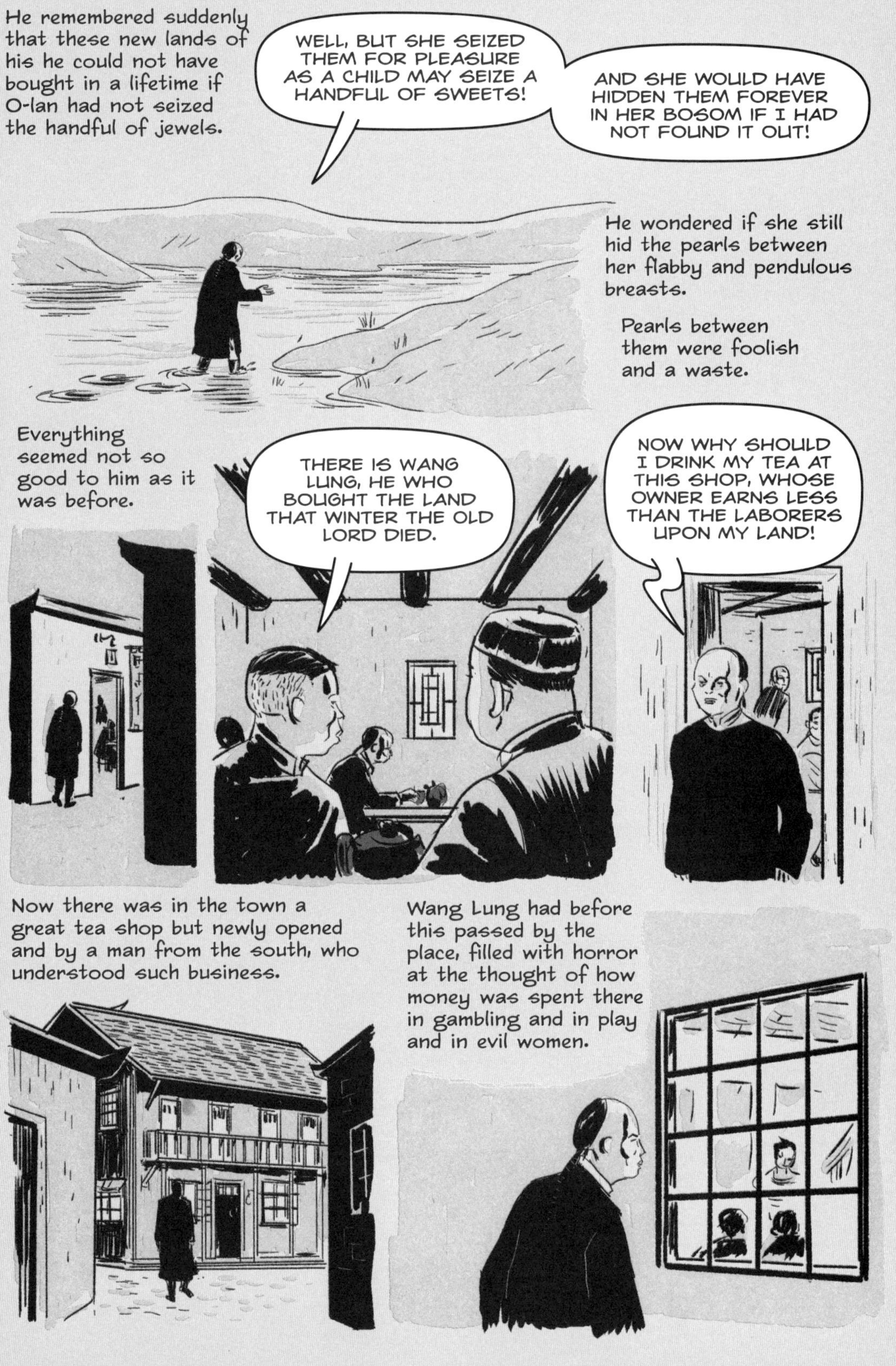
He remembered suddenly that these new lands of his he could not have bought in a lifetime if O-lan had not seized the handful of jewels.
WELL, BUT SHE SEIZED THEM FOR PLEASURE AS A CHILD MAY SEIZE A HANDFUL OF SWEETS!
AND SHE WOULD HAVE HIDDEN THEM FOREVER IN HER BOSOM IF I HAD NOT FOUND IT OUT!
He wondered if she still hid the pearls between her flabby and pendulous breasts.
Pearls between them were foolish and a waste.
Everything seemed not so good to him as it was before.
THERE IS WANG LUNG, HE WHO BOUGHT THE LAND THAT WINTER THE OLD LORD DIED.
NOW WHY SHOULD I DRINK MY TEA AT THIS SHOP, WHOSE OWNER EARNS LESS THAN THE LABORERS UPON MY LAND!
Now there was in the town a great tea shop but newly opened and by a man from the south, who understood such business.
Wang Lung had before this passed by the place, filled with horror at the thought of how money was spent there in gambling and in play and in evil women.

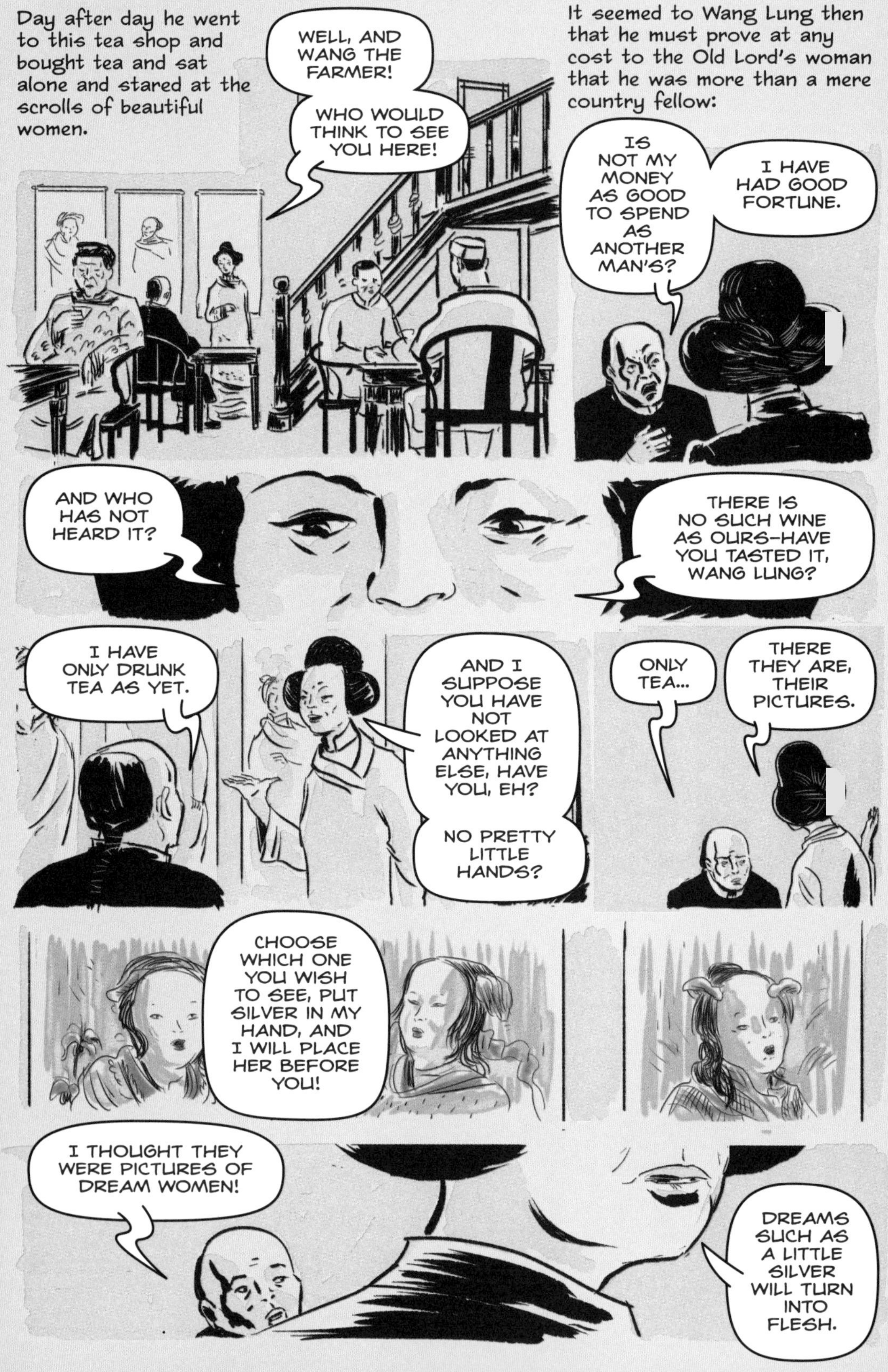
Day after day he went to this tea shop and bought tea and sat alone and stared at the scrolls of beautiful women.
WELL, AND WANG THE FARMER!
WHO WOULD THINK TO SEE YOU HERE!
It seemed to Wang Lung then that he must prove at any cost to the Old Lord's woman that he was more than a mere country fellow:
IS NOT MY MONEY AS GOOD TO SPEND AS ANOTHER MAN'S?
I HAVE HAD GOOD FORTUNE.
AND WHO HAS NOT HEARD IT?
THERE IS NO SUCH WINE AS OURS–HAVE YOU TASTED IT, WANG LUNG?
I HAVE ONLY DRUNK TEA AS YET.
AND I SUPPOSE YOU HAVE NOT LOOKED AT ANYTHING ELSE, HAVE YOU, EH?
NO PRETTY LITTLE HANDS?
ONLY TEA...
THERE THEY ARE, THEIR PICTURES.
CHOOSE WHICH ONE YOU WISH TO SEE, PUT SILVER IN MY HAND, AND I WILL PLACE HER BEFORE YOU!
I THOUGHT THEY WERE PICTURES OF DREAM WOMEN!
DREAMS SUCH AS A LITTLE SILVER WILL TURN INTO FLESH.

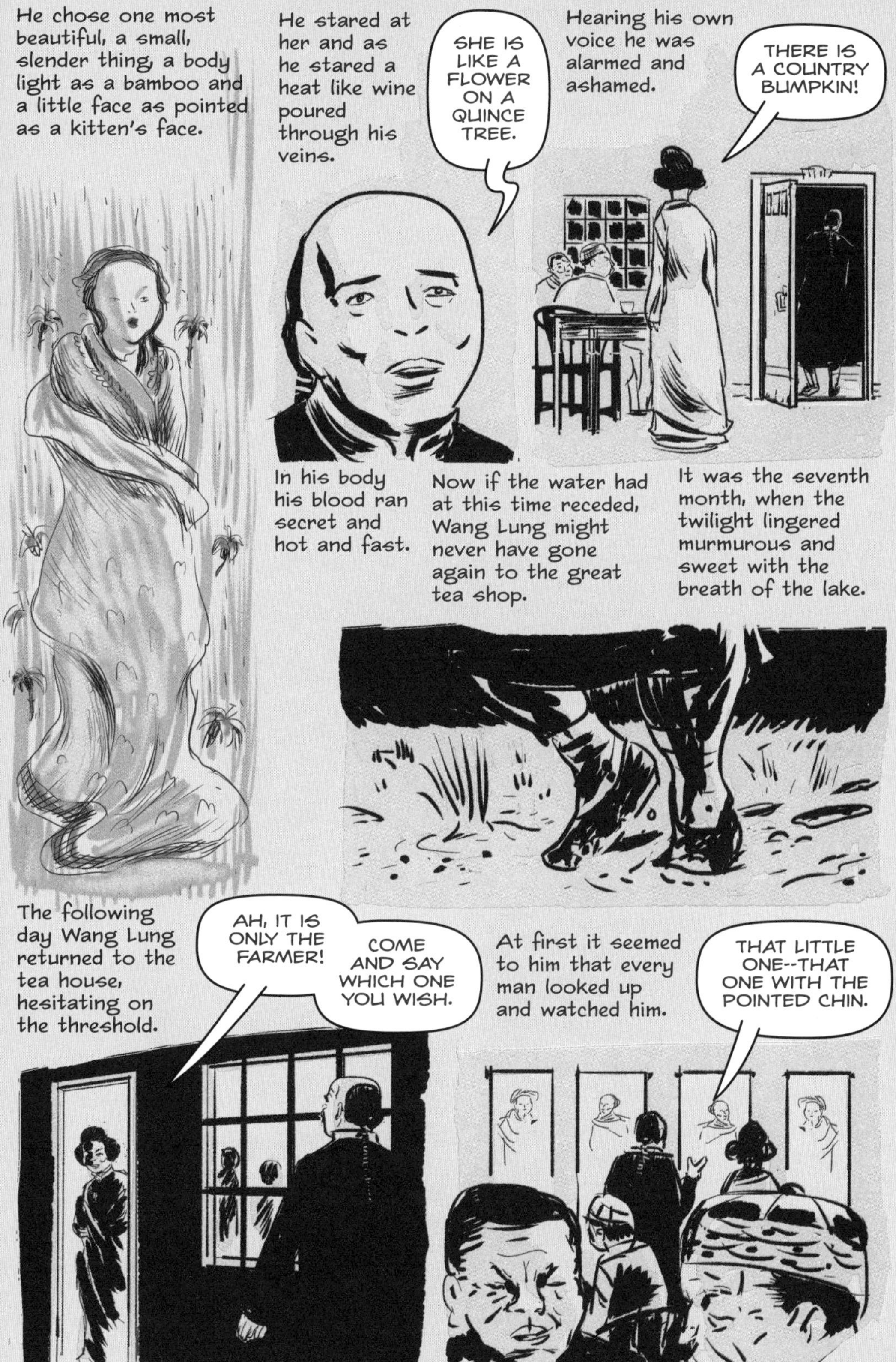
He chose one most beautiful, a small, slender thing, a body light as a bamboo and a little face as pointed as a kitten's face.
He stared at her and as he stared a heat like wine poured through his veins.
SHE IS LIKE A FLOWER ON A QUINCE TREE.
Hearing his own voice he was alarmed and ashamed.
THERE IS A COUNTRY BUMPKIN!
In his body his blood ran secret and hot and fast.
Now if the water had at this time receded, Wang Lung might never have gone again to the great tea shop.
It was the seventh month, when the twilight lingered murmurous and sweet with the breath of the lake.
The following day Wang Lung returned to the tea house, hesitating on the threshold.
AH, IT IS ONLY THE FARMER!
COME AND SAY WHICH ONE YOU WISH.
At first it seemed to him that every man looked up and watched him.
THAT LITTLE ONE--THAT ONE WITH THE POINTED CHIN.

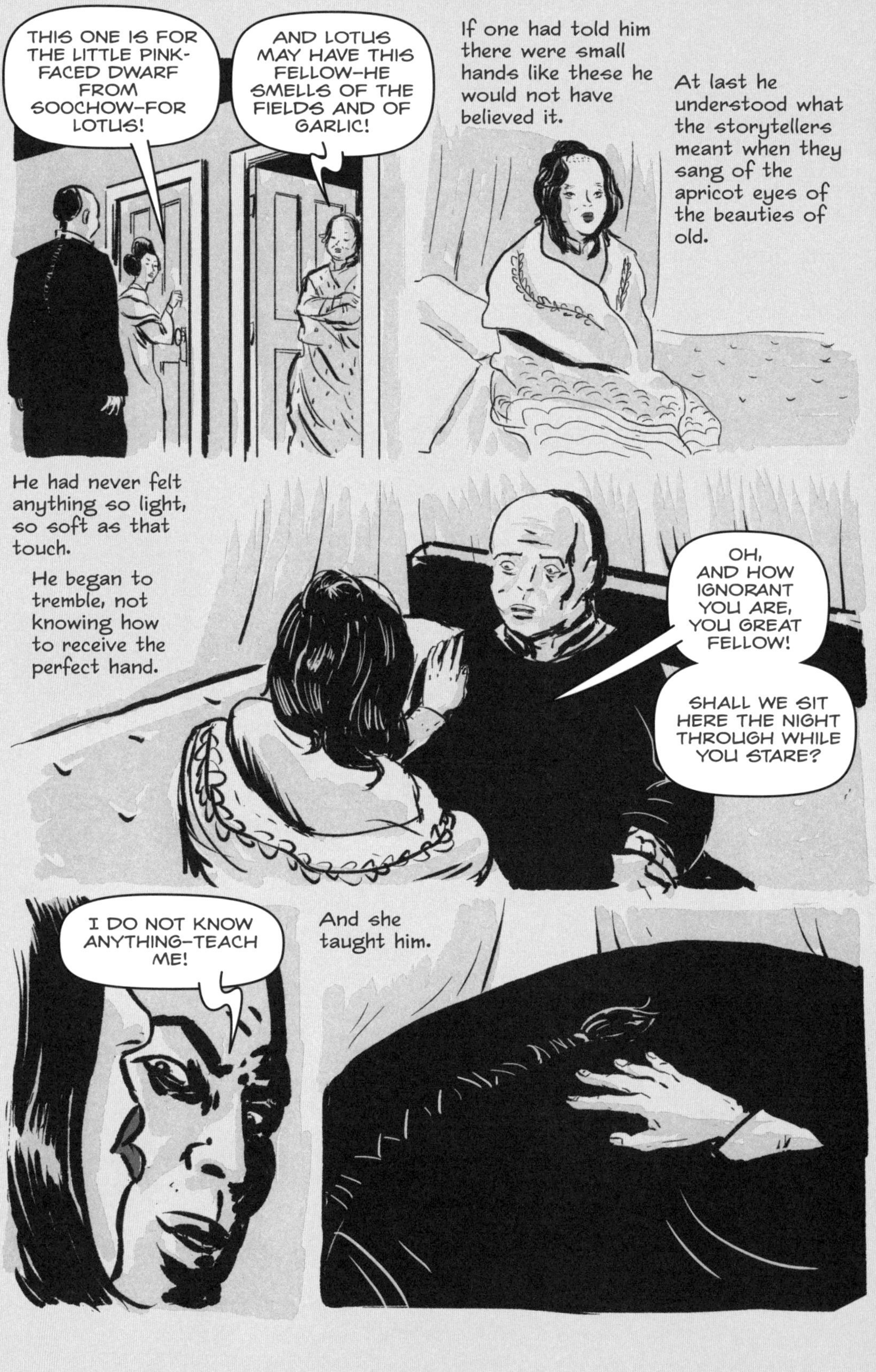
THIS ONE IS FOR THE LITTLE PINK-FACED DWARF FROM SOOCHOW—FOR LOTUS!
AND LOTUS MAY HAVE THIS FELLOW—HE SMELLS OF THE FIELDS AND OF GARLIC!
If one had told him there were small hands like these he would not have believed it.
At last he understood what the storytellers meant when they sang of the apricot eyes of the beauties of old.
He had never felt anything so light, so soft as that touch.
He began to tremble, not knowing how to receive the perfect hand.
OH, AND HOW IGNORANT YOU ARE, YOU GREAT FELLOW!
SHALL WE SIT HERE THE NIGHT THROUGH WHILE YOU STARE?
I DO NOT KNOW ANYTHING—TEACH ME!
And she taught him.

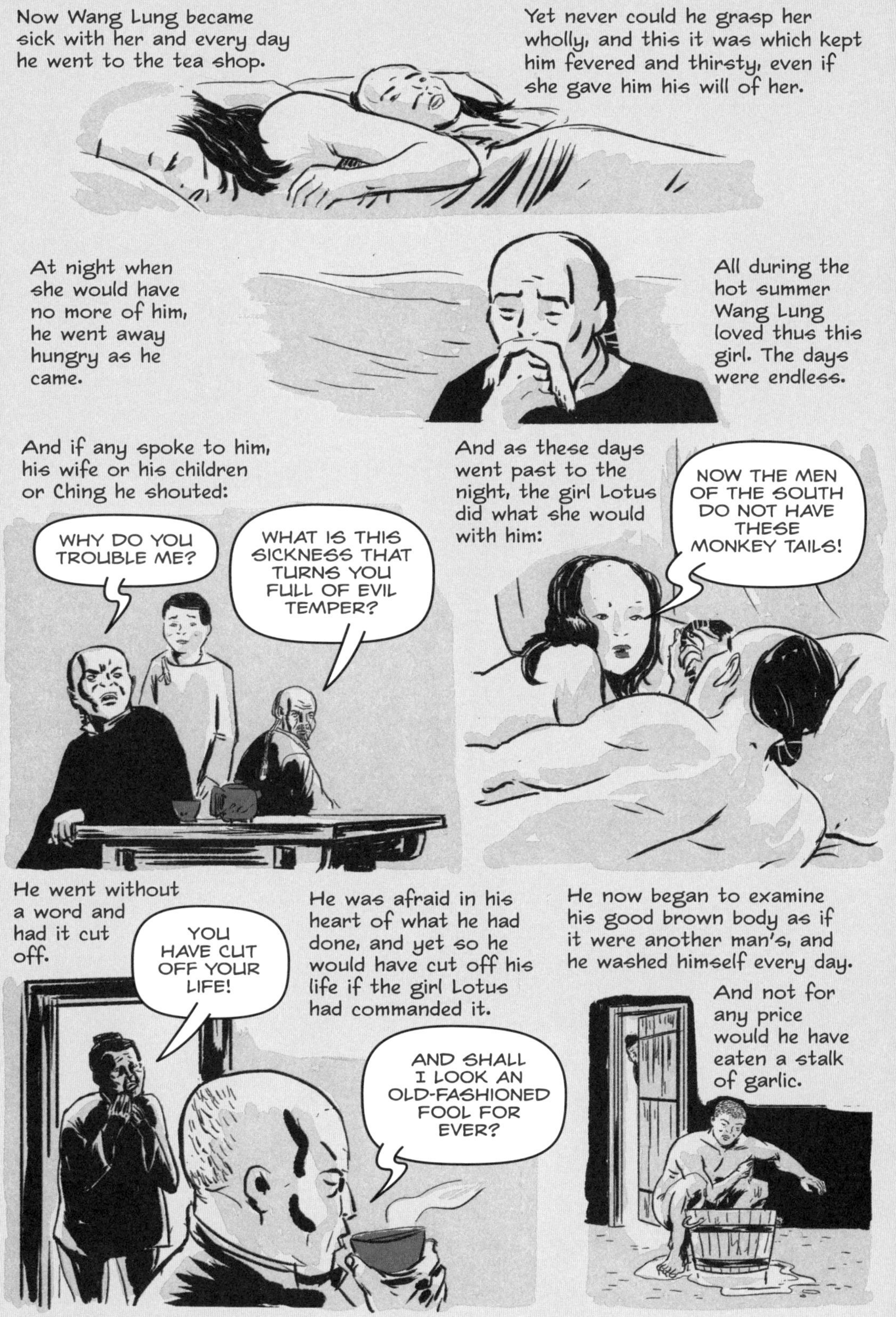
Now Wang Lung became sick with her and every day he went to the tea shop.
Yet never could he grasp her wholly, and this it was which kept him fevered and thirsty, even if she gave him his will of her.
At night when she would have no more of him, he went away hungry as he came.
All during the hot summer Wang Lung loved thus this girl. The days were endless.
And if any spoke to him, his wife or his children or Ching he shouted:
WHY DO YOU TROUBLE ME?
WHAT IS THIS SICKNESS THAT TURNS YOU FULL OF EVIL TEMPER?
And as these days went past to the night, the girl Lotus did what she would with him:
NOW THE MEN OF THE SOUTH DO NOT HAVE THESE MONKEY TAILS!
He went without a word and had it cut off.
YOU HAVE CUT OFF YOUR LIFE!
He was afraid in his heart of what he had done, and yet so he would have cut off his life if the girl Lotus had commanded it.
AND SHALL I LOOK AN OLD-FASHIONED FOOL FOR EVER?
He now began to examine his good brown body as if it were another man's, and he washed himself every day.
And not for any price would he have eaten a stalk of garlic.

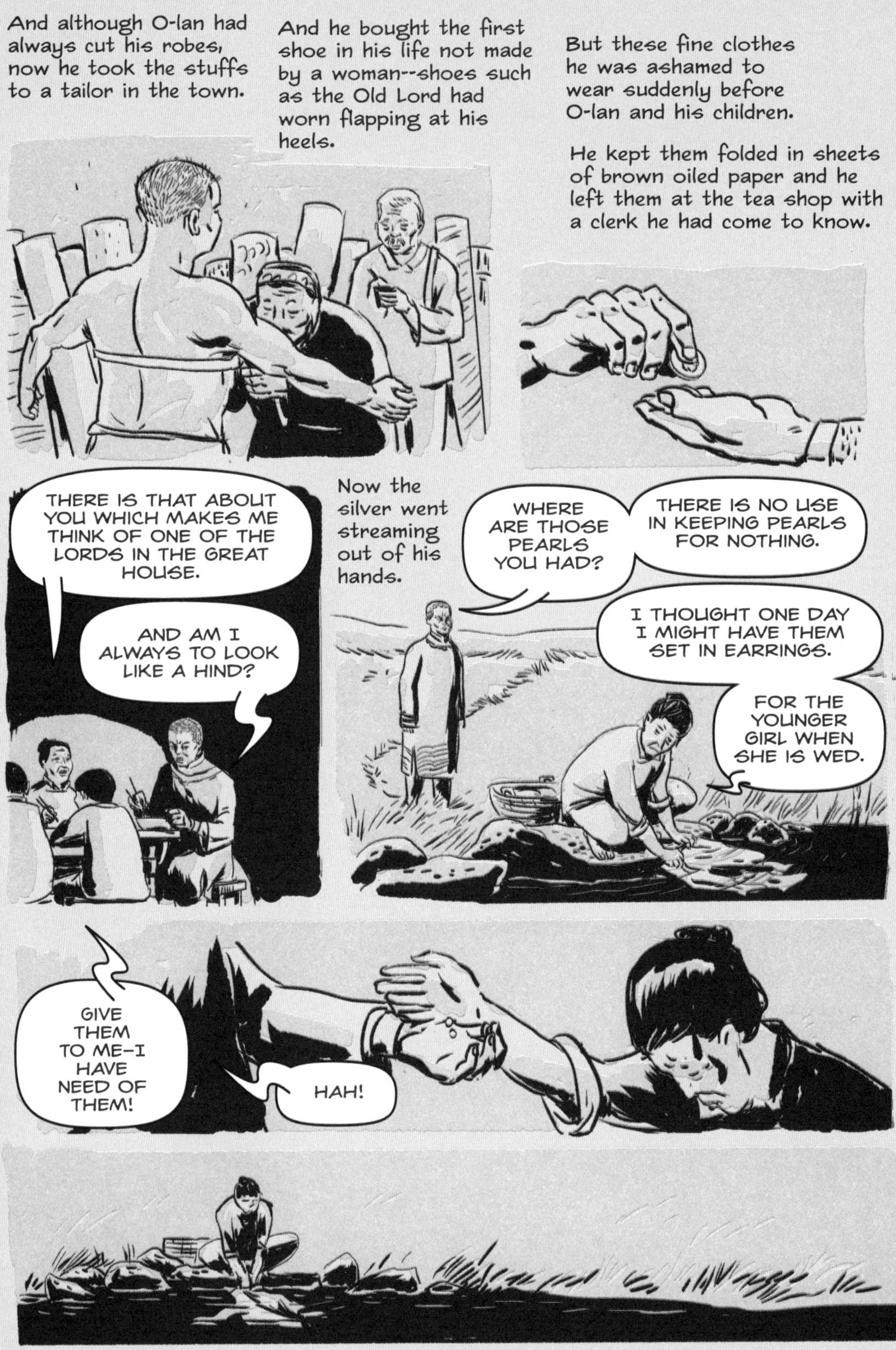
And although O-lan had always cut his robes, now he took the stuffs to a tailor in the town.
And he bought the first shoe in his life not made by a woman--shoes such as the Old Lord had worn flapping at his heels.
But these fine clothes he was ashamed to wear suddenly before O-lan and his children.
He kept them folded in sheets of brown oiled paper and he left them at the tea shop with a clerk he had come to know.
THERE IS THAT ABOUT YOU WHICH MAKES ME THINK OF ONE OF THE LORDS IN THE GREAT HOUSE.
AND AM I ALWAYS TO LOOK LIKE A HIND?
Now the silver went streaming out of his hands.
WHERE ARE THOSE PEARLS YOU HAD?
THERE IS NO USE IN KEEPING PEARLS FOR NOTHING.
I THOUGHT ONE DAY I MIGHT HAVE THEM SET IN EARRINGS.
FOR THE YOUNGER GIRL WHEN SHE IS WED.
GIVE THEM TO ME–I HAVE NEED OF THEM!
HAH!

6

And thus it might have gone on until all the silver was spent, had not Wang Lung's uncle returned suddenly.

It was as though he dropped from a cloud--without explanation of where he had been or of what he had done.

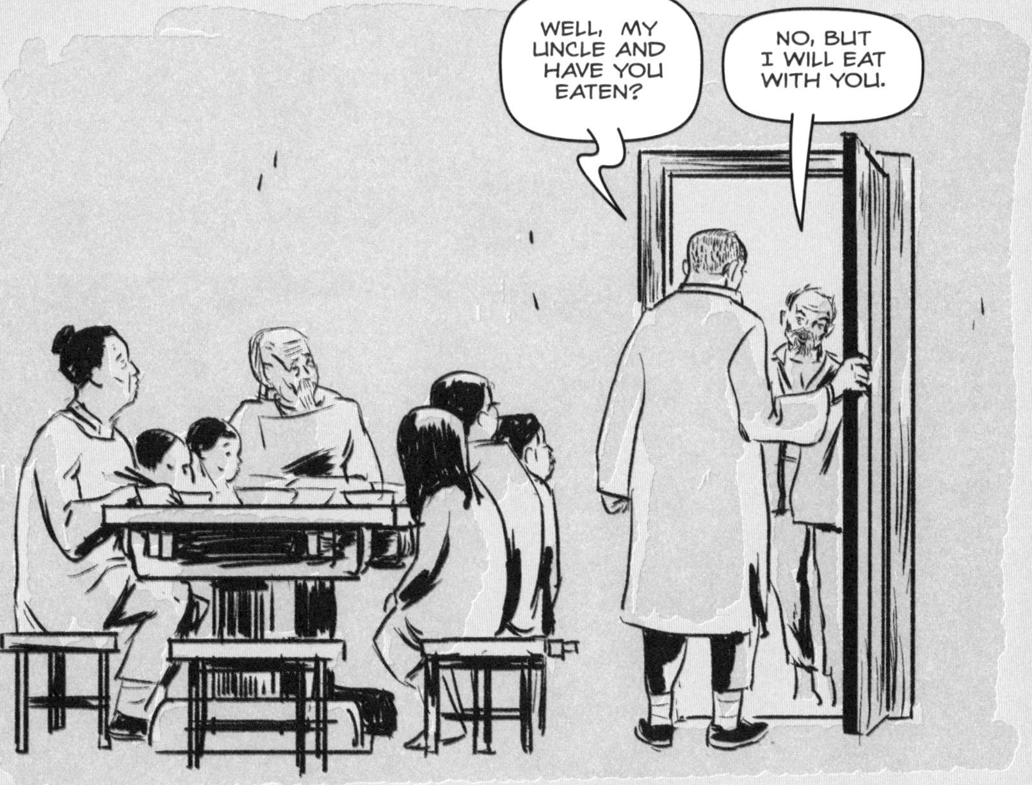
WELL, MY UNCLE AND HAVE YOU EATEN?
NO, BUT I WILL EAT WITH YOU.

Wang Lung thought of his uncle's wife and saw that they would come to his house and none could stop them.

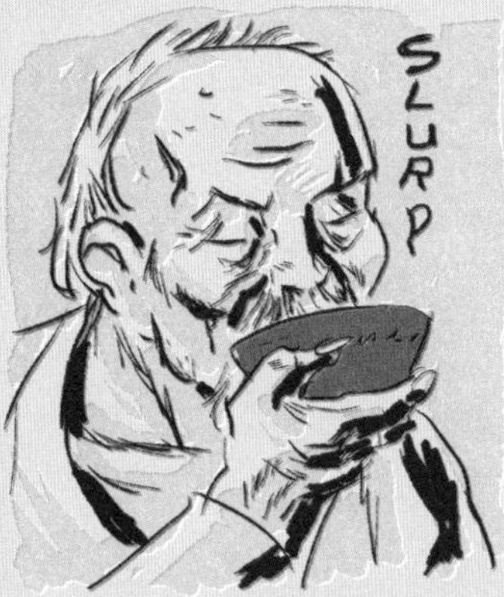
SLURP

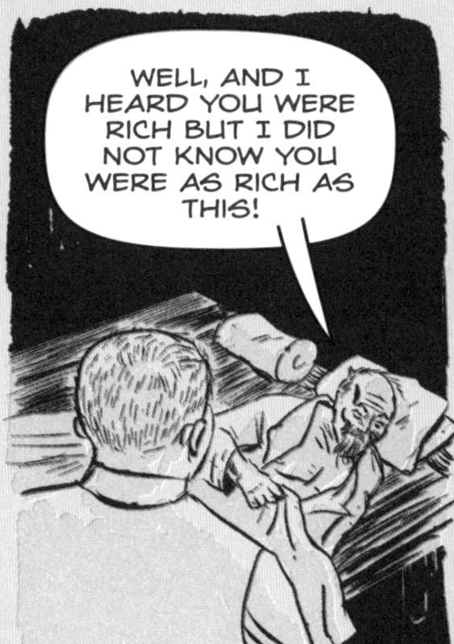
WELL, AND I HEARD YOU WERE RICH BUT I DID NOT KNOW YOU WERE AS RICH AS THIS!

As he feared, so it happened.

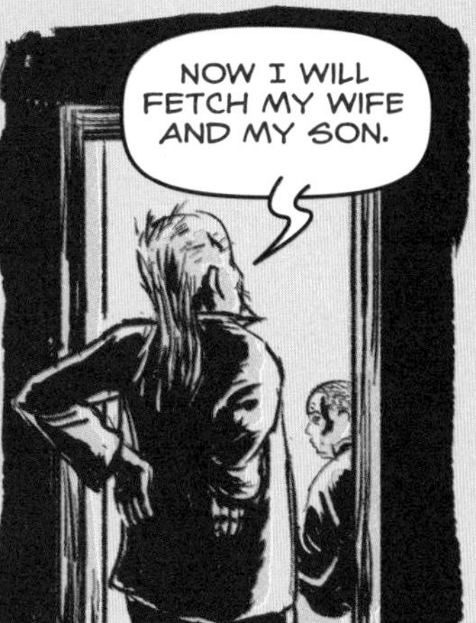
NOW I WILL FETCH MY WIFE AND MY SON.

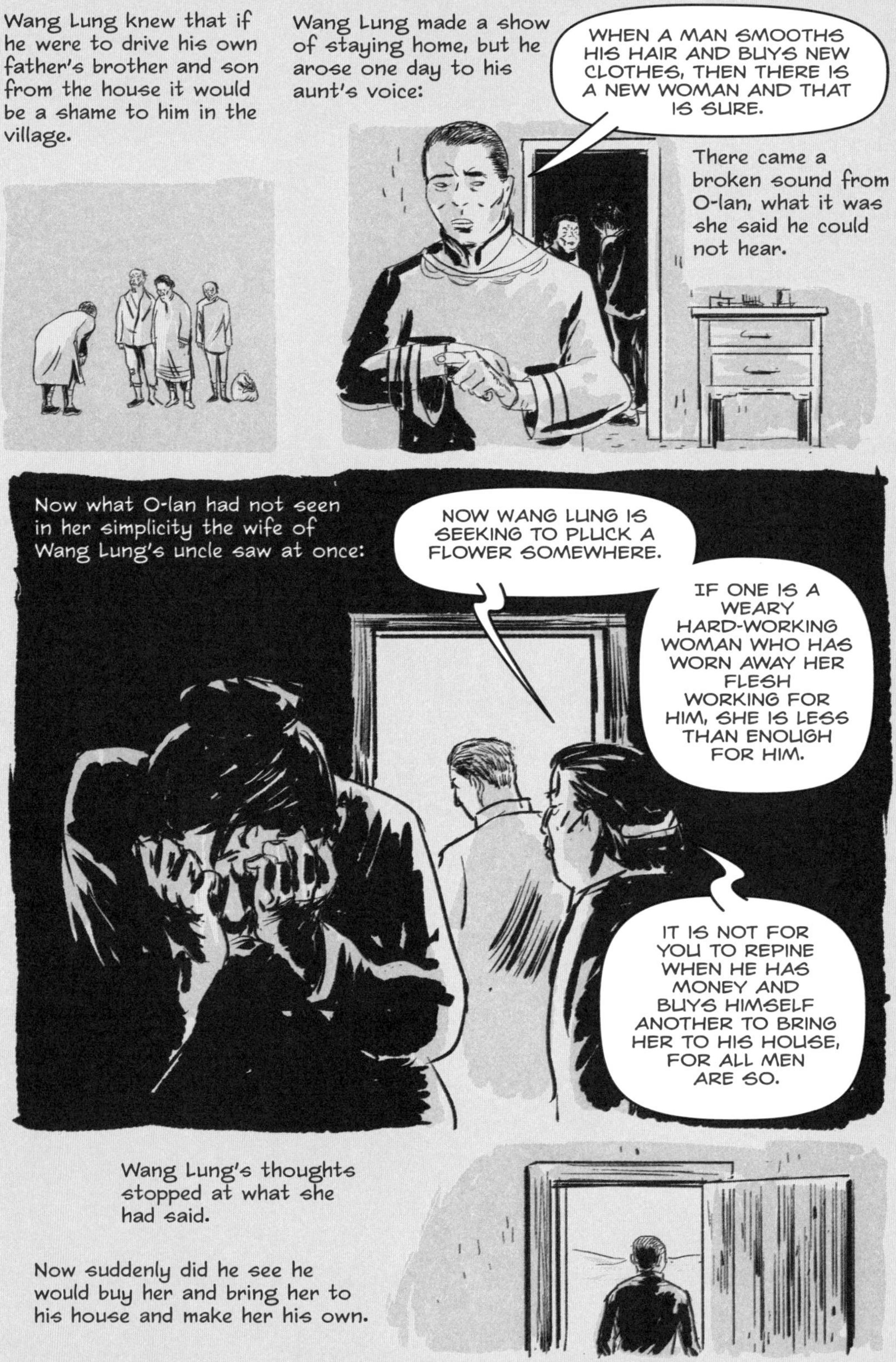
Wang Lung knew that if he were to drive his own father's brother and son from the house it would be a shame to him in the village.
Wang Lung made a show of staying home, but he arose one day to his aunt's voice:
WHEN A MAN SMOOTHS HIS HAIR AND BUYS NEW CLOTHES, THEN THERE IS A NEW WOMAN AND THAT IS SURE.
There came a broken sound from O-lan, what it was she said he could not hear.
Now what O-lan had not seen in her simplicity the wife of Wang Lung's uncle saw at once:
NOW WANG LUNG IS SEEKING TO PLUCK A FLOWER SOMEWHERE.
IF ONE IS A WEARY HARD-WORKING WOMAN WHO HAS WORN AWAY HER FLESH WORKING FOR HIM, SHE IS LESS THAN ENOUGH FOR HIM.
IT IS NOT FOR YOU TO REPINE WHEN HE HAS MONEY AND BUYS HIMSELF ANOTHER TO BRING HER TO HIS HOUSE, FOR ALL MEN ARE SO.
Wang Lung's thoughts stopped at what she had said.
Now suddenly did he see he would buy her and bring her to his house and make her his own.

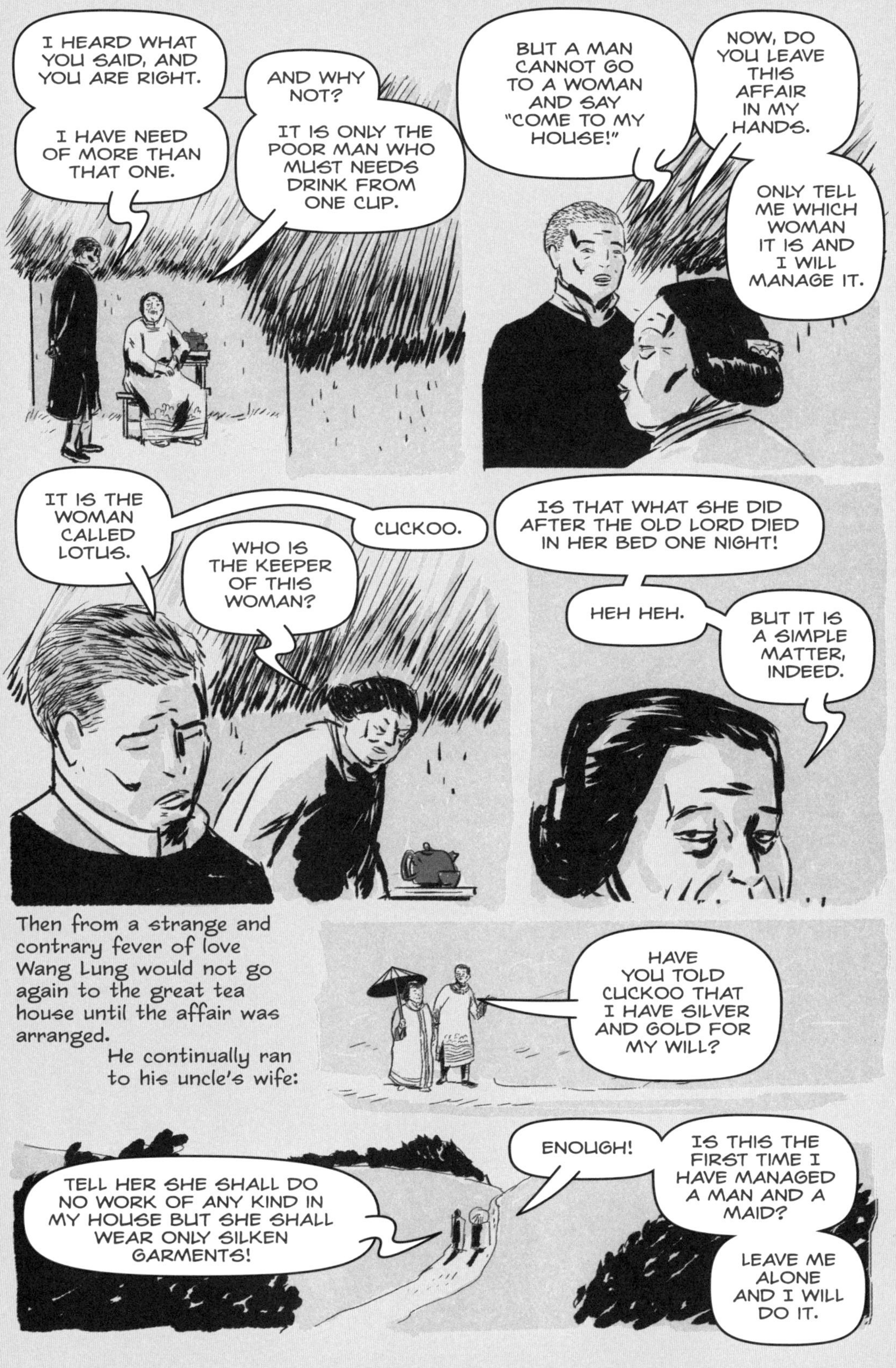
I HEARD WHAT YOU SAID, AND YOU ARE RIGHT.
I HAVE NEED OF MORE THAN THAT ONE.
AND WHY NOT?
IT IS ONLY THE POOR MAN WHO MUST NEEDS DRINK FROM ONE CUP.
BUT A MAN CANNOT GO TO A WOMAN AND SAY "COME TO MY HOUSE!"
NOW, DO YOU LEAVE THIS AFFAIR IN MY HANDS.
ONLY TELL ME WHICH WOMAN IT IS AND I WILL MANAGE IT.
IT IS THE WOMAN CALLED LOTUS.
CUCKOO.
WHO IS THE KEEPER OF THIS WOMAN?
IS THAT WHAT SHE DID AFTER THE OLD LORD DIED IN HER BED ONE NIGHT!
HEH HEH.
BUT IT IS A SIMPLE MATTER, INDEED.
Then from a strange and contrary fever of love Wang Lung would not go again to the great tea house until the affair was arranged.
He continually ran to his uncle's wife:
HAVE YOU TOLD CUCKOO THAT I HAVE SILVER AND GOLD FOR MY WILL?
TELL HER SHE SHALL DO NO WORK OF ANY KIND IN MY HOUSE BUT SHE SHALL WEAR ONLY SILKEN GARMENTS!
ENOUGH!
IS THIS THE FIRST TIME I HAVE MANAGED A MAN AND A MAID?
LEAVE ME ALONE AND I WILL DO IT.

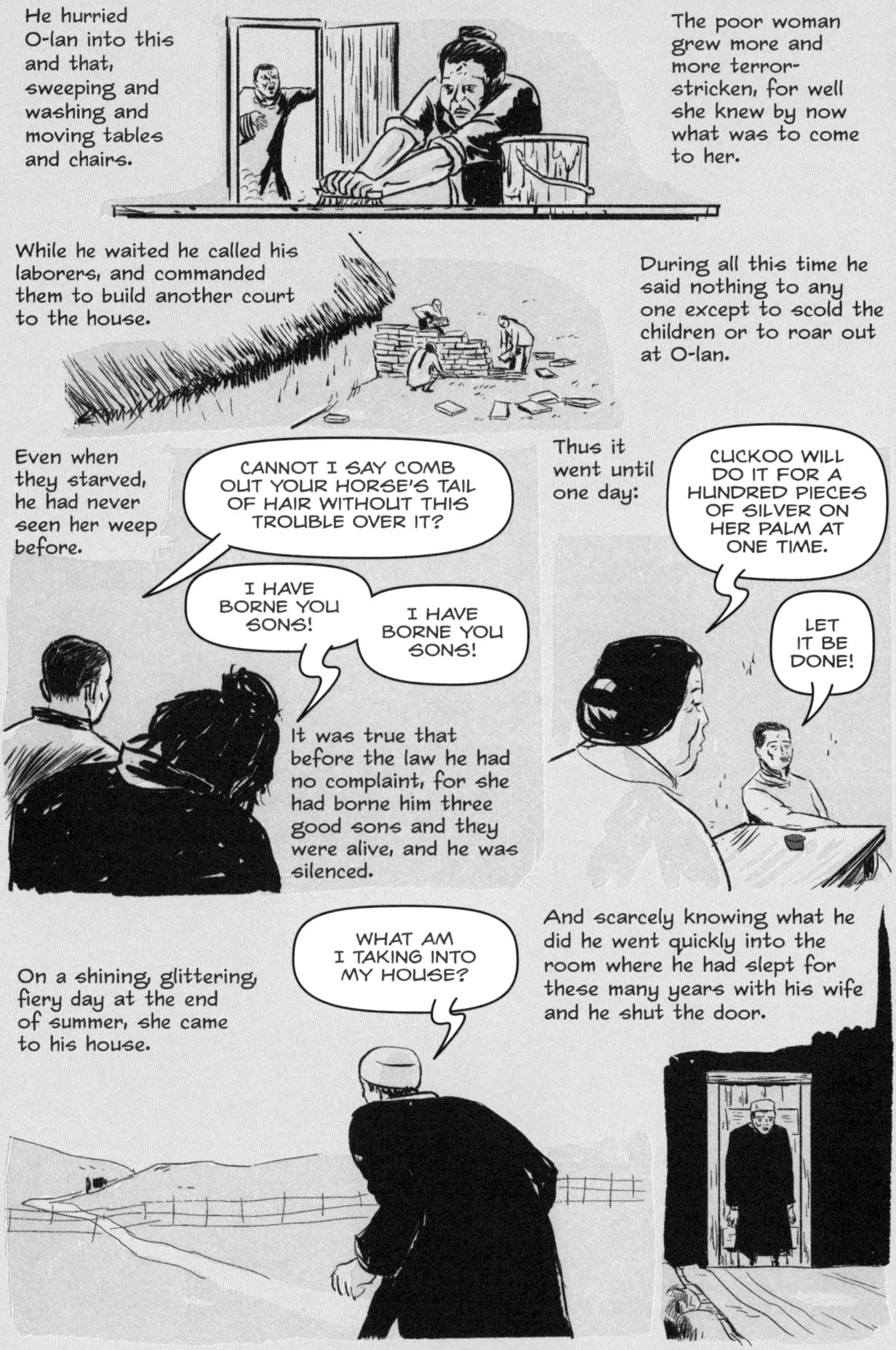
He hurried O-lan into this and that, sweeping and washing and moving tables and chairs.
The poor woman grew more and more terror-stricken, for well she knew by now what was to come to her.
While he waited he called his laborers, and commanded them to build another court to the house.
During all this time he said nothing to any one except to scold the children or to roar out at O-lan.
Even when they starved, he had never seen her weep before.
CANNOT I SAY COMB OUT YOUR HORSE'S TAIL OF HAIR WITHOUT THIS TROUBLE OVER IT?
I HAVE BORNE YOU SONS!
I HAVE BORNE YOU SONS!
It was true that before the law he had no complaint, for she had borne him three good sons and they were alive, and he was silenced.
Thus it went until one day:
CUCKOO WILL DO IT FOR A HUNDRED PIECES OF SILVER ON HER PALM AT ONE TIME.
LET IT BE DONE!
On a shining, glittering, fiery day at the end of summer, she came to his house.
WHAT AM I TAKING INTO MY HOUSE?
And scarcely knowing what he did he went quickly into the room where he had slept for these many years with his wife and he shut the door.

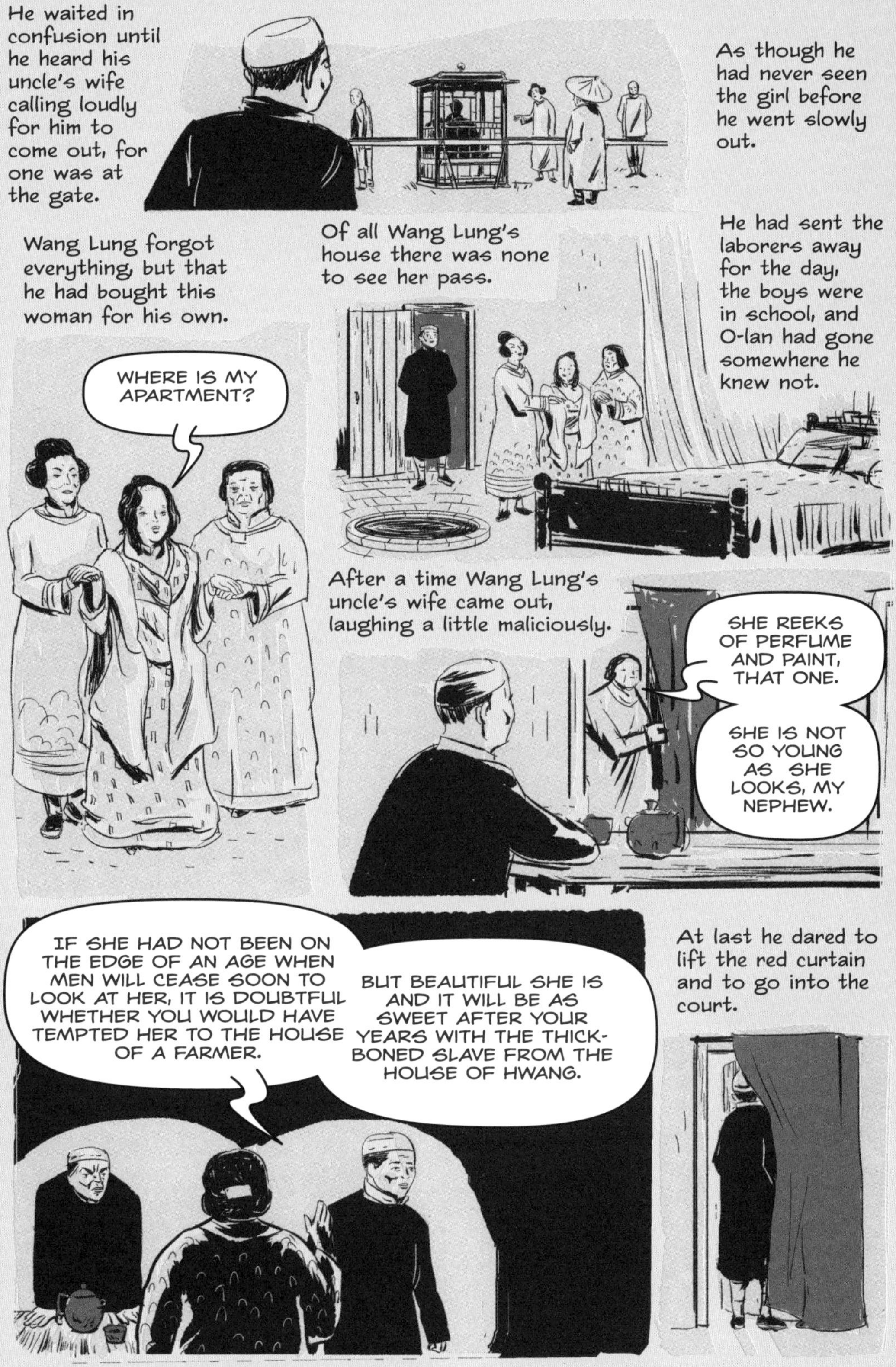
He waited in confusion until he heard his uncle's wife calling loudly for him to come out, for one was at the gate.
As though he had never seen the girl before he went slowly out.
Wang Lung forgot everything, but that he had bought this woman for his own.
Of all Wang Lung's house there was none to see her pass.
He had sent the laborers away for the day, the boys were in school, and O-lan had gone somewhere he knew not.
WHERE IS MY APARTMENT?
After a time Wang Lung's uncle's wife came out, laughing a little maliciously.
SHE REEKS OF PERFUME AND PAINT, THAT ONE.
SHE IS NOT SO YOUNG AS SHE LOOKS, MY NEPHEW.
IF SHE HAD NOT BEEN ON THE EDGE OF AN AGE WHEN MEN WILL CEASE SOON TO LOOK AT HER, IT IS DOUBTFUL WHETHER YOU WOULD HAVE TEMPTED HER TO THE HOUSE OF A FARMER.
BUT BEAUTIFUL SHE IS AND IT WILL BE AS SWEET AFTER YOUR YEARS WITH THE THICK-BONED SLAVE FROM THE HOUSE OF HWANG.
At last he dared to lift the red curtain and to go into the court.

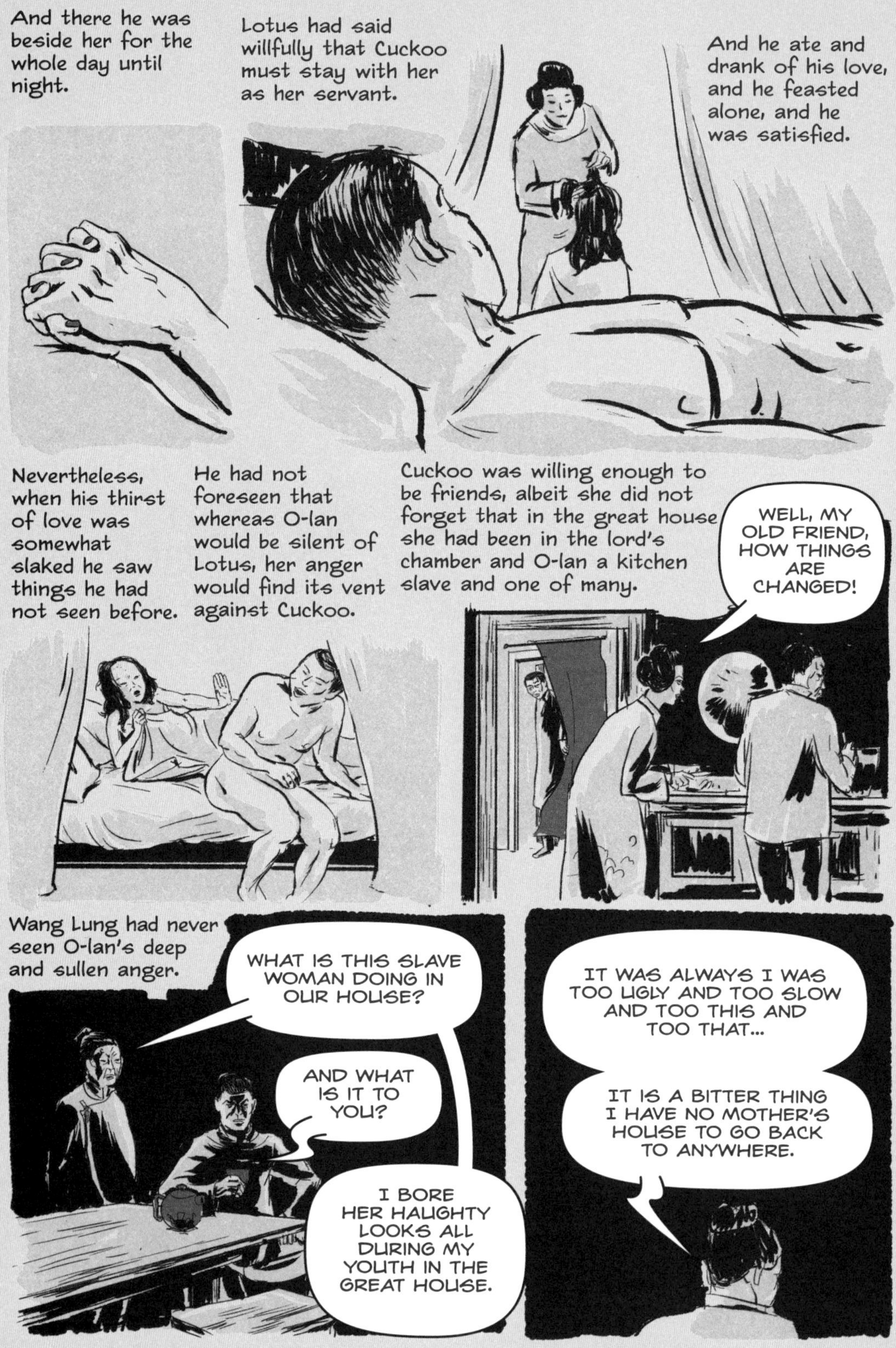
And there he was beside her for the whole day until night.
Lotus had said willfully that Cuckoo must stay with her as her servant.
And he ate and drank of his love, and he feasted alone, and he was satisfied.
Nevertheless, when his thirst of love was somewhat slaked he saw things he had not seen before.
He had not foreseen that whereas O-lan would be silent of Lotus, her anger would find its vent against Cuckoo.
Cuckoo was willing enough to be friends, albeit she did not forget that in the great house she had been in the lord's chamber and O-lan a kitchen slave and one of many.
WELL, MY OLD FRIEND, HOW THINGS ARE CHANGED!
Wang Lung had never seen O-lan's deep and sullen anger.
WHAT IS THIS SLAVE WOMAN DOING IN OUR HOUSE?
AND WHAT IS IT TO YOU?
I BORE HER HAUGHTY LOOKS ALL DURING MY YOUTH IN THE GREAT HOUSE.
IT WAS ALWAYS I WAS TOO UGLY AND TOO SLOW AND TOO THIS AND TOO THAT...
IT IS A BITTER THING I HAVE NO MOTHER'S HOUSE TO GO BACK TO ANYWHERE.

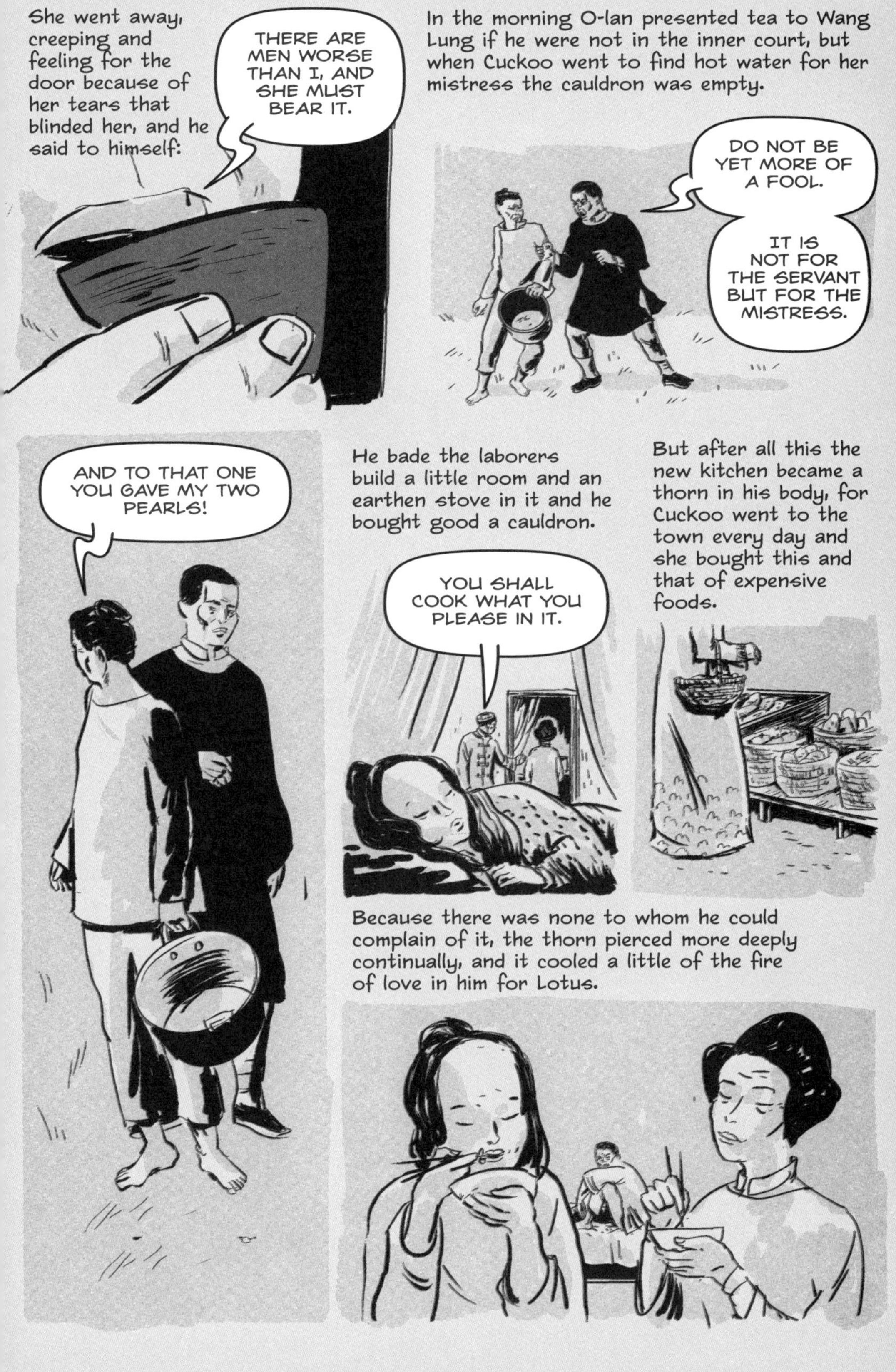
She went away, creeping and feeling for the door because of her tears that blinded her, and he said to himself:
THERE ARE MEN WORSE THAN I, AND SHE MUST BEAR IT.
In the morning O-lan presented tea to Wang Lung if he were not in the inner court, but when Cuckoo went to find hot water for her mistress the cauldron was empty.
DO NOT BE YET MORE OF A FOOL.
IT IS NOT FOR THE SERVANT BUT FOR THE MISTRESS.
AND TO THAT ONE YOU GAVE MY TWO PEARLS!
He bade the laborers build a little room and an earthen stove in it and he bought good a cauldron.
YOU SHALL COOK WHAT YOU PLEASE IN IT.
But after all this the new kitchen became a thorn in his body, for Cuckoo went to the town every day and she bought this and that of expensive foods.
Because there was none to whom he could complain of it, the thorn pierced more deeply continually, and it cooled a little of the fire of love in him for Lotus.

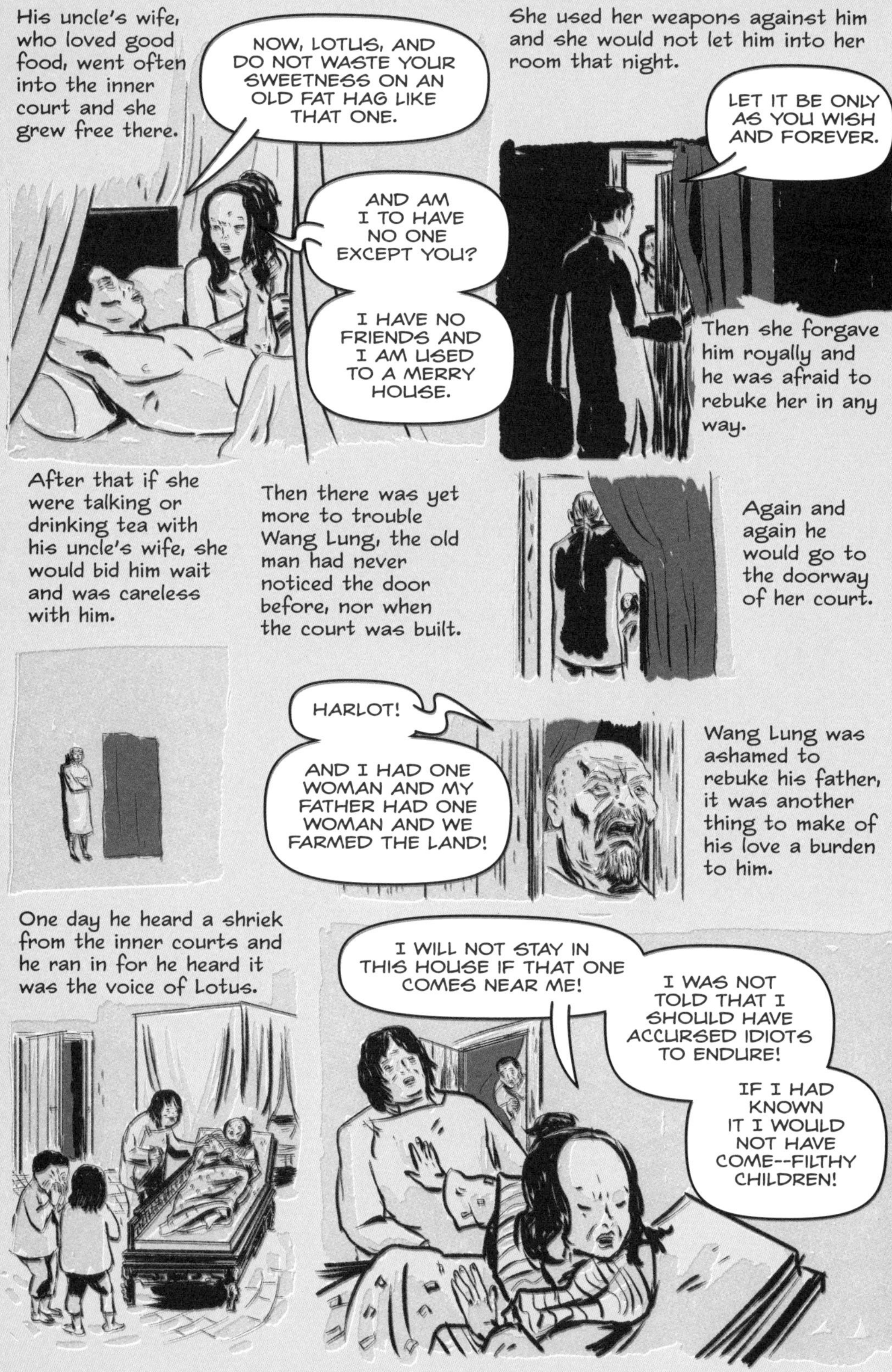
His uncle's wife, who loved good food, went often into the inner court and she grew free there.
NOW, LOTUS, AND DO NOT WASTE YOUR SWEETNESS ON AN OLD FAT HAG LIKE THAT ONE.
AND AM I TO HAVE NO ONE EXCEPT YOU?
I HAVE NO FRIENDS AND I AM USED TO A MERRY HOUSE.
She used her weapons against him and she would not let him into her room that night.
LET IT BE ONLY AS YOU WISH AND FOREVER.
Then she forgave him royally and he was afraid to rebuke her in any way.
After that if she were talking or drinking tea with his uncle's wife, she would bid him wait and was careless with him.
Then there was yet more to trouble Wang Lung, the old man had never noticed the door before, nor when the court was built.
Again and again he would go to the doorway of her court.
HARLOT!
AND I HAD ONE WOMAN AND MY FATHER HAD ONE WOMAN AND WE FARMED THE LAND!
Wang Lung was ashamed to rebuke his father, it was another thing to make of his love a burden to him.
One day he heard a shriek from the inner courts and he ran in for he heard it was the voice of Lotus.
I WILL NOT STAY IN THIS HOUSE IF THAT ONE COMES NEAR ME!
I WAS NOT TOLD THAT I SHOULD HAVE ACCURSED IDIOTS TO ENDURE!
IF I HAD KNOWN IT I WOULD NOT HAVE COME--FILTHY CHILDREN!

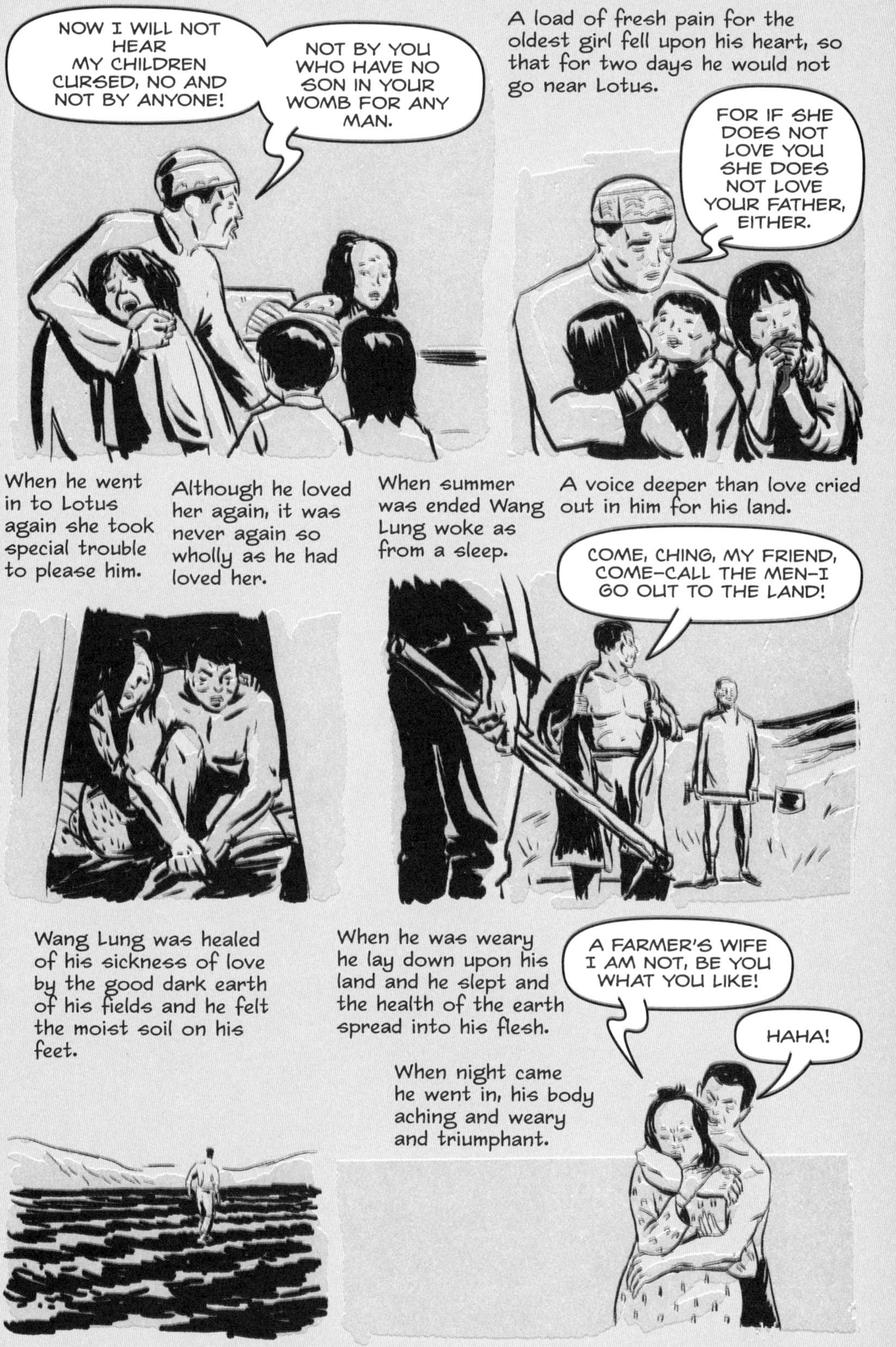
NOW I WILL NOT HEAR MY CHILDREN CURSED, NO AND NOT BY ANYONE!
NOT BY YOU WHO HAVE NO SON IN YOUR WOMB FOR ANY MAN.
A load of fresh pain for the oldest girl fell upon his heart, so that for two days he would not go near Lotus.
FOR IF SHE DOES NOT LOVE YOU SHE DOES NOT LOVE YOUR FATHER, EITHER.
When he went in to Lotus again she took special trouble to please him.
Although he loved her again, it was never again so wholly as he had loved her.
When summer was ended Wang Lung woke as from a sleep.
A voice deeper than love cried out in him for his land.
COME, CHING, MY FRIEND, COME—CALL THE MEN—I GO OUT TO THE LAND!
Wang Lung was healed of his sickness of love by the good dark earth of his fields and he felt the moist soil on his feet.
When he was weary he lay down upon his land and he slept and the health of the earth spread into his flesh.
When night came he went in, his body aching and weary and triumphant.
A FARMER'S WIFE I AM NOT, BE YOU WHAT YOU LIKE!
HAHA!

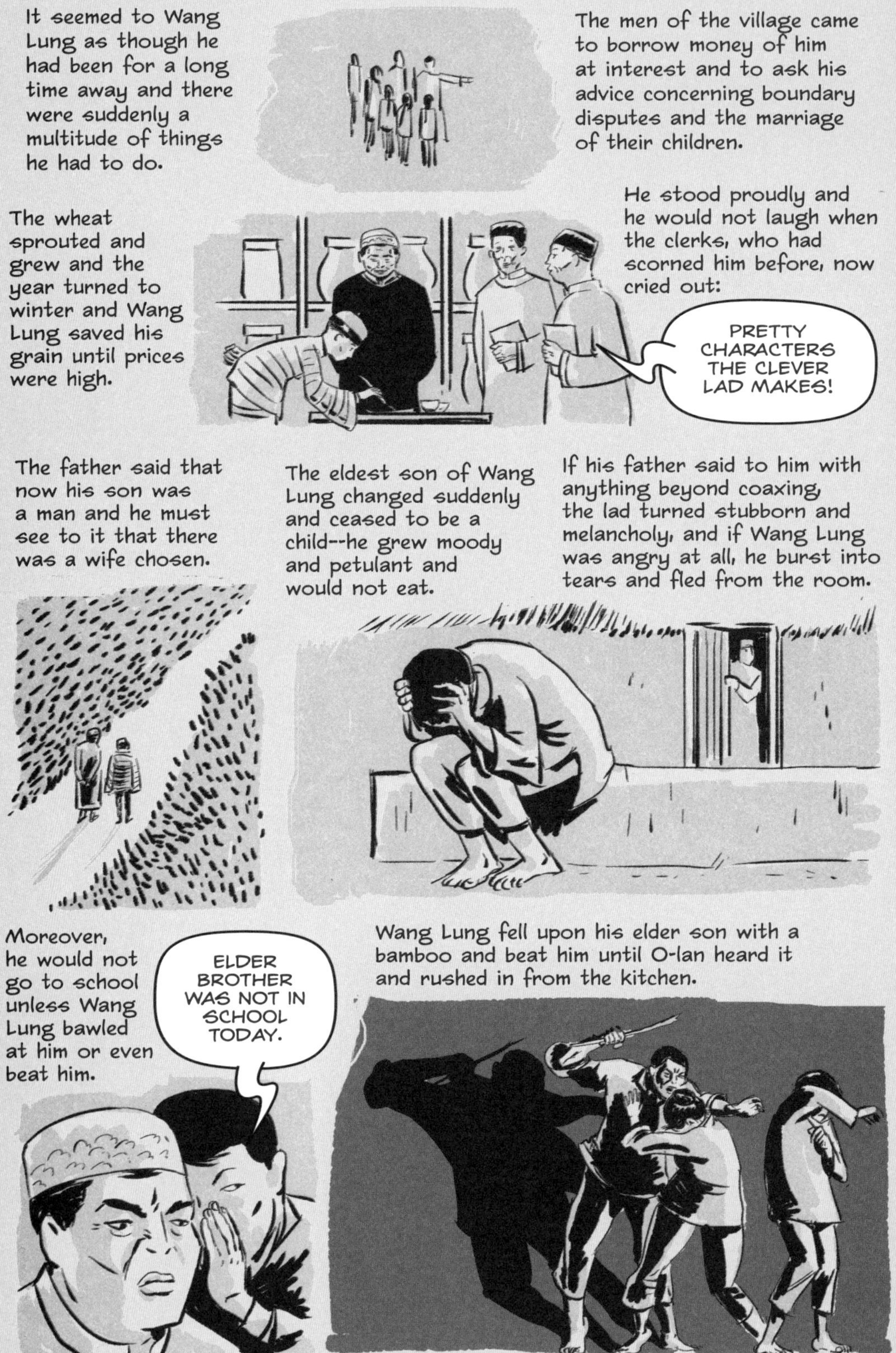
It seemed to Wang Lung as though he had been for a long time away and there were suddenly a multitude of things he had to do.
The men of the village came to borrow money of him at interest and to ask his advice concerning boundary disputes and the marriage of their children.
The wheat sprouted and grew and the year turned to winter and Wang Lung saved his grain until prices were high.
He stood proudly and he would not laugh when the clerks, who had scorned him before, now cried out:
PRETTY CHARACTERS THE CLEVER LAD MAKES!
The father said that now his son was a man and he must see to it that there was a wife chosen.
The eldest son of Wang Lung changed suddenly and ceased to be a child--he grew moody and petulant and would not eat.
If his father said to him with anything beyond coaxing, the lad turned stubborn and melancholy, and if Wang Lung was angry at all, he burst into tears and fled from the room.
Moreover, he would not go to school unless Wang Lung bawled at him or even beat him.
ELDER BROTHER WAS NOT IN SCHOOL TODAY.
Wang Lung fell upon his elder son with a bamboo and beat him until O-lan heard it and rushed in from the kitchen.

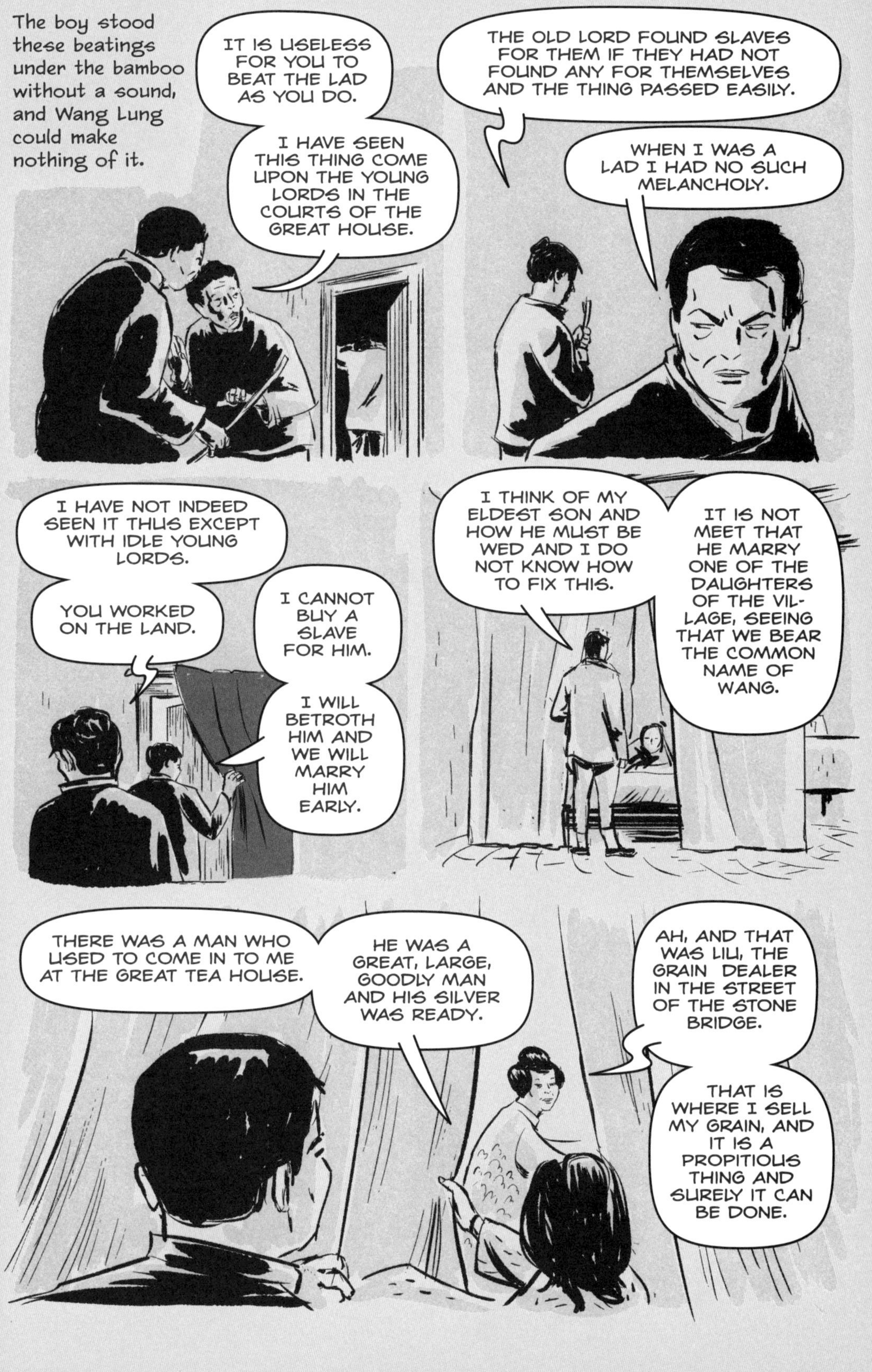
The boy stood these beatings under the bamboo without a sound, and Wang Lung could make nothing of it.
IT IS USELESS FOR YOU TO BEAT THE LAD AS YOU DO.
I HAVE SEEN THIS THING COME UPON THE YOUNG LORDS IN THE COURTS OF THE GREAT HOUSE.
THE OLD LORD FOUND SLAVES FOR THEM IF THEY HAD NOT FOUND ANY FOR THEMSELVES AND THE THING PASSED EASILY.
WHEN I WAS A LAD I HAD NO SUCH MELANCHOLY.
I HAVE NOT INDEED SEEN IT THUS EXCEPT WITH IDLE YOUNG LORDS.
YOU WORKED ON THE LAND.
I CANNOT BUY A SLAVE FOR HIM.
I WILL BETROTH HIM AND WE WILL MARRY HIM EARLY.
I THINK OF MY ELDEST SON AND HOW HE MUST BE WED AND I DO NOT KNOW HOW TO FIX THIS.
IT IS NOT MEET THAT HE MARRY ONE OF THE DAUGHTERS OF THE VIL-LAGE, SEEING THAT WE BEAR THE COMMON NAME OF WANG.
THERE WAS A MAN WHO USED TO COME IN TO ME AT THE GREAT TEA HOUSE.
HE WAS A GREAT, LARGE, GOODLY MAN AND HIS SILVER WAS READY.
AH, AND THAT WAS LIU, THE GRAIN DEALER IN THE STREET OF THE STONE BRIDGE.
THAT IS WHERE I SELL MY GRAIN, AND IT IS A PROPITIOUS THING AND SURELY IT CAN BE DONE.

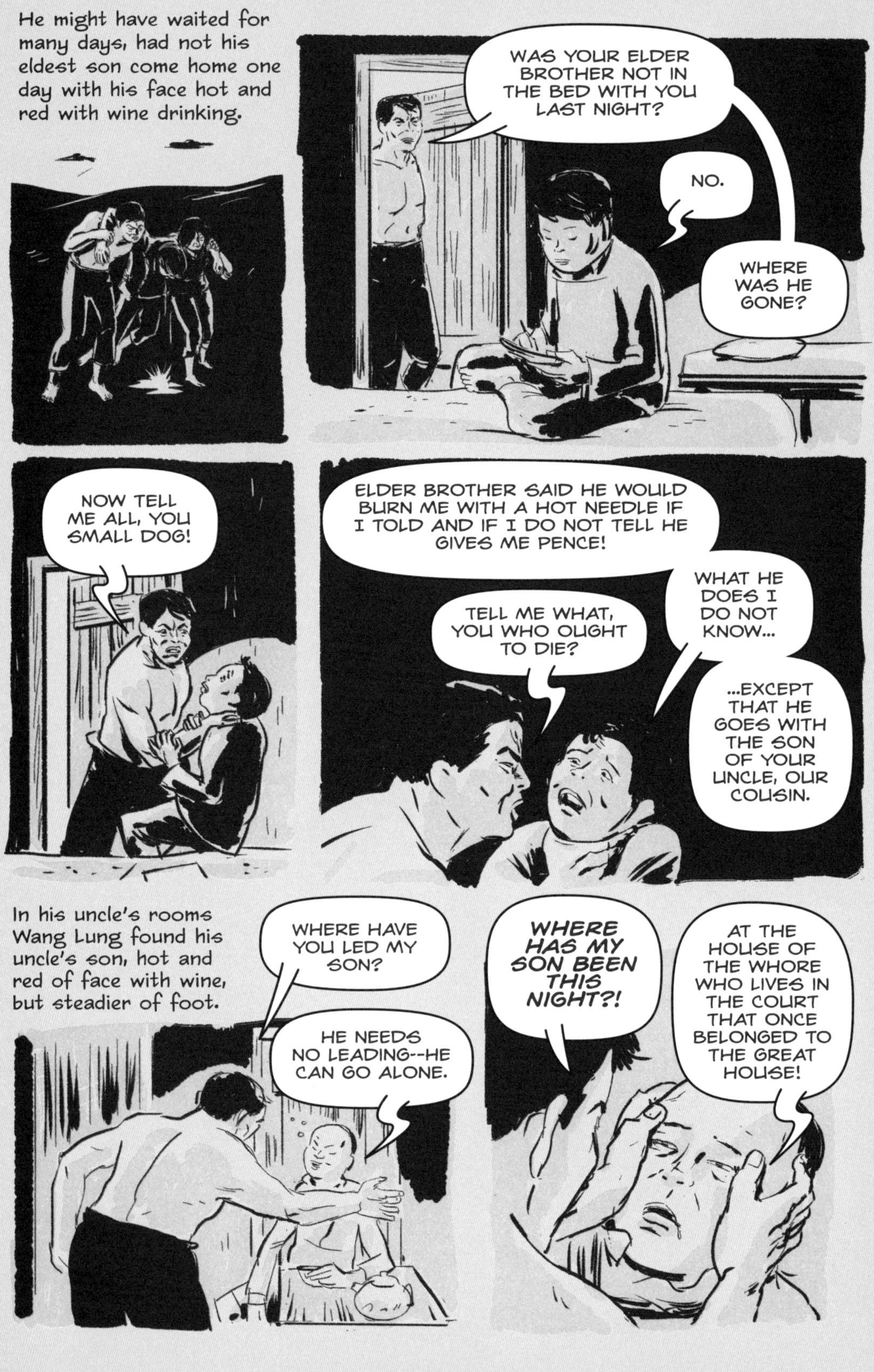
He might have waited for many days, had not his eldest son come home one day with his face hot and red with wine drinking.
WAS YOUR ELDER BROTHER NOT IN THE BED WITH YOU LAST NIGHT?
NO.
WHERE WAS HE GONE?
NOW TELL ME ALL, YOU SMALL DOG!
ELDER BROTHER SAID HE WOULD BURN ME WITH A HOT NEEDLE IF I TOLD AND IF I DO NOT TELL HE GIVES ME PENCE!
TELL ME WHAT, YOU WHO OUGHT TO DIE?
WHAT HE DOES I DO NOT KNOW...
...EXCEPT THAT HE GOES WITH THE SON OF YOUR UNCLE, OUR COUSIN.
In his uncle's rooms Wang Lung found his uncle's son, hot and red of face with wine, but steadier of foot.
WHERE HAVE YOU LED MY SON?
HE NEEDS NO LEADING--HE CAN GO ALONE.
WHERE HAS MY SON BEEN THIS NIGHT?!
AT THE HOUSE OF THE WHORE WHO LIVES IN THE COURT THAT ONCE BELONGED TO THE GREAT HOUSE!

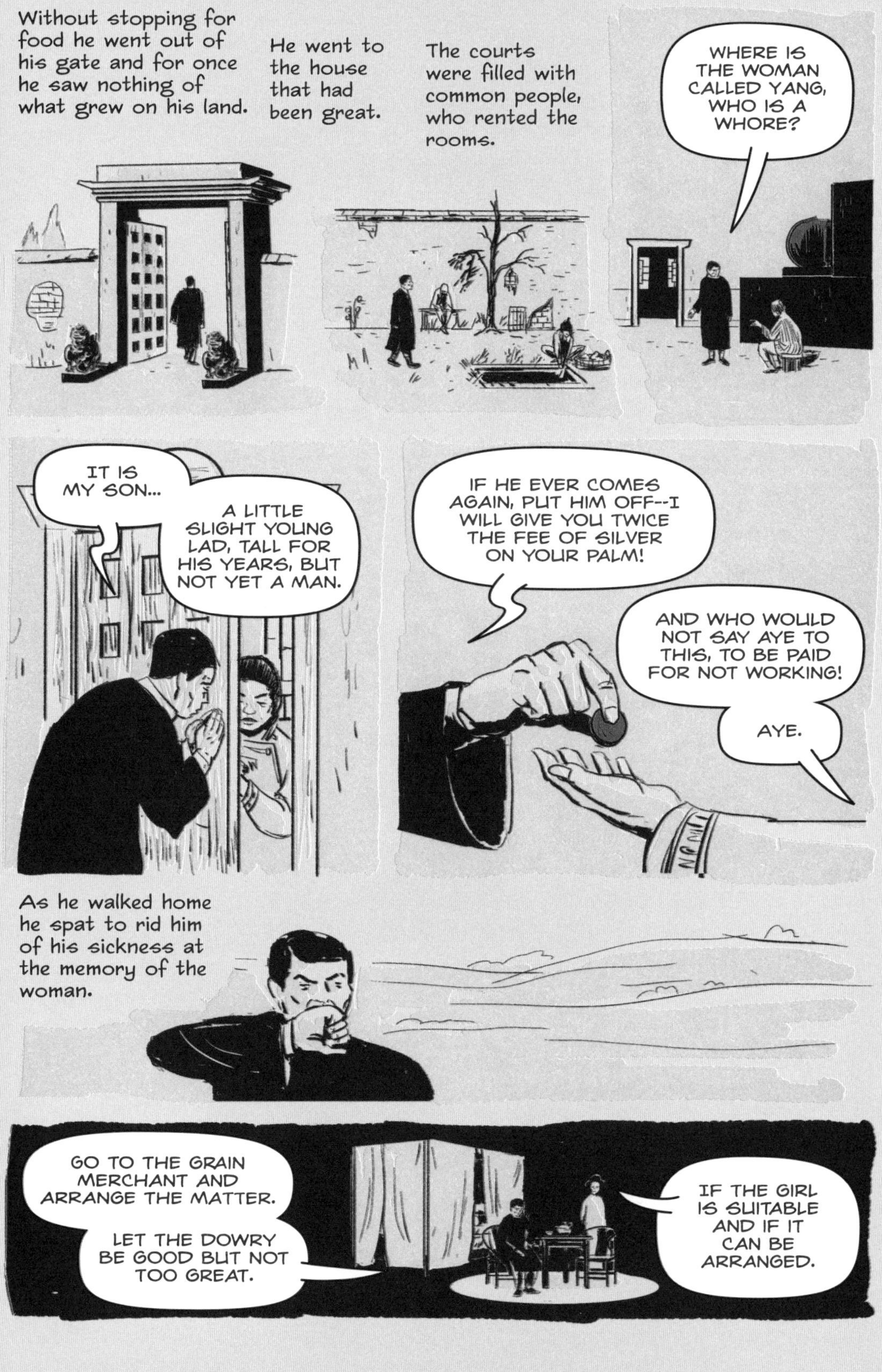
Without stopping for food he went out of his gate and for once he saw nothing of what grew on his land.
He went to the house that had been great.
The courts were filled with common people, who rented the rooms.
WHERE IS THE WOMAN CALLED YANG, WHO IS A WHORE?
IT IS MY SON...
A LITTLE SLIGHT YOUNG LAD, TALL FOR HIS YEARS, BUT NOT YET A MAN.
IF HE EVER COMES AGAIN, PUT HIM OFF--I WILL GIVE YOU TWICE THE FEE OF SILVER ON YOUR PALM!
AND WHO WOULD NOT SAY AYE TO THIS, TO BE PAID FOR NOT WORKING!
AYE.
As he walked home he spat to rid him of his sickness at the memory of the woman.
GO TO THE GRAIN MERCHANT AND ARRANGE THE MATTER.
LET THE DOWRY BE GOOD BUT NOT TOO GREAT.
IF THE GIRL IS SUITABLE AND IF IT CAN BE ARRANGED.

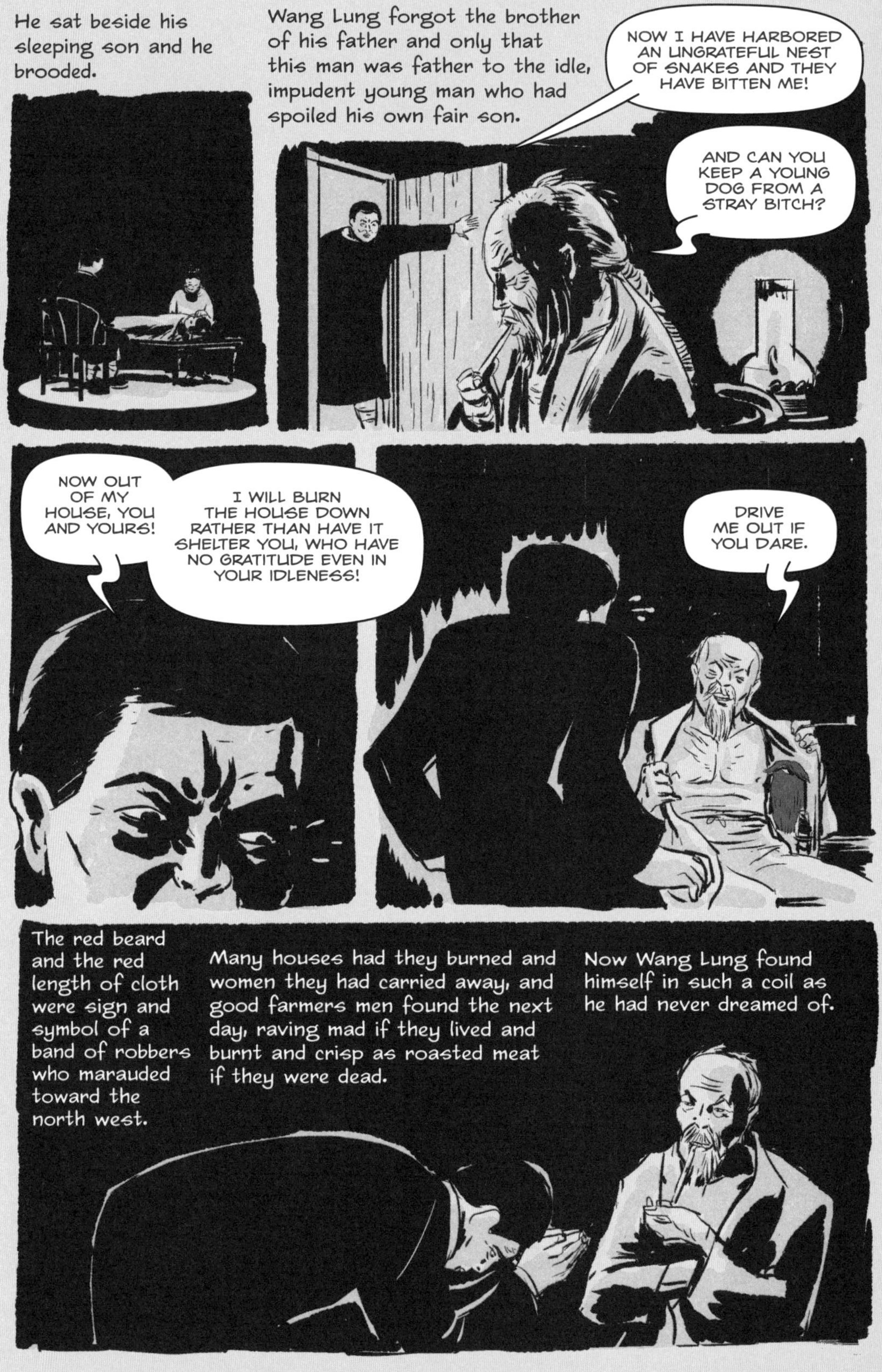
He sat beside his sleeping son and he brooded.
Wang Lung forgot the brother of his father and only that this man was father to the idle, impudent young man who had spoiled his own fair son.
NOW I HAVE HARBORED AN UNGRATEFUL NEST OF SNAKES AND THEY HAVE BITTEN ME!
AND CAN YOU KEEP A YOUNG DOG FROM A STRAY BITCH?
NOW OUT OF MY HOUSE, YOU AND YOURS!
I WILL BURN THE HOUSE DOWN RATHER THAN HAVE IT SHELTER YOU, WHO HAVE NO GRATITUDE EVEN IN YOUR IDLENESS!
DRIVE ME OUT IF YOU DARE.
The red beard and the red length of cloth were sign and symbol of a band of robbers who marauded toward the north west.
Many houses had they burned and women they had carried away, and good farmers men found the next day, raving mad if they lived and burnt and crisp as roasted meat if they were dead.
Now Wang Lung found himself in such a coil as he had never dreamed of.

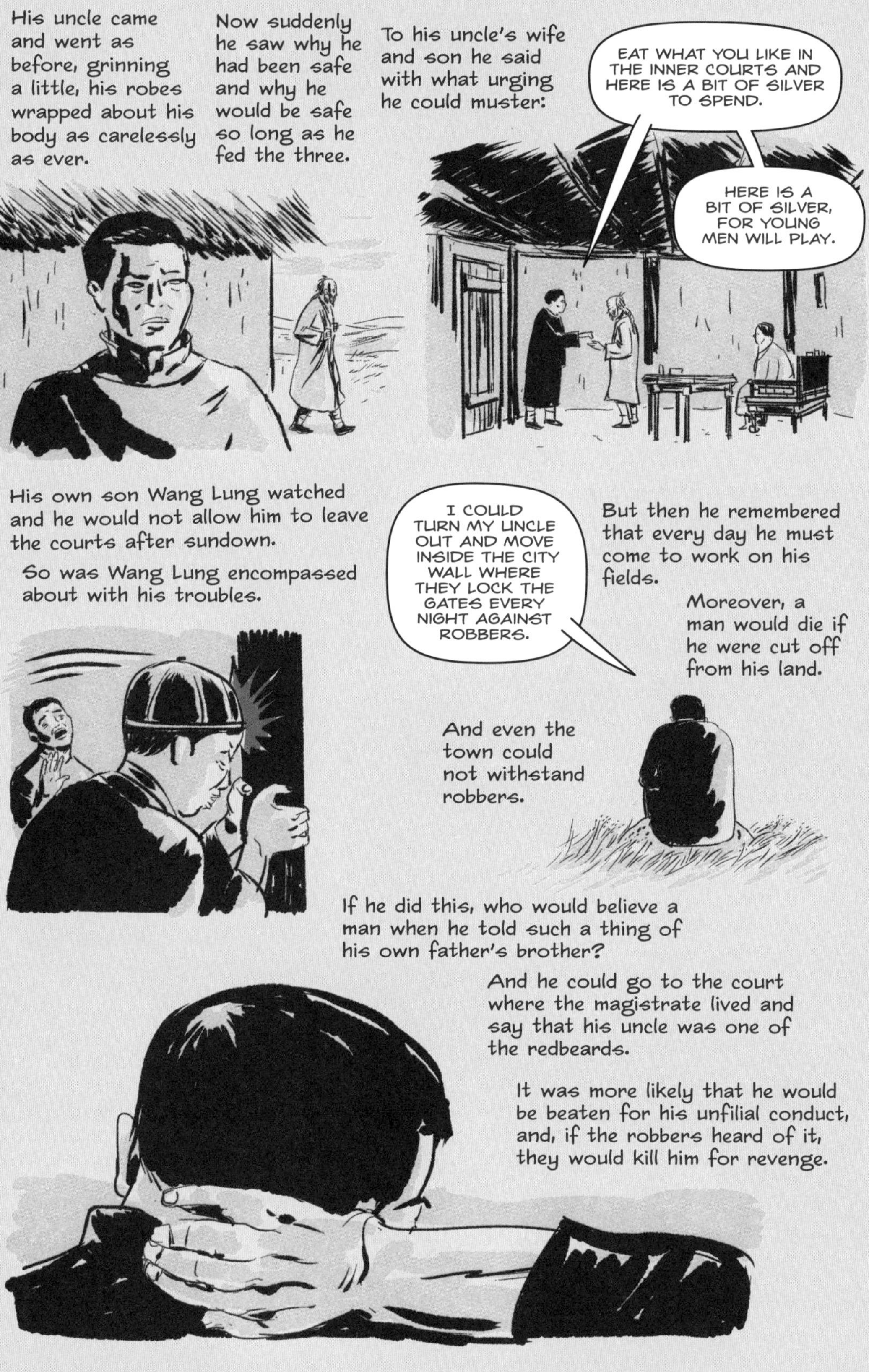

His uncle came and went as before, grinning a little, his robes wrapped about his body as carelessly as ever.
Now suddenly he saw why he had been safe and why he would be safe so long as he fed the three.
To his uncle's wife and son he said with what urging he could muster:
EAT WHAT YOU LIKE IN THE INNER COURTS AND HERE IS A BIT OF SILVER TO SPEND.
HERE IS A BIT OF SILVER, FOR YOUNG MEN WILL PLAY.
His own son Wang Lung watched and he would not allow him to leave the courts after sundown.
So was Wang Lung encompassed about with his troubles.
I COULD TURN MY UNCLE OUT AND MOVE INSIDE THE CITY WALL WHERE THEY LOCK THE GATES EVERY NIGHT AGAINST ROBBERS.
But then he remembered that every day he must come to work on his fields.
Moreover, a man would die if he were cut off from his land.
And even the town could not withstand robbers.
If he did this, who would believe a man when he told such a thing of his own father's brother?
And he could go to the court where the magistrate lived and say that his uncle was one of the redbeards.
It was more likely that he would be beaten for his unfilial conduct, and, if the robbers heard of it, they would kill him for revenge.

Then the good land did again its healing work and the sun shone on him and healed him.

And as if to cure him of his ceaseless thought of his own troubles, there came out of the south one day a small cloud.

At first it stood steady until it spread fanwise up into the air.

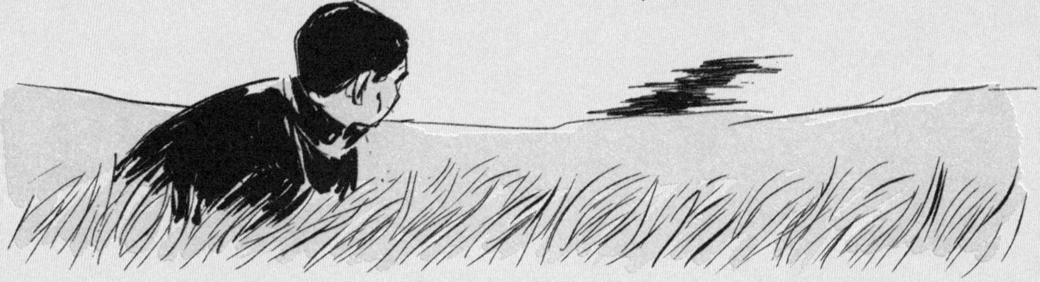

At last a wind blew something to their feet and Wang Lung forgot about everything that troubled him.

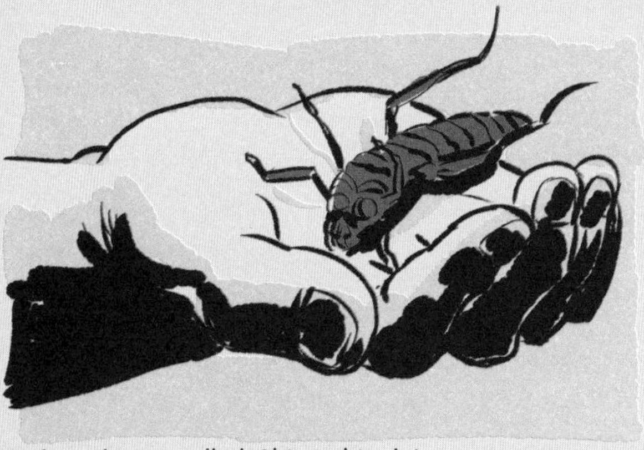

Wang Lung rushed among the frightened villagers:

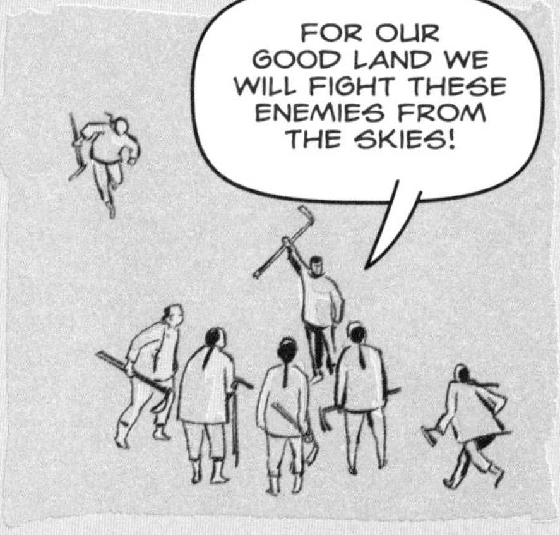
FOR OUR GOOD LAND WE WILL FIGHT THESE ENEMIES FROM THE SKIES!

Wang Lung called Ching, his laborers, and others of the younger farmers, and these set fire to certain fields and they dug wide moat, and they worked without sleeping.

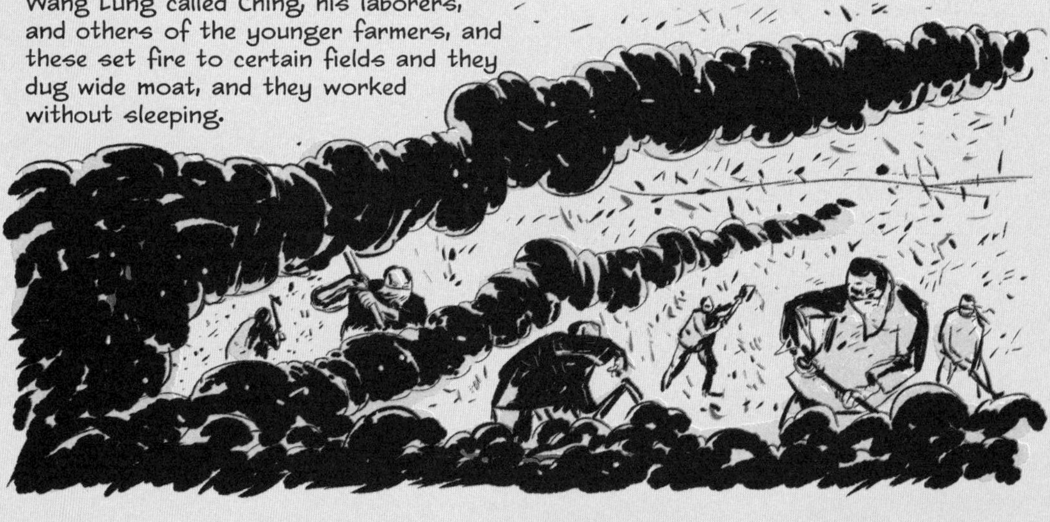

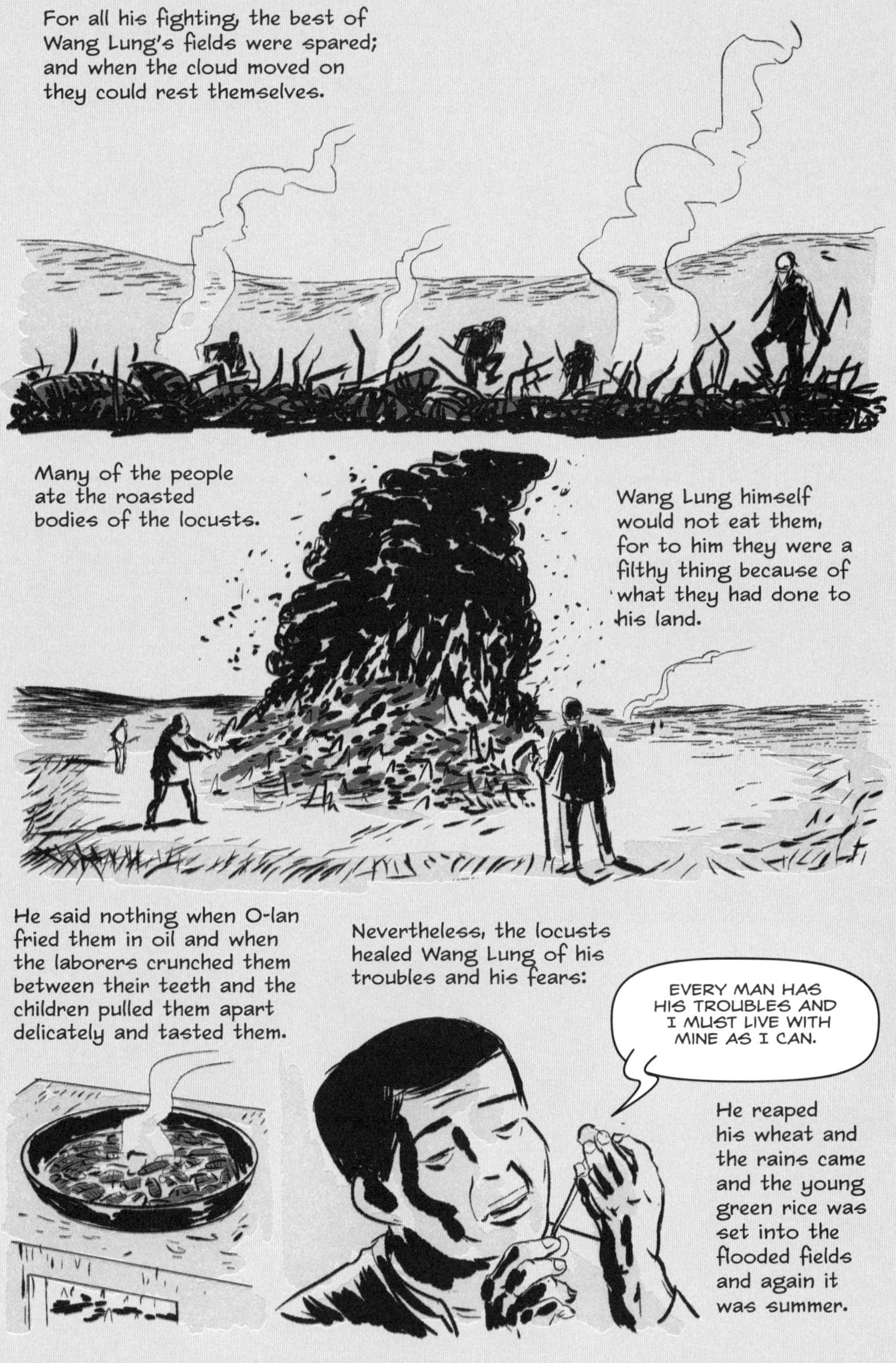
For all his fighting, the best of Wang Lung's fields were spared; and when the cloud moved on they could rest themselves.
Many of the people ate the roasted bodies of the locusts.
Wang Lung himself would not eat them, for to him they were a filthy thing because of what they had done to his land.
He said nothing when O-lan fried them in oil and when the laborers crunched them between their teeth and the children pulled them apart delicately and tasted them.
Nevertheless, the locusts healed Wang Lung of his troubles and his fears:
EVERY MAN HAS HIS TROUBLES AND I MUST LIVE WITH MINE AS I CAN.
He reaped his wheat and the rains came and the young green rice was set into the flooded fields and again it was summer.

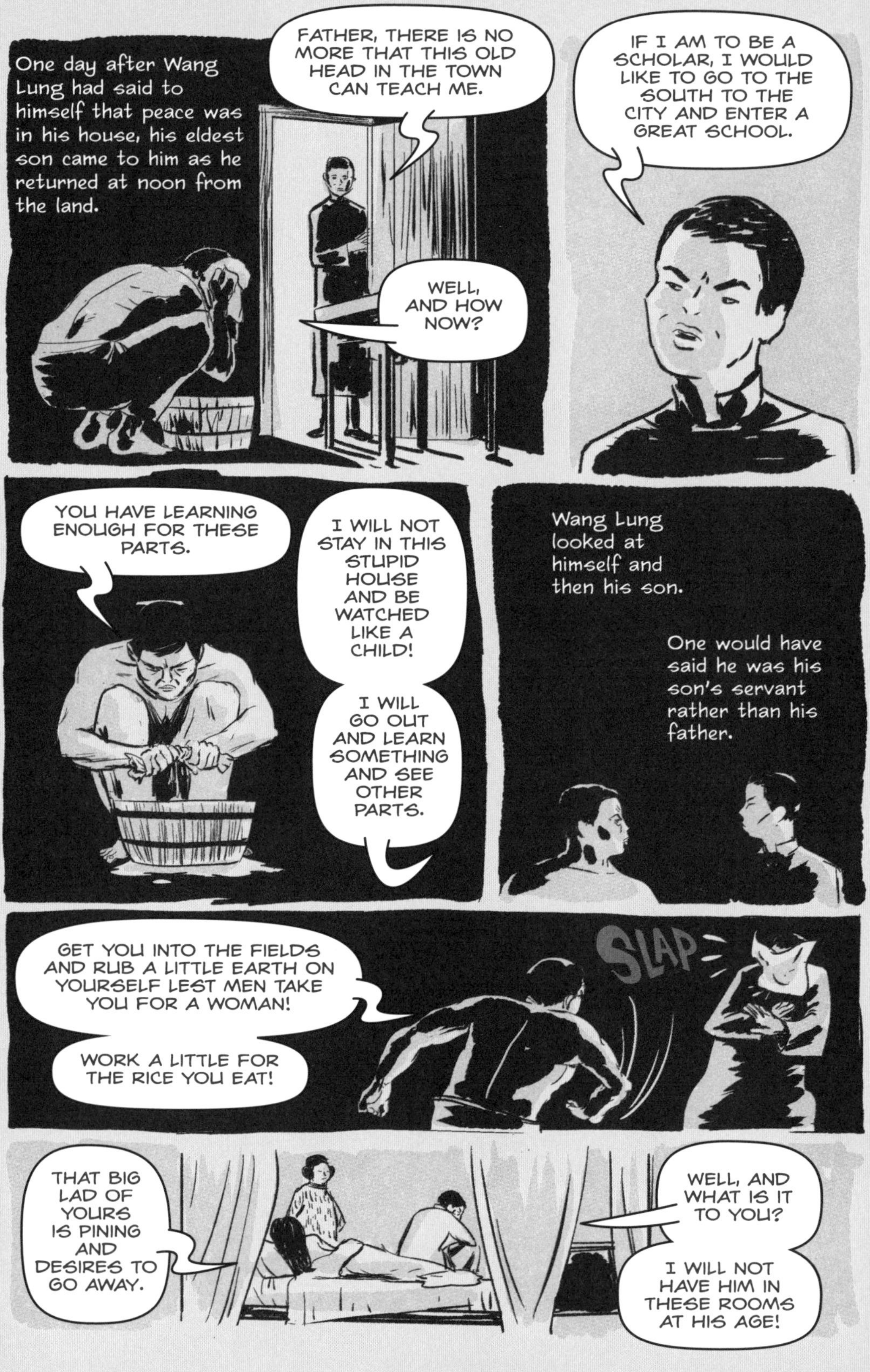
One day after Wang Lung had said to himself that peace was in his house, his eldest son came to him as he returned at noon from the land.
FATHER, THERE IS NO MORE THAT THIS OLD HEAD IN THE TOWN CAN TEACH ME.
WELL, AND HOW NOW?
IF I AM TO BE A SCHOLAR, I WOULD LIKE TO GO TO THE SOUTH TO THE CITY AND ENTER A GREAT SCHOOL.
YOU HAVE LEARNING ENOUGH FOR THESE PARTS.
I WILL NOT STAY IN THIS STUPID HOUSE AND BE WATCHED LIKE A CHILD!
I WILL GO OUT AND LEARN SOMETHING AND SEE OTHER PARTS.
Wang Lung looked at himself and then his son.
One would have said he was his son's servant rather than his father.
GET YOU INTO THE FIELDS AND RUB A LITTLE EARTH ON YOURSELF LEST MEN TAKE YOU FOR A WOMAN!
WORK A LITTLE FOR THE RICE YOU EAT!
SLAP
THAT BIG LAD OF YOURS IS PINING AND DESIRES TO GO AWAY.
WELL, AND WHAT IS IT TO YOU?
I WILL NOT HAVE HIM IN THESE ROOMS AT HIS AGE!

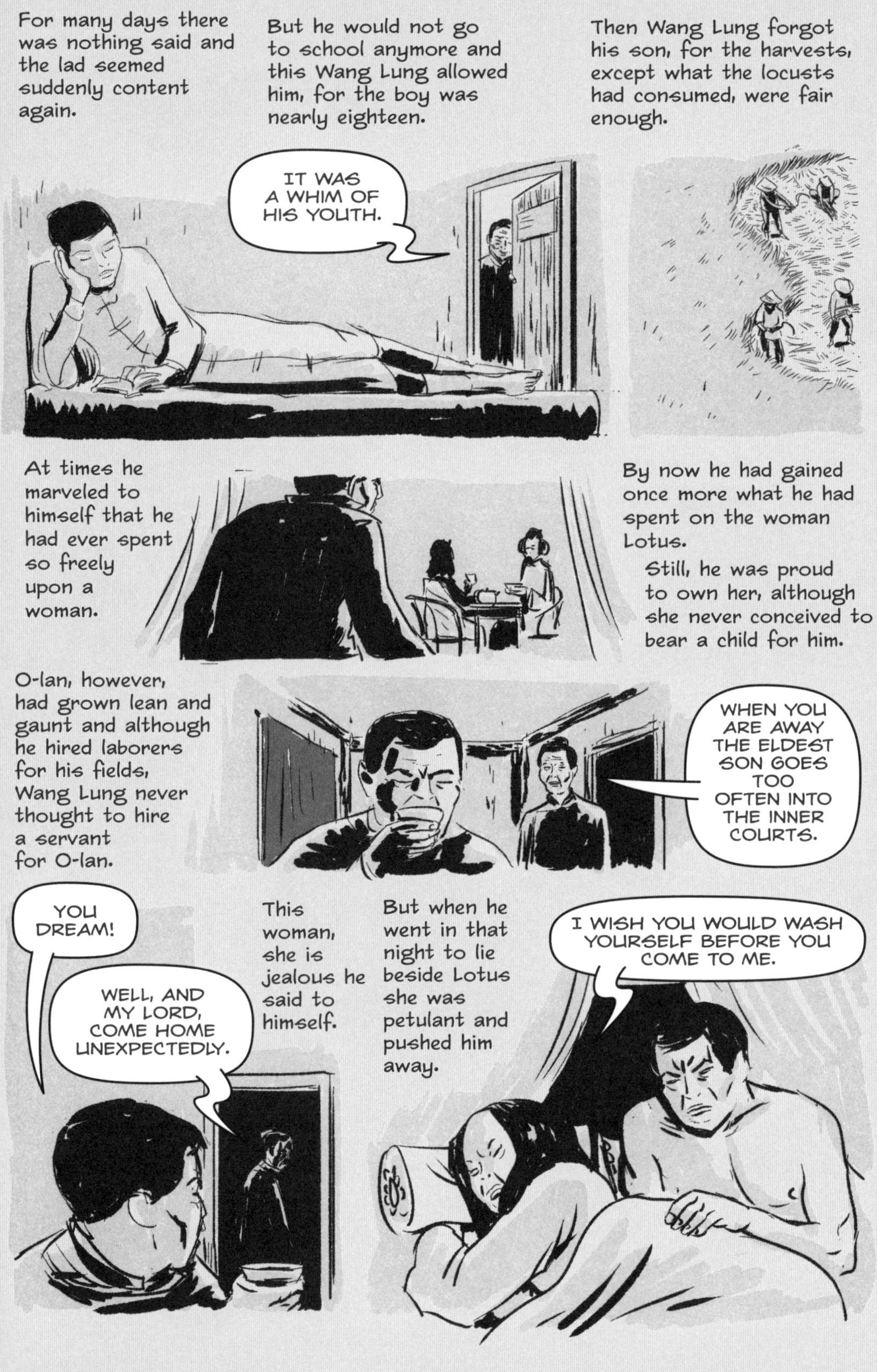

For many days there was nothing said and the lad seemed suddenly content again.
But he would not go to school anymore and this Wang Lung allowed him, for the boy was nearly eighteen.
Then Wang Lung forgot his son, for the harvests, except what the locusts had consumed, were fair enough.
IT WAS A WHIM OF HIS YOUTH.
At times he marveled to himself that he had ever spent so freely upon a woman.
By now he had gained once more what he had spent on the woman Lotus.
Still, he was proud to own her, although she never conceived to bear a child for him.
O-lan, however, had grown lean and gaunt and although he hired laborers for his fields, Wang Lung never thought to hire a servant for O-lan.
WHEN YOU ARE AWAY THE ELDEST SON GOES TOO OFTEN INTO THE INNER COURTS.
YOU DREAM!
WELL, AND MY LORD, COME HOME UNEXPECTEDLY.
This woman, she is jealous he said to himself.
But when he went in that night to lie beside Lotus she was petulant and pushed him away.
I WISH YOU WOULD WASH YOURSELF BEFORE YOU COME TO ME.

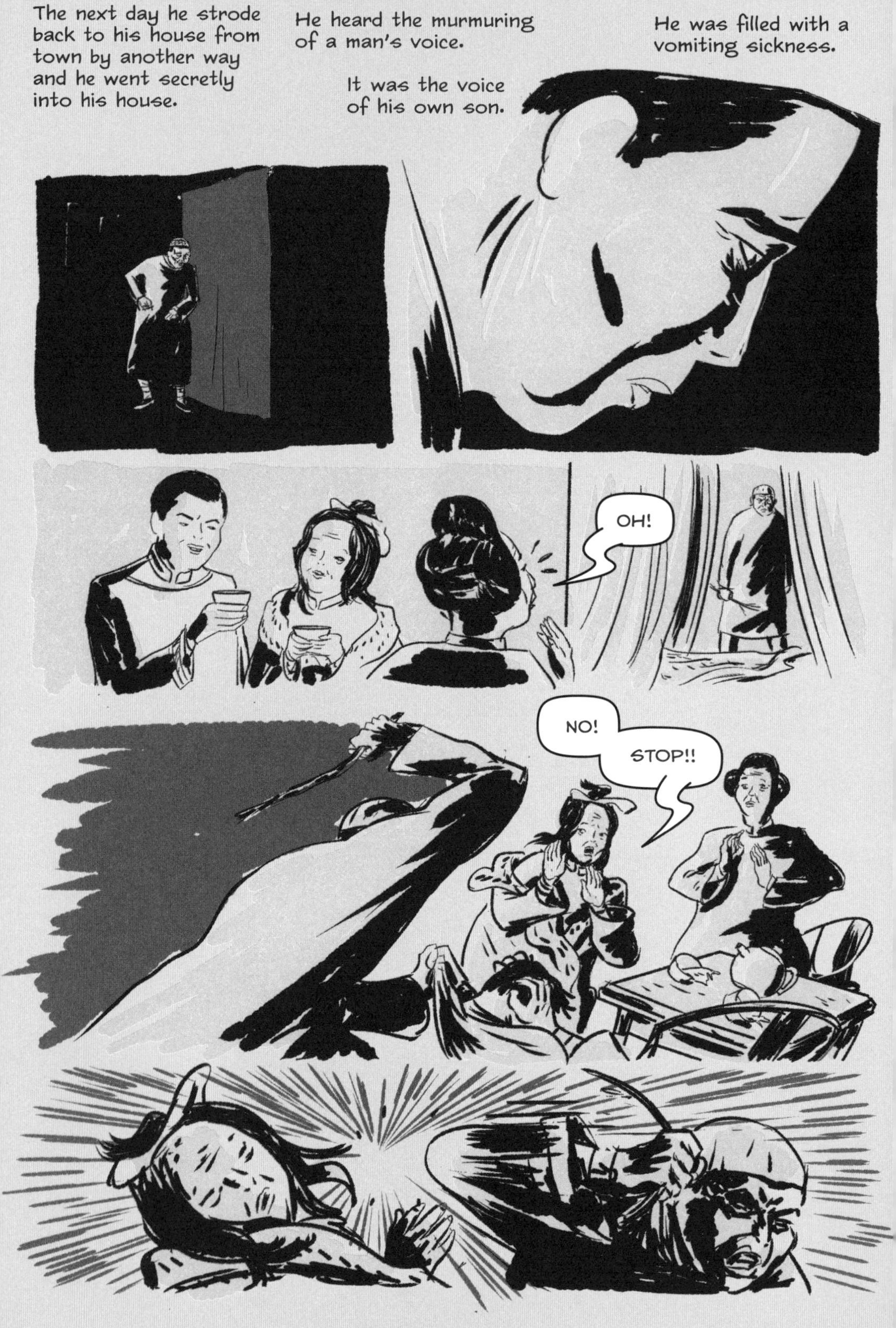
The next day he strode back to his house from town by another way and he went secretly into his house.
He heard the murmuring of a man's voice.
It was the voice of his own son.
He was filled with a vomiting sickness.
OH!
NO!
STOP!!

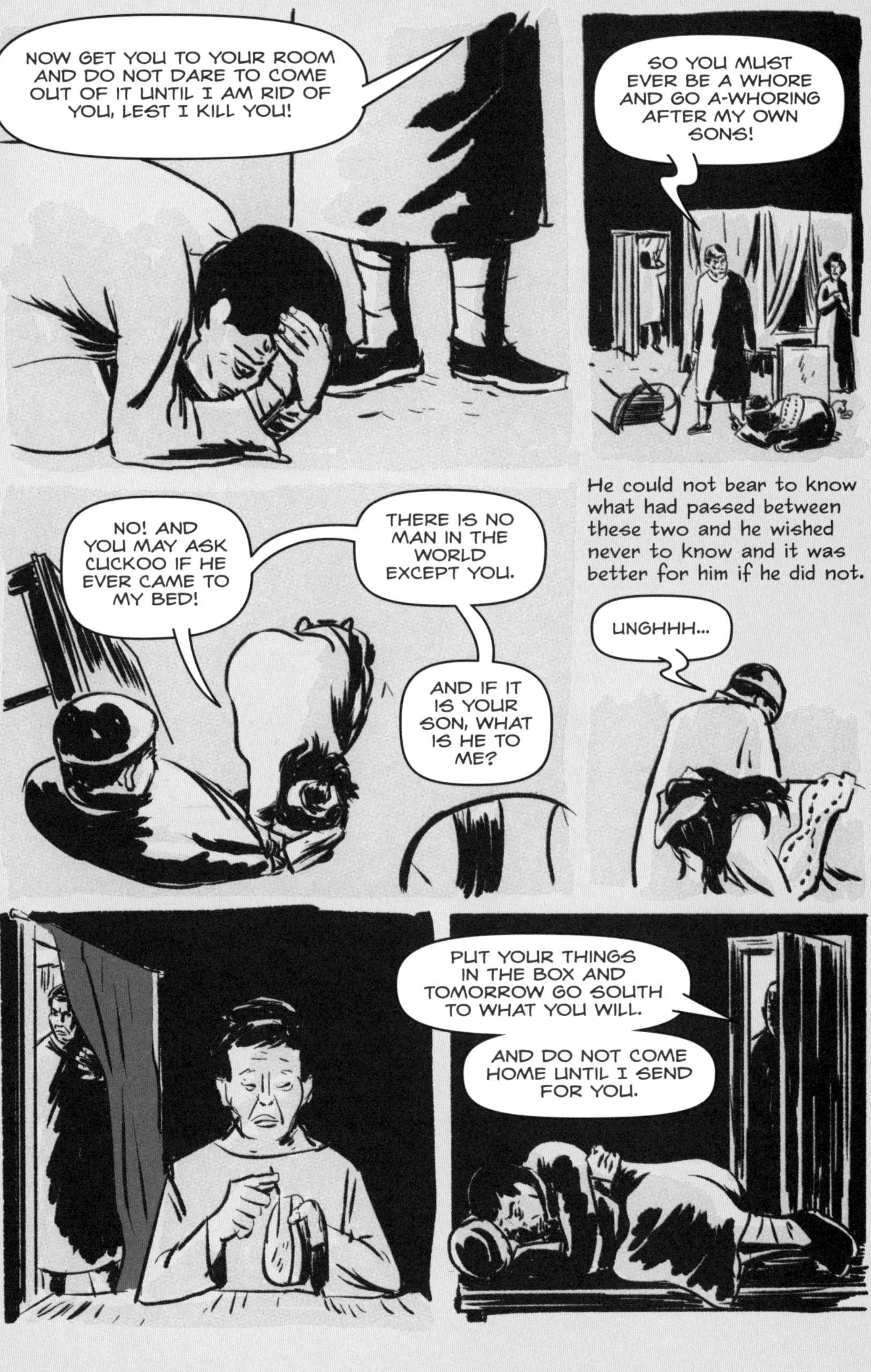
NOW GET YOU TO YOUR ROOM AND DO NOT DARE TO COME OUT OF IT UNTIL I AM RID OF YOU, LEST I KILL YOU!
SO YOU MUST EVER BE A WHORE AND GO A-WHORING AFTER MY OWN SONS!
NO! AND YOU MAY ASK CUCKOO IF HE EVER CAME TO MY BED!
THERE IS NO MAN IN THE WORLD EXCEPT YOU.
AND IF IT IS YOUR SON, WHAT IS HE TO ME?
He could not bear to know what had passed between these two and he wished never to know and it was better for him if he did not.
UNGHHH...
PUT YOUR THINGS IN THE BOX AND TOMORROW GO SOUTH TO WHAT YOU WILL.
AND DO NOT COME HOME UNTIL I SEND FOR YOU.

When the eldest son was gone Wang Lung felt the house was purged of unrest.

This son reminded Wang Lung of his own father—a crafty, sharp, humorous eye.

Now he could look to his other chidren and see what they were.

WELL, I WILL TAKE HIM OUT OF SCHOOL AND SEE IF HE CAN BE APPRENTICED IN THE GRAIN MARKET.

NOW GO AND TELL THE FATHER OF MY ELDEST SON'S BETROTHED THAT I HAVE SOMETHING TO SAY TO HIM.

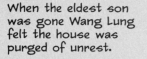

He went to the Street of Bridges, and to a respectable gate built plainly of wood.

Wang Lung was pleased, for there was evidence of good living but not of extreme wealth.

He did not want a rich daughter-in-law lest she be haughty and disobedient and cry for this and that of food and clothes and turn aside his son's heart from his parents.

When the eldery man entered they both bowed.

IF YOU HAVE NEED FOR A SERVANT IN YOUR GREAT MARKET, THERE IS MY SECOND SON.

AND A SHARP ONE HE IS.

I HAVE SUCH NEED OF A YOUNG MAN, IF HE READS AND WRITES.

MY SONS ARE BOTH GOOD SCHOLARS.

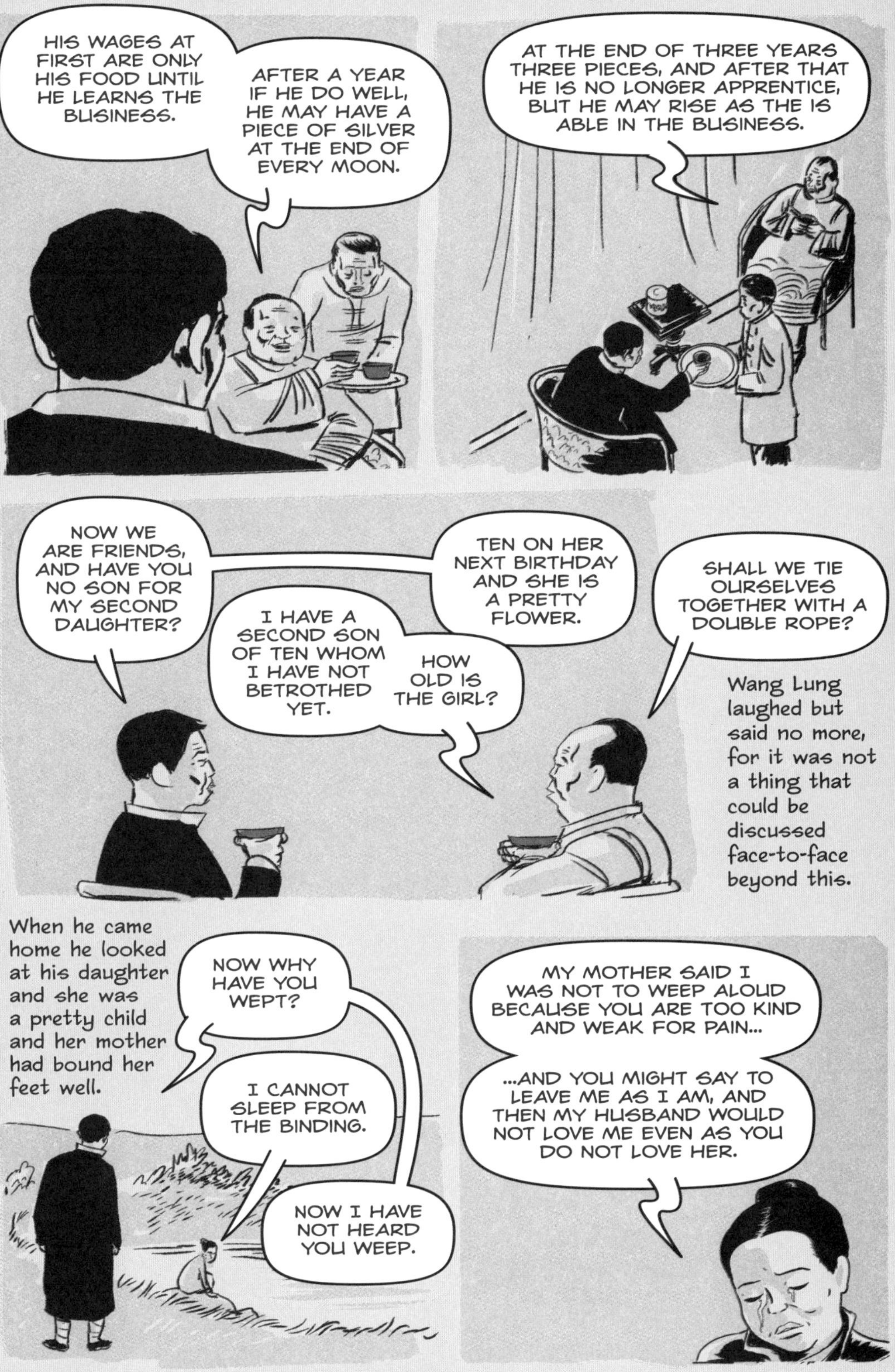

HIS WAGES AT FIRST ARE ONLY HIS FOOD UNTIL HE LEARNS THE BUSINESS.
AFTER A YEAR IF HE DO WELL, HE MAY HAVE A PIECE OF SILVER AT THE END OF EVERY MOON.
AT THE END OF THREE YEARS THREE PIECES, AND AFTER THAT HE IS NO LONGER APPRENTICE, BUT HE MAY RISE AS THE IS ABLE IN THE BUSINESS.
NOW WE ARE FRIENDS, AND HAVE YOU NO SON FOR MY SECOND DAUGHTER?
I HAVE A SECOND SON OF TEN WHOM I HAVE NOT BETROTHED YET.
HOW OLD IS THE GIRL?
TEN ON HER NEXT BIRTHDAY AND SHE IS A PRETTY FLOWER.
SHALL WE TIE OURSELVES TOGETHER WITH A DOUBLE ROPE?
Wang Lung laughed but said no more, for it was not a thing that could be discussed face-to-face beyond this.
When he came home he looked at his daughter and she was a pretty child and her mother had bound her feet well.
NOW WHY HAVE YOU WEPT?
I CANNOT SLEEP FROM THE BINDING.
NOW I HAVE NOT HEARD YOU WEEP.
MY MOTHER SAID I WAS NOT TO WEEP ALOUD BECAUSE YOU ARE TOO KIND AND WEAK FOR PAIN...
...AND YOU MIGHT SAY TO LEAVE ME AS I AM, AND THEN MY HUSBAND WOULD NOT LOVE ME EVEN AS YOU DO NOT LOVE HER.

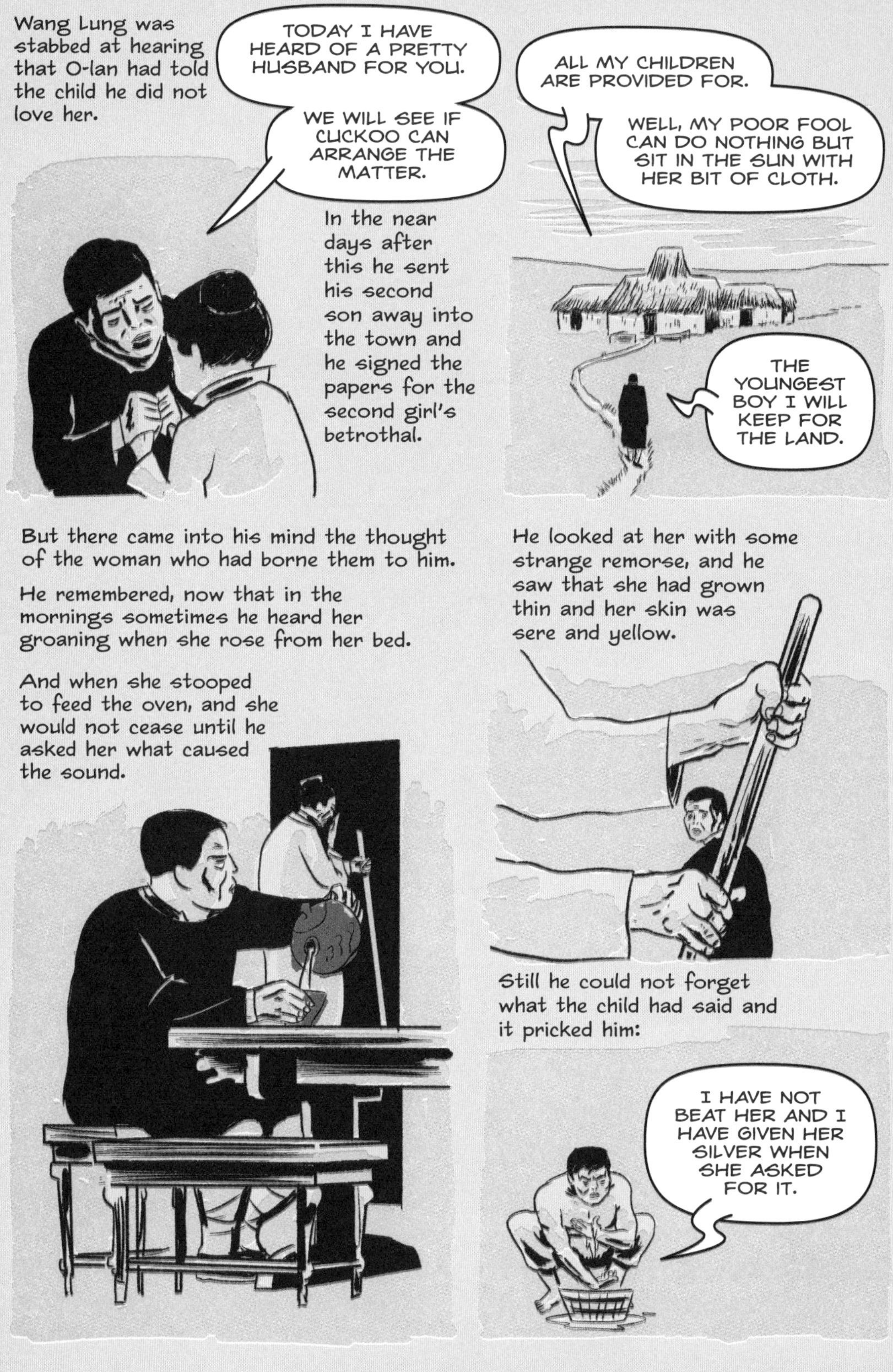
Wang Lung was stabbed at hearing that O-lan had told the child he did not love her.
TODAY I HAVE HEARD OF A PRETTY HUSBAND FOR YOU.
WE WILL SEE IF CUCKOO CAN ARRANGE THE MATTER.
In the near days after this he sent his second son away into the town and he signed the papers for the second girl's betrothal.
ALL MY CHILDREN ARE PROVIDED FOR.
WELL, MY POOR FOOL CAN DO NOTHING BUT SIT IN THE SUN WITH HER BIT OF CLOTH.
THE YOUNGEST BOY I WILL KEEP FOR THE LAND.
But there came into his mind the thought of the woman who had borne them to him.
He remembered, now that in the mornings sometimes he heard her groaning when she rose from her bed.
And when she stooped to feed the oven, and she would not cease until he asked her what caused the sound.
He looked at her with some strange remorse, and he saw that she had grown thin and her skin was sere and yellow.
Still he could not forget what the child had said and it pricked him:
I HAVE NOT BEAT HER AND I HAVE GIVEN HER SILVER WHEN SHE ASKED FOR IT.

He could not be rid of this unease toward her, and kept looking at her as she brought in his food or as she moved about.

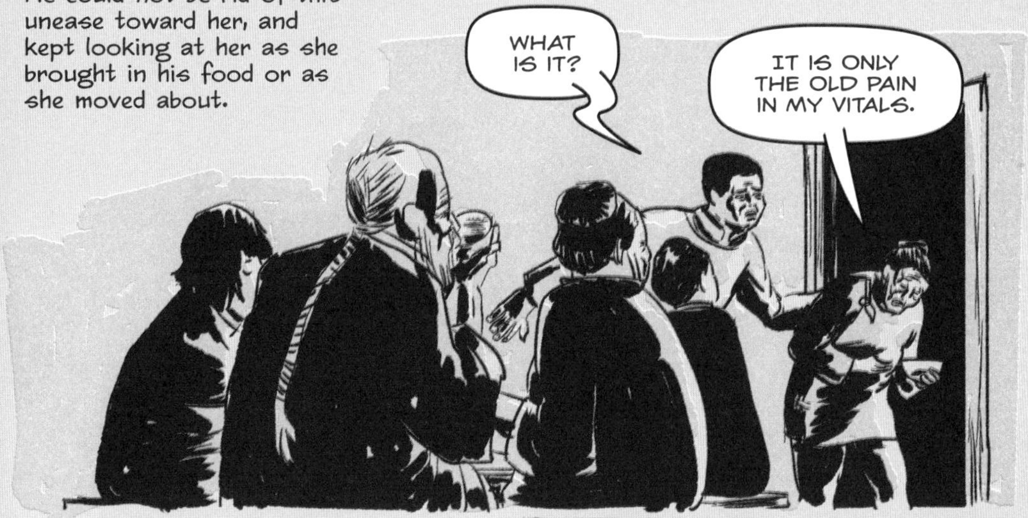
WHAT IS IT?
IT IS ONLY THE OLD PAIN IN MY VITALS.

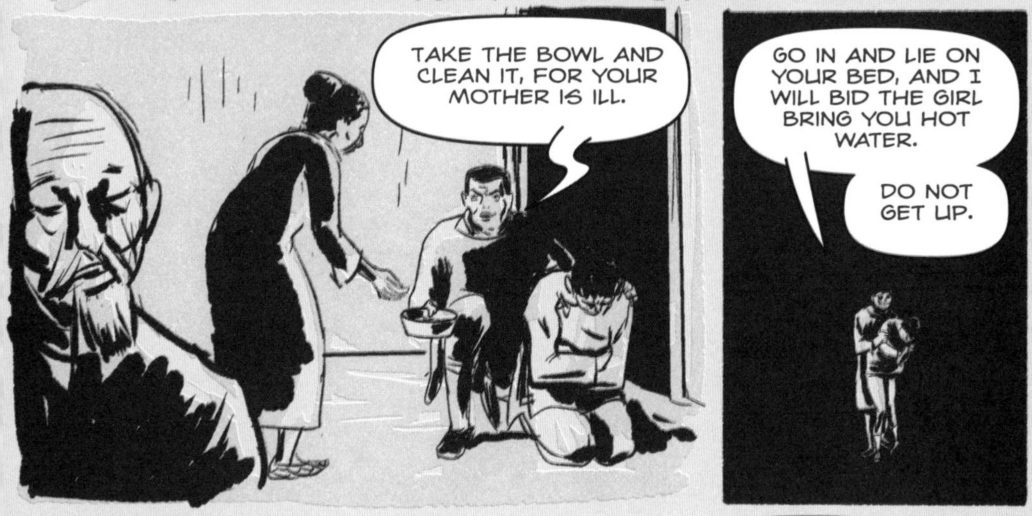
TAKE THE BOWL AND CLEAN IT, FOR YOUR MOTHER IS ILL.
GO IN AND LIE ON YOUR BED, AND I WILL BID THE GIRL BRING YOU HOT WATER.
DO NOT GET UP.

He sat listening to her moaning until he could not bear it, and he rose and went in to the town to ask where a doctor's shop was.

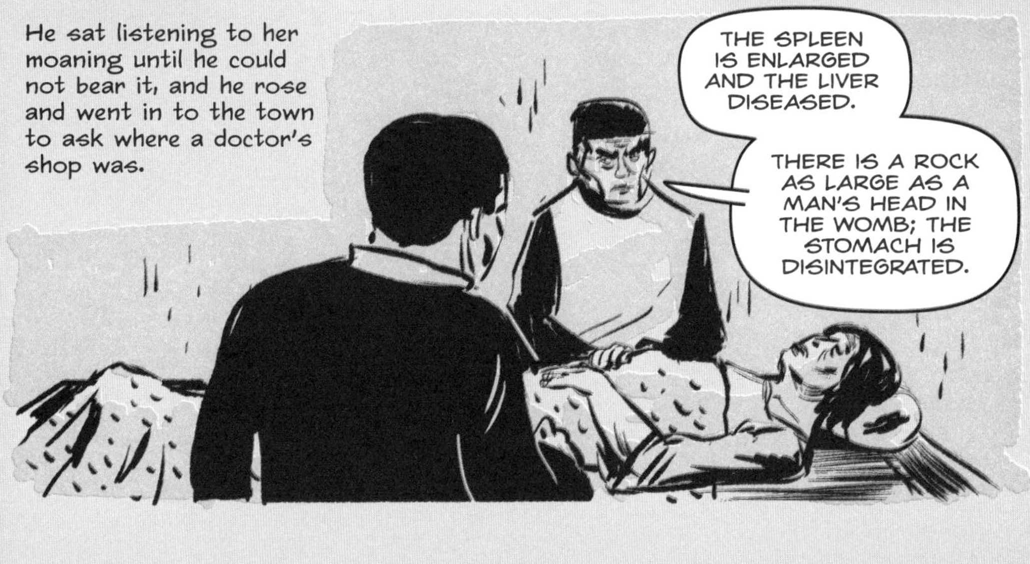
THE SPLEEN IS ENLARGED AND THE LIVER DISEASED.
THERE IS A ROCK AS LARGE AS A MAN'S HEAD IN THE WOMB; THE STOMACH IS DISINTEGRATED.

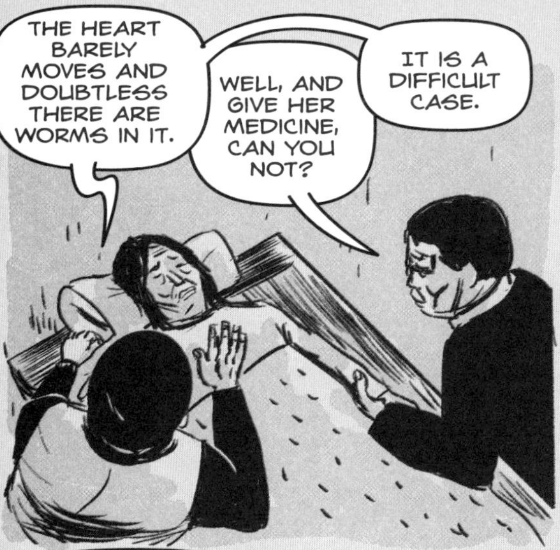
THE HEART BARELY MOVES AND DOUBTLESS THERE ARE WORMS IN IT.
IT IS A DIFFICULT CASE.
WELL, AND GIVE HER MEDICINE, CAN YOU NOT?

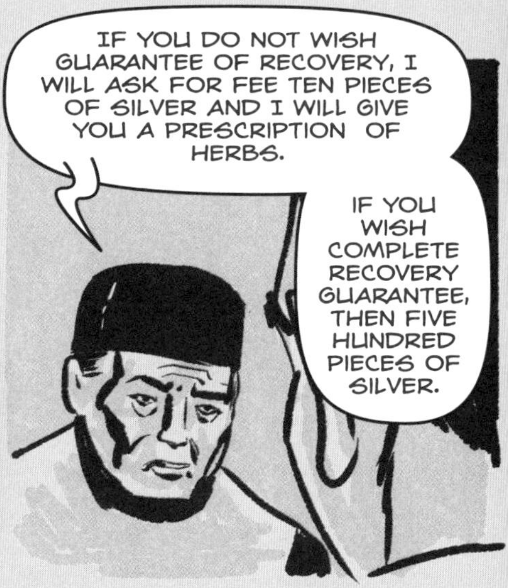
IF YOU DO NOT WISH GUARANTEE OF RECOVERY, I WILL ASK FOR FEE TEN PIECES OF SILVER AND I WILL GIVE YOU A PRESCRIPTION OF HERBS.
IF YOU WISH COMPLETE RECOVERY GUARANTEE, THEN FIVE HUNDRED PIECES OF SILVER.

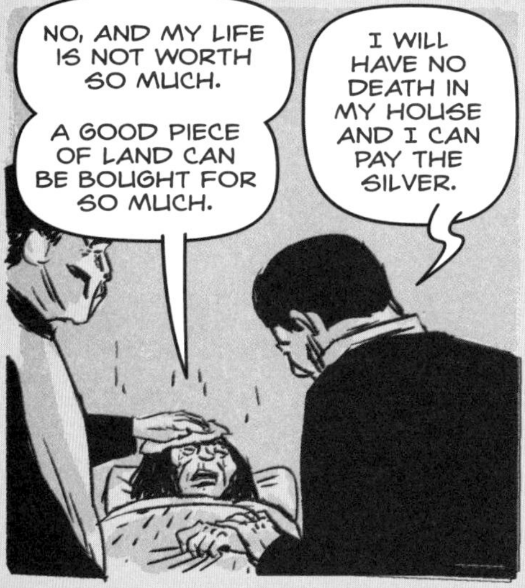
NO, AND MY LIFE IS NOT WORTH SO MUCH.
A GOOD PIECE OF LAND CAN BE BOUGHT FOR SO MUCH.
I WILL HAVE NO DEATH IN MY HOUSE AND I CAN PAY THE SILVER.

The old doctor's eyes shone greedily enough, but he knew the penalty of the law if he did not keep his word and the woman died, and so he said with regret:

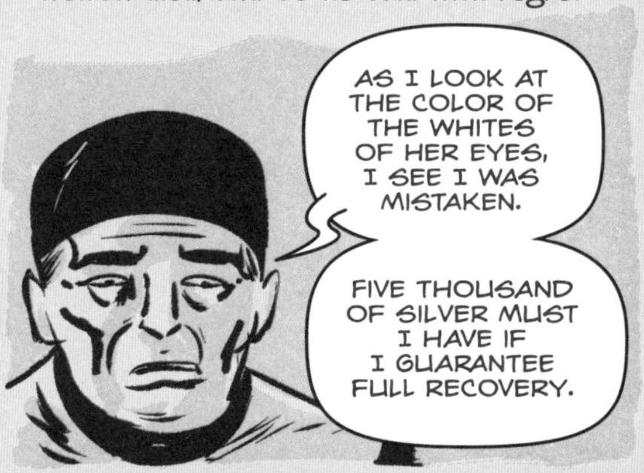
AS I LOOK AT THE COLOR OF THE WHITES OF HER EYES, I SEE I WAS MISTAKEN.
FIVE THOUSAND OF SILVER MUST I HAVE IF I GUARANTEE FULL RECOVERY.

Then Wang Lung looked at the doctor in silence and in sad understanding, and he paid him the ten pieces of silver.

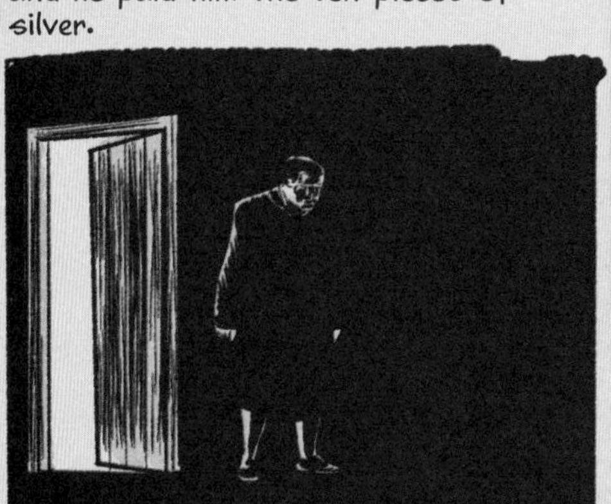

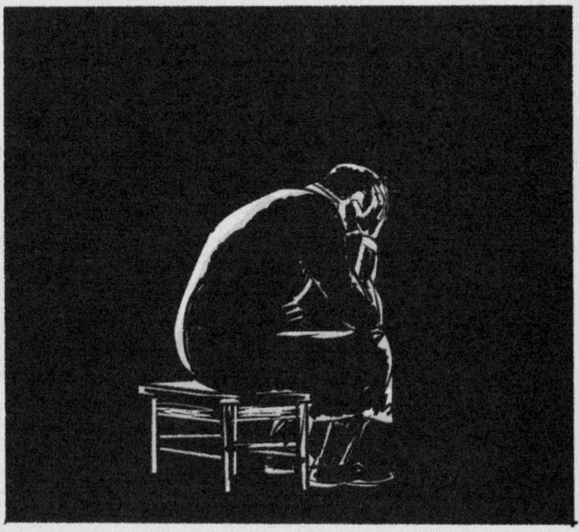

7

But there was no sudden dying of life in O-lan's body.

All through the long months of winter Wang Lung and his children came to understand what value she had been in the house.

It seemed now that none knew how to light the grass and keep it burning in the oven, and none knew how to turn a fish in the cauldron without breaking it.

Wang Lung could not make the old man understand what had happened that O-lan no longer came to bring him tea.

At last the old man was shown O-lan and he wept.

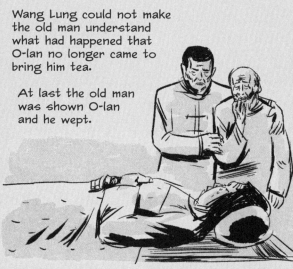

Only the poor fool knew nothing and she only smiled and twisted her bit of cloth.

Yet one had to think of her to bring her in to sleep at night and to feed her.

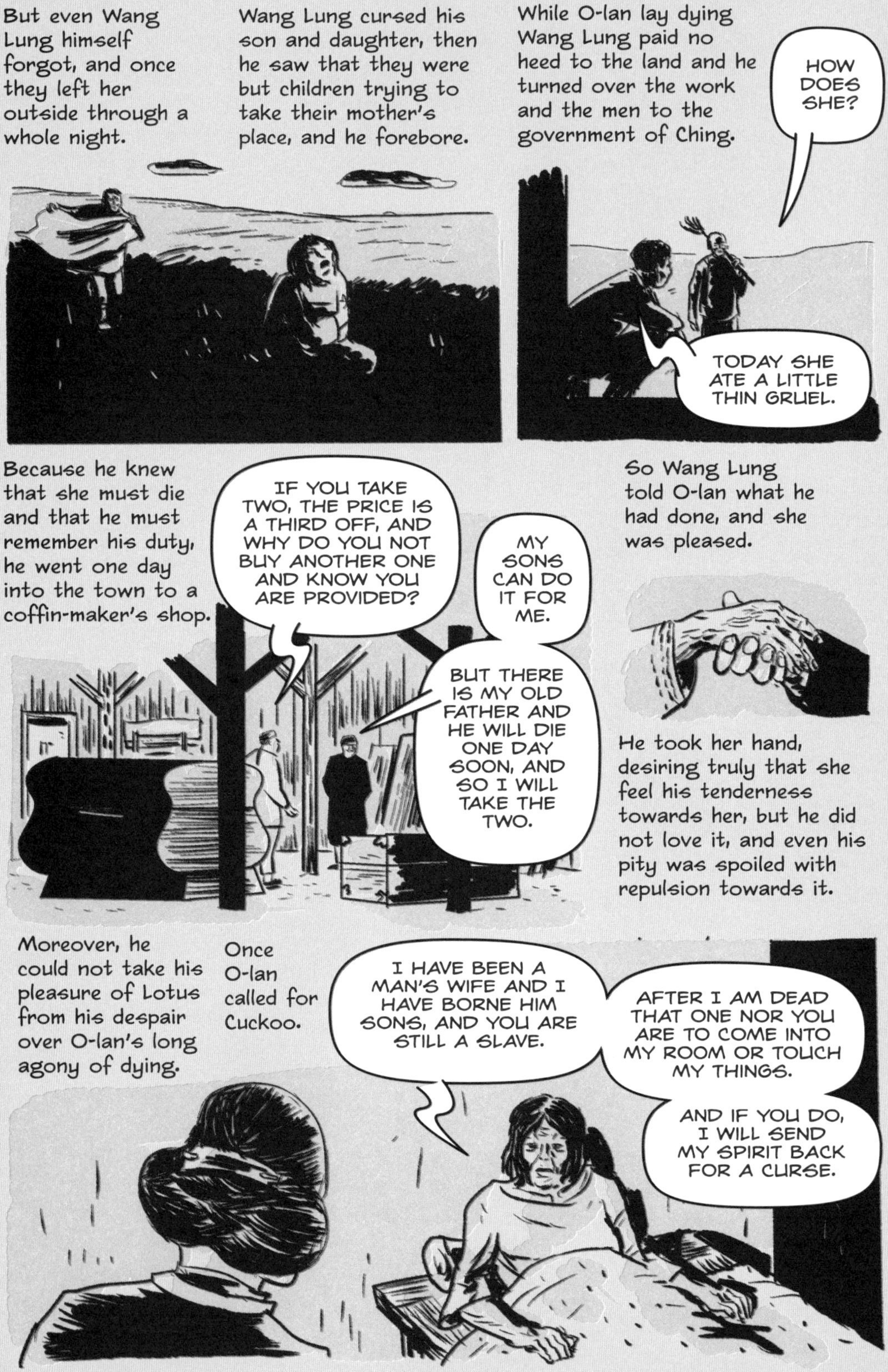
But even Wang Lung himself forgot, and once they left her outside through a whole night.
Wang Lung cursed his son and daughter, then he saw that they were but children trying to take their mother's place, and he forebore.
While O-lan lay dying Wang Lung paid no heed to the land and he turned over the work and the men to the government of Ching.
HOW DOES SHE?
TODAY SHE ATE A LITTLE THIN GRUEL.
Because he knew that she must die and that he must remember his duty, he went one day into the town to a coffin-maker's shop.
IF YOU TAKE TWO, THE PRICE IS A THIRD OFF, AND WHY DO YOU NOT BUY ANOTHER ONE AND KNOW YOU ARE PROVIDED?
MY SONS CAN DO IT FOR ME.
BUT THERE IS MY OLD FATHER AND HE WILL DIE ONE DAY SOON, AND SO I WILL TAKE THE TWO.
So Wang Lung told O-lan what he had done, and she was pleased.
He took her hand, desiring truly that she feel his tenderness towards her, but he did not love it, and even his pity was spoiled with repulsion towards it.
Moreover, he could not take his pleasure of Lotus from his despair over O-lan's long agony of dying.
Once O-lan called for Cuckoo.
I HAVE BEEN A MAN'S WIFE AND I HAVE BORNE HIM SONS, AND YOU ARE STILL A SLAVE.
AFTER I AM DEAD THAT ONE NOR YOU ARE TO COME INTO MY ROOM OR TOUCH MY THINGS.
AND IF YOU DO, I WILL SEND MY SPIRIT BACK FOR A CURSE.

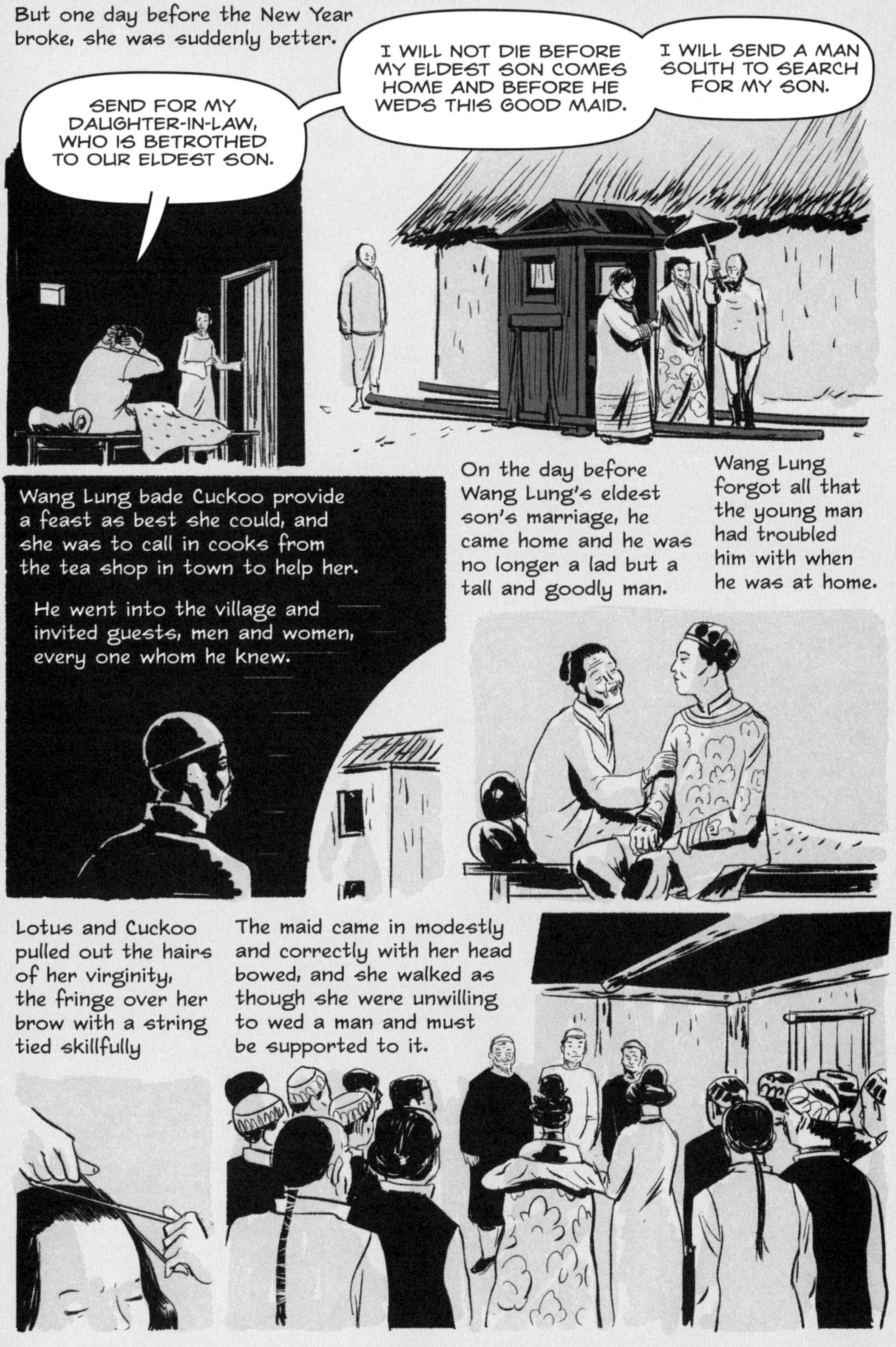
But one day before the New Year broke, she was suddenly better.
SEND FOR MY DAUGHTER-IN-LAW, WHO IS BETROTHED TO OUR ELDEST SON.
I WILL NOT DIE BEFORE MY ELDEST SON COMES HOME AND BEFORE HE WEDS THIS GOOD MAID.
I WILL SEND A MAN SOUTH TO SEARCH FOR MY SON.
Wang Lung bade Cuckoo provide a feast as best she could, and she was to call in cooks from the tea shop in town to help her.
He went into the village and invited guests, men and women, every one whom he knew.
On the day before Wang Lung's eldest son's marriage, he came home and he was no longer a lad but a tall and goodly man.
Wang Lung forgot all that the young man had troubled him with when he was at home.
Lotus and Cuckoo pulled out the hairs of her virginity, the fringe over her brow with a string tied skillfully
The maid came in modestly and correctly with her head bowed, and she walked as though she were unwilling to wed a man and must be supported to it.

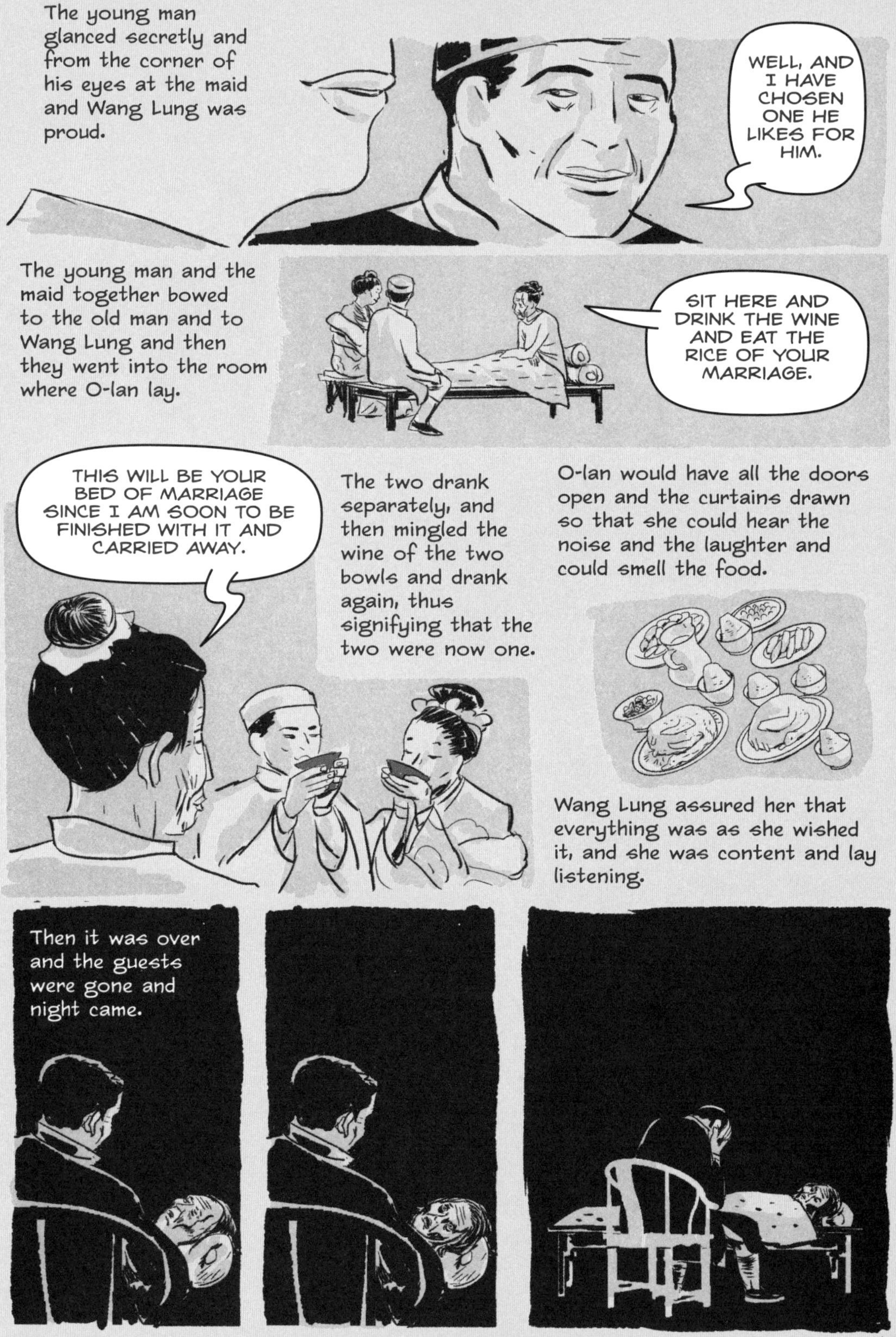

The young man glanced secretly and from the corner of his eyes at the maid and Wang Lung was proud.
WELL, AND I HAVE CHOSEN ONE HE LIKES FOR HIM.
The young man and the maid together bowed to the old man and to Wang Lung and then they went into the room where O-lan lay.
SIT HERE AND DRINK THE WINE AND EAT THE RICE OF YOUR MARRIAGE.
THIS WILL BE YOUR BED OF MARRIAGE SINCE I AM SOON TO BE FINISHED WITH IT AND CARRIED AWAY.
The two drank separately, and then mingled the wine of the two bowls and drank again, thus signifying that the two were now one.
O-lan would have all the doors open and the curtains drawn so that she could hear the noise and the laughter and could smell the food.
Wang Lung assured her that everything was as she wished it, and she was content and lay listening.
Then it was over and the guests were gone and night came.

Once she lay dead it seemed to Wang Lung that he could not bear to be near O-lan.

To comfort himself he went and found a geomancer and asked him for a lucky day for burials.

Wang Lung paid the man and went to the temple and bargained with the abbot there and rented a space for a coffin for three months.

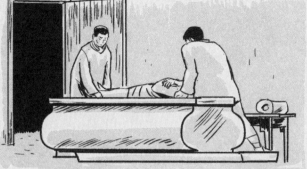

Wang Lung took his possessions and moved altogether into the inner court where Lotus lived.

GO WITH YOUR WIFE INTO THAT ROOM AND BEGET THERE YOUR OWN SONS.

Then one morning the old man died and Wang Lung washed the old man himself.

WE WILL BURY THESE TWO ON A GOOD PIECE OF MY HILL LAND.

For the first time Wang Lung rode on men's shoulders, and mourning and weeping loudly they went to the graves.

He wished he had not taken the two pearls from O-lan that day, and he would never bear to see Lotus put them in her ears again.

THERE IN THAT LAND OF MINE IS BURIED THE FIRST GOOD HALF OF MY LIFE AND MORE.

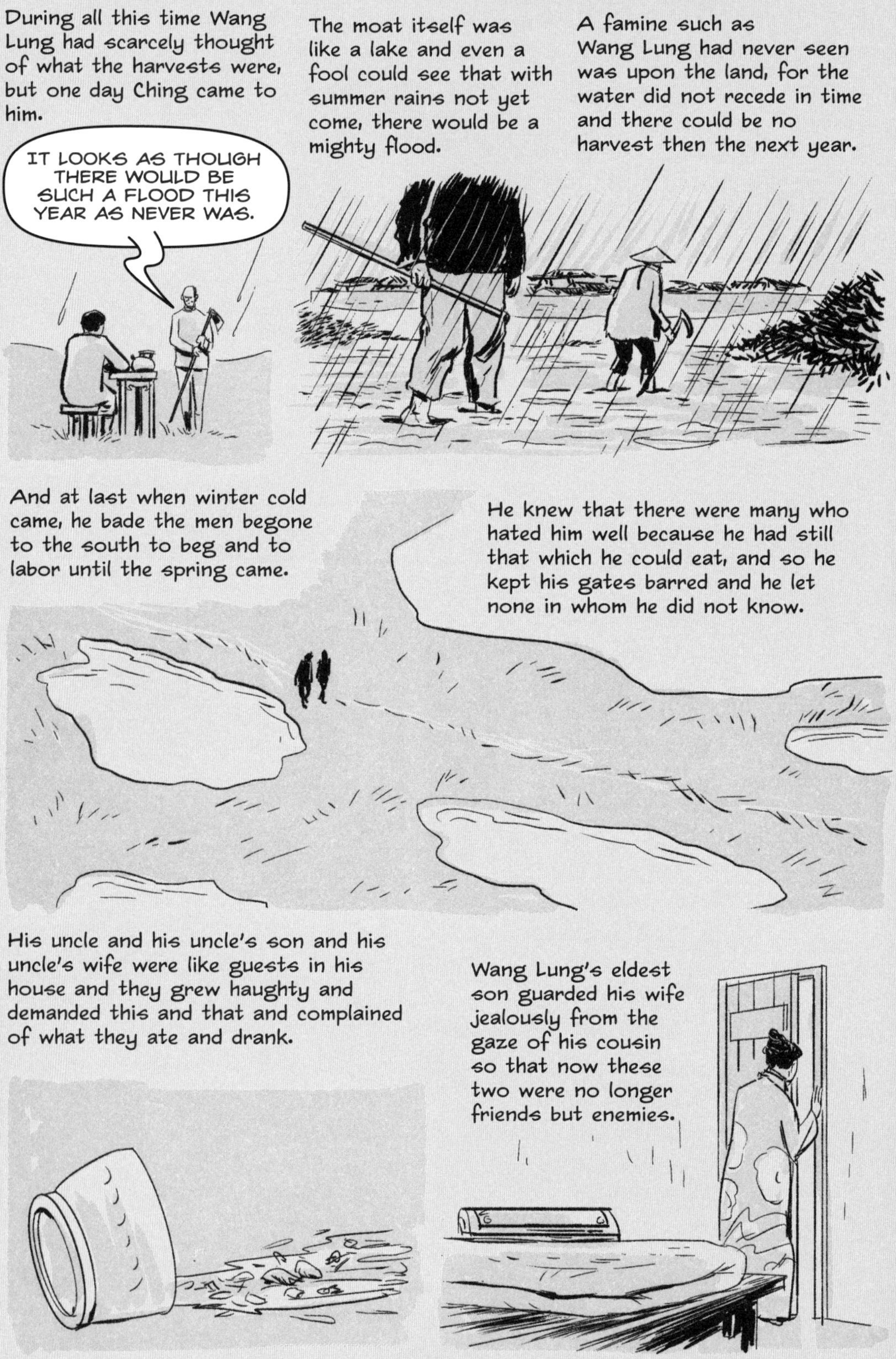
During all this time Wang Lung had scarcely thought of what the harvests were, but one day Ching came to him.
IT LOOKS AS THOUGH THERE WOULD BE SUCH A FLOOD THIS YEAR AS NEVER WAS.
The moat itself was like a lake and even a fool could see that with summer rains not yet come, there would be a mighty flood.
A famine such as Wang Lung had never seen was upon the land, for the water did not recede in time and there could be no harvest then the next year.
And at last when winter cold came, he bade the men begone to the south to beg and to labor until the spring came.
He knew that there were many who hated him well because he had still that which he could eat, and so he kept his gates barred and he let none in whom he did not know.
His uncle and his uncle's son and his uncle's wife were like guests in his house and they grew haughty and demanded this and that and complained of what they ate and drank.
Wang Lung's eldest son guarded his wife jealously from the gaze of his cousin so that now these two were no longer friends but enemies.

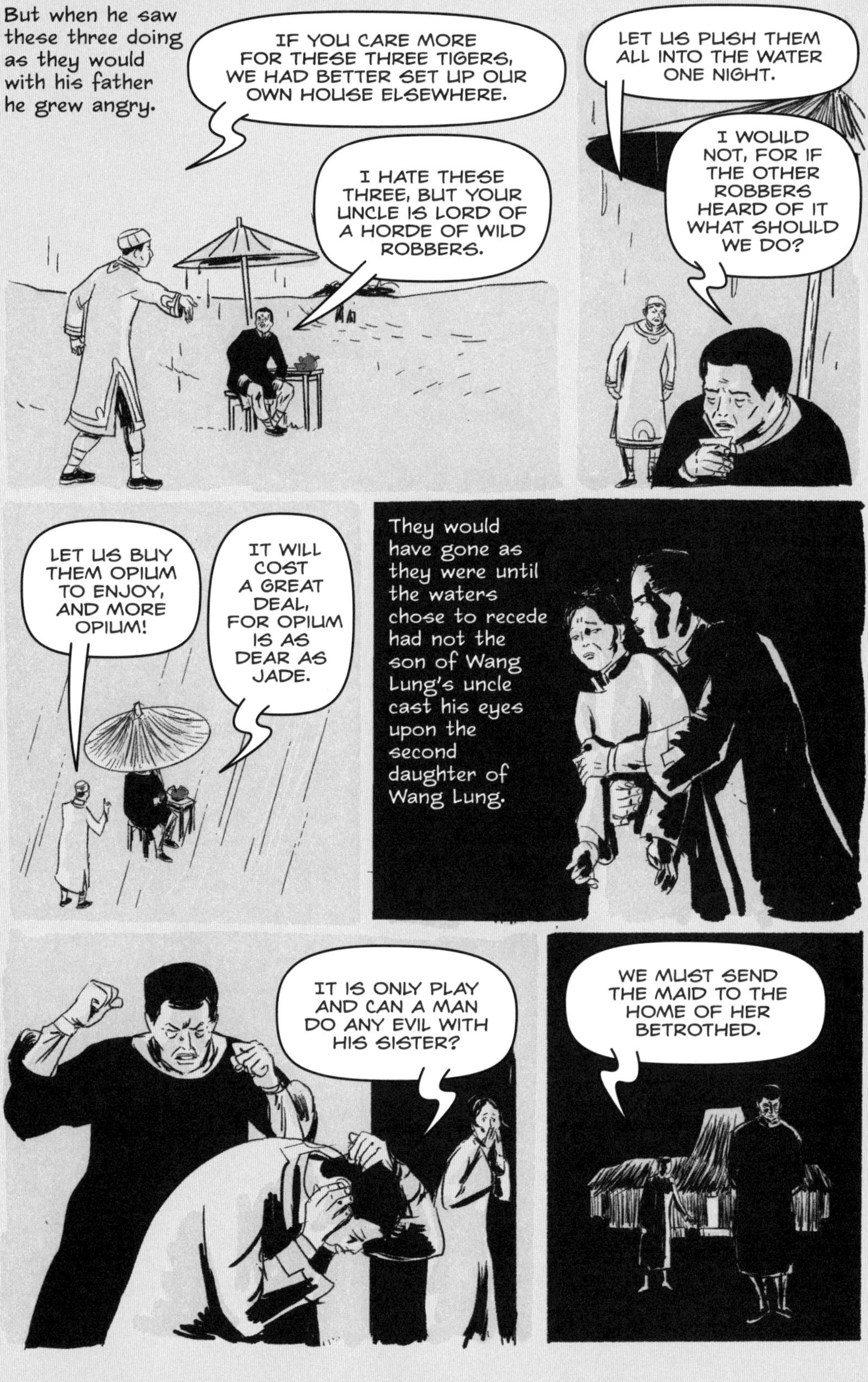
But when he saw these three doing as they would with his father he grew angry.
IF YOU CARE MORE FOR THESE THREE TIGERS, WE HAD BETTER SET UP OUR OWN HOUSE ELSEWHERE.
I HATE THESE THREE, BUT YOUR UNCLE IS LORD OF A HORDE OF WILD ROBBERS.
LET US PUSH THEM ALL INTO THE WATER ONE NIGHT.
I WOULD NOT, FOR IF THE OTHER ROBBERS HEARD OF IT WHAT SHOULD WE DO?
LET US BUY THEM OPIUM TO ENJOY, AND MORE OPIUM!
IT WILL COST A GREAT DEAL, FOR OPIUM IS AS DEAR AS JADE.
They would have gone as they were until the waters chose to recede had not the son of Wang Lung's uncle cast his eyes upon the second daughter of Wang Lung.
IT IS ONLY PLAY AND CAN A MAN DO ANY EVIL WITH HIS SISTER?
WE MUST SEND THE MAID TO THE HOME OF HER BETROTHED.

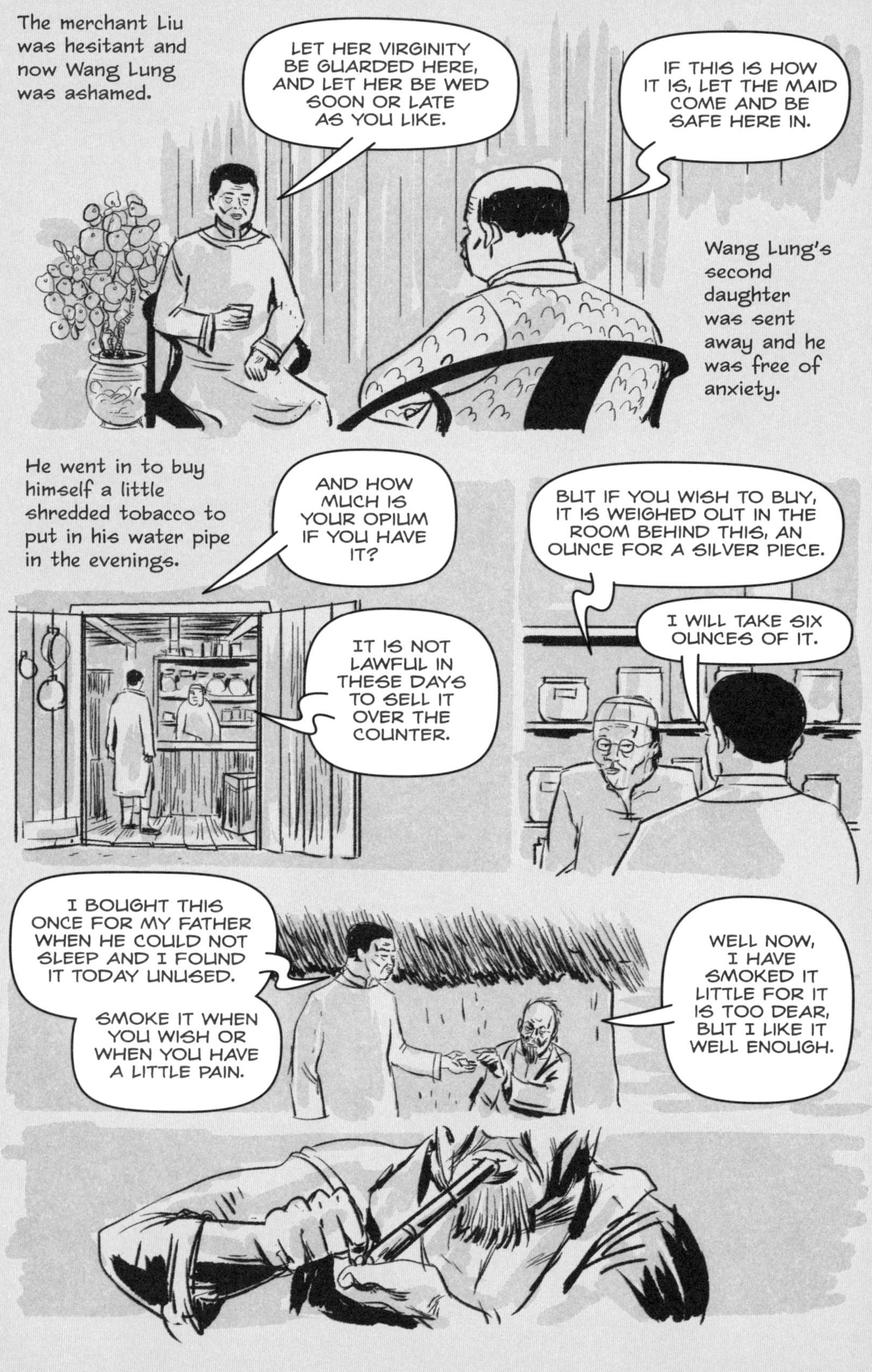
The merchant Liu was hesitant and now Wang Lung was ashamed.
LET HER VIRGINITY BE GUARDED HERE, AND LET HER BE WED SOON OR LATE AS YOU LIKE.
IF THIS IS HOW IT IS, LET THE MAID COME AND BE SAFE HERE IN.
Wang Lung's second daughter was sent away and he was free of anxiety.
He went in to buy himself a little shredded tobacco to put in his water pipe in the evenings.
AND HOW MUCH IS YOUR OPIUM IF YOU HAVE IT?
IT IS NOT LAWFUL IN THESE DAYS TO SELL IT OVER THE COUNTER.
BUT IF YOU WISH TO BUY, IT IS WEIGHED OUT IN THE ROOM BEHIND THIS, AN OUNCE FOR A SILVER PIECE.
I WILL TAKE SIX OUNCES OF IT.
I BOUGHT THIS ONCE FOR MY FATHER WHEN HE COULD NOT SLEEP AND I FOUND IT TODAY UNUSED.
SMOKE IT WHEN YOU WISH OR WHEN YOU HAVE A LITTLE PAIN.
WELL NOW, I HAVE SMOKED IT LITTLE FOR IT IS TOO DEAR, BUT I LIKE IT WELL ENOUGH.

Wang Lung pretended to smoke, but he only took a pipe to his room and left it there cold.

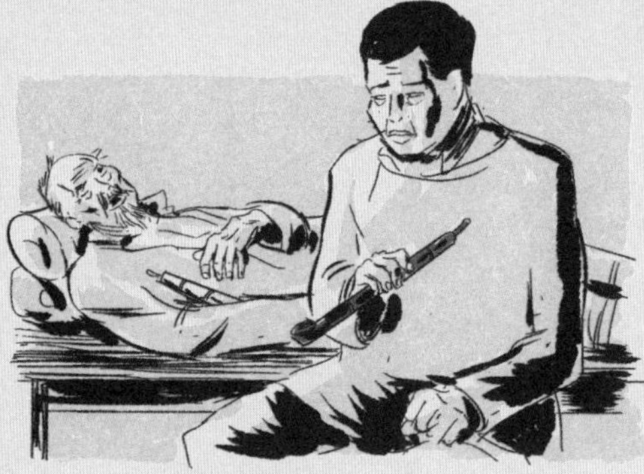

The smoke, and the silver for this Wang Lung did not begrudge because it bought him peace.

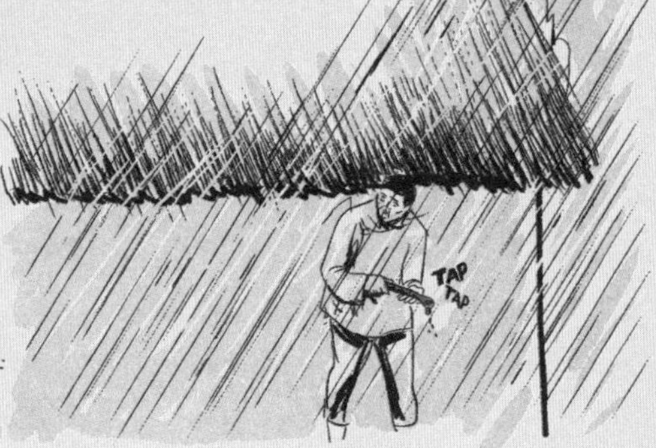
TAP TAP

The winter wore away and the waters began to recede.

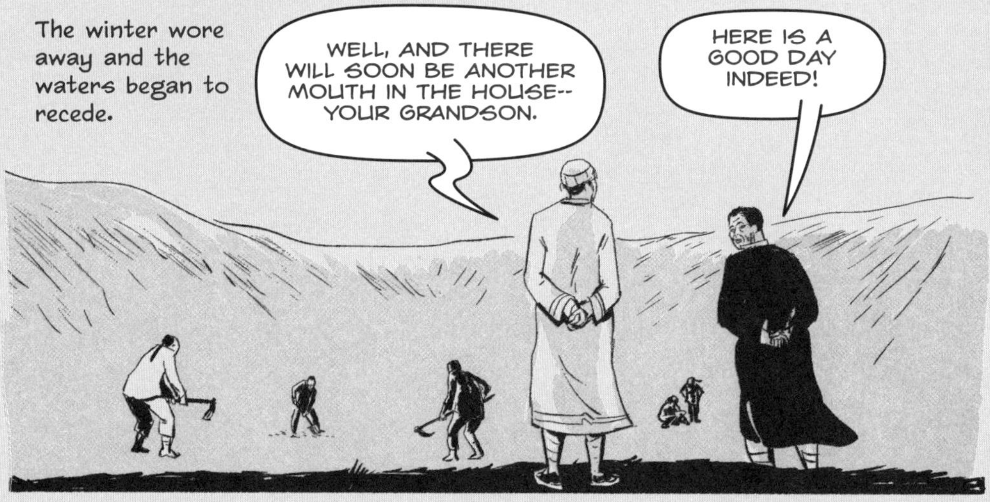
WELL, AND THERE WILL SOON BE ANOTHER MOUTH IN THE HOUSE-- YOUR GRANDSON.
HERE IS A GOOD DAY INDEED!

And as the spring grew into summer, the people who had gone away from the floods came back again.

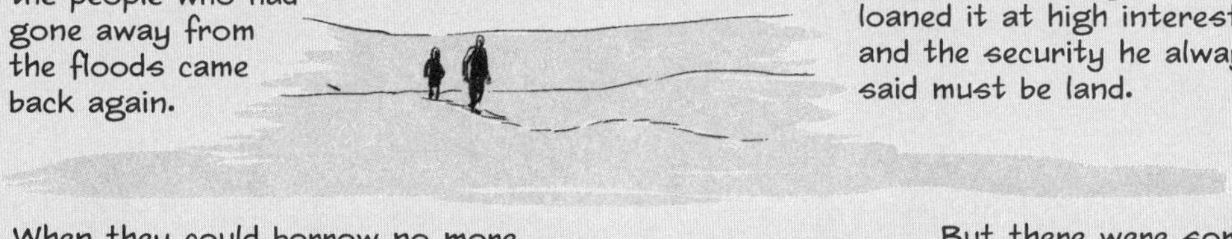

Many came to Wang Lung to borrow money, and he loaned it at high interest, and the security he always said must be land.

When they could borrow no more money, some sold land and part of their fields that they might plant what was left.

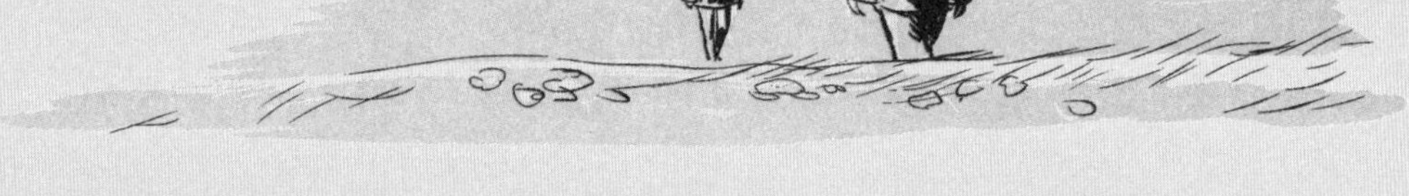

But there were some who would not sell their land, and when they had nothing, they sold their daughters.

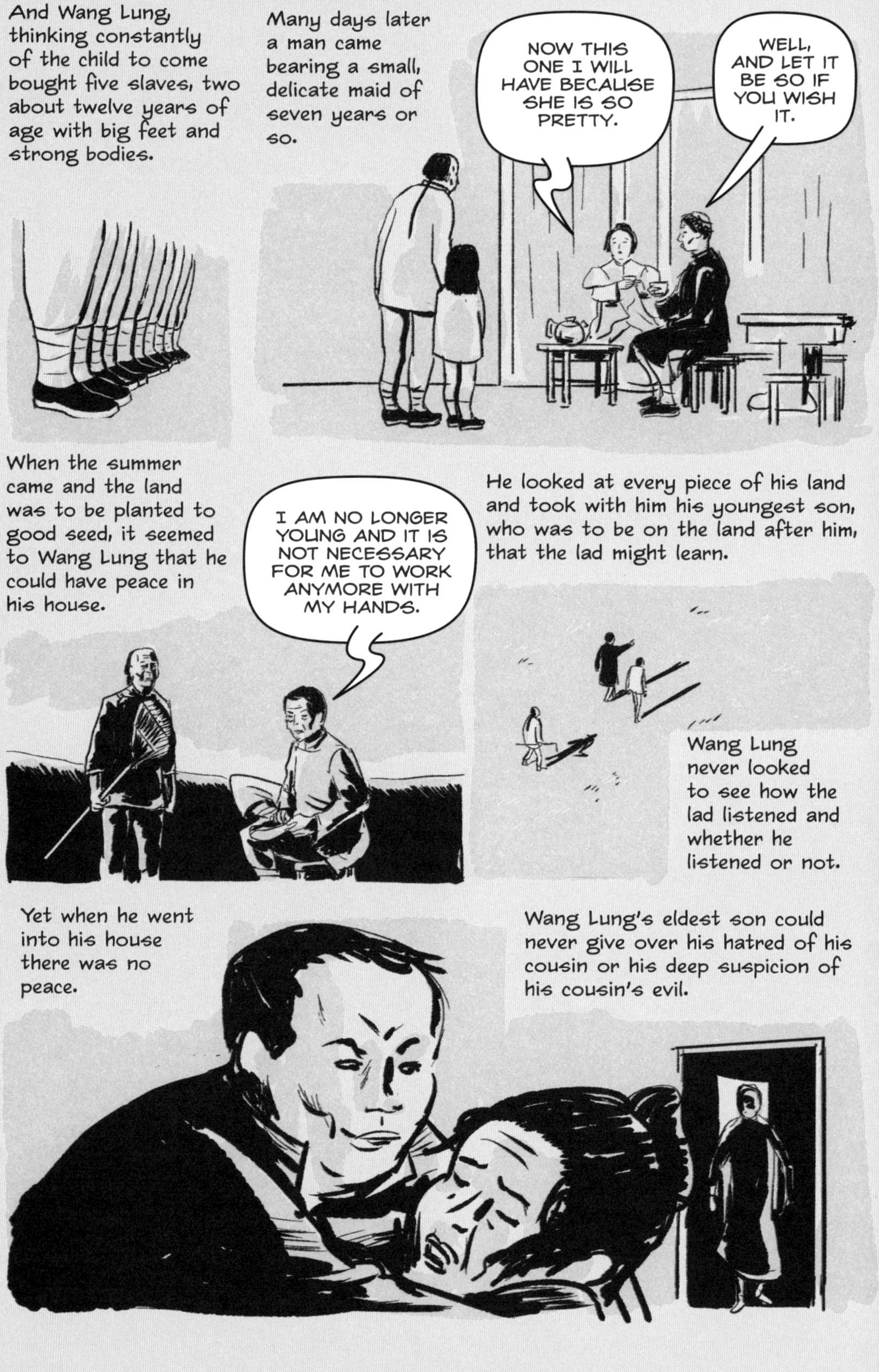
And Wang Lung, thinking constantly of the child to come bought five slaves, two about twelve years of age with big feet and strong bodies.
Many days later a man came bearing a small, delicate maid of seven years or so.
NOW THIS ONE I WILL HAVE BECAUSE SHE IS SO PRETTY.
WELL, AND LET IT BE SO IF YOU WISH IT.
When the summer came and the land was to be planted to good seed, it seemed to Wang Lung that he could have peace in his house.
I AM NO LONGER YOUNG AND IT IS NOT NECESSARY FOR ME TO WORK ANYMORE WITH MY HANDS.
He looked at every piece of his land and took with him his youngest son, who was to be on the land after him, that the lad might learn.
Wang Lung never looked to see how the lad listened and whether he listened or not.
Yet when he went into his house there was no peace.
Wang Lung's eldest son could never give over his hatred of his cousin or his deep suspicion of his cousin's evil.

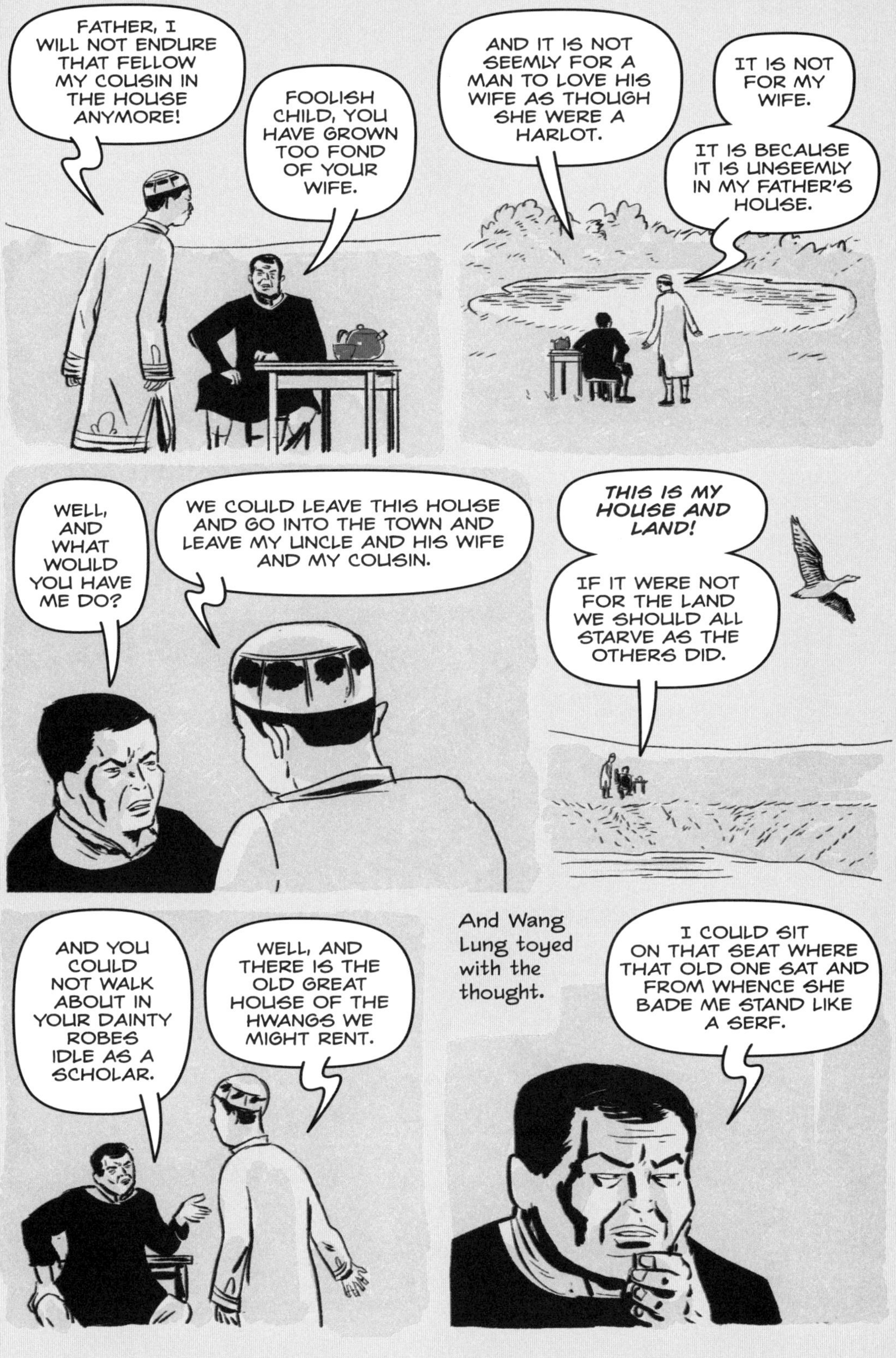
FATHER, I WILL NOT ENDURE THAT FELLOW MY COUSIN IN THE HOUSE ANYMORE!
FOOLISH CHILD, YOU HAVE GROWN TOO FOND OF YOUR WIFE.
AND IT IS NOT SEEMLY FOR A MAN TO LOVE HIS WIFE AS THOUGH SHE WERE A HARLOT.
IT IS NOT FOR MY WIFE.
IT IS BECAUSE IT IS UNSEEMLY IN MY FATHER'S HOUSE.
WELL, AND WHAT WOULD YOU HAVE ME DO?
WE COULD LEAVE THIS HOUSE AND GO INTO THE TOWN AND LEAVE MY UNCLE AND HIS WIFE AND MY COUSIN.
THIS IS MY HOUSE AND LAND!
IF IT WERE NOT FOR THE LAND WE SHOULD ALL STARVE AS THE OTHERS DID.
AND YOU COULD NOT WALK ABOUT IN YOUR DAINTY ROBES IDLE AS A SCHOLAR.
WELL, AND THERE IS THE OLD GREAT HOUSE OF THE HWANGS WE MIGHT RENT.
And Wang Lung toyed with the thought.
I COULD SIT ON THAT SEAT WHERE THAT OLD ONE SAT AND FROM WHENCE SHE BADE ME STAND LIKE A SERF.

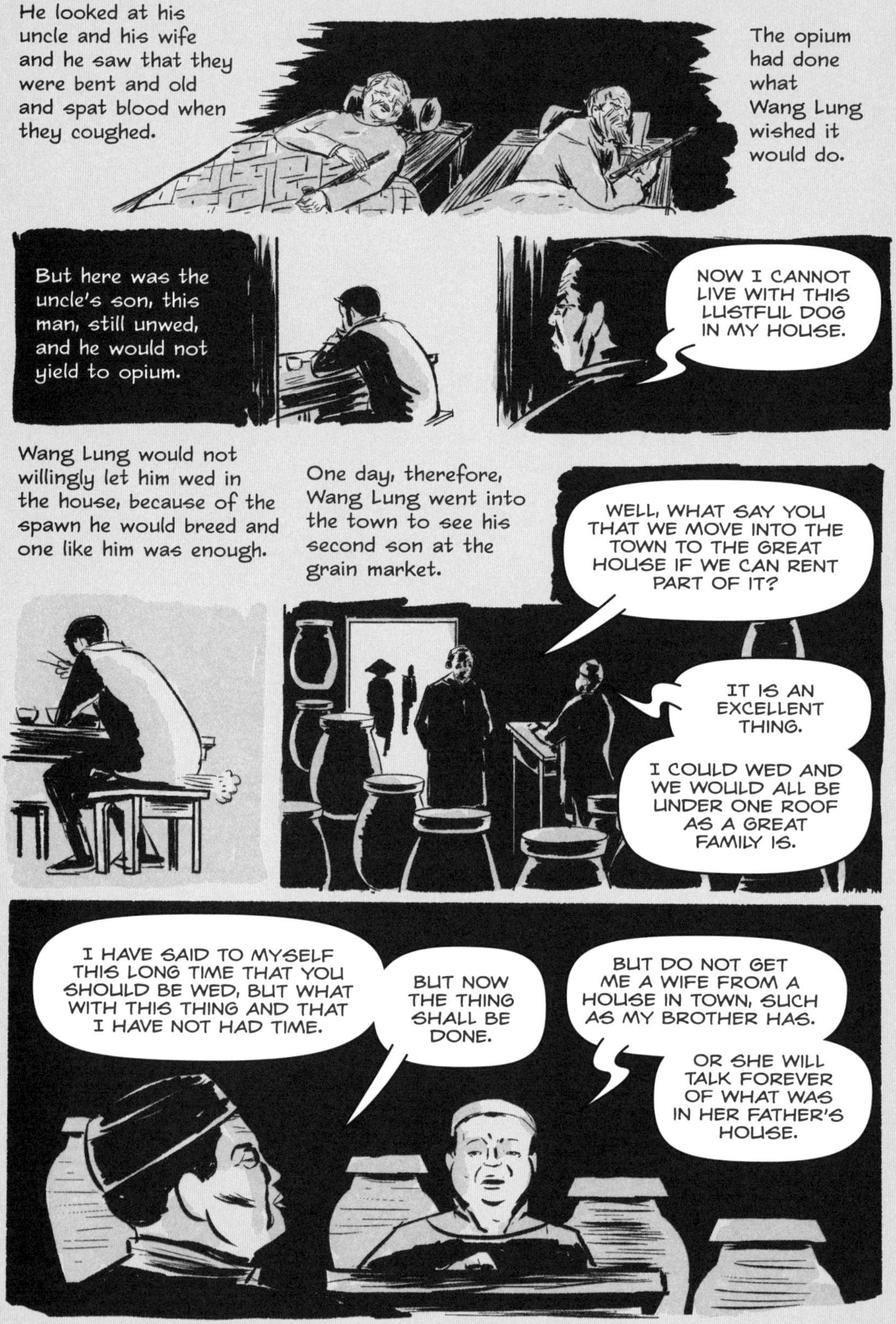
He looked at his uncle and his wife and he saw that they were bent and old and spat blood when they coughed.
The opium had done what Wang Lung wished it would do.
But here was the uncle's son, this man, still unwed, and he would not yield to opium.
NOW I CANNOT LIVE WITH THIS LUSTFUL DOG IN MY HOUSE.
Wang Lung would not willingly let him wed in the house, because of the spawn he would breed and one like him was enough.
One day, therefore, Wang Lung went into the town to see his second son at the grain market.
WELL, WHAT SAY YOU THAT WE MOVE INTO THE TOWN TO THE GREAT HOUSE IF WE CAN RENT PART OF IT?
IT IS AN EXCELLENT THING.
I COULD WED AND WE WOULD ALL BE UNDER ONE ROOF AS A GREAT FAMILY IS.
I HAVE SAID TO MYSELF THIS LONG TIME THAT YOU SHOULD BE WED, BUT WHAT WITH THIS THING AND THAT I HAVE NOT HAD TIME.
BUT NOW THE THING SHALL BE DONE.
BUT DO NOT GET ME A WIFE FROM A HOUSE IN TOWN, SUCH AS MY BROTHER HAS.
OR SHE WILL TALK FOREVER OF WHAT WAS IN HER FATHER'S HOUSE.

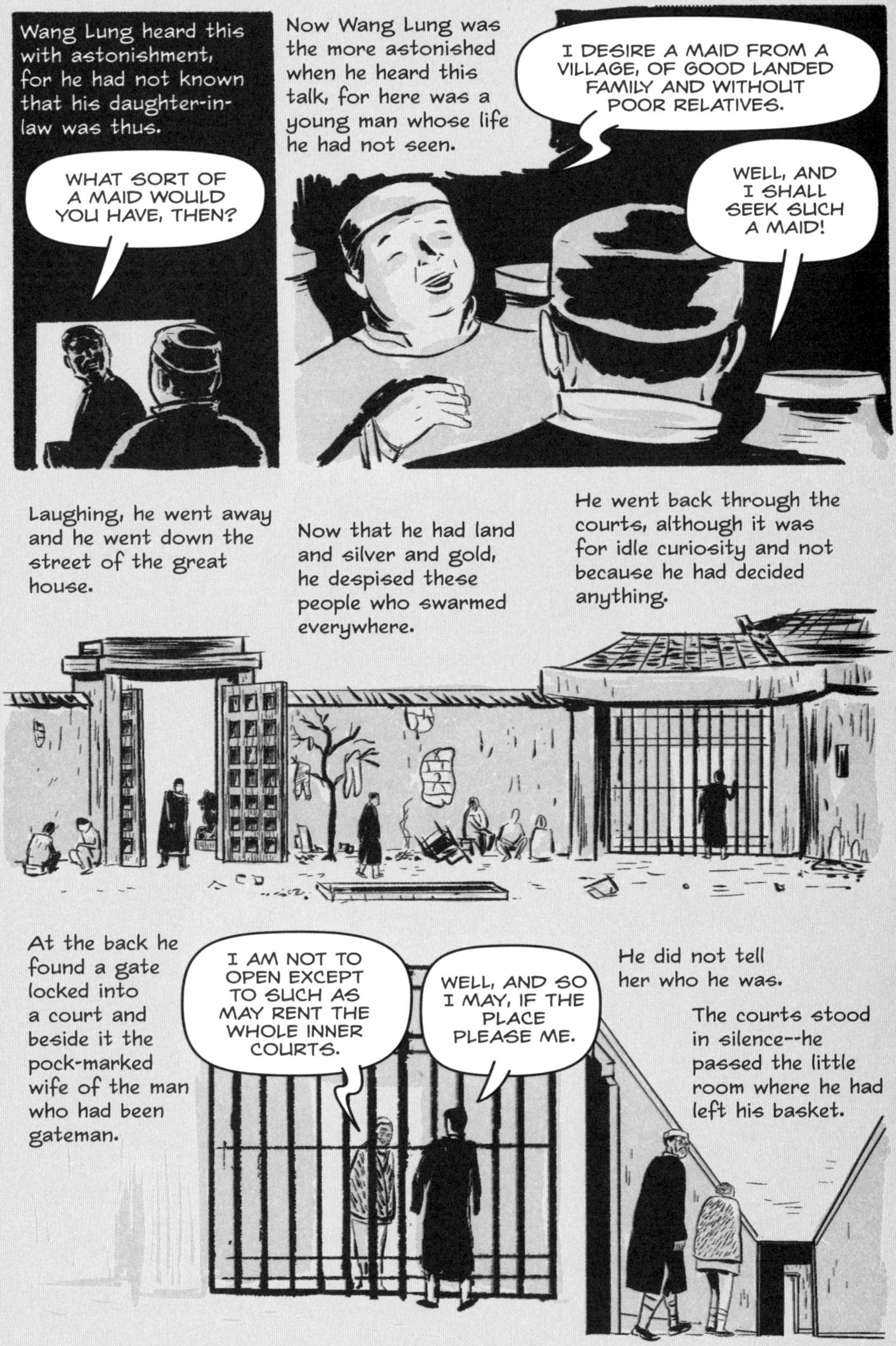
Wang Lung heard this with astonishment, for he had not known that his daughter-in-law was thus.
WHAT SORT OF A MAID WOULD YOU HAVE, THEN?
Now Wang Lung was the more astonished when he heard this talk, for here was a young man whose life he had not seen.
I DESIRE A MAID FROM A VILLAGE, OF GOOD LANDED FAMILY AND WITHOUT POOR RELATIVES.
WELL, AND I SHALL SEEK SUCH A MAID!
Laughing, he went away and he went down the street of the great house.
Now that he had land and silver and gold, he despised these people who swarmed everywhere.
He went back through the courts, although it was for idle curiosity and not because he had decided anything.
At the back he found a gate locked into a court and beside it the pock-marked wife of the man who had been gateman.
I AM NOT TO OPEN EXCEPT TO SUCH AS MAY RENT THE WHOLE INNER COURTS.
WELL, AND SO I MAY, IF THE PLACE PLEASE ME.
He did not tell her who he was.
The courts stood in silence--he passed the little room where he had left his basket.

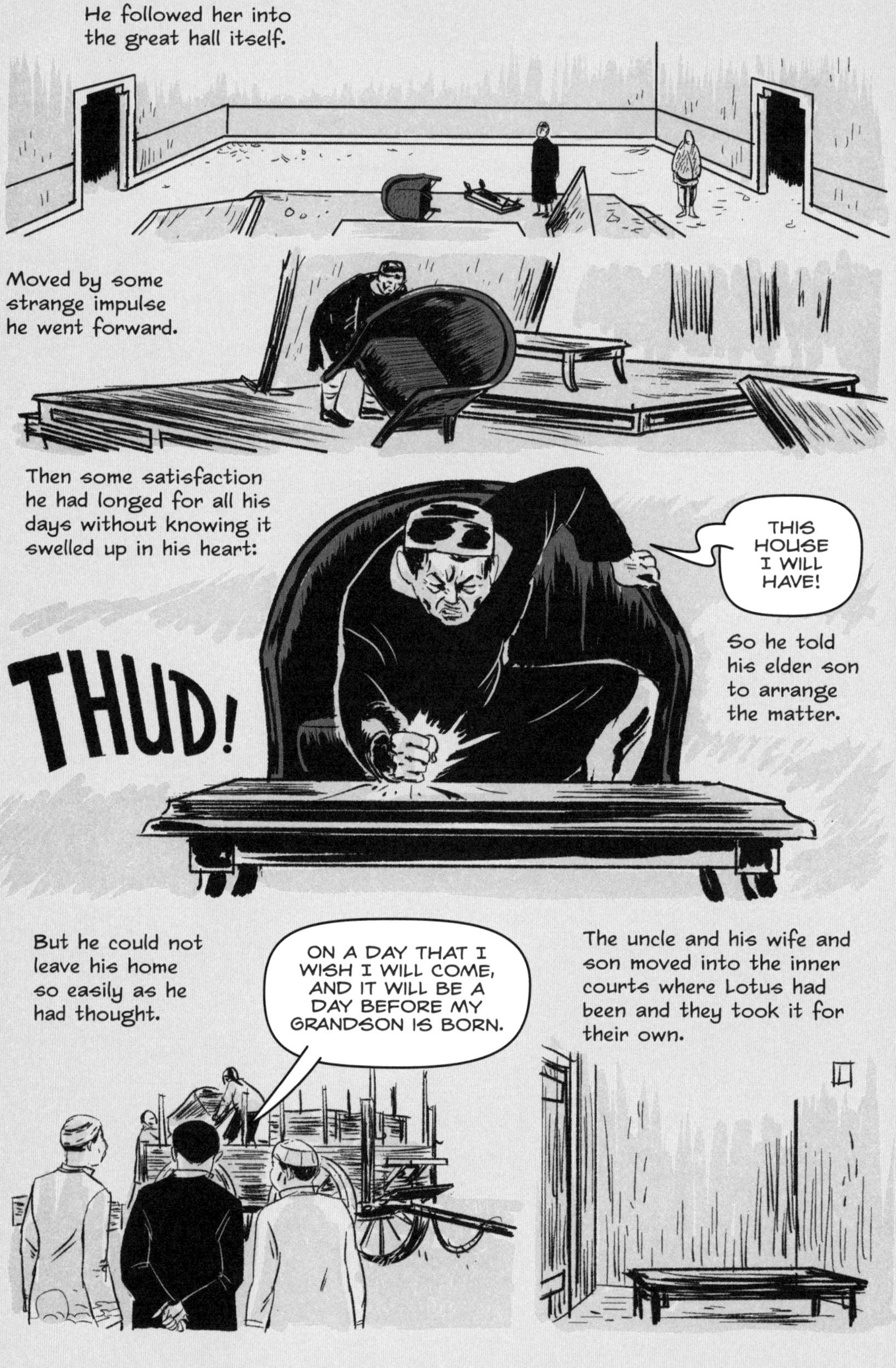
He followed her into the great hall itself.
Moved by some strange impulse he went forward.
Then some satisfaction he had longed for all his days without knowing it swelled up in his heart:
THIS HOUSE I WILL HAVE!
THUD!
So he told his elder son to arrange the matter.
But he could not leave his home so easily as he had thought.
ON A DAY THAT I WISH I WILL COME, AND IT WILL BE A DAY BEFORE MY GRANDSON IS BORN.
The uncle and his wife and son moved into the inner courts where Lotus had been and they took it for their own.

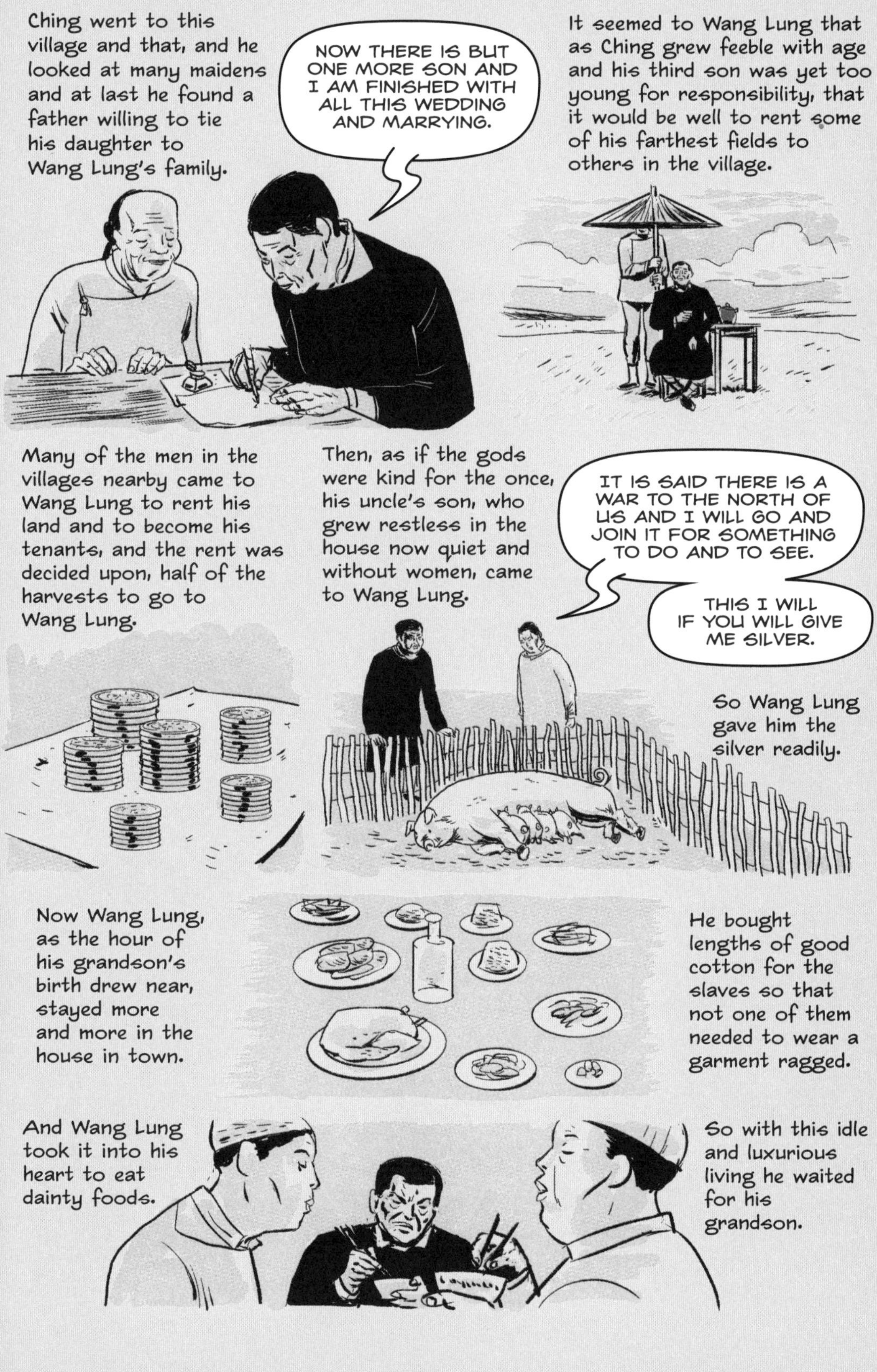
Ching went to this village and that, and he looked at many maidens and at last he found a father willing to tie his daughter to Wang Lung's family.
NOW THERE IS BUT ONE MORE SON AND I AM FINISHED WITH ALL THIS WEDDING AND MARRYING.
It seemed to Wang Lung that as Ching grew feeble with age and his third son was yet too young for responsibility, that it would be well to rent some of his farthest fields to others in the village.
Many of the men in the villages nearby came to Wang Lung to rent his land and to become his tenants, and the rent was decided upon, half of the harvests to go to Wang Lung.
Then, as if the gods were kind for the once, his uncle's son, who grew restless in the house now quiet and without women, came to Wang Lung.
IT IS SAID THERE IS A WAR TO THE NORTH OF US AND I WILL GO AND JOIN IT FOR SOMETHING TO DO AND TO SEE.
THIS I WILL IF YOU WILL GIVE ME SILVER.
So Wang Lung gave him the silver readily.
Now Wang Lung, as the hour of his grandson's birth drew near, stayed more and more in the house in town.
He bought lengths of good cotton for the slaves so that not one of them needed to wear a garment ragged.
And Wang Lung took it into his heart to eat dainty foods.
So with this idle and luxurious living he waited for his grandson.

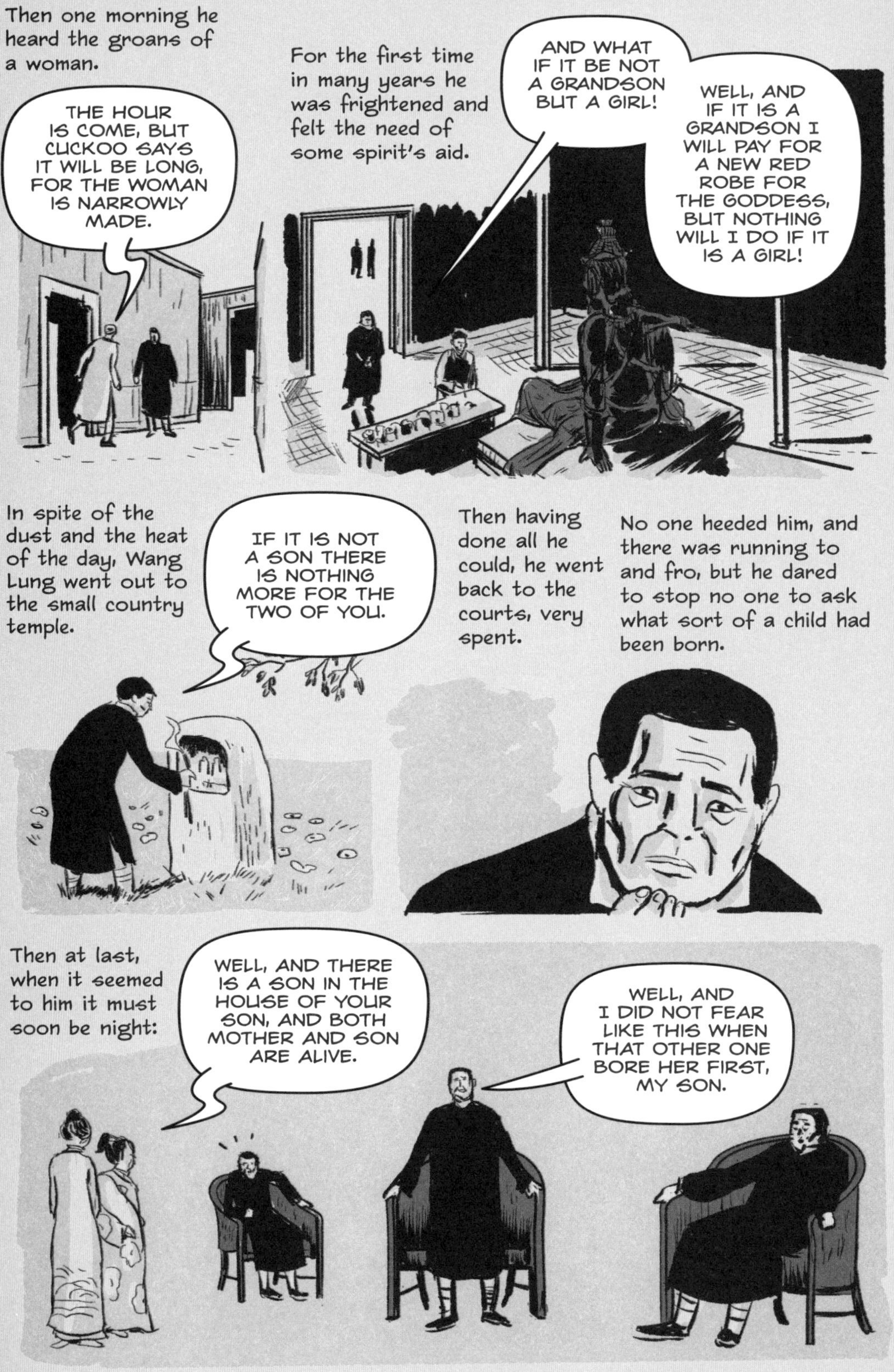

Then one morning he heard the groans of a woman.
THE HOUR IS COME, BUT CUCKOO SAYS IT WILL BE LONG, FOR THE WOMAN IS NARROWLY MADE.
For the first time in many years he was frightened and felt the need of some spirit's aid.
AND WHAT IF IT BE NOT A GRANDSON BUT A GIRL!
WELL, AND IF IT IS A GRANDSON I WILL PAY FOR A NEW RED ROBE FOR THE GODDESS, BUT NOTHING WILL I DO IF IT IS A GIRL!
In spite of the dust and the heat of the day, Wang Lung went out to the small country temple.
IF IT IS NOT A SON THERE IS NOTHING MORE FOR THE TWO OF YOU.
Then having done all he could, he went back to the courts, very spent.
No one heeded him, and there was running to and fro, but he dared to stop no one to ask what sort of a child had been born.
Then at last, when it seemed to him it must soon be night:
WELL, AND THERE IS A SON IN THE HOUSE OF YOUR SON, AND BOTH MOTHER AND SON ARE ALIVE.
WELL, AND I DID NOT FEAR LIKE THIS WHEN THAT OTHER ONE BORE HER FIRST, MY SON.

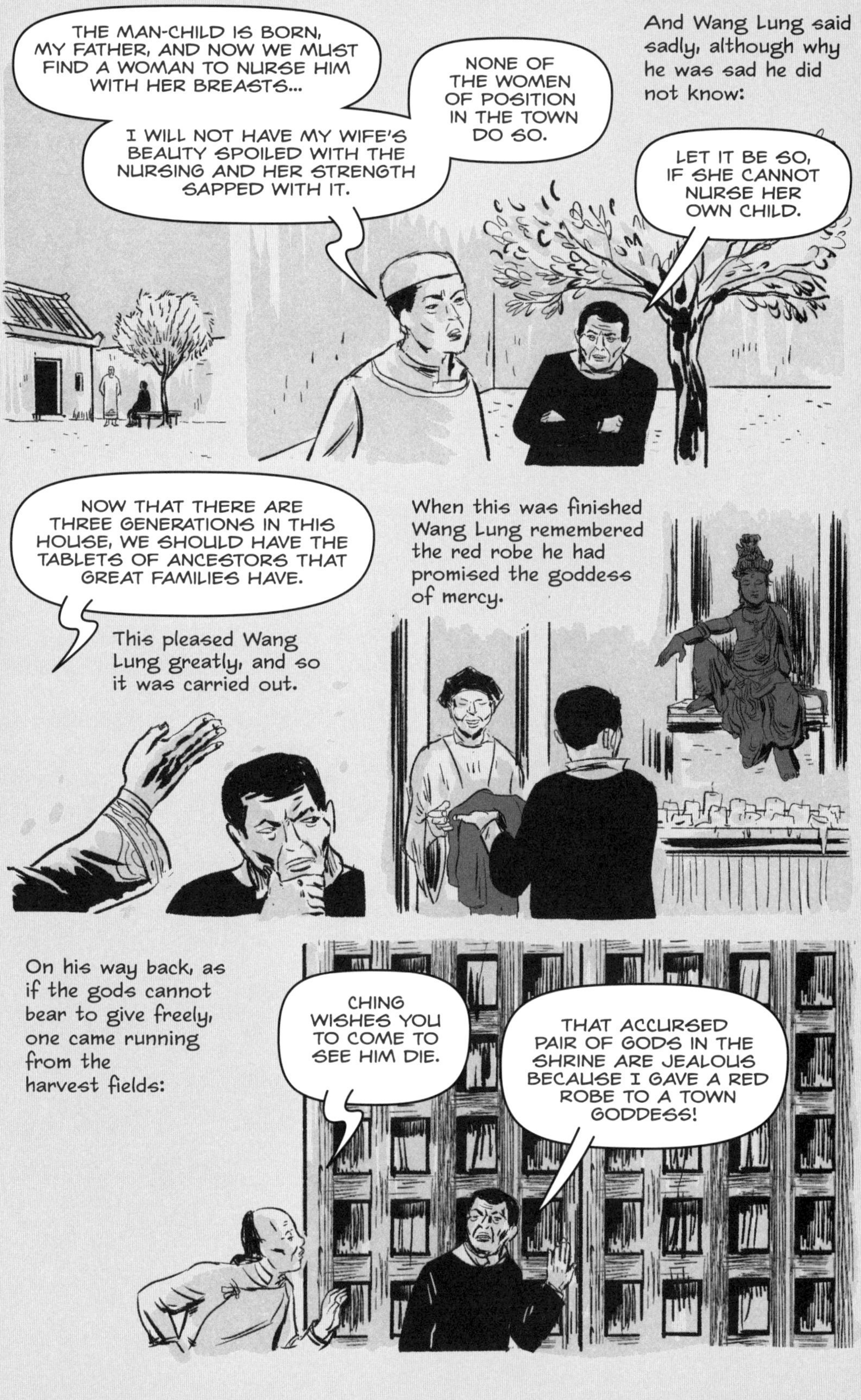
THE MAN-CHILD IS BORN, MY FATHER, AND NOW WE MUST FIND A WOMAN TO NURSE HIM WITH HER BREASTS...
I WILL NOT HAVE MY WIFE'S BEAUTY SPOILED WITH THE NURSING AND HER STRENGTH SAPPED WITH IT.
NONE OF THE WOMEN OF POSITION IN THE TOWN DO SO.
And Wang Lung said sadly, although why he was sad he did not know:
LET IT BE SO, IF SHE CANNOT NURSE HER OWN CHILD.
NOW THAT THERE ARE THREE GENERATIONS IN THIS HOUSE, WE SHOULD HAVE THE TABLETS OF ANCESTORS THAT GREAT FAMILIES HAVE.
This pleased Wang Lung greatly, and so it was carried out.
When this was finished Wang Lung remembered the red robe he had promised the goddess of mercy.
On his way back, as if the gods cannot bear to give freely, one came running from the harvest fields:
CHING WISHES YOU TO COME TO SEE HIM DIE.
THAT ACCURSED PAIR OF GODS IN THE SHRINE ARE JEALOUS BECAUSE I GAVE A RED ROBE TO A TOWN GODDESS!

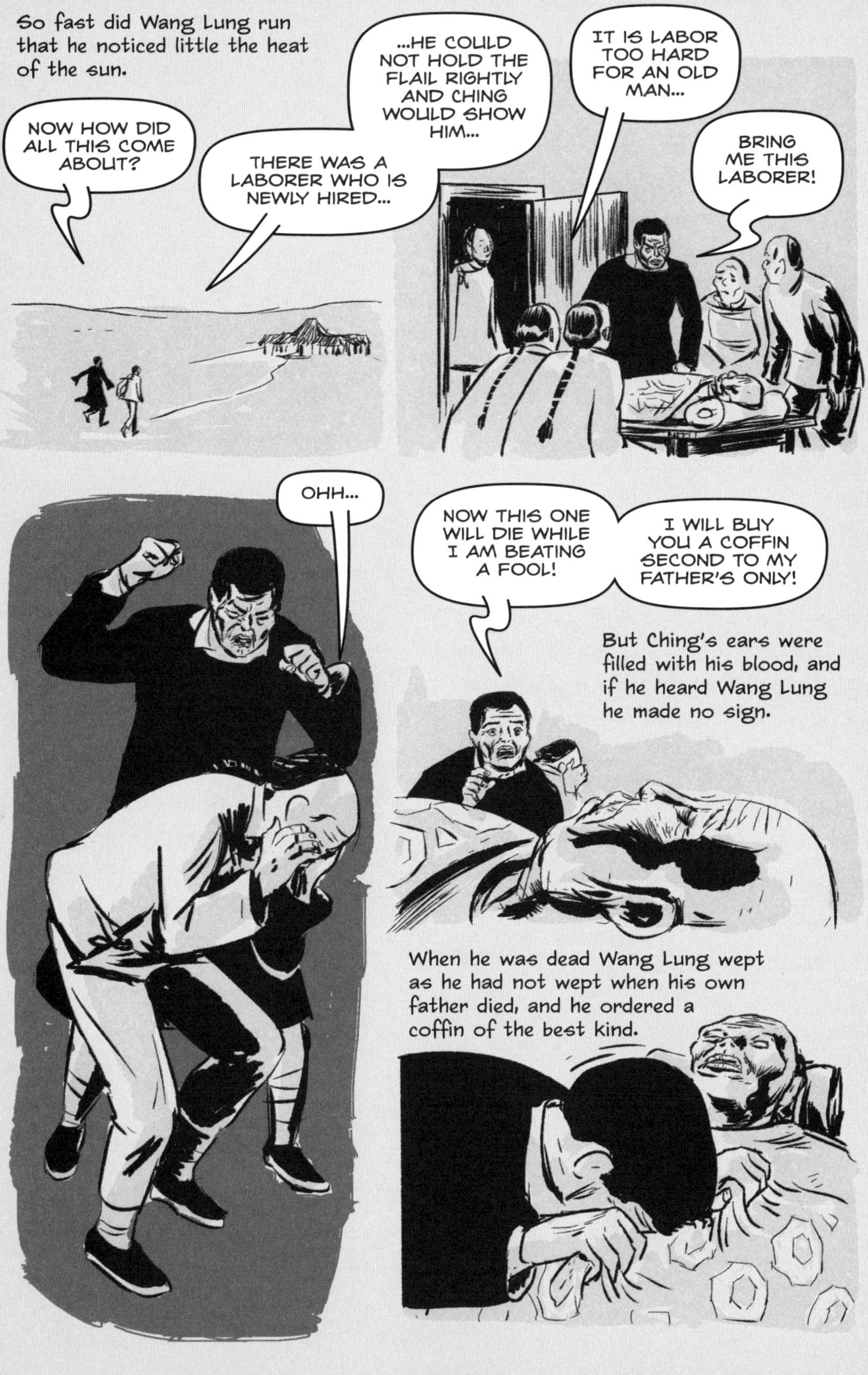
So fast did Wang Lung run that he noticed little the heat of the sun.
NOW HOW DID ALL THIS COME ABOUT?
THERE WAS A LABORER WHO IS NEWLY HIRED...
...HE COULD NOT HOLD THE FLAIL RIGHTLY AND CHING WOULD SHOW HIM...
IT IS LABOR TOO HARD FOR AN OLD MAN...
BRING ME THIS LABORER!
OHH...
NOW THIS ONE WILL DIE WHILE I AM BEATING A FOOL!
I WILL BUY YOU A COFFIN SECOND TO MY FATHER'S ONLY!
But Ching's ears were filled with his blood, and if he heard Wang Lung he made no sign.
When he was dead Wang Lung wept as he had not wept when his own father died, and he ordered a coffin of the best kind.

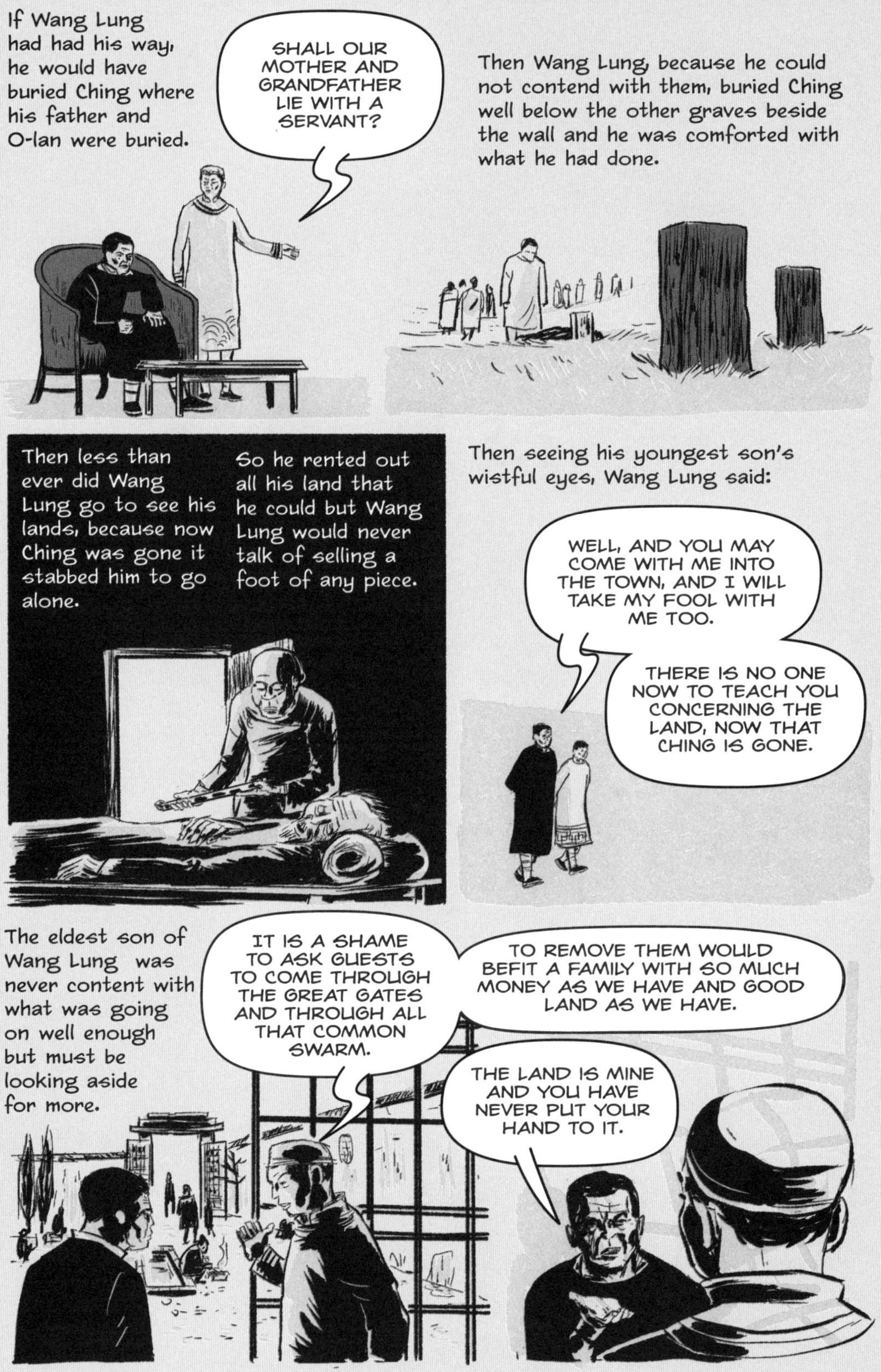

If Wang Lung had had his way, he would have buried Ching where his father and O-lan were buried.
SHALL OUR MOTHER AND GRANDFATHER LIE WITH A SERVANT?
Then Wang Lung, because he could not contend with them, buried Ching well below the other graves beside the wall and he was comforted with what he had done.
Then less than ever did Wang Lung go to see his lands, because now Ching was gone it stabbed him to go alone.
So he rented out all his land that he could but Wang Lung would never talk of selling a foot of any piece.
Then seeing his youngest son's wistful eyes, Wang Lung said:
WELL, AND YOU MAY COME WITH ME INTO THE TOWN, AND I WILL TAKE MY FOOL WITH ME TOO.
THERE IS NO ONE NOW TO TEACH YOU CONCERNING THE LAND, NOW THAT CHING IS GONE.
The eldest son of Wang Lung was never content with what was going on well enough but must be looking aside for more.
IT IS A SHAME TO ASK GUESTS TO COME THROUGH THE GREAT GATES AND THROUGH ALL THAT COMMON SWARM.
TO REMOVE THEM WOULD BEFIT A FAMILY WITH SO MUCH MONEY AS WE HAVE AND GOOD LAND AS WE HAVE.
THE LAND IS MINE AND YOU HAVE NEVER PUT YOUR HAND TO IT.

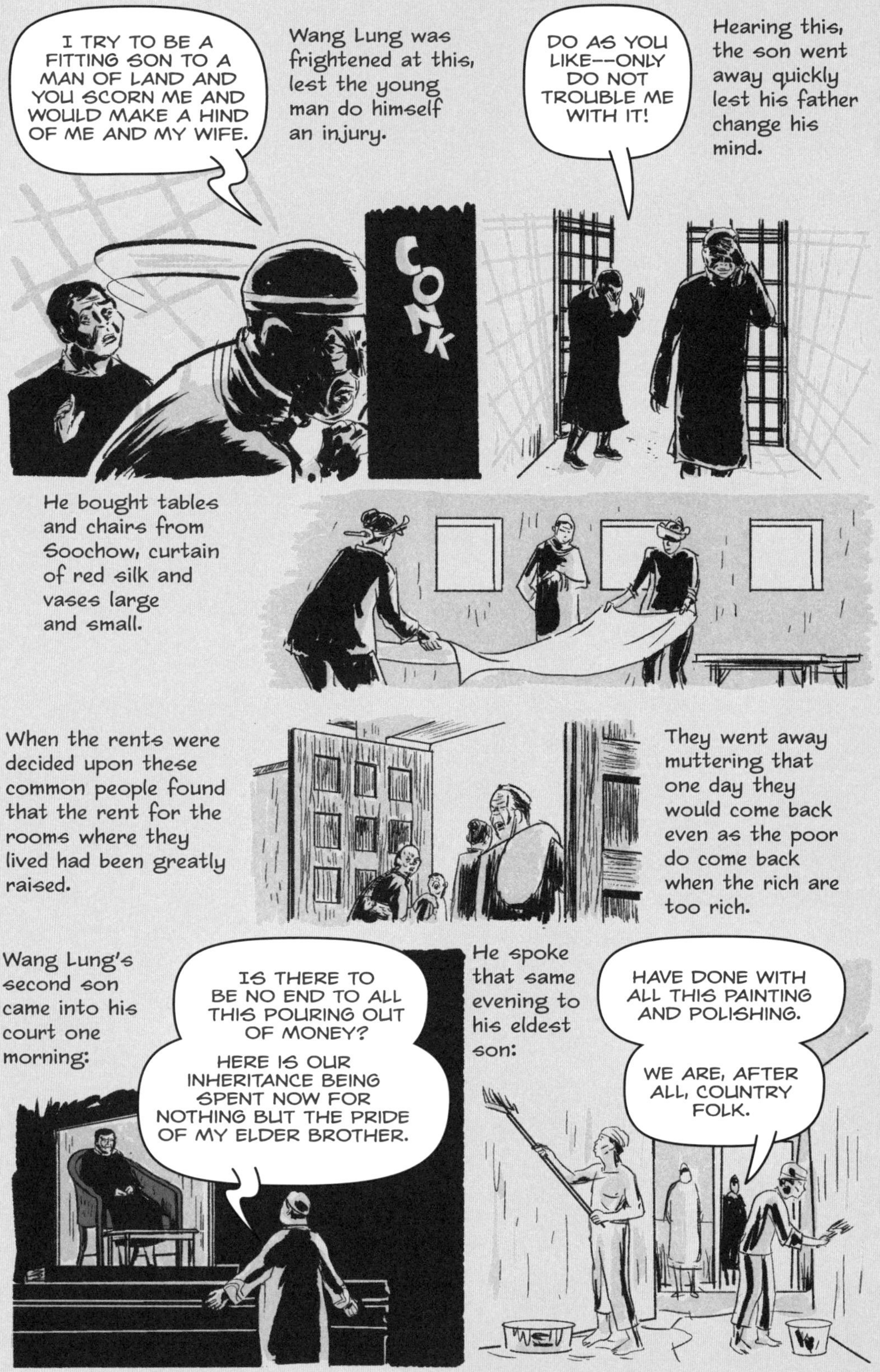
I TRY TO BE A FITTING SON TO A MAN OF LAND AND YOU SCORN ME AND WOULD MAKE A HIND OF ME AND MY WIFE.
Wang Lung was frightened at this, lest the young man do himself an injury.
CONK
DO AS YOU LIKE--ONLY DO NOT TROUBLE ME WITH IT!
Hearing this, the son went away quickly lest his father change his mind.
He bought tables and chairs from Soochow, curtain of red silk and vases large and small.
When the rents were decided upon these common people found that the rent for the rooms where they lived had been greatly raised.
They went away muttering that one day they would come back even as the poor do come back when the rich are too rich.
Wang Lung's second son came into his court one morning:
IS THERE TO BE NO END TO ALL THIS POURING OUT OF MONEY?
HERE IS OUR INHERITANCE BEING SPENT NOW FOR NOTHING BUT THE PRIDE OF MY ELDER BROTHER.
He spoke that same evening to his eldest son:
HAVE DONE WITH ALL THIS PAINTING AND POLISHING.
WE ARE, AFTER ALL, COUNTRY FOLK.

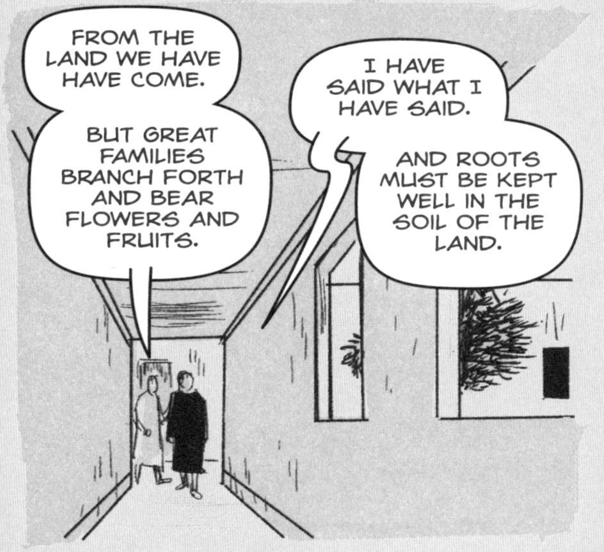
FROM THE LAND WE HAVE HAVE COME.
BUT GREAT FAMILIES BRANCH FORTH AND BEAR FLOWERS AND FRUITS.
I HAVE SAID WHAT I HAVE SAID.
AND ROOTS MUST BE KEPT WELL IN THE SOIL OF THE LAND.

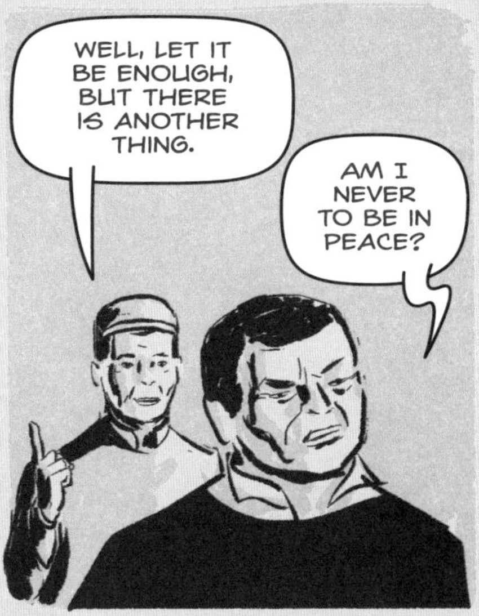
WELL, LET IT BE ENOUGH, BUT THERE IS ANOTHER THING.
AM I NEVER TO BE IN PEACE?

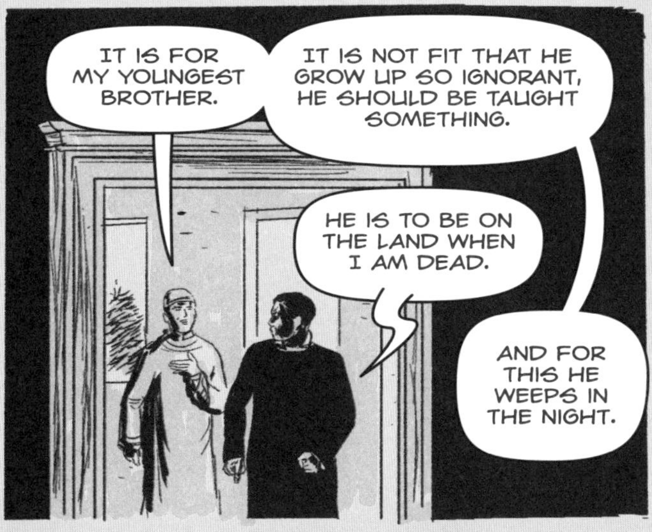
IT IS FOR MY YOUNGEST BROTHER.
IT IS NOT FIT THAT HE GROW UP SO IGNORANT, HE SHOULD BE TAUGHT SOMETHING.
HE IS TO BE ON THE LAND WHEN I AM DEAD.
AND FOR THIS HE WEEPS IN THE NIGHT.

This struck Wang Lung between the brows.

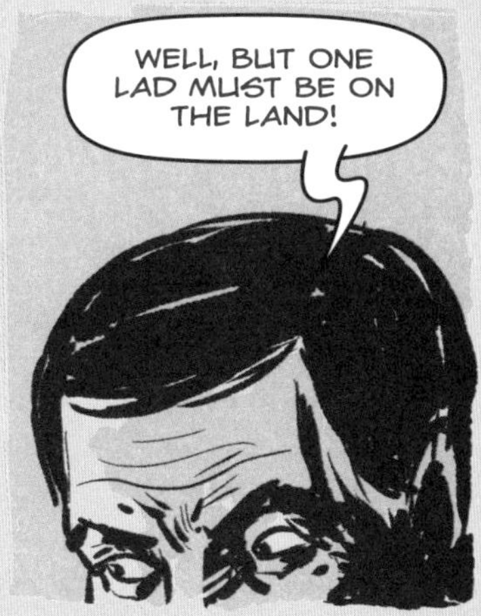
WELL, BUT ONE LAD MUST BE ON THE LAND!

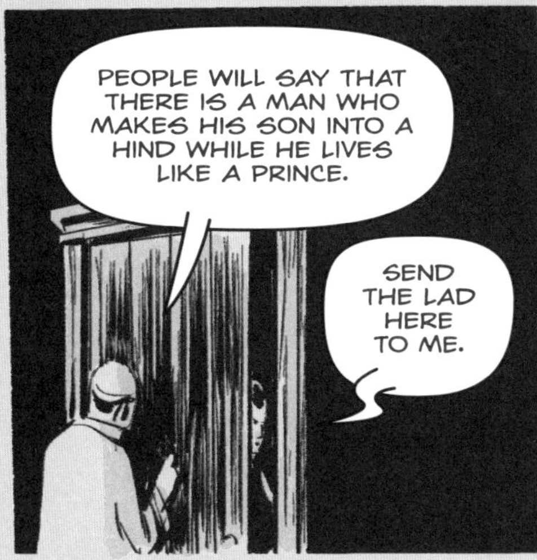
PEOPLE WILL SAY THAT THERE IS A MAN WHO MAKES HIS SON INTO A HIND WHILE HE LIVES LIKE A PRINCE.
SEND THE LAD HERE TO ME.

His third son was a lad as silent as his mother, and because he was silent none paid any attention to him.

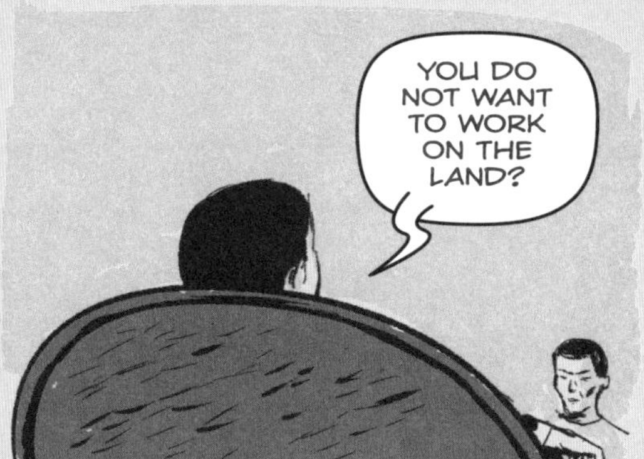
YOU DO NOT WANT TO WORK ON THE LAND?

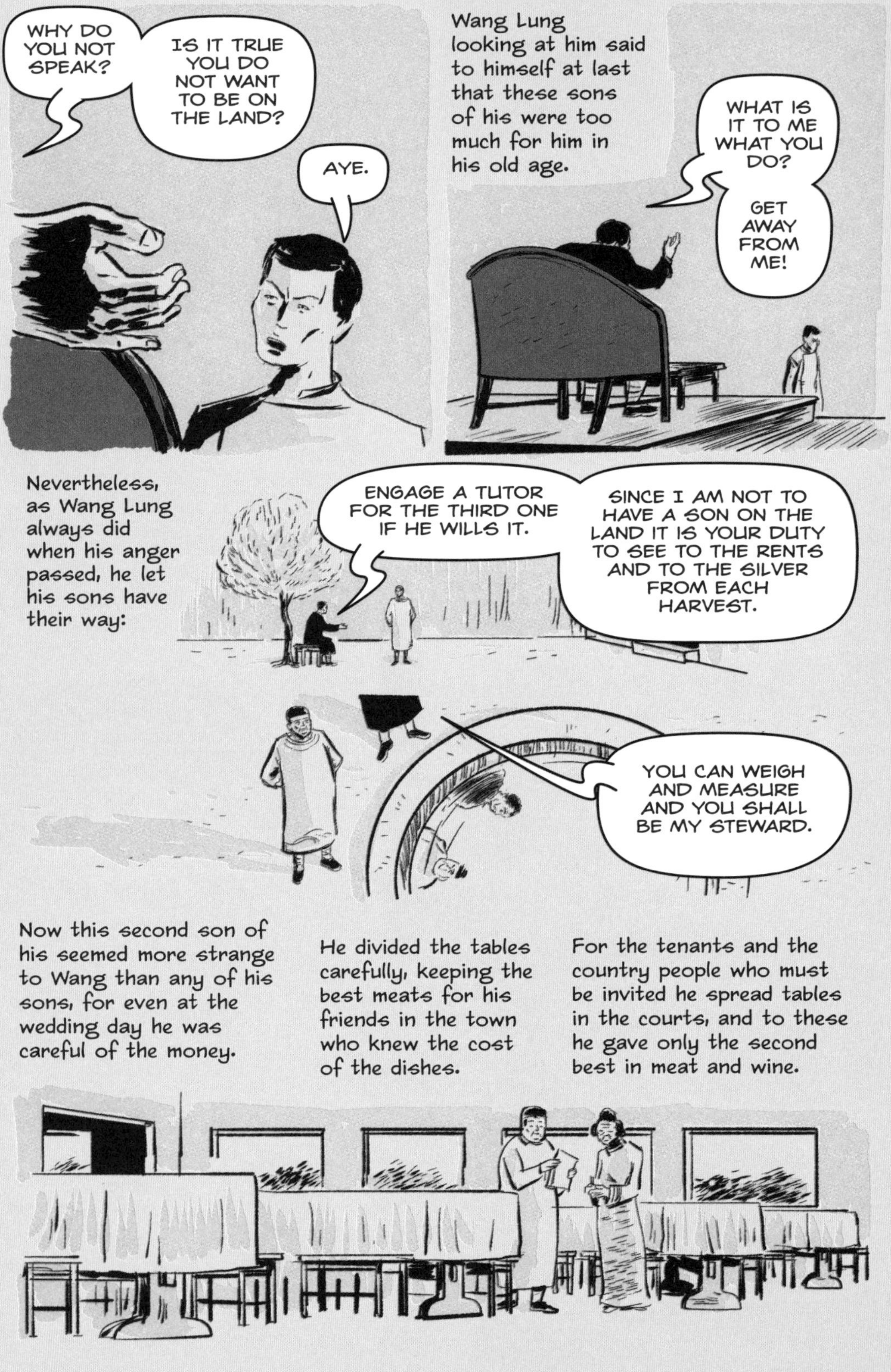
WHY DO YOU NOT SPEAK?
IS IT TRUE YOU DO NOT WANT TO BE ON THE LAND?
AYE.
Wang Lung looking at him said to himself at last that these sons of his were too much for him in his old age.
WHAT IS IT TO ME WHAT YOU DO?
GET AWAY FROM ME!
Nevertheless, as Wang Lung always did when his anger passed, he let his sons have their way:
ENGAGE A TUTOR FOR THE THIRD ONE IF HE WILLS IT.
SINCE I AM NOT TO HAVE A SON ON THE LAND IT IS YOUR DUTY TO SEE TO THE RENTS AND TO THE SILVER FROM EACH HARVEST.
YOU CAN WEIGH AND MEASURE AND YOU SHALL BE MY STEWARD.
Now this second son of his seemed more strange to Wang than any of his sons, for even at the wedding day he was careful of the money.
He divided the tables carefully, keeping the best meats for his friends in the town who knew the cost of the dishes.
For the tenants and the country people who must be invited he spread tables in the courts, and to these he gave only the second best in meat and wine.

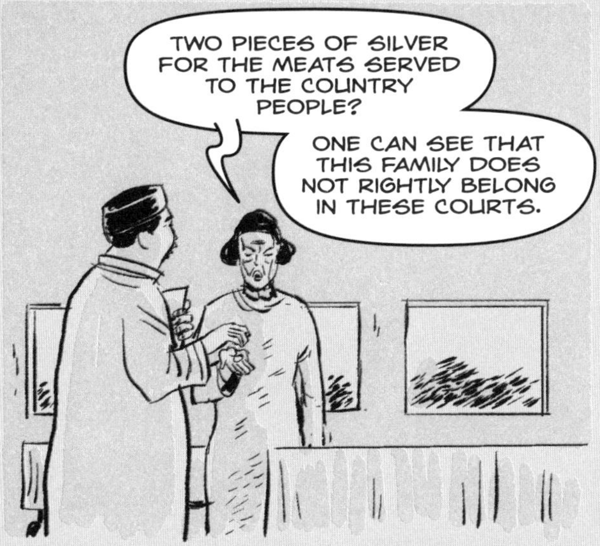
TWO PIECES OF SILVER FOR THE MEATS SERVED TO THE COUNTRY PEOPLE?
ONE CAN SEE THAT THIS FAMILY DOES NOT RIGHTLY BELONG IN THESE COURTS.

The eldest son heard this, and he was ashamed and he gave her more silver secretly and he was angry with his second brother.

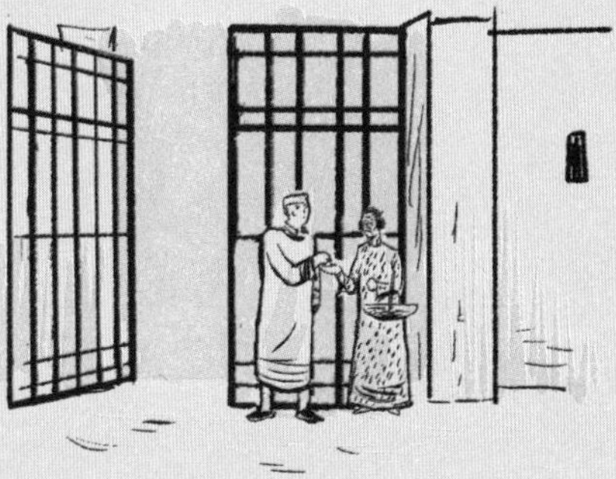

Now of all of them who lived in these courts there was none wholly at peace and comfortable there except the small grandson.

And from this one did Wang Lung secure peace, and he could never have enough of watching him.

He remembered also what his own father had done, and he delighted to take a girdle and put it about the child.

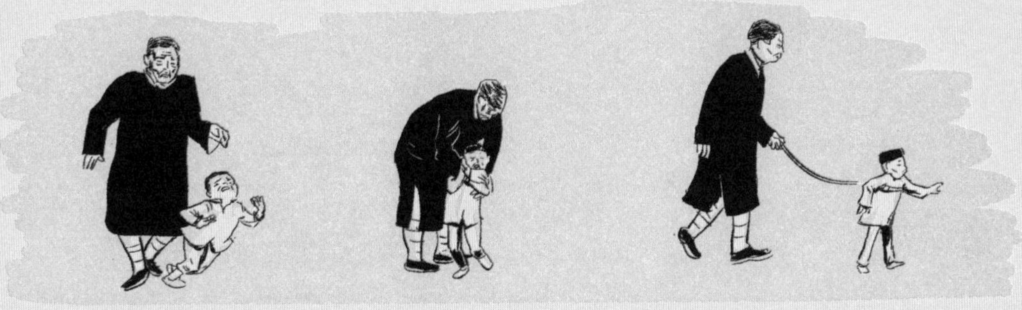

In the space of five years, Wang Lung had four grandsons and three granddaughters and the courts were filled with their laughter and their weeping.

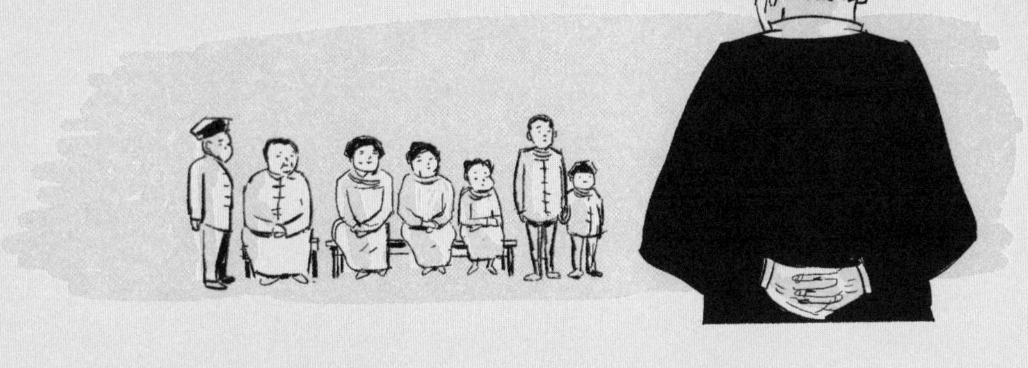

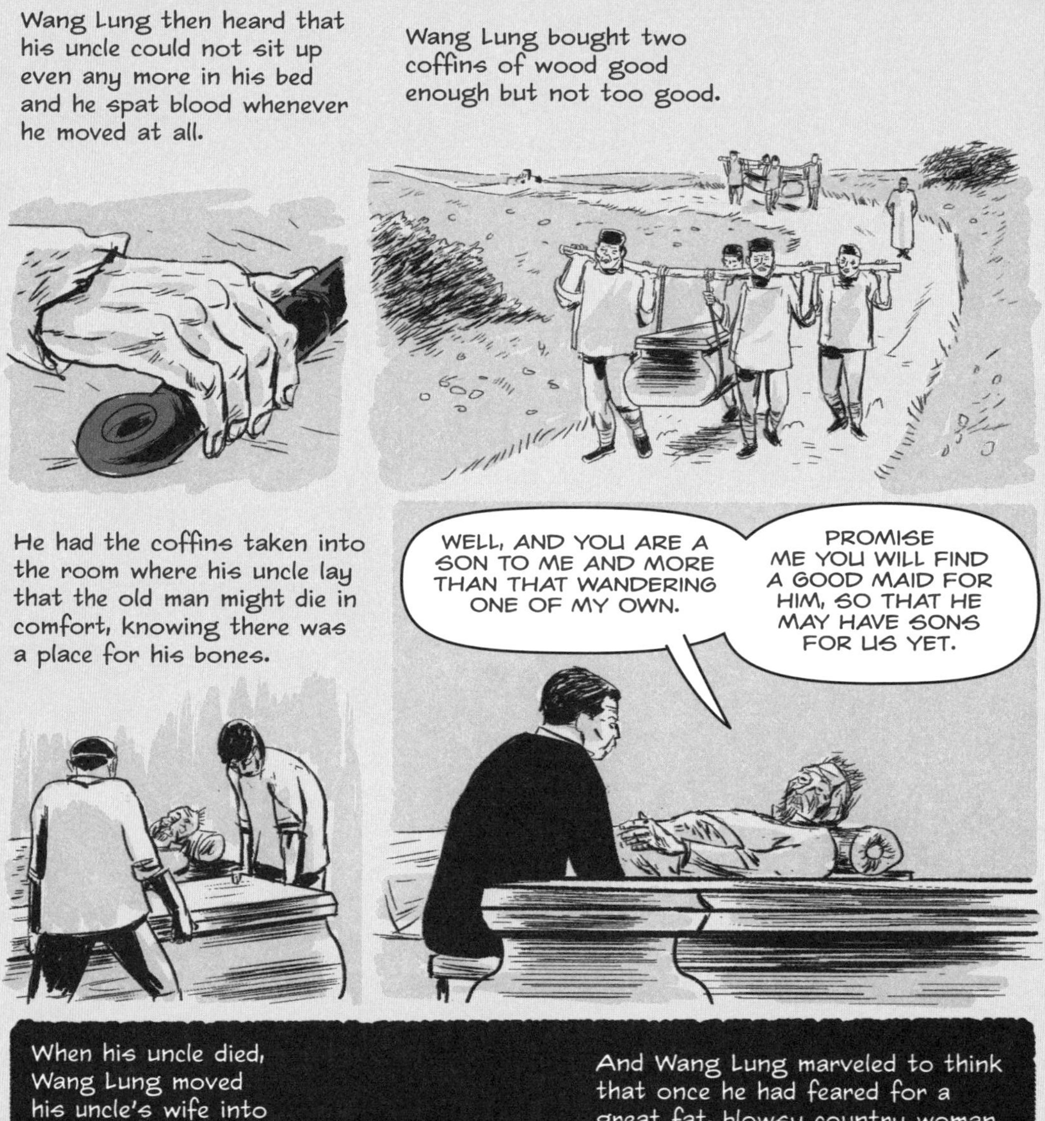

Wang Lung then heard that his uncle could not sit up even any more in his bed and he spat blood whenever he moved at all.

Wang Lung bought two coffins of wood good enough but not too good.

He had the coffins taken into the room where his uncle lay that the old man might die in comfort, knowing there was a place for his bones.

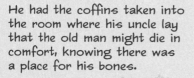

WELL, AND YOU ARE A SON TO ME AND MORE THAN THAT WANDERING ONE OF MY OWN.

PROMISE ME YOU WILL FIND A GOOD MAID FOR HIM, SO THAT HE MAY HAVE SONS FOR US YET.

When his uncle died, Wang Lung moved his uncle's wife into the town and he told Cuckoo to supervise a slave in the care of her.

And Wang Lung marveled to think that once he had feared for a great fat, blowsy country woman, idle and loud, she who lay there now, shriveled and silent as the Old Mistress had been in the fallen House of Hwang.

8

Now and again Wang Lung heard men say:

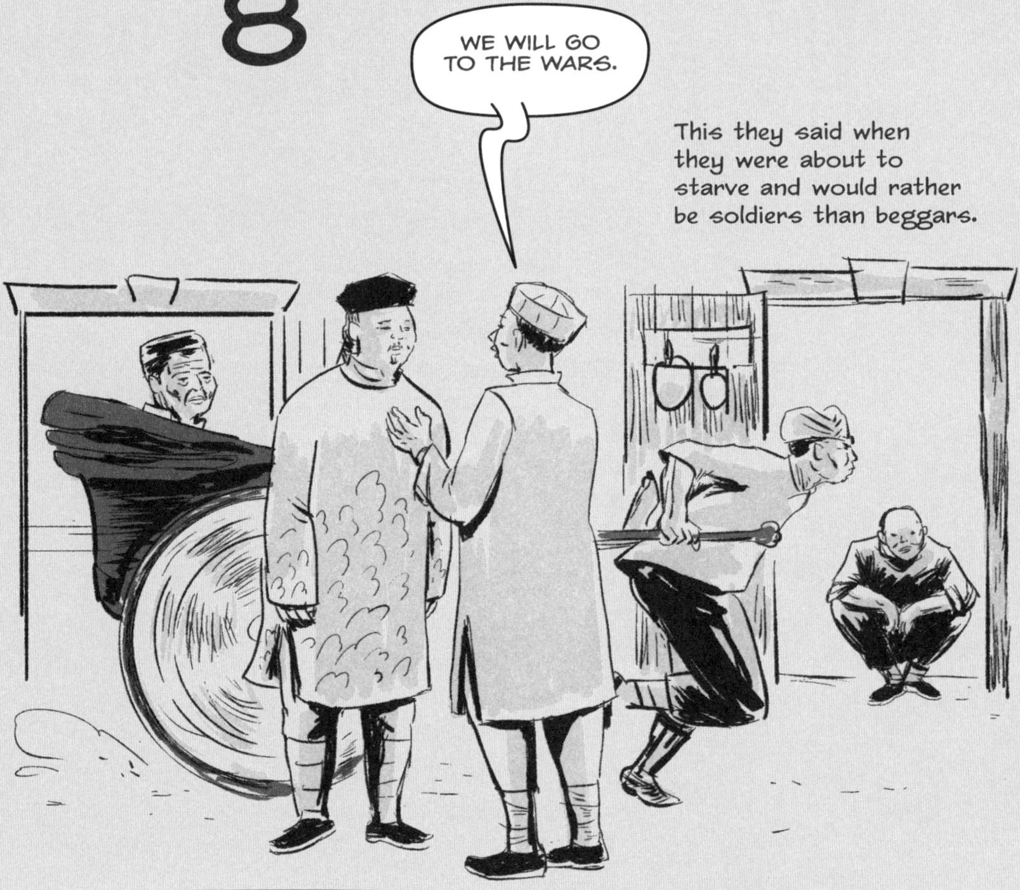
WE WILL GO TO THE WARS.

This they said when they were about to starve and would rather be soldiers than beggars.

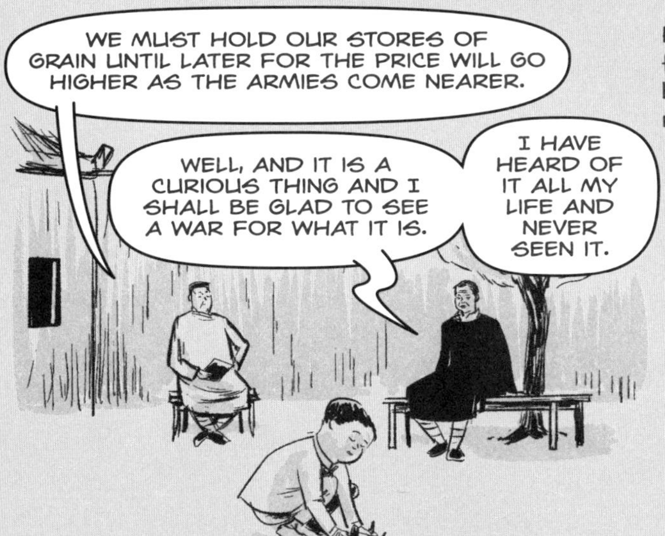
WE MUST HOLD OUR STORES OF GRAIN UNTIL LATER FOR THE PRICE WILL GO HIGHER AS THE ARMIES COME NEARER.
WELL, AND IT IS A CURIOUS THING AND I SHALL BE GLAD TO SEE A WAR FOR WHAT IT IS.
I HAVE HEARD OF IT ALL MY LIFE AND NEVER SEEN IT.

He was too old to be seized for an army's use and besides he was rich and the rich need not fear anything.

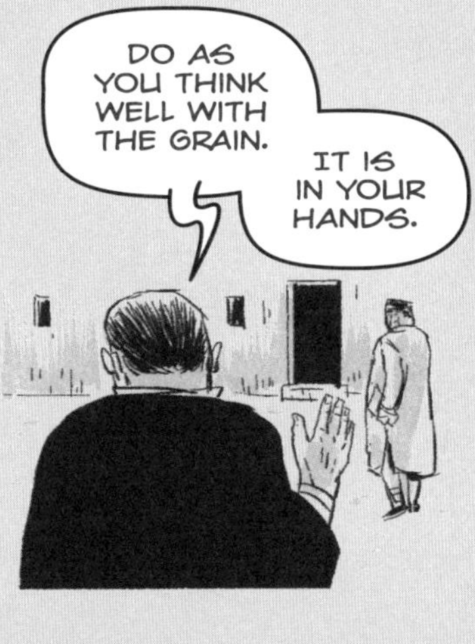
DO AS YOU THINK WELL WITH THE GRAIN.
IT IS IN YOUR HANDS.

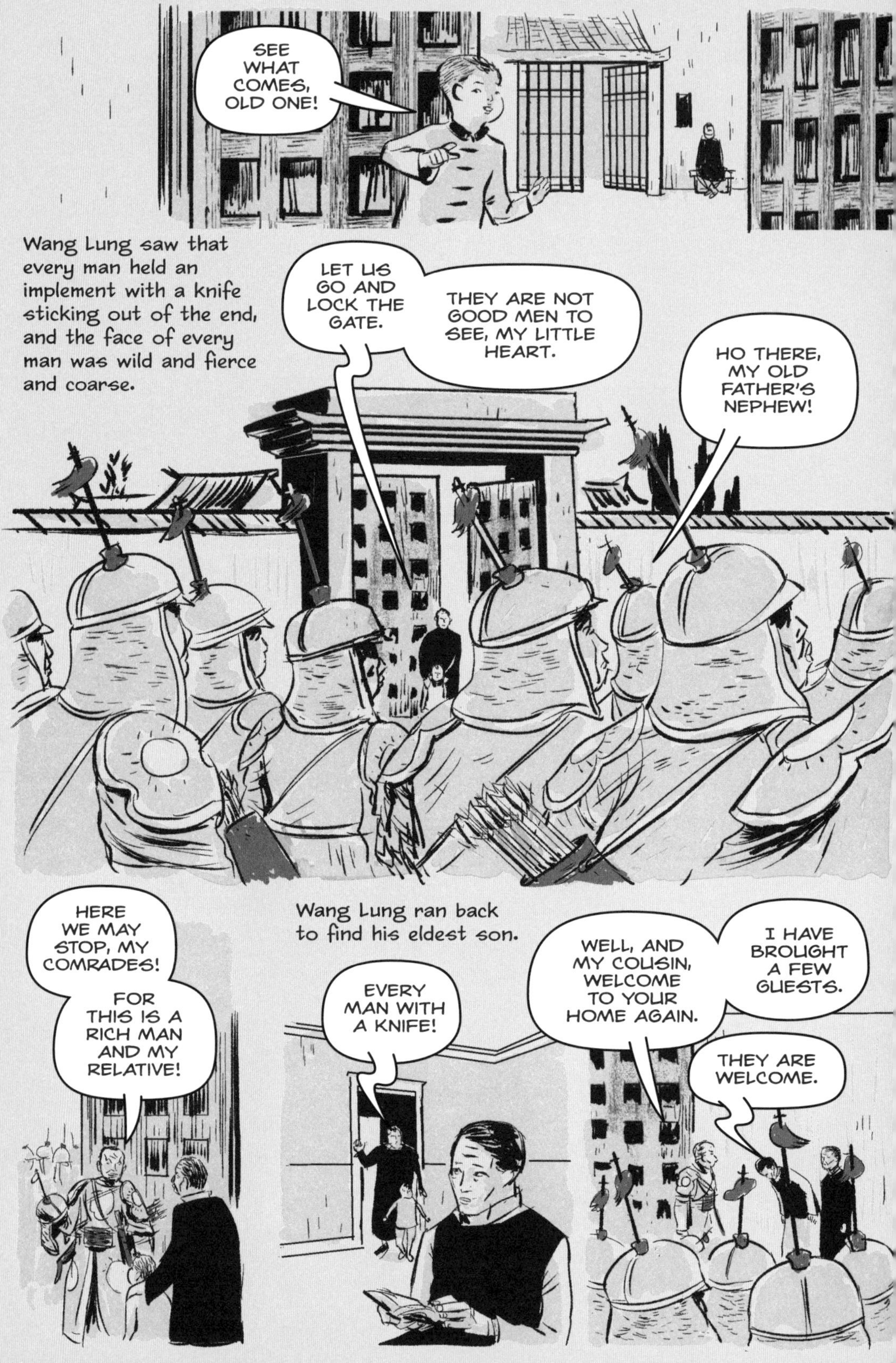
SEE WHAT COMES, OLD ONE!
Wang Lung saw that every man held an implement with a knife sticking out of the end, and the face of every man was wild and fierce and coarse.
LET US GO AND LOCK THE GATE.
THEY ARE NOT GOOD MEN TO SEE, MY LITTLE HEART.
HO THERE, MY OLD FATHER'S NEPHEW!
HERE WE MAY STOP, MY COMRADES!
FOR THIS IS A RICH MAN AND MY RELATIVE!
Wang Lung ran back to find his eldest son.
EVERY MAN WITH A KNIFE!
WELL, AND MY COUSIN, WELCOME TO YOUR HOME AGAIN.
I HAVE BROUGHT A FEW GUESTS.
THEY ARE WELCOME.

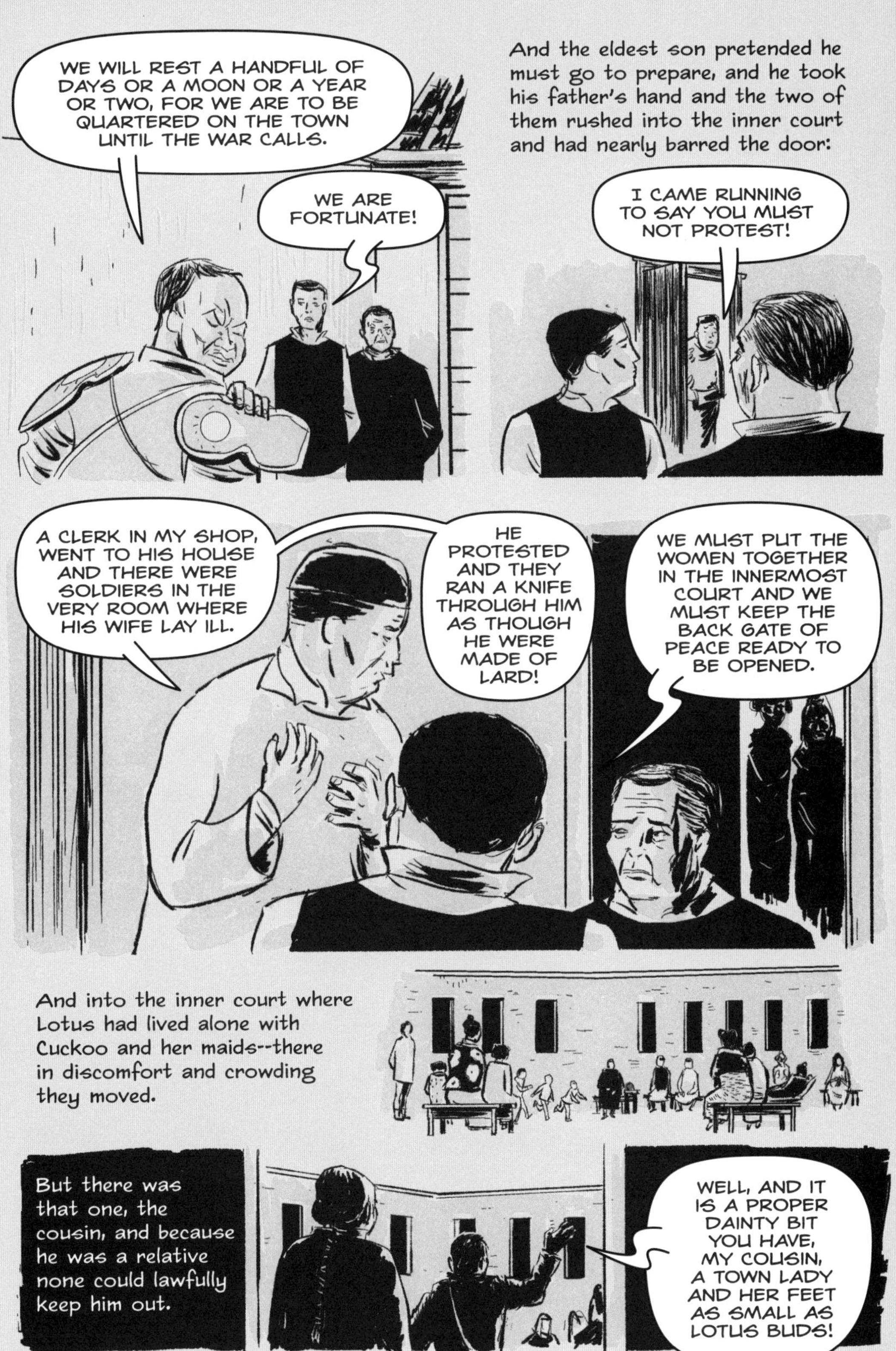
WE WILL REST A HANDFUL OF DAYS OR A MOON OR A YEAR OR TWO, FOR WE ARE TO BE QUARTERED ON THE TOWN UNTIL THE WAR CALLS.
WE ARE FORTUNATE!
And the eldest son pretended he must go to prepare, and he took his father's hand and the two of them rushed into the inner court and had nearly barred the door:
I CAME RUNNING TO SAY YOU MUST NOT PROTEST!
A CLERK IN MY SHOP, WENT TO HIS HOUSE AND THERE WERE SOLDIERS IN THE VERY ROOM WHERE HIS WIFE LAY ILL.
HE PROTESTED AND THEY RAN A KNIFE THROUGH HIM AS THOUGH HE WERE MADE OF LARD!
WE MUST PUT THE WOMEN TOGETHER IN THE INNERMOST COURT AND WE MUST KEEP THE BACK GATE OF PEACE READY TO BE OPENED.
And into the inner court where Lotus had lived alone with Cuckoo and her maids--there in discomfort and crowding they moved.
But there was that one, the cousin, and because he was a relative none could lawfully keep him out.
WELL, AND IT IS A PROPER DAINTY BIT YOU HAVE, MY COUSIN, A TOWN LADY AND HER FEET AS SMALL AS LOTUS BUDS!

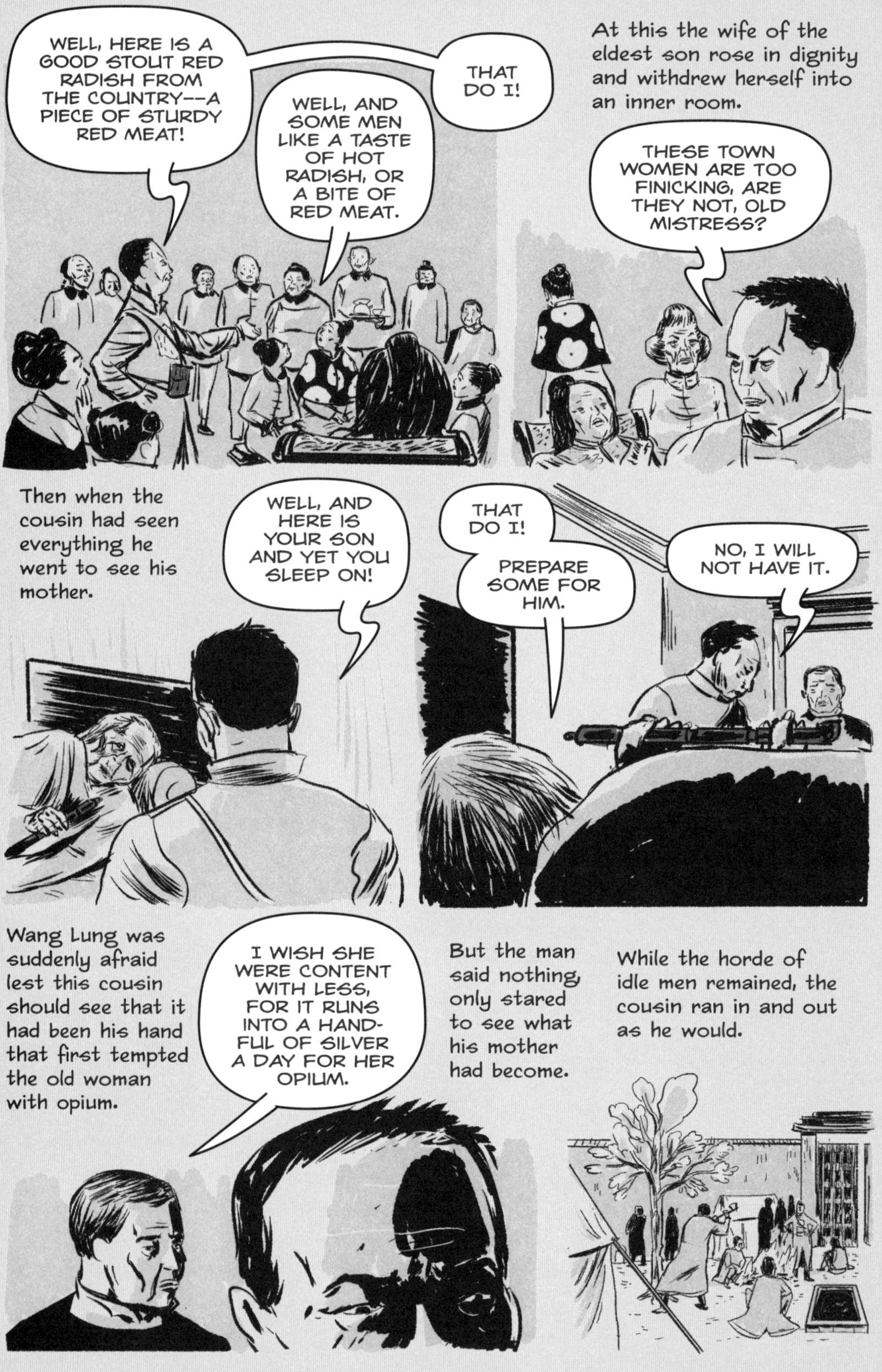
WELL, HERE IS A GOOD STOUT RED RADISH FROM THE COUNTRY--A PIECE OF STURDY RED MEAT!
WELL, AND SOME MEN LIKE A TASTE OF HOT RADISH, OR A BITE OF RED MEAT.
THAT DO I!
At this the wife of the eldest son rose in dignity and withdrew herself into an inner room.
THESE TOWN WOMEN ARE TOO FINICKING, ARE THEY NOT, OLD MISTRESS?
Then when the cousin had seen everything he went to see his mother.
WELL, AND HERE IS YOUR SON AND YET YOU SLEEP ON!
THAT DO I!
PREPARE SOME FOR HIM.
NO, I WILL NOT HAVE IT.
Wang Lung was suddenly afraid lest this cousin should see that it had been his hand that first tempted the old woman with opium.
I WISH SHE WERE CONTENT WITH LESS, FOR IT RUNS INTO A HAND-FUL OF SILVER A DAY FOR HER OPIUM.
But the man said nothing, only stared to see what his mother had become.
While the horde of idle men remained, the cousin ran in and out as he would.

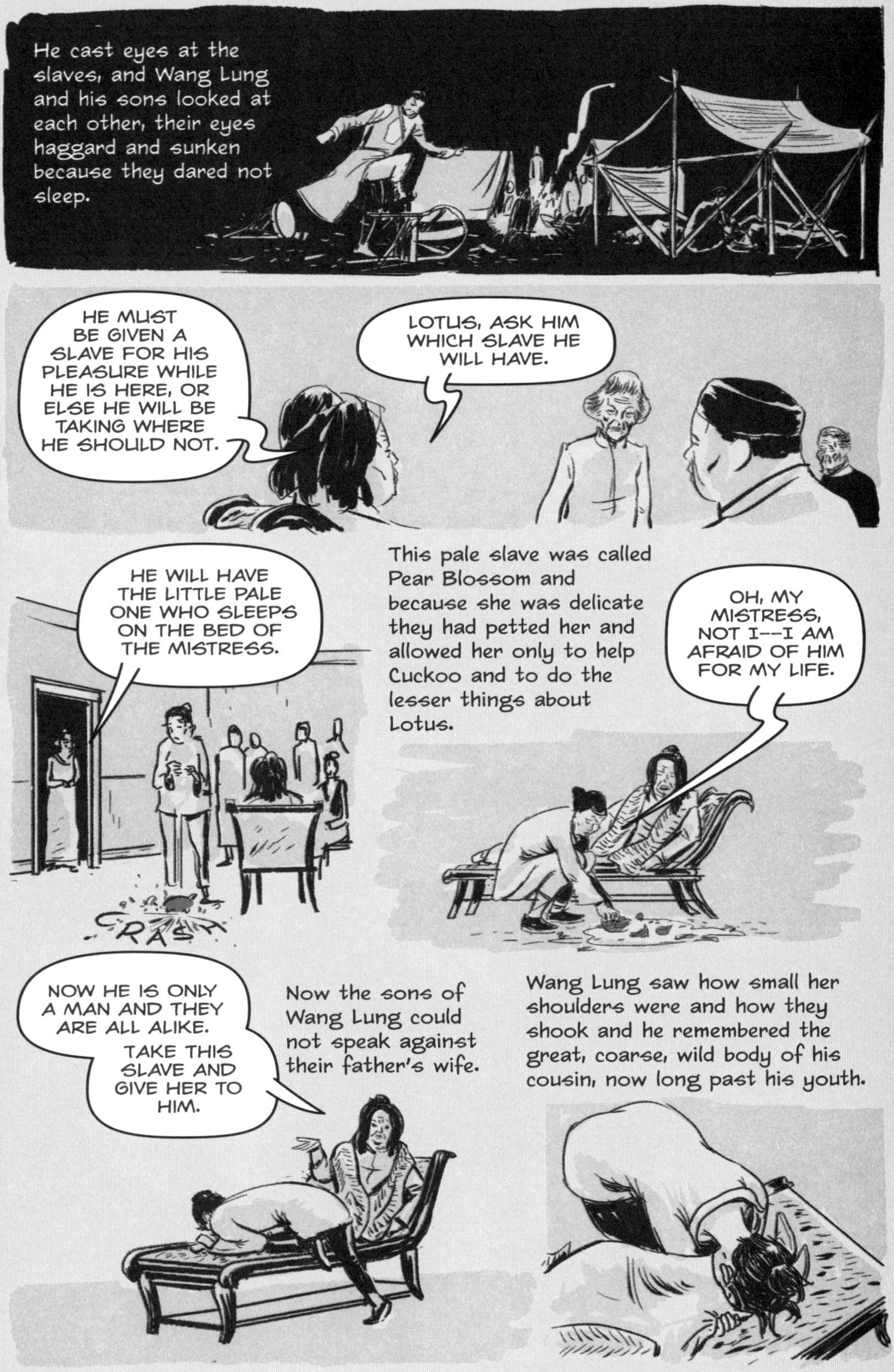
He cast eyes at the slaves, and Wang Lung and his sons looked at each other, their eyes haggard and sunken because they dared not sleep.
HE MUST BE GIVEN A SLAVE FOR HIS PLEASURE WHILE HE IS HERE, OR ELSE HE WILL BE TAKING WHERE HE SHOULD NOT.
LOTUS, ASK HIM WHICH SLAVE HE WILL HAVE.
HE WILL HAVE THE LITTLE PALE ONE WHO SLEEPS ON THE BED OF THE MISTRESS.
CRASH
This pale slave was called Pear Blossom and because she was delicate they had petted her and allowed her only to help Cuckoo and to do the lesser things about Lotus.
OH, MY MISTRESS, NOT I--I AM AFRAID OF HIM FOR MY LIFE.
NOW HE IS ONLY A MAN AND THEY ARE ALL ALIKE.
TAKE THIS SLAVE AND GIVE HER TO HIM.
Now the sons of Wang Lung could not speak against their father's wife.
Wang Lung saw how small her shoulders were and how they shook and he remembered the great, coarse, wild body of his cousin, now long past his youth.

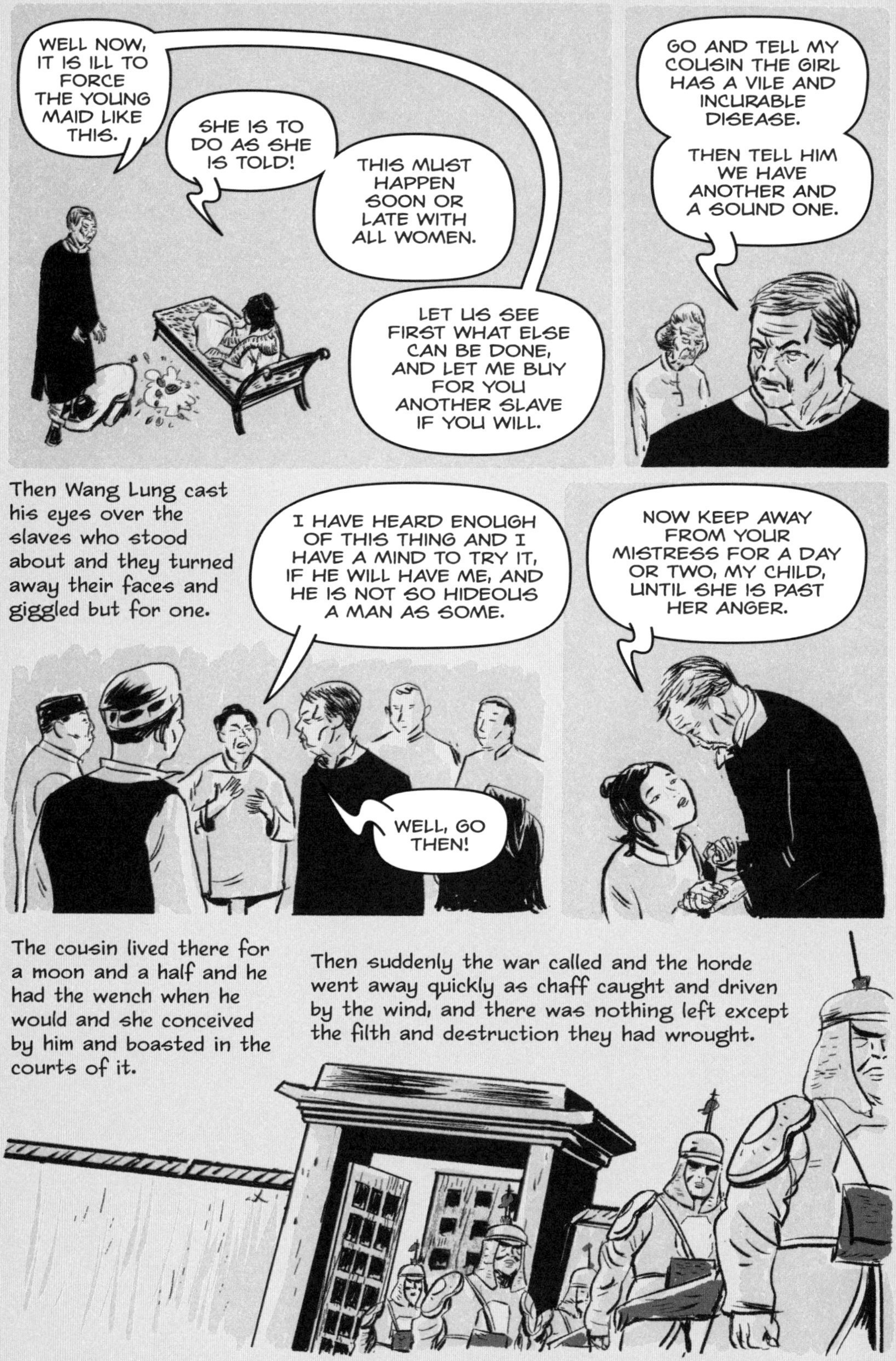
WELL NOW, IT IS ILL TO FORCE THE YOUNG MAID LIKE THIS.
SHE IS TO DO AS SHE IS TOLD!
THIS MUST HAPPEN SOON OR LATE WITH ALL WOMEN.
LET US SEE FIRST WHAT ELSE CAN BE DONE, AND LET ME BUY FOR YOU ANOTHER SLAVE IF YOU WILL.
GO AND TELL MY COUSIN THE GIRL HAS A VILE AND INCURABLE DISEASE.
THEN TELL HIM WE HAVE ANOTHER AND A SOUND ONE.
Then Wang Lung cast his eyes over the slaves who stood about and they turned away their faces and giggled but for one.
I HAVE HEARD ENOUGH OF THIS THING AND I HAVE A MIND TO TRY IT, IF HE WILL HAVE ME, AND HE IS NOT SO HIDEOUS A MAN AS SOME.
WELL, GO THEN!
NOW KEEP AWAY FROM YOUR MISTRESS FOR A DAY OR TWO, MY CHILD, UNTIL SHE IS PAST HER ANGER.
The cousin lived there for a moon and a half and he had the wench when he would and she conceived by him and boasted in the courts of it.
Then suddenly the war called and the horde went away quickly as chaff caught and driven by the wind, and there was nothing left except the filth and destruction they had wrought.

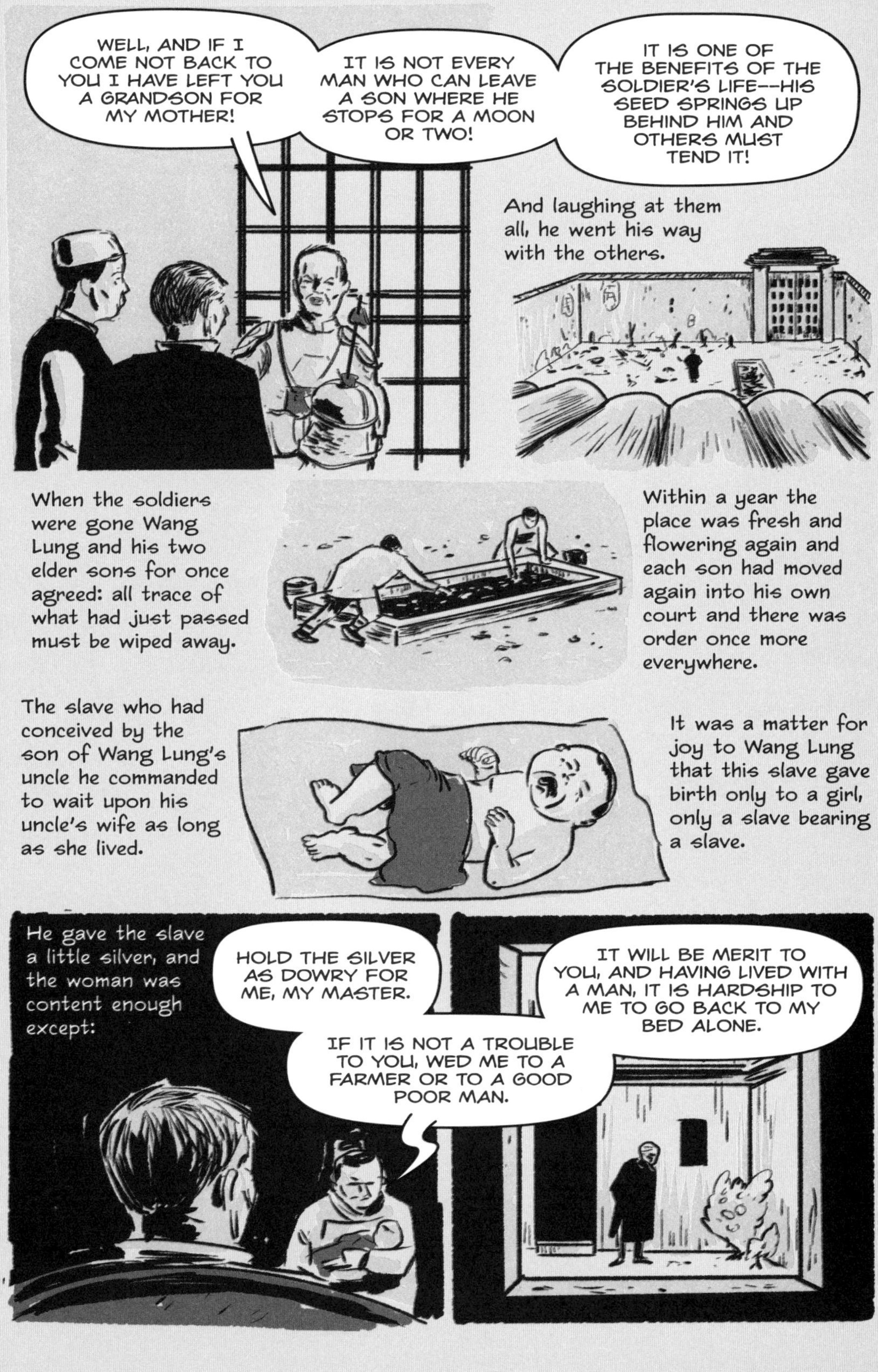

WELL, AND IF I COME NOT BACK TO YOU I HAVE LEFT YOU A GRANDSON FOR MY MOTHER!
IT IS NOT EVERY MAN WHO CAN LEAVE A SON WHERE HE STOPS FOR A MOON OR TWO!
IT IS ONE OF THE BENEFITS OF THE SOLDIER'S LIFE--HIS SEED SPRINGS UP BEHIND HIM AND OTHERS MUST TEND IT!
And laughing at them all, he went his way with the others.
When the soldiers were gone Wang Lung and his two elder sons for once agreed: all trace of what had just passed must be wiped away.
Within a year the place was fresh and flowering again and each son had moved again into his own court and there was order once more everywhere.
The slave who had conceived by the son of Wang Lung's uncle he commanded to wait upon his uncle's wife as long as she lived.
It was a matter for joy to Wang Lung that this slave gave birth only to a girl, only a slave bearing a slave.
He gave the slave a little silver, and the woman was content enough except:
HOLD THE SILVER AS DOWRY FOR ME, MY MASTER.
IF IT IS NOT A TROUBLE TO YOU, WED ME TO A FARMER OR TO A GOOD POOR MAN.
IT WILL BE MERIT TO YOU, AND HAVING LIVED WITH A MAN, IT IS HARDSHIP TO ME TO GO BACK TO MY BED ALONE.

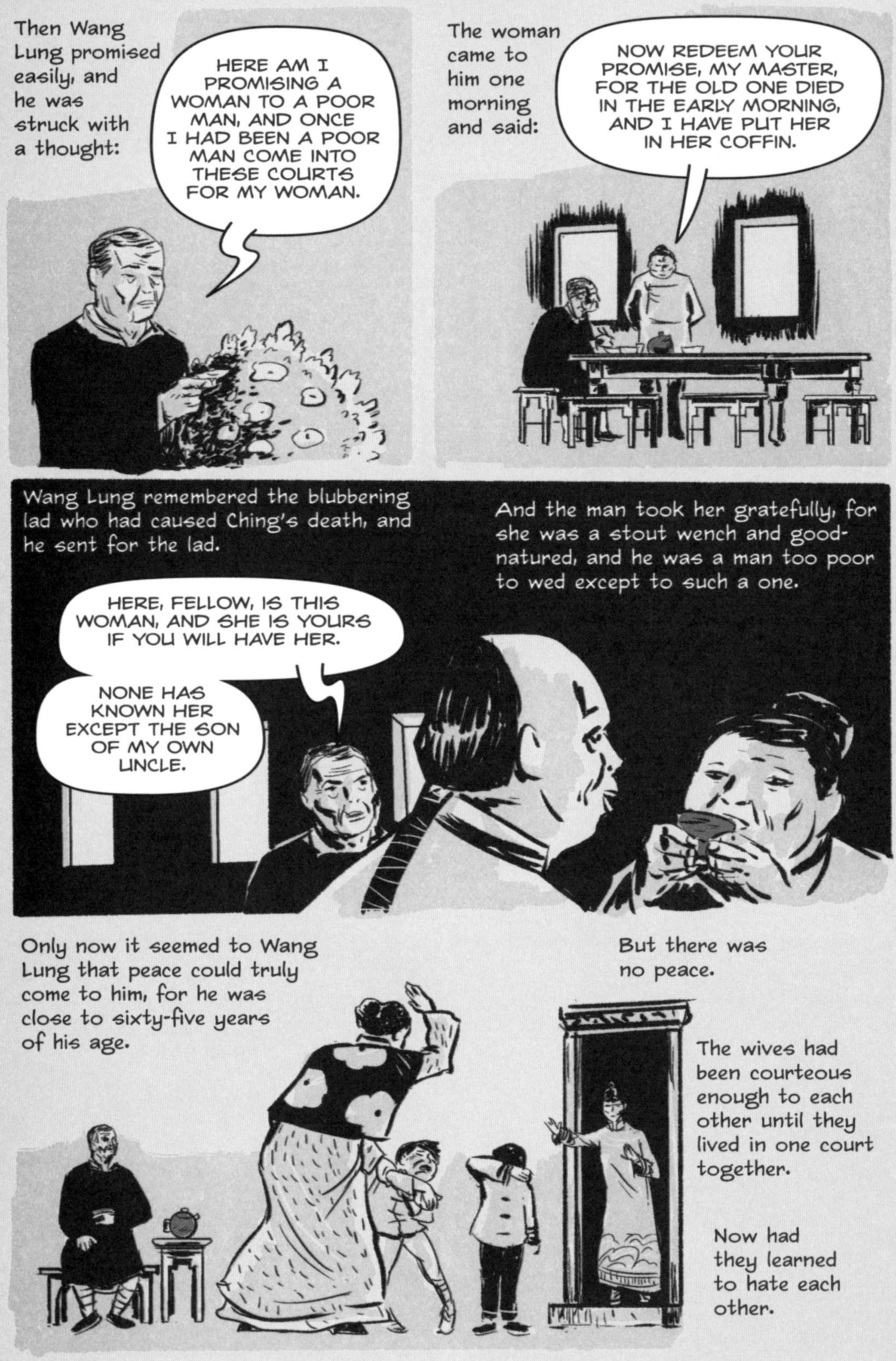

Then Wang Lung promised easily, and he was struck with a thought:
HERE AM I PROMISING A WOMAN TO A POOR MAN, AND ONCE I HAD BEEN A POOR MAN COME INTO THESE COURTS FOR MY WOMAN.
The woman came to him one morning and said:
NOW REDEEM YOUR PROMISE, MY MASTER, FOR THE OLD ONE DIED IN THE EARLY MORNING, AND I HAVE PUT HER IN HER COFFIN.
Wang Lung remembered the blubbering lad who had caused Ching's death, and he sent for the lad.
HERE, FELLOW, IS THIS WOMAN, AND SHE IS YOURS IF YOU WILL HAVE HER.
NONE HAS KNOWN HER EXCEPT THE SON OF MY OWN UNCLE.
And the man took her gratefully, for she was a stout wench and good-natured, and he was a man too poor to wed except to such a one.
Only now it seemed to Wang Lung that peace could truly come to him, for he was close to sixty-five years of his age.
But there was no peace.
The wives had been courteous enough to each other until they lived in one court together.
Now had they learned to hate each other.

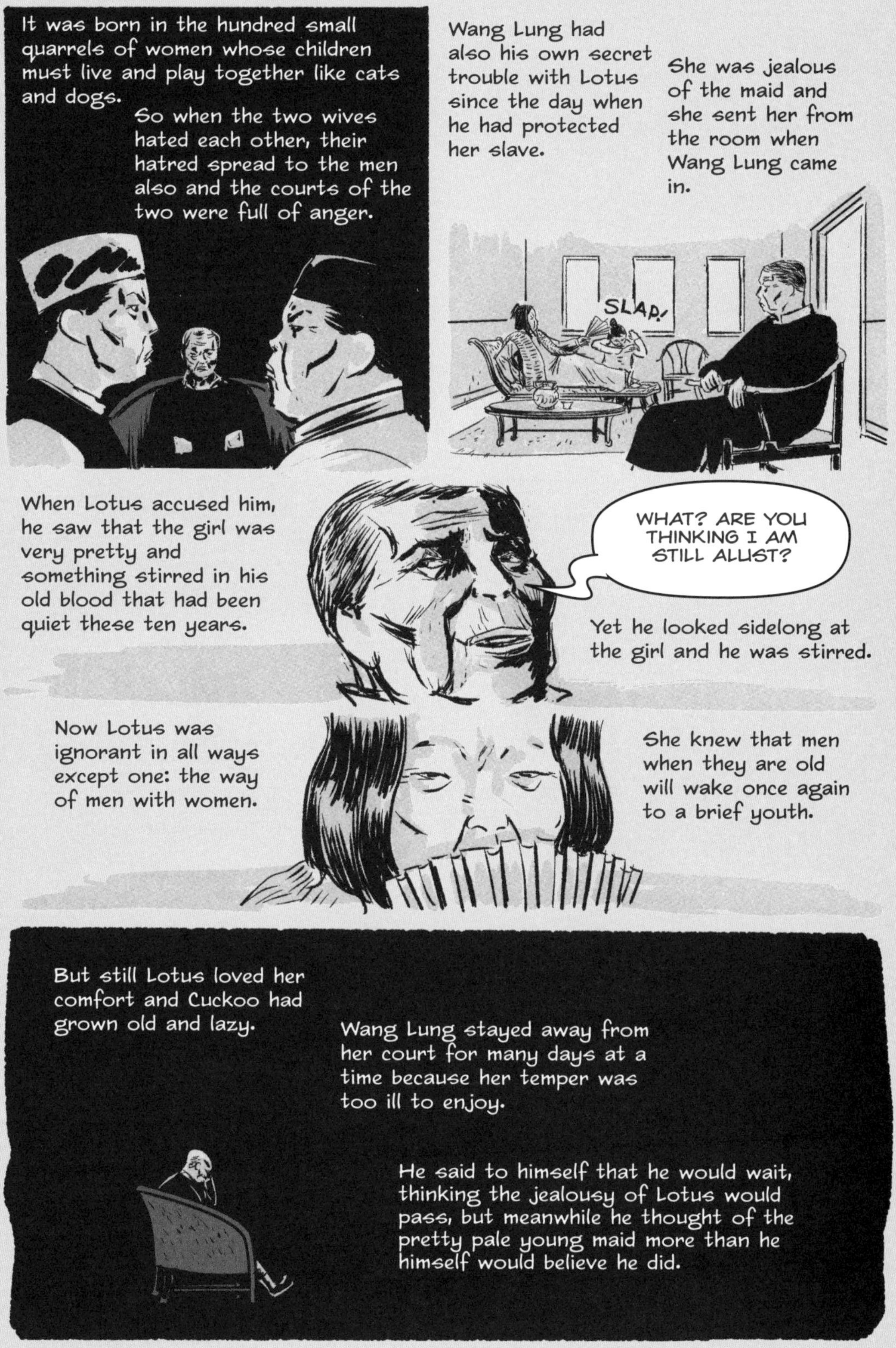
It was born in the hundred small quarrels of women whose children must live and play together like cats and dogs.
So when the two wives hated each other, their hatred spread to the men also and the courts of the two were full of anger.
Wang Lung had also his own secret trouble with Lotus since the day when he had protected her slave.
She was jealous of the maid and she sent her from the room when Wang Lung came in.
SLAP!
When Lotus accused him, he saw that the girl was very pretty and something stirred in his old blood that had been quiet these ten years.
WHAT? ARE YOU THINKING I AM STILL ALUST?
Yet he looked sidelong at the girl and he was stirred.
Now Lotus was ignorant in all ways except one: the way of men with women.
She knew that men when they are old will wake once again to a brief youth.
But still Lotus loved her comfort and Cuckoo had grown old and lazy.
Wang Lung stayed away from her court for many days at a time because her temper was too ill to enjoy.
He said to himself that he would wait, thinking the jealousy of Lotus would pass, but meanwhile he thought of the pretty pale young maid more than he himself would believe he did.

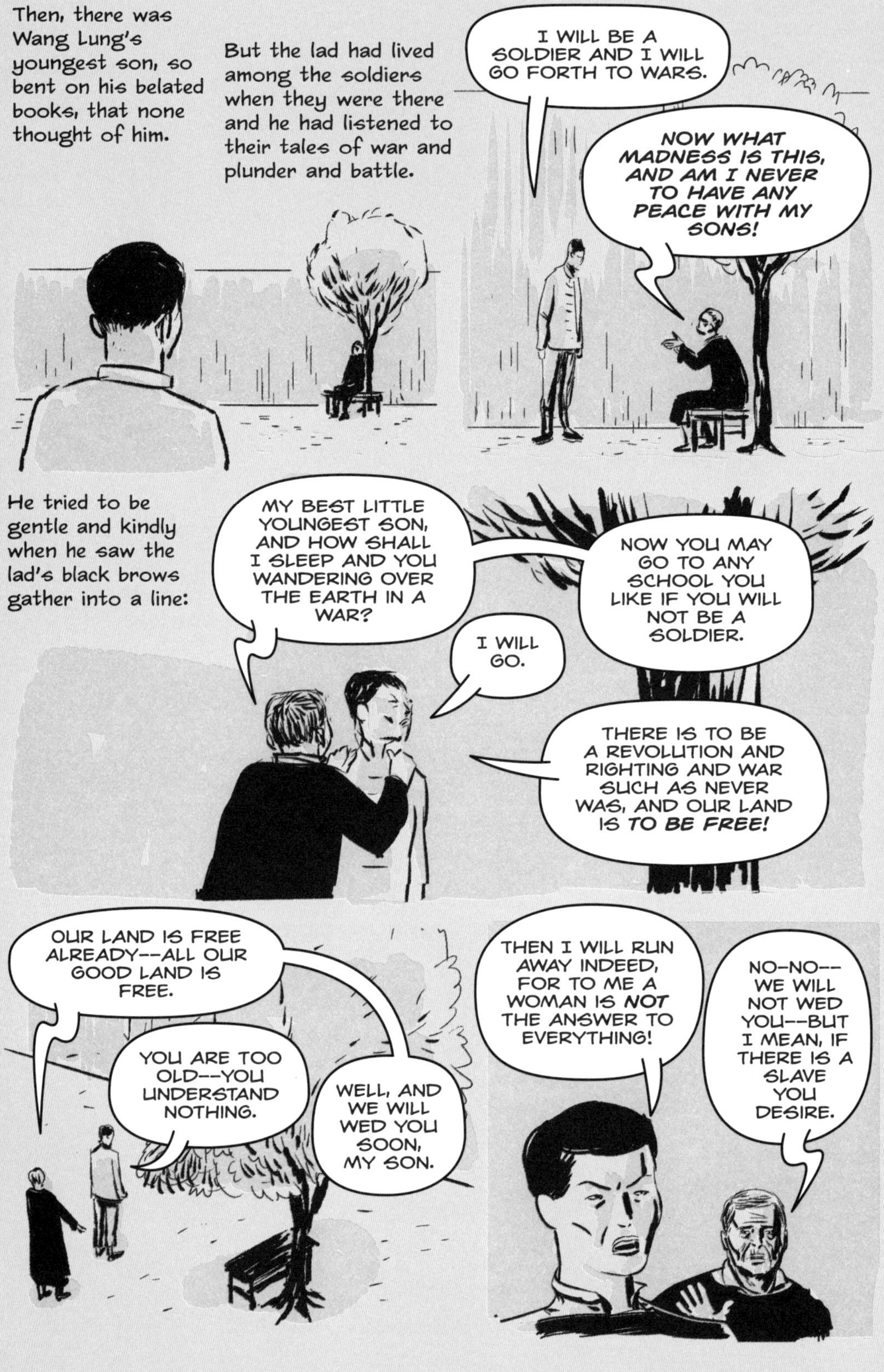
Then, there was Wang Lung's youngest son, so bent on his belated books, that none thought of him.
But the lad had lived among the soldiers when they were there and he had listened to their tales of war and plunder and battle.
I WILL BE A SOLDIER AND I WILL GO FORTH TO WARS.
NOW WHAT MADNESS IS THIS, AND AM I NEVER TO HAVE ANY PEACE WITH MY SONS!
He tried to be gentle and kindly when he saw the lad's black brows gather into a line:
MY BEST LITTLE YOUNGEST SON, AND HOW SHALL I SLEEP AND YOU WANDERING OVER THE EARTH IN A WAR?
NOW YOU MAY GO TO ANY SCHOOL YOU LIKE IF YOU WILL NOT BE A SOLDIER.
I WILL GO.
THERE IS TO BE A REVOLUTION AND RIGHTING AND WAR SUCH AS NEVER WAS, AND OUR LAND IS *TO BE FREE!*
OUR LAND IS FREE ALREADY--ALL OUR GOOD LAND IS FREE.
YOU ARE TOO OLD--YOU UNDERSTAND NOTHING.
WELL, AND WE WILL WED YOU SOON, MY SON.
THEN I WILL RUN AWAY INDEED, FOR TO ME A WOMAN IS *NOT* THE ANSWER TO EVERYTHING!
NO-NO--WE WILL NOT WED YOU--BUT I MEAN, IF THERE IS A SLAVE YOU DESIRE.

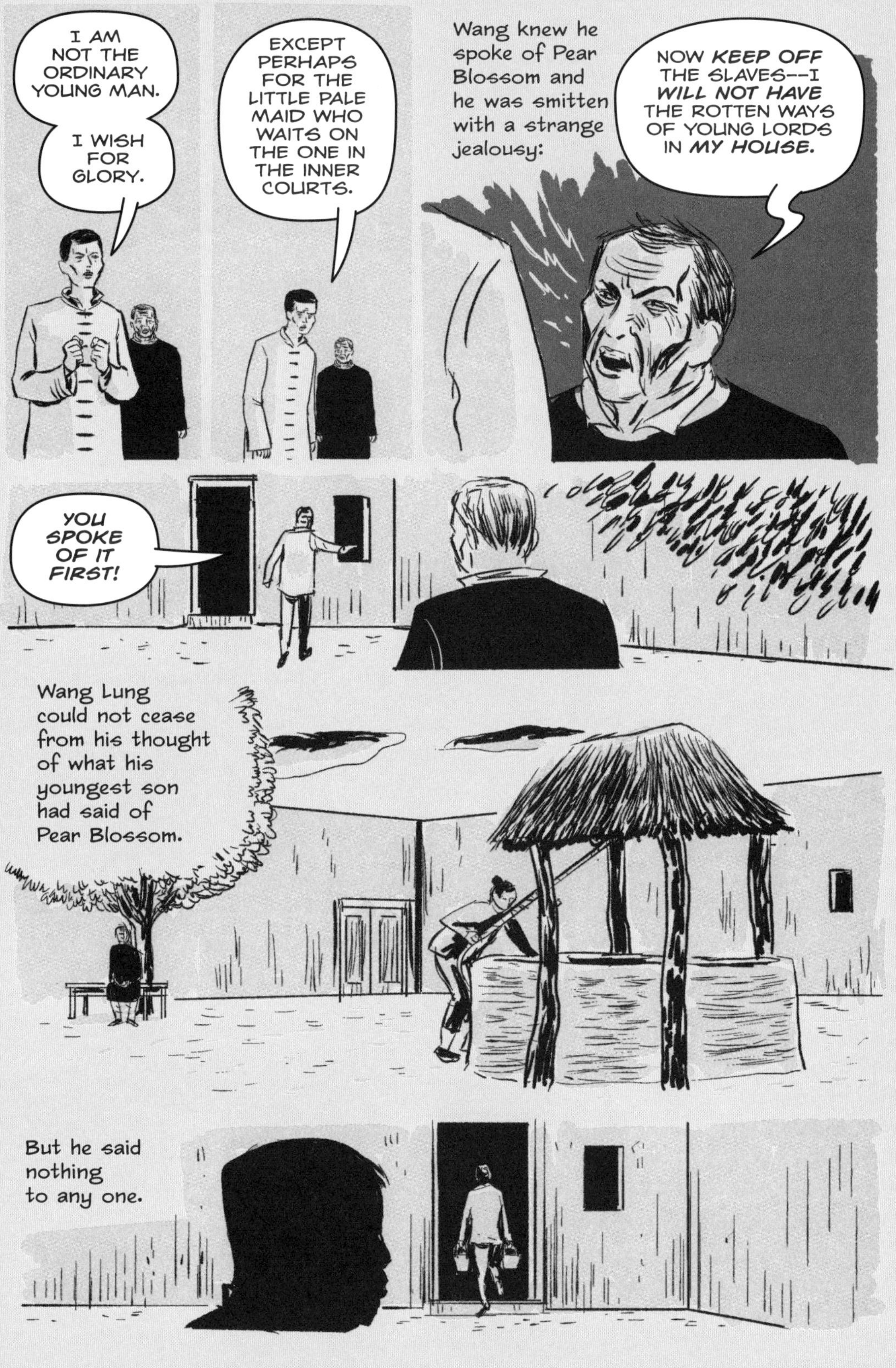
I AM NOT THE ORDINARY YOUNG MAN.
I WISH FOR GLORY.
EXCEPT PERHAPS FOR THE LITTLE PALE MAID WHO WAITS ON THE ONE IN THE INNER COURTS.
Wang knew he spoke of Pear Blossom and he was smitten with a strange jealousy:
NOW KEEP OFF THE SLAVES--I WILL NOT HAVE THE ROTTEN WAYS OF YOUNG LORDS IN MY HOUSE.
YOU SPOKE OF IT FIRST!
Wang Lung could not cease from his thought of what his youngest son had said of Pear Blossom.
But he said nothing to any one.

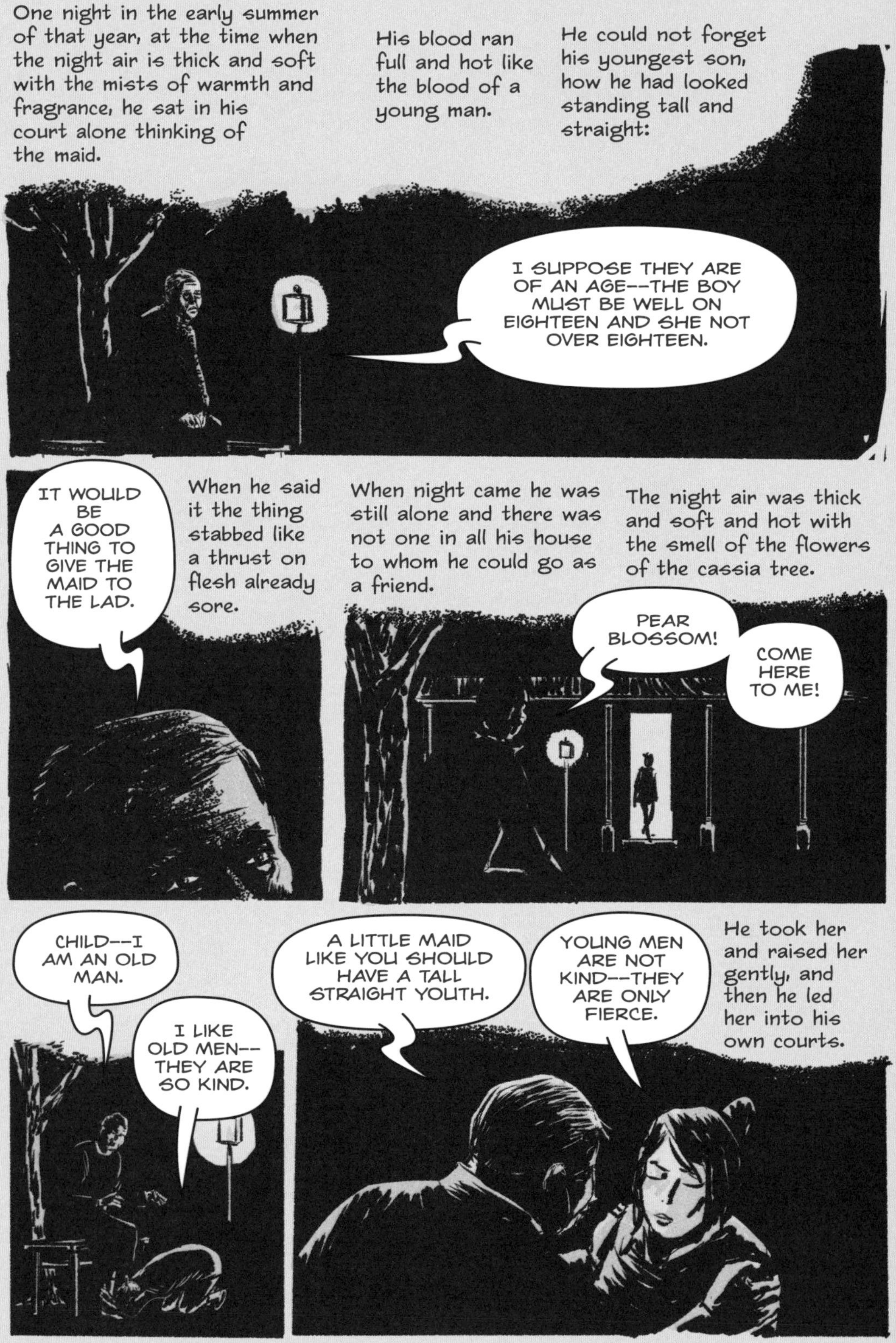
One night in the early summer of that year, at the time when the night air is thick and soft with the mists of warmth and fragrance, he sat in his court alone thinking of the maid.
His blood ran full and hot like the blood of a young man.
He could not forget his youngest son, how he had looked standing tall and straight:
I SUPPOSE THEY ARE OF AN AGE--THE BOY MUST BE WELL ON EIGHTEEN AND SHE NOT OVER EIGHTEEN.
IT WOULD BE A GOOD THING TO GIVE THE MAID TO THE LAD.
When he said it the thing stabbed like a thrust on flesh already sore.
When night came he was still alone and there was not one in all his house to whom he could go as a friend.
The night air was thick and soft and hot with the smell of the flowers of the cassia tree.
PEAR BLOSSOM!
COME HERE TO ME!
CHILD--I AM AN OLD MAN.
I LIKE OLD MEN--THEY ARE SO KIND.
A LITTLE MAID LIKE YOU SHOULD HAVE A TALL STRAIGHT YOUTH.
YOUNG MEN ARE NOT KIND--THEY ARE ONLY FIERCE.
He took her and raised her gently, and then he led her into his own courts.

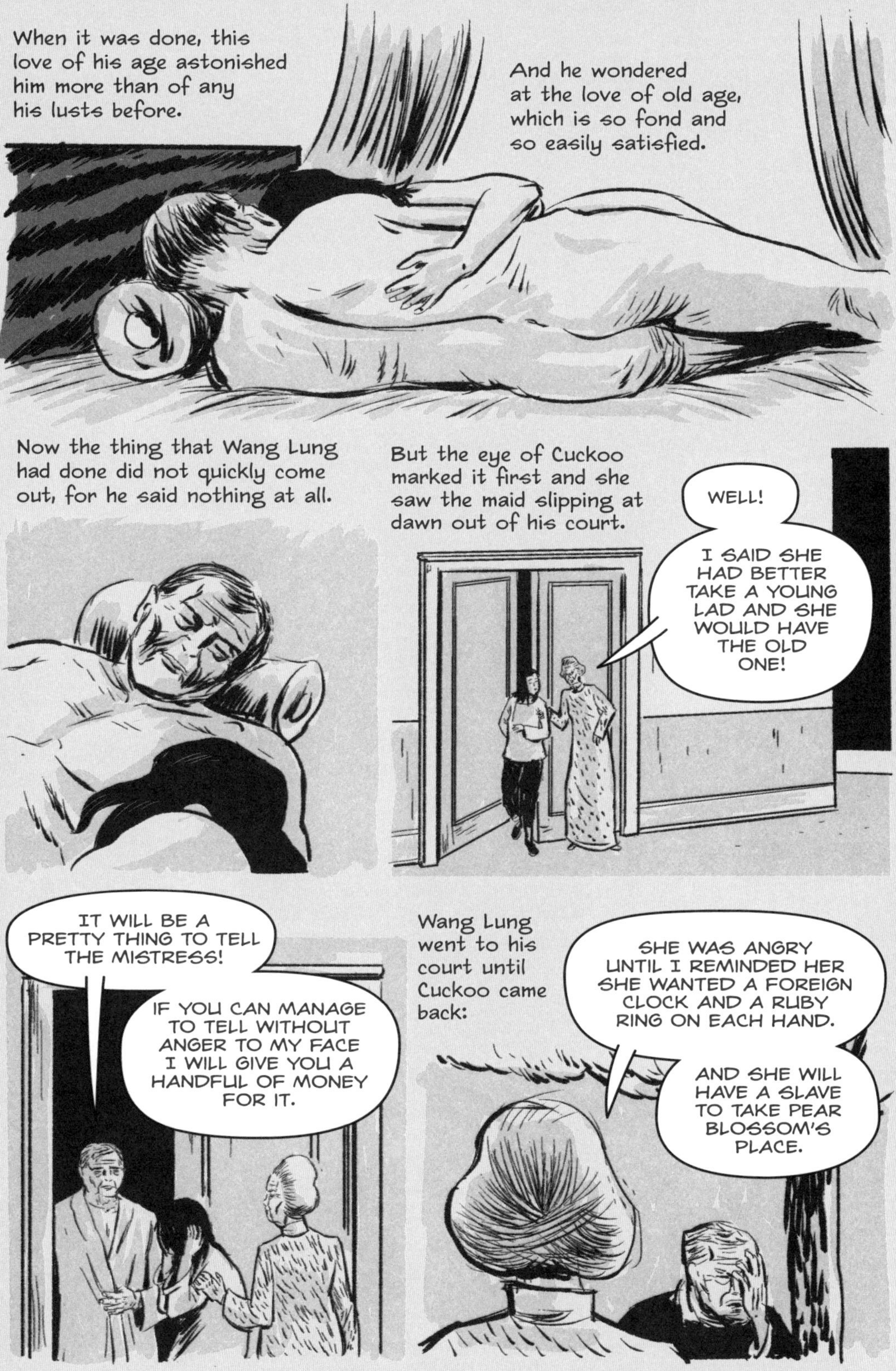
When it was done, this love of his age astonished him more than of any his lusts before.
And he wondered at the love of old age, which is so fond and so easily satisfied.
Now the thing that Wang Lung had done did not quickly come out, for he said nothing at all.
But the eye of Cuckoo marked it first and she saw the maid slipping at dawn out of his court.
WELL!
I SAID SHE HAD BETTER TAKE A YOUNG LAD AND SHE WOULD HAVE THE OLD ONE!
IT WILL BE A PRETTY THING TO TELL THE MISTRESS!
IF YOU CAN MANAGE TO TELL WITHOUT ANGER TO MY FACE I WILL GIVE YOU A HANDFUL OF MONEY FOR IT.
Wang Lung went to his court until Cuckoo came back:
SHE WAS ANGRY UNTIL I REMINDED HER SHE WANTED A FOREIGN CLOCK AND A RUBY RING ON EACH HAND.
AND SHE WILL HAVE A SLAVE TO TAKE PEAR BLOSSOM'S PLACE.

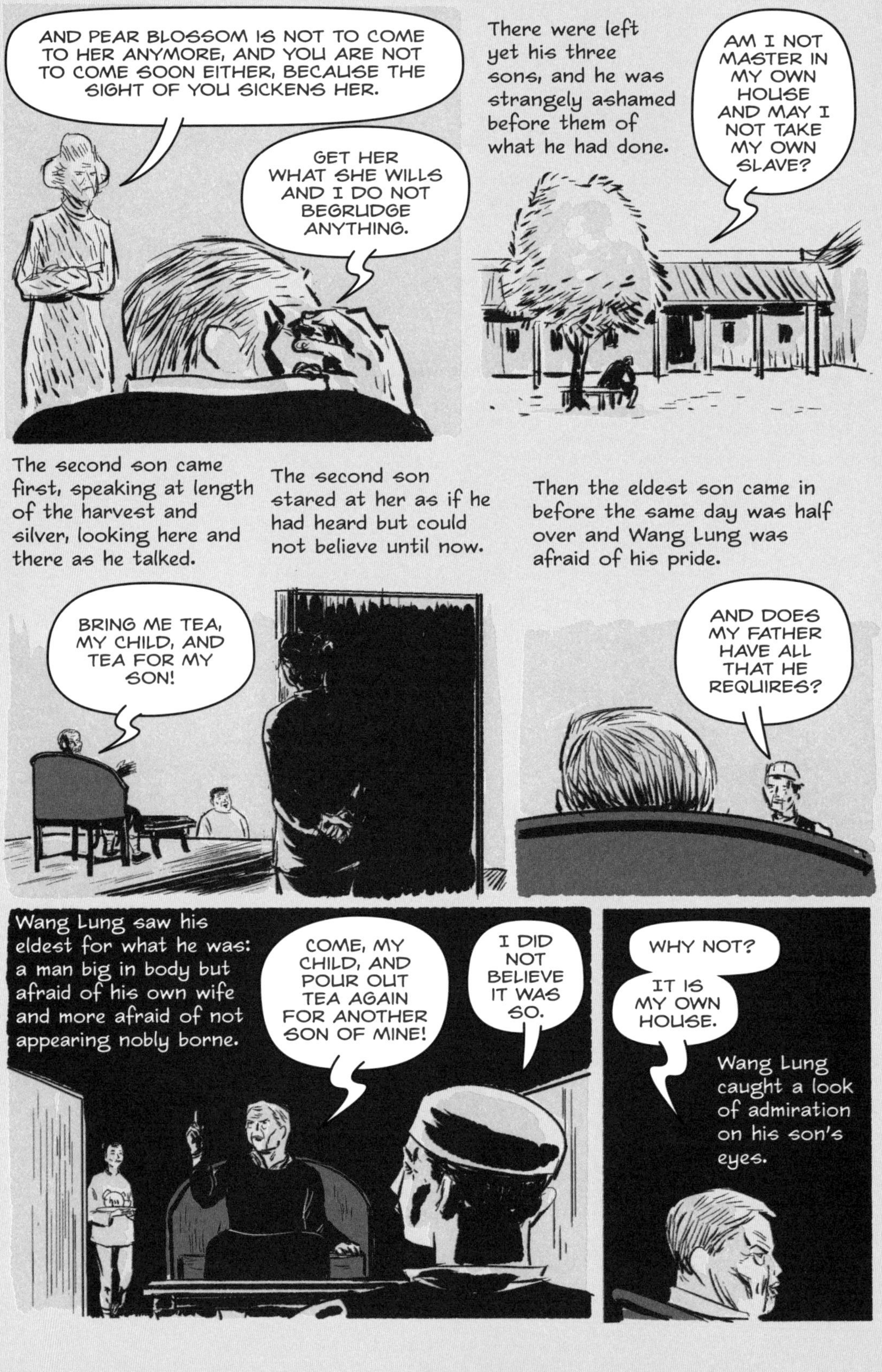
AND PEAR BLOSSOM IS NOT TO COME TO HER ANYMORE, AND YOU ARE NOT TO COME SOON EITHER, BECAUSE THE SIGHT OF YOU SICKENS HER.
GET HER WHAT SHE WILLS AND I DO NOT BEGRUDGE ANYTHING.
There were left yet his three sons, and he was strangely ashamed before them of what he had done.
AM I NOT MASTER IN MY OWN HOUSE AND MAY I NOT TAKE MY OWN SLAVE?
The second son came first, speaking at length of the harvest and silver, looking here and there as he talked.
BRING ME TEA, MY CHILD, AND TEA FOR MY SON!
The second son stared at her as if he had heard but could not believe until now.
Then the eldest son came in before the same day was half over and Wang Lung was afraid of his pride.
AND DOES MY FATHER HAVE ALL THAT HE REQUIRES?
Wang Lung saw his eldest for what he was: a man big in body but afraid of his own wife and more afraid of not appearing nobly borne.
COME, MY CHILD, AND POUR OUT TEA AGAIN FOR ANOTHER SON OF MINE!
I DID NOT BELIEVE IT WAS SO.
WHY NOT?
IT IS MY OWN HOUSE.
Wang Lung caught a look of admiration on his son's eyes.

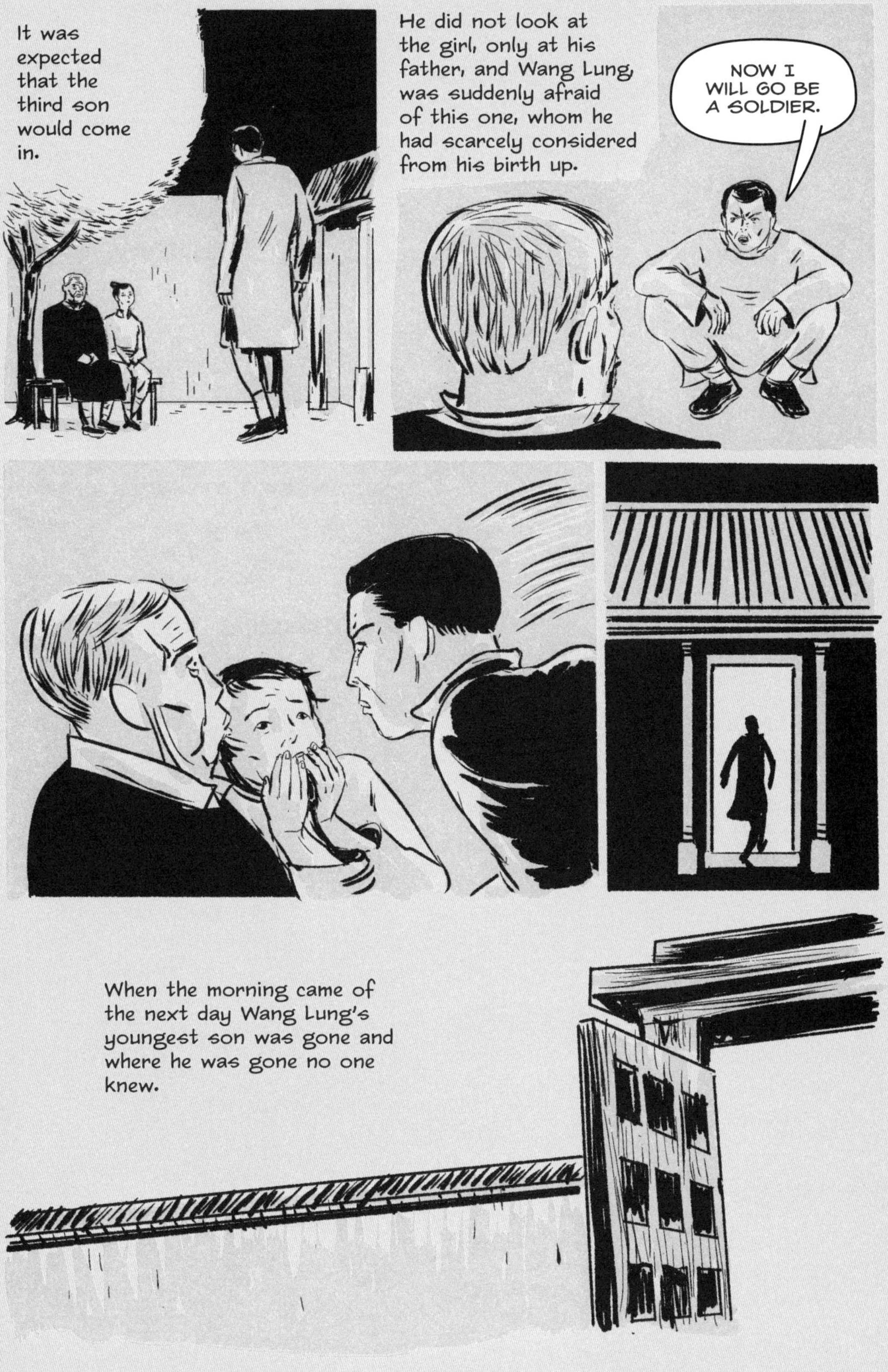
It was expected that the third son would come in.
He did not look at the girl, only at his father, and Wang Lung, was suddenly afraid of this one, whom he had scarcely considered from his birth up.
NOW I WILL GO BE A SOLDIER.
When the morning came of the next day Wang Lung's youngest son was gone and where he was gone no one knew.

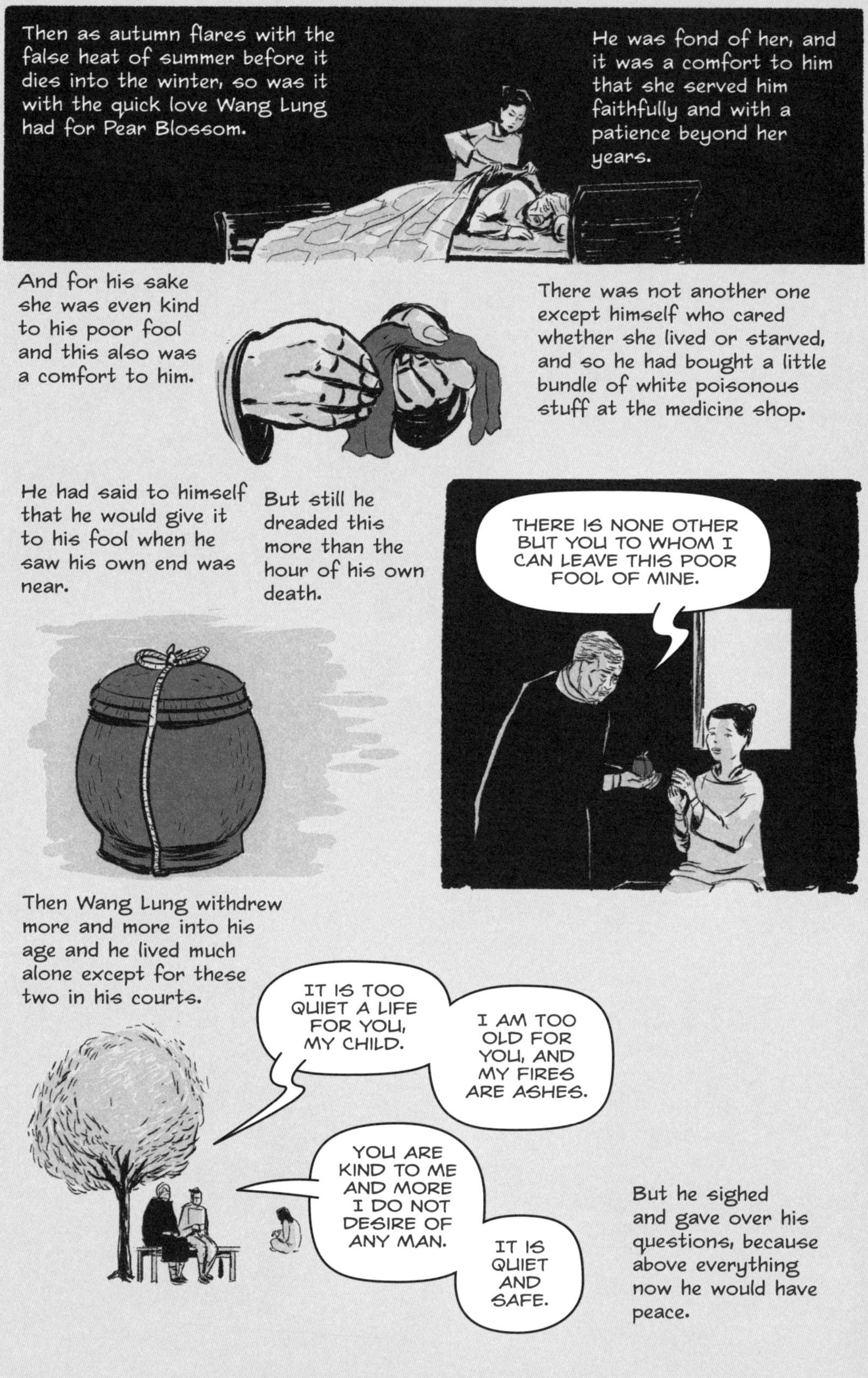
Then as autumn flares with the false heat of summer before it dies into the winter, so was it with the quick love Wang Lung had for Pear Blossom.
He was fond of her, and it was a comfort to him that she served him faithfully and with a patience beyond her years.
And for his sake she was even kind to his poor fool and this also was a comfort to him.
There was not another one except himself who cared whether she lived or starved, and so he had bought a little bundle of white poisonous stuff at the medicine shop.
He had said to himself that he would give it to his fool when he saw his own end was near.
But still he dreaded this more than the hour of his own death.
THERE IS NONE OTHER BUT YOU TO WHOM I CAN LEAVE THIS POOR FOOL OF MINE.
Then Wang Lung withdrew more and more into his age and he lived much alone except for these two in his courts.
IT IS TOO QUIET A LIFE FOR YOU, MY CHILD.
I AM TOO OLD FOR YOU, AND MY FIRES ARE ASHES.
YOU ARE KIND TO ME AND MORE I DO NOT DESIRE OF ANY MAN.
IT IS QUIET AND SAFE.
But he sighed and gave over his questions, because above everything now he would have peace.

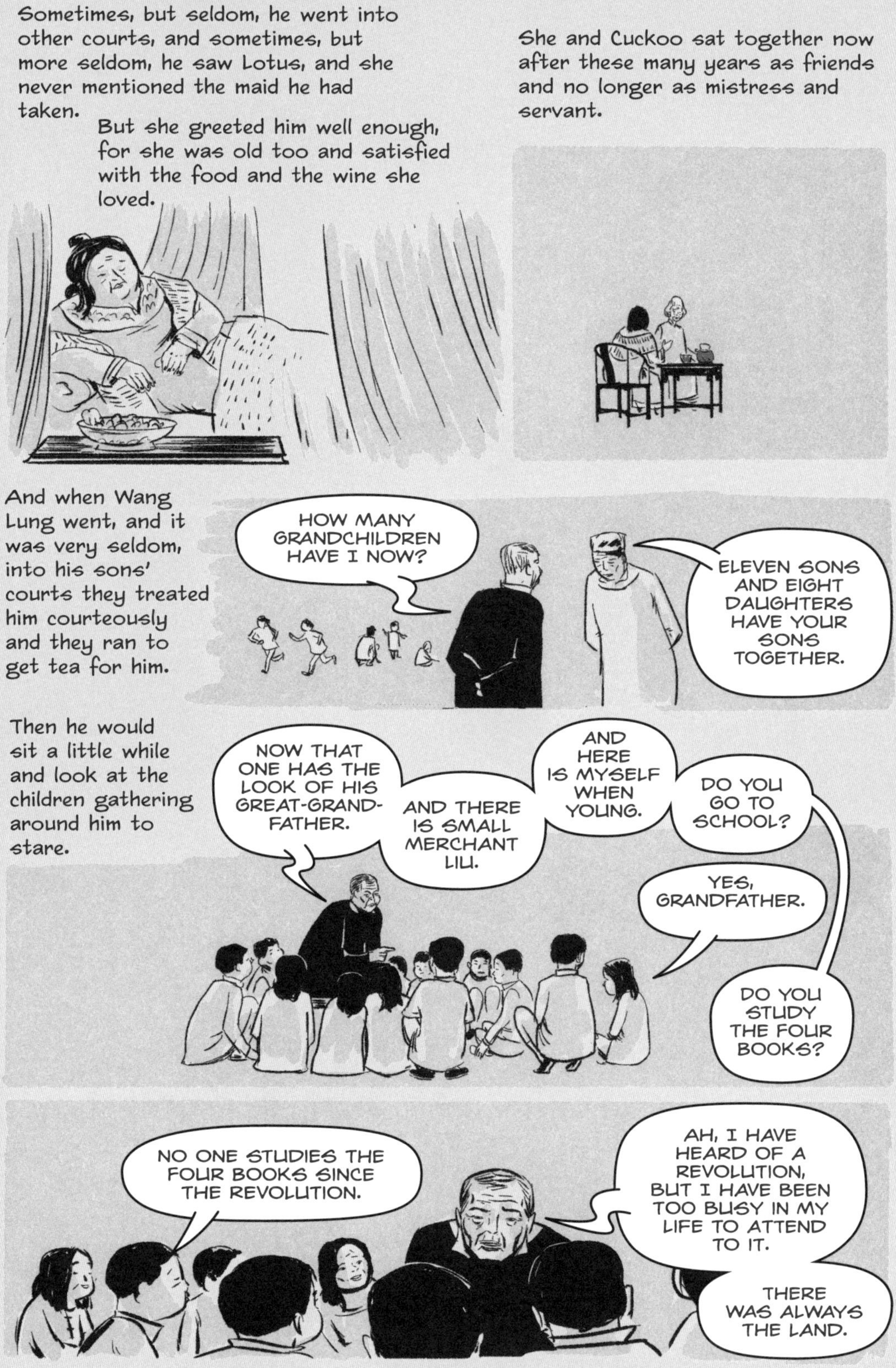
Sometimes, but seldom, he went into other courts, and sometimes, but more seldom, he saw Lotus, and she never mentioned the maid he had taken.
But she greeted him well enough, for she was old too and satisfied with the food and the wine she loved.
She and Cuckoo sat together now after these many years as friends and no longer as mistress and servant.
And when Wang Lung went, and it was very seldom, into his sons' courts they treated him courteously and they ran to get tea for him.
HOW MANY GRANDCHILDREN HAVE I NOW?
ELEVEN SONS AND EIGHT DAUGHTERS HAVE YOUR SONS TOGETHER.
Then he would sit a little while and look at the children gathering around him to stare.
NOW THAT ONE HAS THE LOOK OF HIS GREAT-GRANDFATHER.
AND THERE IS SMALL MERCHANT LIU.
AND HERE IS MYSELF WHEN YOUNG.
DO YOU GO TO SCHOOL?
YES, GRANDFATHER.
DO YOU STUDY THE FOUR BOOKS?
NO ONE STUDIES THE FOUR BOOKS SINCE THE REVOLUTION.
AH, I HAVE HEARD OF A REVOLUTION, BUT I HAVE BEEN TOO BUSY IN MY LIFE TO ATTEND TO IT.
THERE WAS ALWAYS THE LAND.

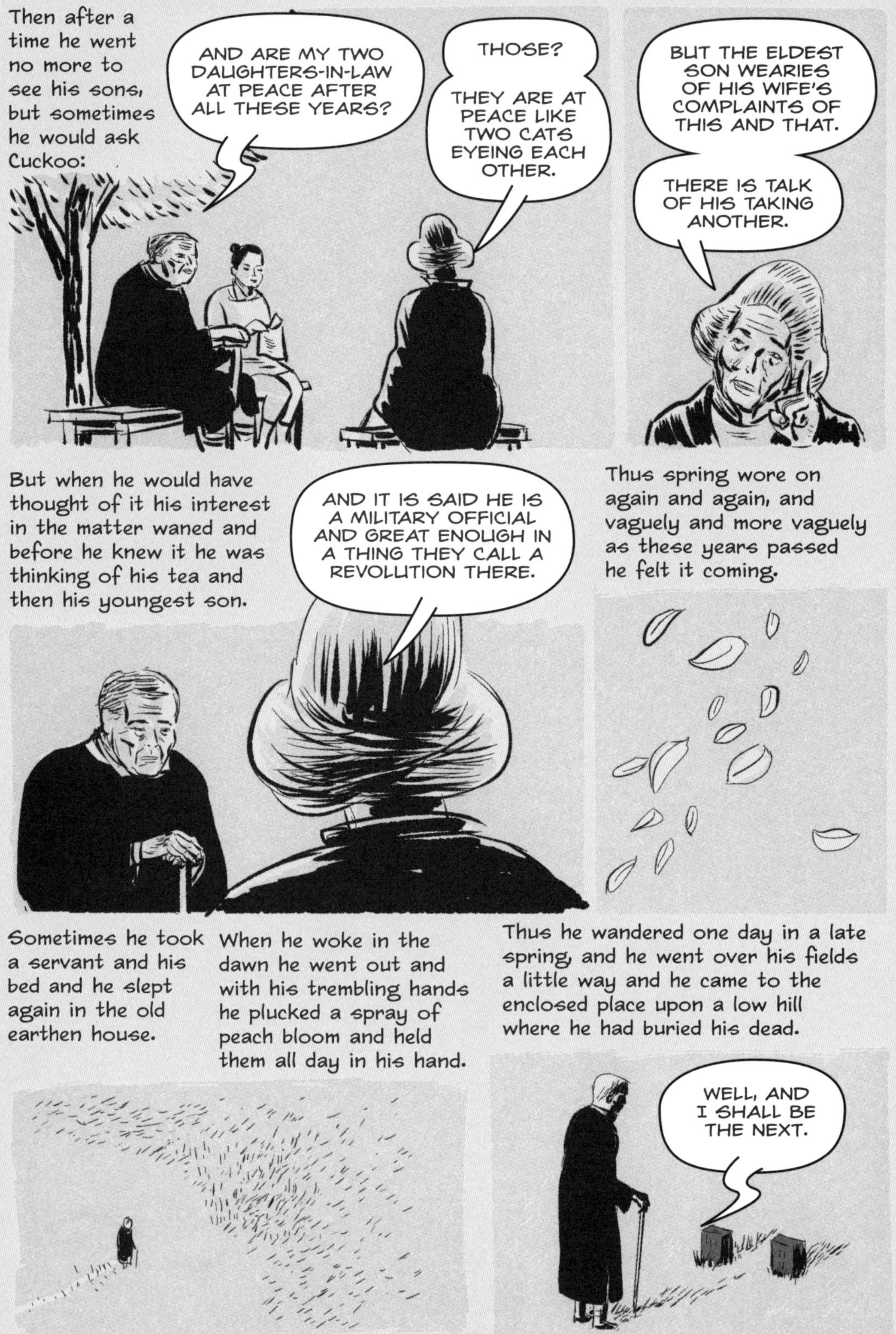

Then after a time he went no more to see his sons, but sometimes he would ask Cuckoo:
AND ARE MY TWO DAUGHTERS-IN-LAW AT PEACE AFTER ALL THESE YEARS?
THOSE?
THEY ARE AT PEACE LIKE TWO CATS EYEING EACH OTHER.
BUT THE ELDEST SON WEARIES OF HIS WIFE'S COMPLAINTS OF THIS AND THAT.
THERE IS TALK OF HIS TAKING ANOTHER.
But when he would have thought of it his interest in the matter waned and before he knew it he was thinking of his tea and then his youngest son.
AND IT IS SAID HE IS A MILITARY OFFICIAL AND GREAT ENOUGH IN A THING THEY CALL A REVOLUTION THERE.
Thus spring wore on again and again, and vaguely and more vaguely as these years passed he felt it coming.
Sometimes he took a servant and his bed and he slept again in the old earthen house.
When he woke in the dawn he went out and with his trembling hands he plucked a spray of peach bloom and held them all day in his hand.
Thus he wandered one day in a late spring, and he went over his fields a little way and he came to the enclosed place upon a low hill where he had buried his dead.
WELL, AND I SHALL BE THE NEXT.

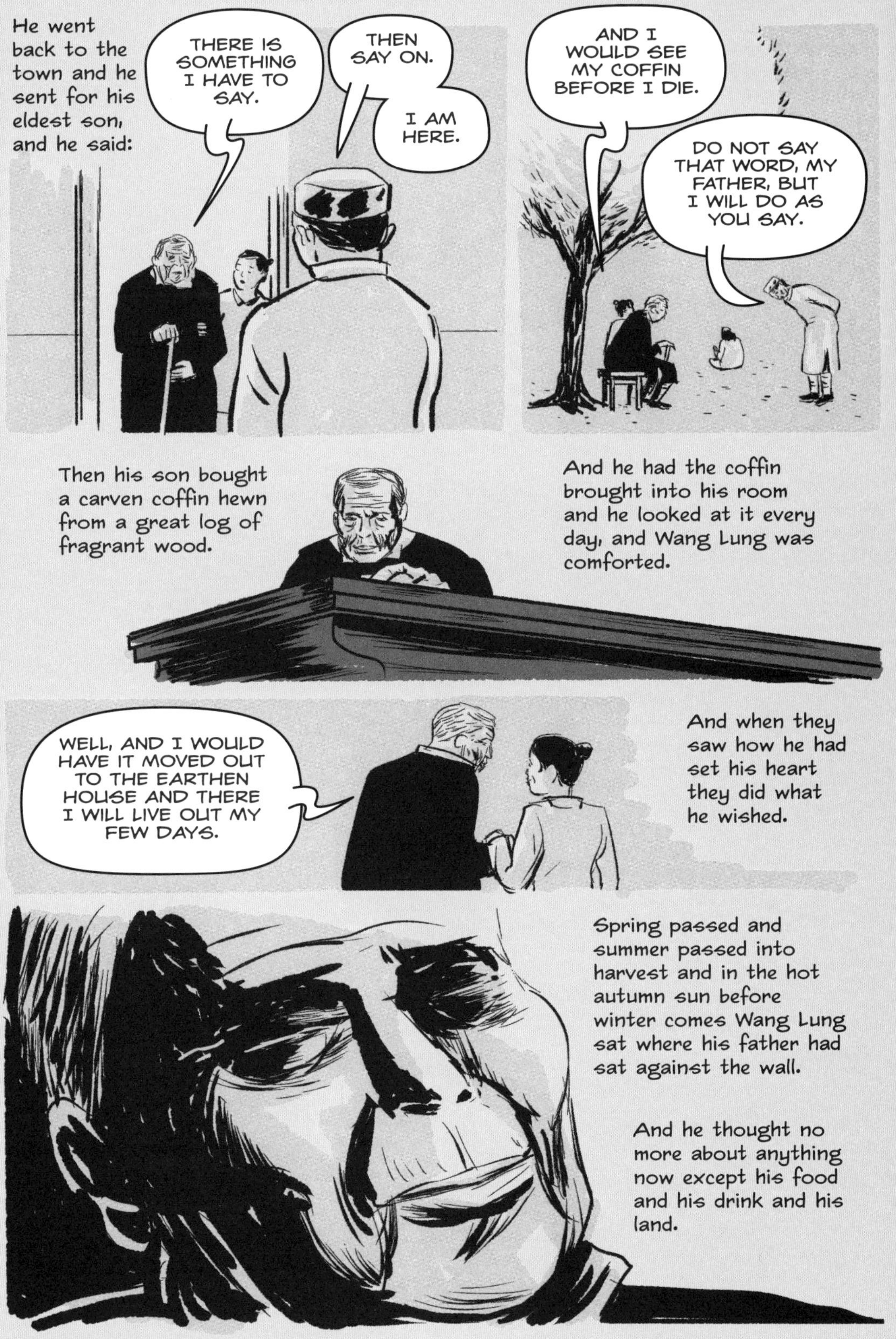
He went back to the town and he sent for his eldest son, and he said:
THERE IS SOMETHING I HAVE TO SAY.
THEN SAY ON.
I AM HERE.
AND I WOULD SEE MY COFFIN BEFORE I DIE.
DO NOT SAY THAT WORD, MY FATHER, BUT I WILL DO AS YOU SAY.
Then his son bought a carven coffin hewn from a great log of fragrant wood.
And he had the coffin brought into his room and he looked at it every day, and Wang Lung was comforted.
WELL, AND I WOULD HAVE IT MOVED OUT TO THE EARTHEN HOUSE AND THERE I WILL LIVE OUT MY FEW DAYS.
And when they saw how he had set his heart they did what he wished.
Spring passed and summer passed into harvest and in the hot autumn sun before winter comes Wang Lung sat where his father had sat against the wall.
And he thought no more about anything now except his food and his drink and his land.

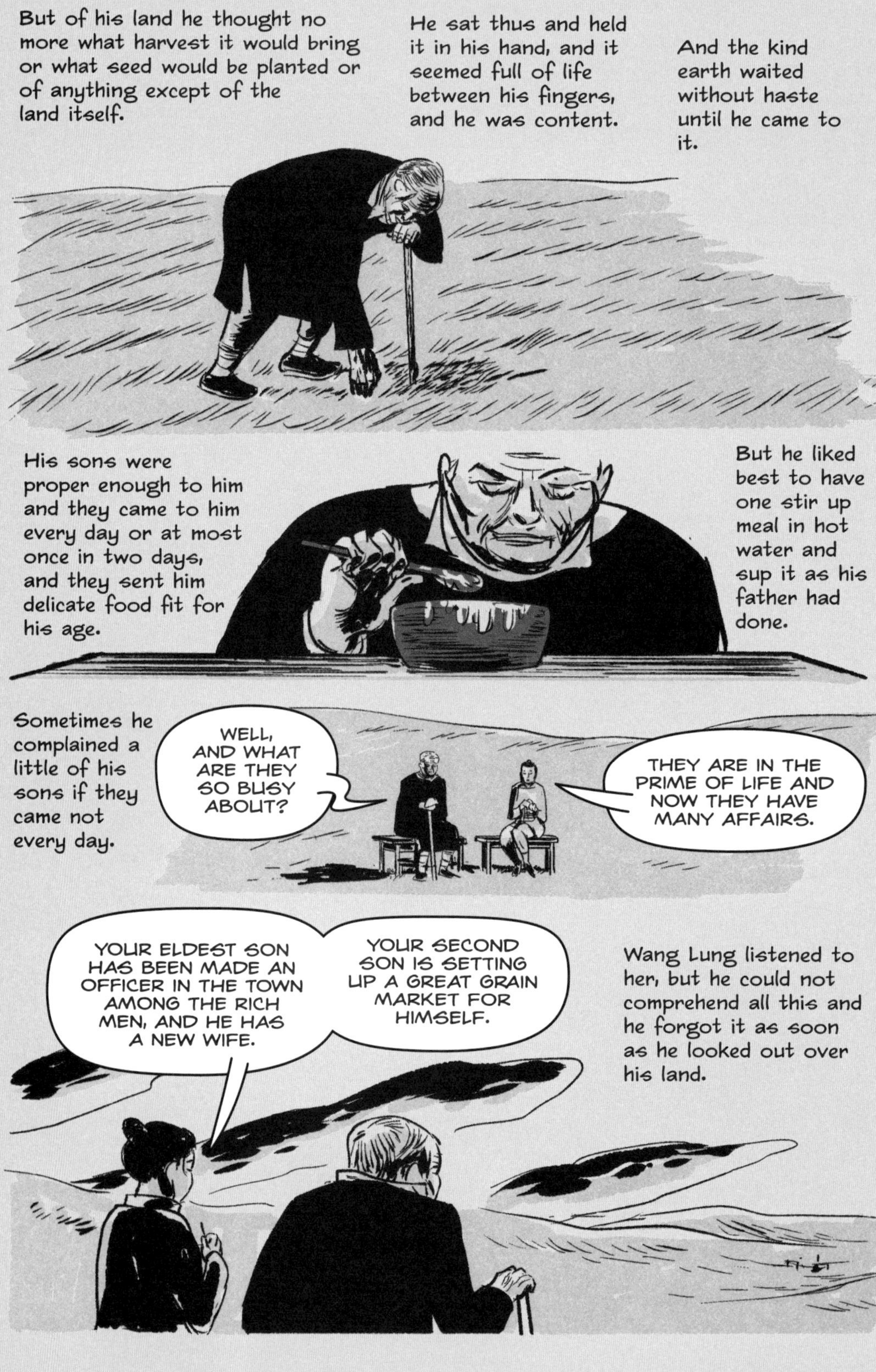
But of his land he thought no more what harvest it would bring or what seed would be planted or of anything except of the land itself.
He sat thus and held it in his hand, and it seemed full of life between his fingers, and he was content.
And the kind earth waited without haste until he came to it.
His sons were proper enough to him and they came to him every day or at most once in two days, and they sent him delicate food fit for his age.
But he liked best to have one stir up meal in hot water and sup it as his father had done.
Sometimes he complained a little of his sons if they came not every day.
WELL, AND WHAT ARE THEY SO BUSY ABOUT?
THEY ARE IN THE PRIME OF LIFE AND NOW THEY HAVE MANY AFFAIRS.
YOUR ELDEST SON HAS BEEN MADE AN OFFICER IN THE TOWN AMONG THE RICH MEN, AND HE HAS A NEW WIFE.
YOUR SECOND SON IS SETTING UP A GREAT GRAIN MARKET FOR HIMSELF.
Wang Lung listened to her, but he could not comprehend all this and he forgot it as soon as he looked out over his land.

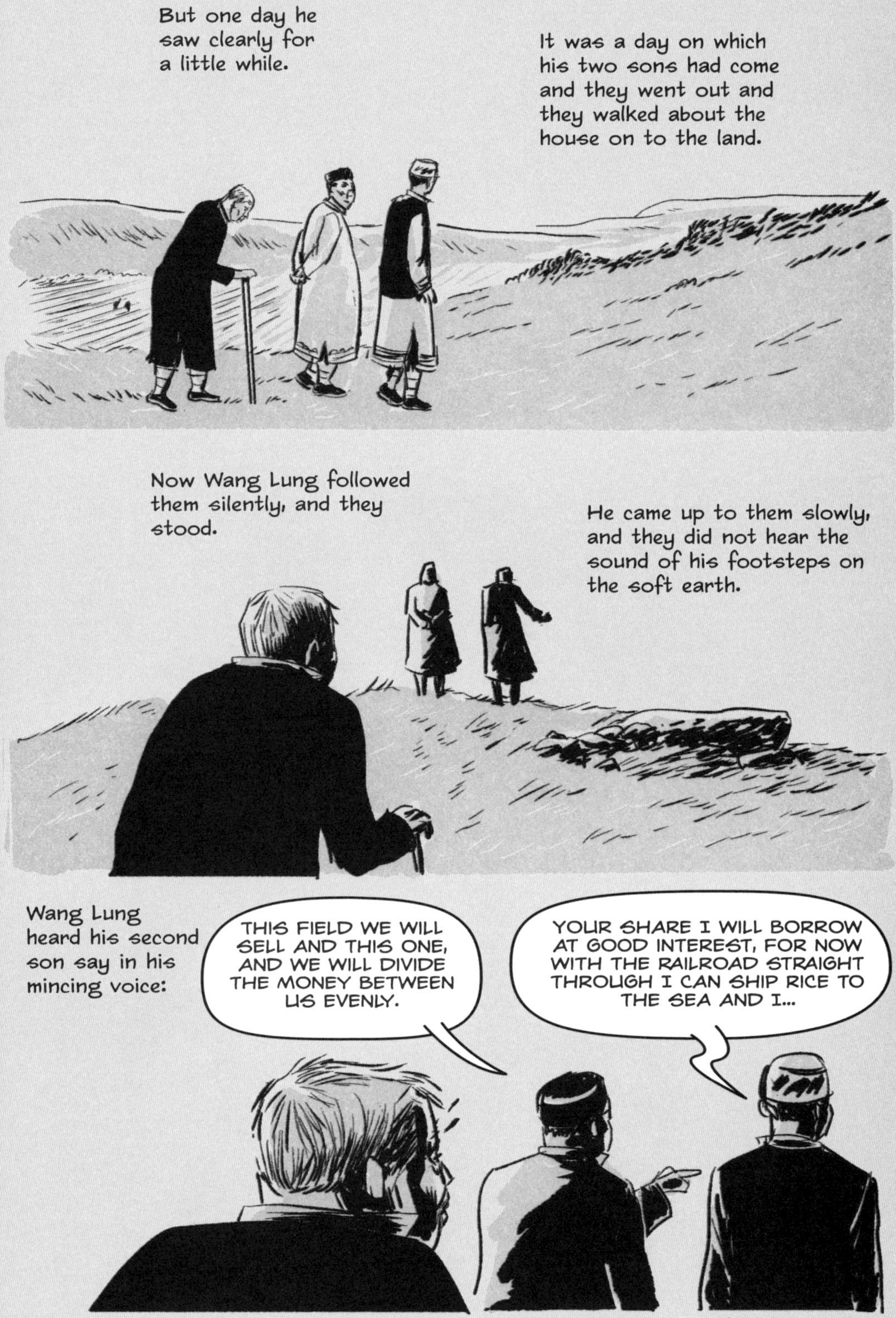
But one day he saw clearly for a little while.
It was a day on which his two sons had come and they went out and they walked about the house on to the land.
Now Wang Lung followed them silently, and they stood.
He came up to them slowly, and they did not hear the sound of his footsteps on the soft earth.
Wang Lung heard his second son say in his mincing voice:
THIS FIELD WE WILL SELL AND THIS ONE, AND WE WILL DIVIDE THE MONEY BETWEEN US EVENLY.
YOUR SHARE I WILL BORROW AT GOOD INTEREST, FOR NOW WITH THE RAILROAD STRAIGHT THROUGH I CAN SHIP RICE TO THE SEA AND I...

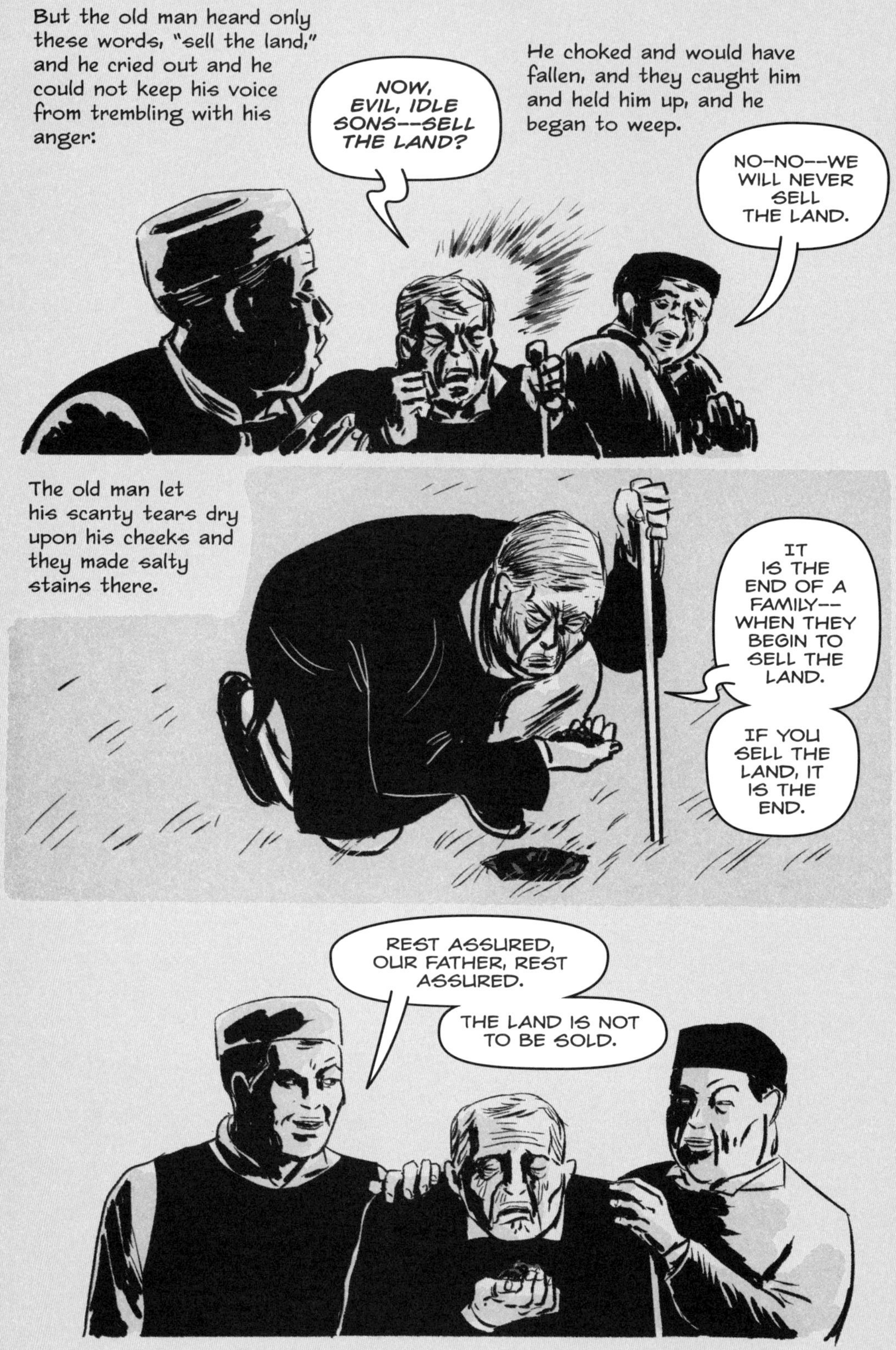
But the old man heard only these words, "sell the land," and he cried out and he could not keep his voice from trembling with his anger:
NOW, EVIL, IDLE SONS--SELL THE LAND?
He choked and would have fallen, and they caught him and held him up, and he began to weep.
NO-NO--WE WILL NEVER SELL THE LAND.
The old man let his scanty tears dry upon his cheeks and they made salty stains there.
IT IS THE END OF A FAMILY--WHEN THEY BEGIN TO SELL THE LAND.
IF YOU SELL THE LAND, IT IS THE END.
REST ASSURED, OUR FATHER, REST ASSURED.
THE LAND IS NOT TO BE SOLD.